BLACK AND WHITE, BLUE AND GOLD

By Jay Bender

Black and White, Blue and Gold

1

CHAPTER 1

For Page B1, *The North Coast Press*

May 9

By Cliff O'Brien

CLEVELAND – Police are investigating the stabbing death of a young man, who was killed last night in the area of E. 37th and Woodland.

According to CPD spokesperson Lt. Wilson Young, emergency dispatchers received a 9-1-1 call at 10:18 p.m., saying the victim, who is still unidentified, was found near a vacant lot, bleeding heavily. EMS and CPD units who responded to scene were unable to revive the victim, and he was pronounced dead at the scene.

Young would not specify the number or location of the stab wounds but did describe them as "obviously lethal." He referred further questions to the Cuyahoga County Medical Examiner's Office.

"Clearly, we're at a very early stage in this investigation," Young said. "We're going to do all we can to find out what happened and who was responsible. Right now, it's just too early to speculate."

According to Young, it is unknown whether the incident is drug related, although the area is "well-known" to police as a busy location for narcotics activity.

The victim was described as a Black male, between 18 and 24 years old, six feet tall and 190 pounds. Police stated the victim also had extensive tattoos on his upper body, including a large "Grim Reaper" on his right arm.

Anyone with information regarding the victim or the crime is asked to contact the Cleveland Police Department.

Cliff O'Brien tapped the final period onto the computer screen in front of him and read the text over. It wasn't exactly Pulitzer material, but it was done in time, just barely, to make tomorrow's edition. He was reasonably sure the print competition wouldn't have it that soon, so if it were long enough, he had what he needed. Another quick stab at the keyboard and the monitor told him the story would run just under eight inches when converted to newsprint. With a four-deck, single-column headline, O'Brien figured it would be long enough to avert any embarrassing void of newsprint on the cover of the metro section. He hit the "send" key and called over the cubicle wall to the night city editor, Leo Nelson.

"It's in the pipeline," he near shouted.

O'Brien heard a muffled response, which might have been "OK" He leaned back in his chair and took a sip of herbal tea from his mug, grimacing. Long gone cold, and not all that tempting in the first place, the flavor formerly known as "Wild Berry" had degraded well past palatability. He would have preferred coffee, but he was trying to cut back. At a newspaper, which was like trying to cut back on gossip, or breathing. From over the wall, he heard a quick laugh.

"Did he really say, 'obviously lethal'?" Leo called.

"Verbatim, of course," Cliff replied.

"For an official spokesman, Young says some strange things."

"You should hear him off the record," O'Brien replied, loudly enough to hear a thin chorus of voices join the refrain.

"There's no such thing as off the record," his co-workers chimed in with mock glee. They all knew better. "Off the record" meant "off the record," if you wanted to keep your sources, and subsequently, your job. Journalism professors who hadn't worked long enough in the field to really make a living at it before running back to campus still preached that hard line. On the street, friendly sources were a priceless commodity.

Cliff had to smile. The jokes meant Leo was happy with the story, or happy enough to send it to the news editor for final layout. It was a weak piece written quickly and without much background, but he had it first and he had it right. Tomorrow he would really start digging. The police would know more, the coroner might talk, and the neighbors would be fueling the rumor mill. Tomorrow would be a busy day.

Doreen Ellis poked her head up over the cubicle wall.

"We're heading to Griff's for a beer," she said. "Interested?"

"Hmmm," O'Brien exaggerated, stroking his chin, and looking off into the distance. "The end of a workday, a cold beer, good friends, and an American reporter of Irish descent? According to the laws of nature and genetics, I am *compelled* to join you."

Doreen laughed, her smile quick and infectious.

"The cold beer alone would have gotten me," she said before dropping out of sight behind the wall, reappearing almost instantly with a backpack slung over one shoulder and heading toward a tiny group of co-workers, already gathering at the newsroom door.

"Let me grab the boss first," he said. O'Brien picked up a reporter's notebook and stuck it into the pocket of his windbreaker. Early May is still chilly at night in Cleveland. Leo was just standing up and shrugging into his own jacket.

"Save your breath, O'Brien," the older man said. "I'm way ahead of you, as usual. As a sign of my faith in our good working relationship however, I will let you buy the first round."

Cliff laughed again as they headed out of the newsroom. Tomorrow would be busy, he reminded himself. But it was still a day away.

CHAPTER 2

For Detective Sergeant Jack Brickman, today had already turned into tomorrow without notice. His busy afternoon had turned into a busy night and promised to be a busy morning. The first hours of a homicide investigation were vital.

The crime scene was rapidly thinning out. The Cuyahoga County Medical Examiner's Office had picked up the body and transported "John Doe" to the new facilities near Case Western Reserve University after the crime scene was painstakingly studied, charted, photographed, and swabbed by the trace evidence experts. Brickman had gotten to the scene quickly, just after maybe half a dozen uniformed cops. The detective had been pleased to see that the blue shirts had quickly taped off the areas and had assigned an officer to log the comings and goings of everyone approaching the body. A detail that was occasionally and unfortunately overlooked in the grim excitement of a murder could be vital later as defense attorneys scoured police records for the tiniest crack in the case. Chain-of-evidence errors were always a favorite target.

For their part, Brickman and his partner, the aging but still sharp veteran Al Sladky, had moved through the crowd of onlookers quickly, asking the obvious questions, and getting the obvious answers. It was rare that a bystander would offer more than "I didn't see anything" or some version of the response, often seasoned with profanity. Nobody, it seemed, ever wanted to get involved, at least in front of the neighbors. People talked, and if the crime appeared drug related, which this probably was, word usually filtered back to the dealers themselves. Brickman couldn't blame the onlookers for their fear. While drugs and the violence they fostered were hated by cops and civilians alike, taking a stand in public wasn't always a smart idea. As they worked the small crowd, they passed out business cards with the usual plea for help, "if you think of anything that might help us, please call right away."

But Brickman, although young for a detective sergeant at thirty-three, wasn't just listening to answers. He had long learned the veteran investigator's trick of trying to hear what wasn't being said. If witnesses hesitated, coughed, mumbled, or pretended not to understand the question, there was a good chance they weren't telling the truth. He mentally logged those nuances and faces that went with them for later inquiry. Tonight, though, he was faced with a group of people who really hadn't seen anything. Surprisingly, the person who had found the body, a Miss Algeria White, was also the person who called 9-1-1 on her cell phone and had waited for police and EMS to arrive so she could tell them what she had seen, which wasn't much. White, a first-year student working her way through Cuyahoga Community College, had been on her way home from a late spring class at nearby "Tri-C" and had stumbled across the victim. Other than White, the neighborhood had only come alive after the sudden arrival of two zone cars.

Brickman was surprised at that. In the inner city, many people spent spring, summer, and autumn nights on their front porches. The crime scene was near a public housing project. The weather was chilly, yes, but not uncomfortably so. It was unusual that nobody had been outside on this night. So, they were left with one witness and a crowd of speculators. Well, they had closed many cases that started with less. Time meant nothing to the dead, but the clock was already ticking for Brickman. He could feel things start to speed up the way they always did in the first 48 hours of a homicide investigation.

From across the dwindling crowd, Al Sladky caught his eye and nodded. Time to go. Jack pushed one more business card into somebody's hand and joined his partner as they walked on the edge of the crime scene.

"Anything?" Jack asked.

Sladky answered by shrugging his shoulders and grunting. For somebody else, the gesture might be construed as apathetic or condescending. Brickman had worked with Sladky for three years and had known him for a few years before that. He knew not to read anything into the gesture. It meant exactly what it was supposed to mean, "I didn't find anything out and I don't know anything more than you."

As they walked toward their car, a non-descript Ford anybody could identify as a police car from ten blocks away, Brickman took another look at the location of the crime scene. The body itself had been found at the corner of the Longwood housing complex, next to a vacant lot that used to house a chemical plant or machine shop, Brickman forgot which. There wasn't much light in the area, as many of the streetlights had been smashed out or had just died of neglect. A chain-link fence that had separated the housing complex from the vacant lot was a wall of vines, just starting to sprout new leaves. All in all, a fairly private little spot for a murder, even if it was next to a four-lane road.

Brickman got into the passenger side of the Ford. Sladky eased himself in behind the wheel. Al usually drove, but he never made an issue about it. Brickman was the same way, not getting hung up on little issues that burdened some partnerships. Sladky started the car and asked the obvious question.

"Now what?" he said.

"Same as always," Brickman replied. "Let's start knocking on doors."

CHAPTER 3

Cliff O'Brien woke up at ten, about his usual time. Because *The North Coast Press* was a morning paper, and deadlines were at night, Cliff generally didn't get to the office until after noon. There were exceptions, of course, such as press conferences and breaking news, but O'Brien, unlike most Clevelanders, usually enjoyed a leisurely morning. Faint street sounds drifted up to his bedroom as the light filtered in through the vertical blinds.

Cliff rolled onto his back and stretched, slightly stuffy from what he would call a light hangover. Although he hadn't closed Griff's the previous night, he had stayed long enough to down four pints of Guiness. He'd meant to stop at three, but Leo Nelson had insisted on buying him one for the road. Since Cliff was walking home, and because it was bad form to turn down a free beer, especially from your boss, he had accepted the offer. Luckily, he had escaped at that point, just as a round of shots was being poured. Their staff outings often deteriorated into duels of cordiality, with reciprocating drinks traveling in every direction.

Not that Cliff minded. The paper's staff got along well with each other. Like the paper itself, the reporters and editors were young, and had the energy and thirst of many new professionals. O'Brien expected the day to be busy, and he wanted a reasonably clear head. Plus, he wanted to get a workout in before heading to the paper. He knew from experience that every beer he downed would make it just a little harder to get to the pool. A swimmer in high school, Cliff tried to keep himself in reasonably good shape. Admittedly, he was a little thicker around the middle than he would have liked, but all in all he considered himself a fairly fit 27-year-old. Although vain about nothing except his writing, O'Brien was single and looking. The lack of a beer belly was a noticeable plus in the Cleveland dating market.

Cliff rolled out of bed and threw on some old jeans and a thinning sweatshirt from his alma mater, Ohio University, not to be confused with The Ohio State University. Oh, OSU had a school of journalism, but the E.W. Scripps School of Journalism at OU was easily among the top five "J" schools in the country. A lackluster student in high school, his rapid acceptance into one of Ohio University's most respected colleges still baffled Cliff. He had done well on his college tests, and he had been editor of his school paper, but from what he had heard about the ever-rising admission standards, he counted himself lucky to have made the cut. He had long suspected that his old high school advisor, Mr. Padrowski, a proud OU alum, had made a few calls on his behalf. The right words in the right ears never hurt.

Luckily, he didn't have to go far to get the morning paper. Cliff lived in Reserve Square, a few blocks from *The Press* offices at Rockwell and E. 13th. He opened the apartment's door and grabbed the paper. He spread it open on the butcher's block that served as small kitchen table and reached over to the refrigerator for a bottle of water. Cliff wouldn't be ashamed to admit that the first place he went was to his article. A quick read told him it had been left intact. Although he trusted Leo, he had long ago become wary of editors.

Writing a newspaper article, Cliff had often said, was like sending your child off to war. You hoped his general knew what he was doing, but you just never knew for sure. Your writing could be hacked to pieces for space, content, or "other." Other just plain sucked since it could be anything from political repayment to protecting an advertiser. Luckily, "other" had yet to rear its ugly head at *The Press*.

Cliff made a mental note to thank his source for the tip. Satisfied, he opened the paper to the comics. Cliff noticed he had picked up a habit common to millions of newspaper readers nationwide, but the comics were the first place he turned after his own articles. He was a cynic, and he figured the comics probably told him more about the world than the front page anyway. A few chuckles later, he folded the pages into quarters on clipboard, so the crossword puzzle was accessible and flipped through the other sections of the paper.

The North Coast Press was a fledgling in the newspaper business and was ironically what might be called a stepchild of the computer age. Its owner, Gavin V. Lawson, or "Gav" as he preferred to be called, was a modern media mogul of the first order. True, he had pioneered several software revolutions, and took a second only to Bill Gates as a techno-mogul, but Gav's true passion was news, in the traditional sense. Gavin's dad had been an editor for a paper in the southwest that had been forced out of business by a conglomerate, much as *The Cleveland Press*, among dozens of smaller papers, had been forced in submission by the broad-reaching influence, smart business sense, and aggressive endeavors of *The Cleveland Plain Dealer.*

Regardless, once Gav had enough money to last him several lifetimes, he had turned his fortune and his boundless energy in several directions, one of which was defying the status quo in "one-paper towns," a group to which Cleveland belongs. So, as other techno-brands were running from the print media, Gavin Lawson was waging a unilateral war to keep newsprint relevant.

In moments of clarity, Cliff wondered if Gav wasn't a modern Don Quixote. Still, he wasn't complaining. Cliff had been rescued by Gavin's recruiters from Cincinnati because of his aggressive reporting and writing style and had been granted a premier job at *The Press*, with a good salary to match. So, he had been whisked from southern Ohio to the crime desk at a brand-new paper that wanted his most aggressive investigative reporting. He could live with that deal.

Cliff looked up as he browsed the paper, longingly eyeing the coffee maker despite his goal to cut back.

"Screw it," he said aloud, as he rose and headed over to the counter. He carefully measured out enough coffee for two large mugs and filled the decanter. By the time it was brewed, Cliff was already done with about two-thirds of the crossword. Pouring a cup for himself, he thought fondly of a time, while working for a tiny paper in southeastern Ohio, when he could have "consulted the Oracle" for crossword solutions. Granted, "the Oracle" was just tomorrow's paste-up of the crossword answers, but still, it had been a great safety net.

By eleven, Cliff had finished the crossword and the coffee. He wandered over to his computer and booted it up. His work email was perfectly divided: One reader thought he was too pro-police and one thought he was too anti-police. He had not expected more than that since his morning piece had been so short.

He then switched to his personal email. Cliff was happy to see a simple message from his parents, who had happily taken delivery of their first home computer on the previous Christmas. They were getting a big kick out the computer, which had been hotfooted to Mentor as soon as Cliff's employer consultant had heard they didn't have one. Gavin Lawson was a tech mogul after all, and his companies were more than happy to get the latest computers out to as many people as possible. And it paid to keep his employees happy.

After throwing a bagel in the toaster, Cliff called his voicemail to retrieve messages. There was nothing that couldn't wait until he got to the office. By the time the bagel popped up, Cliff had already polished off a banana. Following a liberal spreading of cream cheese, Cliff was munching and packing his gym bag with a swimsuit, workout clothes, and some work clothes. He threw a baseball cap over his disheveled hair and was out the door just as the local TV news would have been leading with a reread of his story. Twenty minutes later, he was at his health club changing into shorts and a T-shirt and looking forward to a short lifting session followed by a long swim. A swim usually helped him focus.

CHAPTER 4

Jack was working on about four hours sleep, and woke up at ten. Well, actually he had woken up at seven, when his wife Karen got up for work. Jack had been vaguely aware of her alarm going off, the normal morning shuffling through the closet and drawers and the familiar sounds of the shower and sink, punctuated by the soft touch of her lips on his forehead as she kissed him good-bye. Jack was sound asleep again by the time her car pulled out of the driveway.

When he came fully awake, Jack hauled himself out of bed, grabbed a quick shower and a shave. He felt like crap from the short sleep, but he knew he needed to get back to work. It was always like this during the first two or three days of a homicide. The day's uniform was a jacket and tie. He unlocked his home gun safe and retrieved his duty Glock pistol from where it rested with the .38 snubbie he had used as backup piece during his patrol days. Some guys Jack knew didn't lock up their guns at home, and that just didn't make sense to him. The chances of having an unsecured duty handgun stolen from your house, even in the relatively safe Tremont neighborhood Jack and Karen called home, were much higher than having to get to the gun in a split second. And even though they didn't have kids yet, Karen made it clear early on that while she could live with guns in the home, she wanted them stored sensibly.

Jack thought about brewing a quick to-go cup of coffee, but he decided he was going to treat himself on the way in instead. It was a clear day, cloudless and cool. He was focused on the case, as it was, as he headed downtown which was a short drive away.

Last night's canvass had been a bust. Nobody near the crime scene had noticed anything unusual, and by the time they were done, they still had nothing to go on. Jack was not worried about that. They still had no idea who the victim was, and that would be the real starting point anyway. As a rule, people killed people they knew. Random violence against strangers was still a rarity, although it always seemed as though the climate was shifting towards a more violent world. He couldn't judge objectively: He was too deep at the heart of it to look at it holistically.

Jack thought about it as he drove. He had more questions than answers, and he never liked that.

One thing that bothered him was the nature of the wounds. From what he could see last night, there had been only two wounds, and either one could have been the cause of death. One had been a stab wound to the base of victim's skull. The other had been a very deep slash across the inside of the victim's left thigh. The cut, as far as he could see, had not been perfect, considering the man's baggy pants, but it had been effective, long enough and deep enough to sever the femoral artery. The wounds were unique in two vital ways, their location, and their number. Contrary to what most people saw in the movies, stabbings were usually not lethal unless there were multiple wounds. Brickman could hear the words of his first defensive tactics instructor in his head.

"If you have to use a knife, remember three things," the wiry man had said, "cut fast, deep, and often."

And that certainly had been borne out in his years on the street. Knives and edged weapons were the tool of choice in domestics, and he had never seen a fatality caused by just two wounds. His mind was already pointing to limited conclusions: They were dealing with either a lucky first-timer or an experienced knife fighter, likely an ex-con or ex-military. Either way, it pointed towards a grudge killing. Knives were personal weapons.

He pulled up to the curb at the Starbucks on West 6th, longing for a café latte with a few extra shots of espresso. Out of nowhere, a traffic division officer swooped toward him, ticket book at the ready. She stopped short and gave him a resigned wave when he pulled his jacket back to reveal the badge and gun clipped to his belt. There are few perks in police work, and generally not having to worry about getting tickets was one of them. Was it hypocritical? Probably, but it didn't bother him. Sometimes the little things helped get you through the day. Jack was out of the shop in a few minutes, five dollars poorer, but ready to go to work.

Jack pulled into the Justice Center, a 1970's holdover design, imposing in its own way in the heart of Cleveland, made more so by the pillbox slit windows that adorned the Cuyahoga County Jail. The jail primarily housed criminals who had worked their way up through the "farm system" of various municipal courts of the county before making it to the big leagues of more serious crimes. Brickman often wondered if career criminals had a sense of pride over graduating into the ranks of "real" bad guys, and if the dubious accomplishment of receiving a true bill on a felony charge was as meaningful as getting a college diploma. Jack had two of those, both in psychology. One was from the University of Michigan, where he had played baseball, and second, a master's, was from Case Western University, ground out slowly over the course of five years' worth of part time courses.

In addition to the jail, the Justice Center housed the Cleveland Police Department's headquarters, First District offices, the prosecutor's office, the sheriff's department, the court of common pleas, the grand jury, and a host of civil courts. The simple name, in a rare instance of bureaucratic accuracy, fit the structure perfectly. It was the center of justice in Cleveland and Cuyahoga County. At least what passed for justice these days. At any rate, the building was an almost continual hub of activity during the daytime hours, with jurists, criminals, visitors, and cops from every municipality in the county traipsing the lobby on their way to trials, depositions, and grand jury hearings. Only at night was it quiet.

Jack nosed his Toyota into the parking garage under the building, bearing to the right as he turned in. Bearing left would take you to the cramped sallyport of the jail. Brickman idly glanced over and saw a marked unit from one of the suburbs waiting at the metal overhead door. The jail housed prisoners from all over the county, and it looked like a new customer was getting dropped off.

Jack got lucky and found a space close to the elevators. Somebody must have just left. The detective swiped in with an electronic key card and stepped on board the elevator. He pressed a button for his floor. And pressed it again. And again. Finally, he was rewarded with a lit button and a ding. Jack couldn't remember a time when everything in the building worked the way it was supposed to.

Al Sladky was at his desk across from Jack's when he entered the office. It was quiet. Nobody else was in. The space was drab with a few cubicle walls and no windows. It was painted in what nearby paint manufacturer Sherwin Williams probably had labelled "Institutional Yellow."

"Jesus, Al, do you sleep here?" he asked.

"Listen, kid, I've spent more time asleep on the job than you've been on the job," Al responded. It was an old joke.

Jack slid into his desk chair, and glanced at his stained calendar. Sladky nodded towards the Starbuck's cup on the blotter.

"You still overpaying for that fancy stuff?" he said.

"Yes sir," Jack replied. "A bad cup of free coffee is really just a bad cup of coffee."

Sladky laughed, more of a brief rumbly snort. Then they got down to business.

"So, what's your take on this one," Jack asked the older man.

Sladky leaned back a little in his chair.

"Based on my vast experience as a homicide investigator, I have come to several conclusions, none of which are likely to be the correct solution, but what the hell? I may get lucky," he said.

"Judging from the ink, I'd say we got us a dead ex-con. From the neighborhood, probably tied up with drugs. And from the wounds, I'd say we got us another ex-con or a very lucky amateur."

"Which means your first guess is the same as mine," Brickman replied, not surprised.

"Sure, steal my theory," Sladky deadpanned back to Brickman.

"Gang related?" Jack asked.

Sladky shrugged.

"If it is a gang thing, why not a drive-by or an execution?" Jack pressed. "That's the usual MO, right?

"Think about it," Sladky said. "Stuff like drive-by shootings is what got everybody excited about the gangs in the first place. A stabbing might make the news. A shooting definitely will. And if they're unlucky enough to plug a civilian, say a kid or something, then you got everybody from the Feds to the national networks paying attention. It's bad for business."

"Don't ask me why they didn't corner the guy someplace quiet and give him a double tap to the head. Stabbing takes a little work," he concluded.

"That's what I'm trying to figure out," Brickman said. "You could be looking at somebody who really wants to establish himself as a tough guy, maybe somebody who wants a bigger, badder reputation. I think this is going to be more than just a solution to a business problem. Using a blade seems like somebody is trying to send a message."

Sladky rolled his eyes.

"Wait, let me guess," he said. "Is this the conclusion of a cop with a master's degree in psychology? Is my young partner dabbling in criminal profiling again?"

"Yes," Jack replied chuckling. "And I'll need you to clear off your desk so I'll have plenty of free space to throw my chicken bones."

Brickman took the kidding in stride. Sladky had come onto the police in the traditional way, entering the Marine Corps right out of high school, then joining the force after a four-year hitch. That had been twenty-two years ago, more or less, and that meant that Sladky only had three years to go before being able to qualify for a full pension, although Al didn't seem to be in any hurry to leave. Plus, he had three sons, the oldest of whom was just finishing up his junior year at Ohio State. The two younger boys were at St. Ignatius on the city's west side.

Jack had come up a different way, taking the civil service test after graduating from Michigan. While working his way up through the ranks, Jack had taken advantage of the department's tuition reimbursement program and slogged through graduate school, fitting classes in as often as his grueling schedule allowed. The degree had helped him land a short stint as a hostage negotiator, and a trip to the FBI's National Academy for a 16-week intensive training program. The Feds had actually courted Jack, again showing a preference for proven street cops.

Jack and Al both turned to face the door when they heard two more detectives enter the room, interrupting their discussion. The partners were paired up similarly, a veteran and a relative newcomer, Carmen Harris and Tony Willis, respectively.

"Morning boys," Al said. "Where've you been?"

Harris replied.

"Some guy on East 55th decided to start beating' on his wife when he got the latest Visa bill," Harris said. "Seems she was doing a little too much shopping. The beating was apparently one too many, 'cause she ended up showing him one of her latest purchases, a hot little black number in .25 caliber."

"Fatal?" Sladky asked, surprised.

"Well, not at first," Harris said. "He died on the way to the hospital."

"From a .25?" Brickman asked. "How many times did she hit him?"

"Just the one, but it was enough to do the job," he said. "You know, it was the usual. I don't think she wanted him dead, just wanted him to stop. So, she gets to the gun, a cheap little thing by the way, and warns him to stop. He's all like 'go ahead, bitch, do it' so she does and pops him in the chest.

15

"Anyway, now he's pissed, but scared too, yelling, and screaming for help by the time the blue suits get there. His vitals were a little shaky when EMS got there, but he went south in a hurry. They figure the slug nicked a big artery and just worked its way loose while he was carrying on.

"So, what do you guys got?"

As Sladky gave Harris a rundown of their case, Brickman opened the top drawer of his desk and pulled out a yellow pad and started transcribing his meager case notes to fresh paper, rewriting the hastily scrawled data verbatim, and translating the simple shorthand in complete words. The original notebook would end up in the case file eventually, but Jack liked to work from clearer copies. He had just about finished when the phone rang.

"Brickman," he said. It was a technician from the coroner's office.

Jack transferred the phone to his left hand and started writing.

"OK, great, thanks," he said before hanging up. Sladky looked at him expectantly.

"We got an ID," Jack told him.

"AFIS hit?" Al asked, referring to the federal fingerprint database.

"What else?" Jack replied.

Brickman punched in the victim's information into his desktop computer. Again, pulling a complete criminal history from the database was not as simple as television made it appear. You needed special clearance to just summon it to your screen. As a homicide investigator, Jack had that clearance, but he was held accountable for every record he pulled. He got lucky. The victim had a local jacket, so Brickman could pull those reports up from the department's own records without having to track them down through other departments. It seemed like he spent his life waiting.

Scanning the screen, Jack saw two mugshots, one facing him, the other showing a profile. The eyes were defiant and angry as they stared at the detective. Last night, they had been vacant and empty.

Timmons, Jameel R.

Reading through the record, Jack saw that their estimate of Timmons' age had been right on. He had been twenty-four. They had also been right about his criminal history. Since turning eighteen, Timmons, AKA "J-Time," had been mostly in trouble. Like a pro ball player starting in the minor leagues, Timmons had worked his way up from petty theft and possession to carrying a concealed weapon and trafficking. The latter charge had rewarded him with an eighteen-month stay at the Lorain correctional facility. It had probably been a longer sentence, but overcrowding was a constant issue in the state's prisons. As Jack worked his way through Timmons' Computerized Criminal History, or CCH, and field intelligence reports that listed Timmons' known associates as a local faction of the Gangster Disciples, a street gang strong in Detroit and Chicago, he began forming a professional opinion of the young man.

Jack continued flipping through the screens, stopping at one that detailed Timmons' other tattoos, the ones that hadn't been visible at the scene. Over the right chest was a six-pointed star, underneath which was the word "MOM." A casual observer might wrongly assume that the star was a religious affiliation, and that he loved his mother. They would have been wrong on both counts. Jack knew that the star was the primary symbol of the Folk Nation, the parent group of the Gangster Disciples. As for MOM, well, he probably did love his mother, but the term was an acronym common in prison tattoos. It meant "mind over matter." To Jack, that translated to psychoprophylaxis. To the cons, it meant if they were tough enough to take whatever prison threw at them and keep going.

Another gang symbol, this one a heart with wings on it, was tattooed on his right calf in the same sloppy prison style.

Sladky grew impatient.

"You reading or sharing?" he said.

"Sorry," Jack replied, and sent the file to the printer for a hard copy. Jack could be intense, especially at the start of an investigation. And he knew Sladky liked to have something he could page through, not just a screen to stare at.

Jack jotted down a few notes in his field notebook. He now had some facts, including the address of Timmons' next of kin, his mother, and his release information from the department of corrections. Timmons had only been out of jail for about two months. He had either stepped on somebody's toes right away or someone had been holding a grudge for a while.

Finally, Jack read something that explained what Timmons might have been doing in the area. A domestic relations court entry requiring Timmons to pay child support for one James Murphy, son of Lumika Murphy. Murphy's address was in the Longwood apartment complex, not far from the murder scene.

Sladky looked up as Jack leaned back from the computer screen.

"Well, waddya' think?

"This tells us we were probably right about who Timmons was and where he came from," Jack said. " And why he was in that area."

"Yeah, I noticed his last known address was over on Buckeye," Sladky said. "Was he makin' a deal or was there love in the air?

"Maybe he was just visiting his kid."

"Right," Al said. "But the way I see it, this guy was probably into two things: Business and pleasure. He was there to make money or get laid."

"Two safe bets," Jack replied. But if he wasn't just passing by, paying a visit, why did this seem like a hit?

He was about to ask Sladky the same thing when the door opened, and Lt. McNamara walked in. Mac was in his early fifties, overweight and balding. As usual, he was carrying a stack of files and looked harried and disheveled. Jack could tell by the strong odor of tobacco that Mac had just been out on a cigarette break.

When Mac saw them, he nodded in their direction.

"Give me a minute, guys," he said, before disappearing into his office.

Seconds later, they heard a thud from behind the door, obviously made as he dumped the stack of files onto his desk. Mac reappeared and half sat on the desk next to Brickman's. He crossed his arms and looked at them over the top of his glasses.

"So, what do you have?"

Jack gave him a brief rundown of the case so far, updated with the victim's name. Sladky only interrupted a couple times to clarify.

"OK," Mac said, "sounds like a gang thing, like you guys figured. Have you been up to see The Padre yet?"

"Nah," Sladky said. "We both just came in."

"Tell you what," Mac said. "Check with Ramirez, see if he can help you guys out. I'm sure he'll have a file on Timmons. He may ask you to run with it for a while...they're pretty busy upstairs. You two don't have anything pending, do you?"

"We're scheduled for the grand jury tomorrow morning on the Calvin case," Jack said, "and we're scheduled to start the Hawkins trial on Monday."

"Is that going forward?" Mac asked. "I thought he was going to plead out."

"Last we heard, he was going to cop to manslaughter," Sladky said. "He'll probably do the right thing on Monday, so we ain't expecting to be tied up too long."

"Let me know if that changes, Al," their boss replied. "If it does, Ramirez is going to get the Timmons thing. I don't want you two spread that thin."

Jack thought it more likely that the bean counters had been complaining about overtime again.

"What about the coroner's report?" Mac asked.

Jack shook his head.

"Hoping to get it tomorrow," he said.

"OK, do what you can tonight."

"Did patrol make notification yet?" Jack asked.

"Yeah," Mac said. "Some time this morning. They went over with victim's services and talked to mom on Buckeye and gave her the news."

"Any word on how she took it?"

18

"No," Mac said. "I've got the name of the patrolmen who went to the house if you want them. They're probably home by now, though."

"Think we'll be able to squeeze in a visit tomorrow?" he asked Al, who had just finished his coffee and was crumpling the cup into the prerequisite ball before pitching it into the garbage can.

"Don't ask me, ask the grand jury," Al said.

Jack and the lieutenant both smiled.

"What about the media? Did they get the ID yet?" Jack asked.

"They'll get the name at 1600, when Young briefs 'em. Anyway, talk to Ramirez before he leaves, will you?" Mac said, and headed toward his office, the perpetual look of worry already back on his face.

Jack dialed up Luis Ramirez' number and gave the gang task force's leader a brief thumbnail on Timmons. As expected, he said he was overloaded but he would look into it. Ramirez, who was nicknamed "The Padre" due to his tireless efforts to "convert" gang members, was a very busy cop.

"Thanks," Jack said, and hung up.

"Ready, rookie?" Al asked as he stood up. To Al, just about everybody was a rookie.

"Why not?" Jack said, grabbing an extra notebook from his desk before dropping the Timmons file into his desk drawer, which he locked with a small, odd-looking key. Al snatched a portable radio from a charging cradle on his desk and they headed to the door.

"So," Jack said. "Where do you want to start?"

"Where else?" said Sladky. "The girl."

CHAPTER 5

Cliff O'Brien got to *The Press'* office a little before two. He nodded to the security guard manning a console in the huge, ornate lobby as he headed toward the employee entrance. Cliff shifted his gym bag higher onto his shoulder, and moved a water bottle from his right hand to his left so he could dig into his front pocket for his magnetic key card. After a quick swipe, he was rewarded with a heavy click as the electronic deadbolt slid free and a small red light turned to green. He pulled the door open and held it ajar with his foot as he repocketed the swipe card, juggling his water and gym bag as he did so.

The home of *The Press* was another one of Gavin Lawson's signatures. When he decided to start the paper, he had done so, literally, from the ground up. Gav had bought several buildings at Rockwell and East 13th Street and promptly razed them, creating room not only for the editorial and business offices of *The Press*, but also its printing and distribution facilities as well.

After a short wait, Cliff rode one of several elevators to the city newsroom on the fourth floor. He passed through a small waiting area and waved hello to the young receptionist who was busy manning the phone lines through a hands-free headset. She smiled and waved back, still talking to the caller as she did so.

The city newsroom was a large, bustling place, although its setup made it hard for newcomers to really gauge its size. The room consisted of clusters of desks broken up by cubicles found in offices everywhere. Cliff had initially preferred his old paper's layout, where the newsroom was just one open space with desks stuck together and no walls in between. He'd quickly learned to appreciate the cubicles. The prefab walls kept things quieter, making phone calls clearer and helping him focus when he was on a deadline. Which was always. The "quiet down, I'm on the phone" gesture he'd perfected in Cincinnati had been rendered obsolete.

Cliff stopped to say hi to a few co-workers on the way to his cubicle. Some who had obviously stayed later than Cliff at the bar were sporting the "never again" pallor of a world-class hangover, which was impressive considering it was early afternoon. Having been there plenty of times himself, he could relate. One reporter, Brian Katz, looked particularly disheveled.

"I'd like to say you're looking good, Brian," Cliff said. "But you'd know I was lying."

Katz, who covered general interest topics, ventured a half-hearted grin. The effort looked painful.

"Blame Flemming," he said, referring to an assistant sports editor. "He heard about a new drink from a Browns front office guy. All I know is, it was bourbon mixed with tequila."

"Booze mixed with booze," Cliff said. "What a revolting concept. I like things simple. Shot and a beer."

"Yeah. You'd think one would have been enough to let me know it was a bad idea."

"Hey, Cliff, what's the good word?"

Cliff turned to see Doreen Ellis making her way towards her own cubicle, a black canvas briefcase over one shoulder and a carryout coffee mug in the other hand.

"Just trying to wake the dead," he said, gesturing toward Katz with his water bottle.

"You know, you can have a good time without drinking," Ellis said with mock authority.

"So they say," Katz replied. "Personally, I don't believe it. To paraphrase somebody famous, a solid hangover makes you appreciate how good normal life feels."

"I didn't notice you abstaining last night, Dor," Cliff said.

"Two beers do not a hangover make," she said, walking towards her desk. "Besides, I had an interview this morning with a fire inspector. How about you? Working that stabbing from last night?"

"Yeah," Cliff said. "Young's holding his usual press conference at four. I'm hoping to do a follow-up tomorrow, maybe a background piece on Saturday. Depends on if the cops catch the bad guy before then."

They reached the end of the passage between cubicles and Doreen disappeared around the corner of the workspace. Cliff stuffed his gym bag into a corner of his cubicle and headed over to Leo Nelson's office a few feet away. Leo Nelson enjoyed the luxury of real walls. The door was open, and Cliff rapped his knuckles lightly on its metal surface. Leo, his wiry frame hunched over his computer terminal, was obviously in the middle of something, since he let Cliff stand in the open doorway for several minutes before looking up.

"Hey, O'Brien," he said. "How's my star reporter today?"

"So far, so good," Cliff said.

"Well, enough idle chit-chat. What do you have for me today?"

"Leo," Cliff said, "I think all the romance has gone out of our relationship. You used to love our little chats."

"Yeah, well, on a normal day, I'd put my feet up and jaw a spell, as they say down south," Leo said, "But Floyd's story on the waterfront revitalization funding fell short by a couple of sources, and he's going to need a couple of days. What I really need is an in-depth feature with some graphics to tie in. Otherwise, I've got to tell layout to fill a hole on the front page with national news."

"Well, I hope to have some follow-up on that stabbing from last night, but it probably won't be long enough."

"Swell," Leo said. "Nothing on the back burner?"

"How about 22 inches and two charts on police pursuit policies in the area?"

Leo looked up through his glasses, a huge grin on his face.

"You're not kidding, are you?"

Cliff shook his head.

"I've been working on it for a week or so," he said.

"When can it be ready?"

"Ten minutes ago."

The grin grew into a full-grown smile.

"Outstanding," Leo said. "Send it over right away."

"No problem, boss," Cliff replied.

He logged onto his computer and pulled up the story. In seconds, Leo had the story in front of him. Cliff checked his voice mail and made a few notes while his boss read through the story. Cliff was already returning a phone call to a city councilwoman by the time Leo was done with it. When he hung up, Leo was standing at the entrance to his cubicle.

"Kid, you are a life saver," he said. "It's just what I needed."

"Glad to help," Cliff said. "Any chance of getting it above the fold?"

"No, but I'll make sure they spell your name right on the byline."

"Fair enough."

"You know," Leo said, "letting you focus on in-depth stories was probably the best move I've made here."

"Remember that at raise time," Cliff said.

"Seriously," Leo started to say. "Since I put these other guys on scanner duty and making the daily calls to the cops, you keep coming up with good stories."

It was hard to be sure, but Cliff could have sworn Leo was actually walking with a spring in his step as he headed back to his office. Then again, maybe his leg had just fallen asleep while he was editing.

Cliff made a few more phone calls and did a short interview with a source for a story he was working on concerning the rising price of crack cocaine on the street. When he was done, he checked his watch. Grabbing his notebook, he got up and poked his head into Leo's office again.

"We got any cars free, Leo?" he asked.

"For you, sure," Leo replied, and pointed to a key rack near the doorway. "Grab that white keychain. The Escort is in the garage. Where you headed?"

"CPD is doing their press briefing," Cliff said. "I'm sure they got an ID on the DOA. I want to get started on a follow-up."

Leo put his hands up in a placating gesture.

"Spare me the alphabet soup," he said. "We have a beat reporter to cover the briefing you know. Or do you smell something bigger brewing?"

Cliff shrugged.

"Who knows?" he said. "I may look up the family, see where that leads."

"You know the TV guys will be doing that with all kinds of 'honor student, churchgoer' stuff, right?"

"Of course," Cliff said. "I'll just try to stay out of their way."

And with a conspiratorial smile, Cliff was on his way.

CHAPTER 6

The press briefing didn't turn out as productive as Cliff had hoped.

Wilson Young, CPD's Public Information Officer, was his typically engaging self. The lieutenant had a real gift for communication, and was well-known for improvising new but surprisingly accurate phrases and terminology, some of which inevitably worked their way into the city's vernacular. Cliff's favorite was "police brutaliation."

Today, however, no such landmark witticisms had been forthcoming. Young had led off with a bank robbery, an assault on an elderly couple at the West Side Market and the expansion of the department's bicycle patrol. The handful of reporters, flanked and outnumbered two to one by television cameras, dutifully jotted notes and asked a few questions. Cliff could tell they were all champing at the bit to ask about the murder. No one interrupted Young though. As congenial as he was, he didn't like being interrupted. New reporters sometimes ignored the warnings of their peers, only to be rewarded with a blank stare and long, exaggerated pause. Sometimes Young would even cut them off for a week or two. That usually got the message across.

Finally, he addressed the stabbing. Unconsciously, the reporters leaned forward to hear. Even the cameras zoomed closer as Young prepared to speak.

"Now, as some of you already mysteriously know, and have reported," he began, looking pointedly at Cliff, "the city suffered its forty-sixth homicide of the year last night."

Cliff looked at the notebook balanced on his knee and tried to suppress a smug grin. Even as he did so, he felt his ears turn red. It was nice to be acknowledged but it was still a little embarrassing to be the target of several envious glares. Lt. Young and Cliff's peers had long suspected he had a good inside source on the force. They were right, of course, but all the Guiness in the world would never loosen his lips enough to confirm their hunches.

Cliff's pen sailed across the faint blue lines of his notebook as Young launched into the details of the previous night's crime. By the time Young had wrapped up and opened the floor to questions, Cliff hadn't learned much that he didn't already know. Briefings were sometimes like that. The most important thing he had learned was the name of the victim. Coupled with a few phone calls, the name would lead him to the next of kin, and probably another story. Cliff had been disappointed but not surprised to learn that the coroner's report would not be released until at least next week. From experience, Cliff knew the cops would have it much sooner, but if anything remained sacrosanct in the police community, it was the coroner's report.

When Young finished, Cliff fired a couple exploratory questions his way, none of which bagged anything useful. Still, he had a jumping off point for his story, and a couple of ideas for future in-depth pieces.

CHAPTER 7

Jack and Al's visit to Lumika Murphy's apartment in the squalid Longwood complex yielded them little more than a "fuck you" and a door slammed in their faces while a young woman held a screaming child, presumably Jameel Timmons' son, in the background. Police weren't popular here. Al waited a few seconds and knocked again. The same woman opened the door.

"If you here about Jameel, I don't know nothing," she said. "But you find Andre Clark, you ask him. He put a bad beat down on Jameel." And she slammed the door again.

The Longwood apartment complex isn't far from CPD headquarters, and they were back at their desks in less than ten minutes. Jack immediately got to work searching the computer for any record of Andre Clark, and Al dug into his desk drawers for the Calvin case file and started paging through it, grunting occasionally as he flipped through the pages. About halfway through the documents, he stood, grabbed his coffee mug and Jack's, filled them, and brought them to the desktop without comment. Without looking up from the computer screen, Jack reached for the cup and brought it to his lips. With an exaggerated smile he got some of the bitter brew into his mouth.

"Aaaaah," he said. "Now that's what I call a good cup of coffee."

It wasn't. Station house coffee was awful.

Al looked over the top of the Calvin file and rolled his eyes. Jack occasionally enjoyed bugging Al, and slurping coffee was one of the easiest ways to do it.

The database search didn't tell Jack much about Andre Clark. It gave them a current address and a criminal history, but nothing beyond that. As records went, Clark's was fairly impressive. The only thing missing was a murder conviction, and he'd probably get to that eventually based on his past. Or maybe he had graduated to that last night. He had been charged with a staggering variety of crimes in his thirty years of life, from minor drug possession to robbery to felonious assault. Despite his record, though, Clark had done surprisingly little jail time. As Jack scanned the screen, he read a tale too often repeated in the criminal justice field – too many cases had been plea bargained, with short sentences. Even some of the felonies, which should have guaranteed prison time, had only earned Clark probation.

Even with the record, Jack still knew next to nothing about Andre Clark, including known associates or gang affiliations. He certainly didn't know his current whereabouts. One vital piece of information he had obtained, though, was that Clark was still on probation for his last offense. That might give them some leverage to pick him up and have a nice chat.

"Anything good?" Sladky asked from across the desk.

"Only the basics," Jack replied. "It gives his last known address, but that entry is ten years old. Looks like nobody bothered to update it."

"Yeah, probably his mom's house or something," Al said. "I'll bet the guy hasn't lived there in years, but I bet he still stops by."

Sladky shut the Calvin file and pushed it toward Jack.

"Hey, college boy, take a look at that will ya? Refresh that famous memory of yours."

"Come on, Al," Jack said as he wiped his coffee mug out with a paper towel. "You know you love a challenge. Besides, a good thinking exercise keeps you young."

"Too late for that," Al replied.

"Is it too early for dinner?" Jack asked.

Al looked at his watch.

"Nah, let's have a nice leisurely meal and go knock on Clark's door. Maybe we'll be in front of the tube for the Tribe game."

"Won't you scare Paula, coming home that early?" Jack asked as he headed toward the door.

"Who said anything about going home, kid? Budweiser and my favorite bartender need my generous donations."

"Just remember it's a school night," Jack said, laughing.

"Yes, dear."

CHAPTER 8

Page B1, *The North Coast Press*

May 11

By Cliff O'Brien

Jameel Timmons died two nights ago.

Cleveland Police are in the initial phase of investigation into the brutal stabbing death of the 24-year-old man in the area of the Longwood housing complex.

Timmons' family and friends are in the early stages of dealing with the loss of a troubled young man they all seemed to think was finally on the right path.

Jameel's mother, Patrice Campbell, said she had always feared her son's wild lifestyle would catch up with him.

"It's a mother's worst nightmare, you know," she said from her Buckeye Road home. "You just do what you can, try to raise your kids right, and somehow they just end up with the wrong people."

Campbell said her son's troubles started when he was a teen.

"Maybe I didn't do enough," she said. "I have to work a lot, and back then, it was all hours of the day and night."

Campbell, now a cleaning crew supervisor, said she was so desperate for money when Jameel was young that she would work any shift, and fill in for absentee workers at a moments notice. Those shifts, she said, left Timmons under the supervision of his older sister.

"I was just trying to put food on the table and clothes on their backs," Campbell said. "I don't blame my girl, but maybe it was too much to ask of her to watch him all the time. She wanted to have fun, too."

According to Campbell, Timmons had several scrapes with the law.

"A lot of that was just kid stuff," she said. "You know, curfew, maybe breaking some windows and so on. The later stuff they said he did, well, I still don't know if all of that was true."

Campbell said Timmons, who was on probation for his latest "stuff," was really trying to turn his life around.

"First thing he did when he got set free was come and see me," Campbell said, tears in her eyes. "If he was such a bad boy, why would he do that?"

According to Campbell, Timmons was always around for holidays and special occasions, and was trying to be a good father to his infant son, James, who lives with his mother, Lumika Murphy, in the Longwood housing complex. Timmons had probably been on his way to see Lumika and James when he was killed, Campbell said.

"He was really trying," she said. "His own daddy wasn't around much. Maybe he wanted to change things. All I know is he was a good boy who made some mistakes."

Other family members agreed, placing the blame for Timmons' legal troubles on the rough streets of Cleveland, and overzealous police.

Still, others who knew Timmons painted a different picture of the young man.

One neighbor, who didn't wish to be named, said Timmons was what he called "one of the worst punks on the street."

"Since I can remember, he was in trouble," the man said. "And it wasn't no misunderstandings, either. He was always the ringleader, always the kid with the biggest mouth."

He also spoke of Timmons's quick temper and violent habits.

"He didn't take anything from anybody," the neighbor said. "He'd beat down anybody who looked at him sideways."

And those wild ways only got worse when he befriended what another neighbor, who also wished to remain anonymous, called "gangbangers."

"Man, it was all hours of the day and night, cars would be pulling in, pulling out, guys calling for Jameel when he lived at home, and even when he didn't."

Timmons apparently had been moving around the area in the past four years, rarely showing up at his mother's house. More than once, the neighbor said, police had taken him from his mother's house in handcuffs.

"I think it was just his hideout," the man said. "Like his mom needed that at home. Besides, they always found him there anyway."

CPD spokesman Lt. Wilson Young confirmed that Timmons had a lengthy police record, including convictions for carrying a concealed handgun and drug trafficking. Young also stated that Timmons did indeed have ties to the Cleveland gang community, but would not specify whether Timmons was an active member or just an associate. He also did not specify to which gang he may have been connected.

"As of right now, we are following up several leads in this case," Young said. "To elaborate further on this case might hamper the work of detectives in the field."

Young would also not elaborate further on this cause of death beyond confirming that Timmons had been stabbed, adding that the coroner's report was expected to be released early next week.

The death of Jameel Timmons brought Cleveland's to-date total of homicides to forty-six, a twenty-year low.

"Not that it matters to his mom," Cliff thought as he re-read the story in his cubicle at the paper. He had his feet up on his desk and was leaning back in his chair, reading *The Press* like thousands of other Clevelanders were at that very moment. One nice perk of being a journalist was that you could read the paper at work without getting yelled at for wasting time.

Even an inter-office e-mail couldn't dampen Cliff's spirits today. He was holding a paper that held not one, but two bylined stories of his creation. And they were on the front pages of the first two sections of the newspaper. True to his word, Leo Nelson had used the pursuit policy story on A1 and the murder follow-up on B1. He was trying not to appear too smug about it, but he just couldn't seem to wipe the grin off his face.

Neither the errant observation about Timmons' mother, nor being in the office relatively early bothered him today. He had a slow day ahead, with only some follow-up interviews planned. And since it was Friday, he hoped to be holding down a bar stool at Griff's by the time their legendary happy hour started. It would be a welcome way to start the weekend.

Cliff had just started sipping his second cup of coffee when he heard Leo Nelson knocking on the "door" to his cubicle.

"Am I interrupting?" he said, a broad smile on his face.

"Just trying to read the paper and see what the rest of these people do around here," Cliff said.

"Well, you can gloat a little today I guess," Leo said. " Those were two darn good stories. I like the realistic angle you got on the murder victim. You know nobody else is going to go after that kind of thing."

"You're not saying I took a wrong approach, are you?" Cliff asked.

"Hell, no!" Leo said. "That's the kind of stuff they want upstairs, and that's why we hired you. Just because the guy got killed doesn't mean he was a saint. If you only print half of the truth, then it's not really the truth."

"Tell that to the networks," Cliff said, chuckling. They'd had this conversation before.

"By tonight, they'll probably be following up the same angle," Leo said. "You know: 'Misunderstood kid ruined by single parent home, drugs and the mean streets.' Anyway, good work. You're making my job a lot easier."

"You have my stuff for Sunday, right?" Cliff asked.

"Yeah, and it looks pretty solid, too" Leo replied. "Got any surprises for tomorrow?"

"Hey, don't get greedy, OK?" Cliff said. "I have to space out my miracles, and right now I don't have anything ready."

"Sorry, sorry," Leo said. "If nothing breaks, feel free to sneak out a little early. I know you worked pretty late last night. Just try not to make it look too obvious. I have a reputation to protect."

"Speaking of working weird hours, what are you doing in this early?" Cliff asked. "I didn't know you ever got here before noon."

"Editorial staff meeting," Leo said as he turned to leave. "Lord knows we don't have enough meetings around here."

Cliff felt even better after his boss left. He wasn't sure if he should feel guilty about his good mood. After all, it was at the expense of somebody who had been alive a few days ago. From a purely objective viewpoint, he really didn't have anything to feel guilty about. He hadn't killed anybody, nor had he exploited anyone in their time of grief. He had just reported the news, which was his job. He was sure Patrice Campbell wouldn't be happy with the story, but he had at least gotten her feelings about her son into the story. If she wanted to believe her son had been an angel, that was fine. Her neighbors knew better though, and that was where the real story was anyway.

He had spent a lot of time talking to Campbell and her neighbors. As usual, he had needed to jockey for position with the television crews and *The PD* reporter, but he had managed to sit down with Patrice Campbell for an interview. After that, it was just a matter of knocking on

31

doors until somebody answered. Once they found out he wasn't a cop, most people were willing to talk to him.

Cliff made a few phone calls and finished the crossword puzzle while waiting for some callbacks on a couple of other stories he had on the back burner. He was just killing time before lunch, after which he had a meeting with a narcotics detective to explore some new story ideas, and maybe look into a personality profile of the vice division's new commander. He fully intended to take Leo's dispensation and sneak out early. He had already earned his paycheck this week, and could enjoy an early start to the weekend with a clean conscience. Besides, he was likely to be busy on Monday with the kickoff to Police Memorial Week. There would be plenty of events to cover. Who knew? Maybe he'd dig up another angle on the Timmons story, too.

CHAPTER 9

Jack Brickman sat in the waiting area of the grand jury room, well, waiting.

The detective sat in the generic padded chair reading a folded copy of *The Press* when Sladky sat down next to him with a brown paper bag and two paper cups of coffee. He handed one to Jack before settling in. He dug into the bag and produced a cheese Danish, which he offered to his partner.

"Al, you're spoiling me," Jack said as he took the pastry and put the paper down.

"Why go hungry?" Al said as he bit into his own Danish and washed it down with a slug of bitter coffee. A lot of their partnership seemed to revolve around coffee, food, and beer.

"Anything good in there today?" Al asked, nodding toward The Press.

"We made the first page of the metro section," Jack said as he passed the paper to Al, leaving him to pore over the sports section. Al was done with the story in a few minutes.

"Well, he got it about right," he said, referring to the reporter. "At least he didn't try any of that 'honor student' crap."

"O'Brien's usually pretty fair," Jack conceded.

"As long as he gets it right is all I care about," Al said as he handed the paper back to his younger partner. The older man then opened an ancient leather briefcase under his chair and extracted a paperback.

Jack finished the paper and looked at his watch. It was already half past ten, later than he would have liked. They had a meeting with the coroner at 1:30, and they would be lucky to be heard before the grand jury broke for lunch at noon.

Jack was more focused on the Timmons case anyway. They had struck out at the last known address from Andre Clark's file. The people who lived at the house now said they had only been there a few months, and Andre Clark definitely hadn't been one of the previous occupants. They said they thought he might have lived there before the last tenants, but they weren't sure. And no, they didn't have any idea where he could be reached. Even a name search through the Ohio Bureau of Motor Vehicles proved fruitless. That listed the same address as their file.

Sladky had finally gotten through to The Padre on the phone and let him know they wanted to talk to Andre Clark as soon as possible. The lieutenant said they would get right on it, although he didn't recognize the name as a major player. Still, he had a lot of faith in his database, and was relatively certain that if Clark were in any way tied into the drug business, he would be easy enough to track down.

Jack didn't like a trail to go cold, and in the days since the murder, Clark could have easily left town. He'd have plenty of time to produce an alibi or prepare a story for the police. Occasionally, time worked against you and helped the suspect build up courage or whatever other mental defense mechanisms kicked into place after you committed a murder. And other times, it worked for you, letting guilt and fear build up until suspects were practically begging to confess. Judging from Clark's criminal pedigree, Jack doubted he would feel guilty or afraid. A violent predator like Clark would write the crime off as necessary for his own survival, and all other considerations would be unimportant. Pride, Jack predicted, would be Clark's downfall. He'd be proud of taking care of business in such a macho fashion. Hopefully, he would want to brag about it when they caught him.

Jack pulled his laptop computer from its case and brought it to life, ignoring the mocking eye rolls from Sladky. The last thing Jack wanted to do was work on an article, but he was just treading water trying to figure out the Timmons killing with the weak information he had. The coroner's report would be the first hard evidence they had on the case, and they were several hours away from getting that. If the grand jury got them in before lunch.

By the time Al was called, Jack had nearly finished the article he was working on for a police magazine. It was about fifteen minutes before noon, so Jack doubted he would be called, too. The legal profession took its lunch hours seriously. Sure enough, Al emerged from the grand jury room thirteen minutes later, just as the bailiff was picking up his phone. He almost immediately put it back down.

"Sergeant Brickman? They won't need you," he said as he started shuffling subpoenas around his desk.

"Any trouble?" Jack asked as they headed toward the elevators.

"Nah, they know a slam dunk when they see it," Al said. "One guy asked about the search, but the foreman stepped in and explained the exclusionary rule thing. 'Course I coulda done it better, but I guess that's what he gets paid for."

"Right," Jack said.

"You hungry?" he asked Jack as they boarded the crowded elevator.

"Starving despite the Danish."

"How about Primo Vino for lunch?" Al said, "We're going that way anyway."

"Just what we need before a trip to the morgue," Jack said. "A hearty Italian meal."

"Hey, it's just a sit down with the medical examiner, not a slice and dice," Al said as they headed to the parking garage. " 'Sides, you gonna want to eat a big meal *after* we go there?"

"Good point," Jack conceded. "Little Italy it is, then."

"Just remember, it's your turn to buy. After all, I got breakfast."

"Al, we have to start working on your definition of breakfast," Jack said as they reached the car.

The restaurant, at the east end of Murray Hill, in the area known as Little Italy, had not been very crowded, so the detectives made it to the coroner's office in plenty of time for their meeting. Murray Hill was literally just around the corner from University Hospital's main campus, Case Western Reserve University, and the Cuyahoga County Coroner's office. The coroner had only recently moved into their new accommodations, a state-of-the-art facility at the corner of Cedar and Carnegie. The old building had been bought by the hospital to make way for a parking garage. In return, the county had received space in a renovated office building overlooking one of the busiest intersections in Cleveland.

The new facilities reflected the impeccable standards they had established over the years. With a nearly flawless record, the coroner's office enjoyed a position of trust in the law enforcement community. Even the public had come to accept that the coroner was on only one side, and that was the side of scientific truth.

The current coroner, Dr. Ambrose Herlong, had run unopposed in the last election since his predecessor had decided to retire after a lengthy and very accomplished career. Dr. Herlong was in his early fifties, an avid golfer and fly fisherman. He'd been in the medical examiner's office for decades before he took the top post. He was barely into his first term but so far, he had upheld the high standards of his forerunners, people whose dedication and skill had reached nearly legendary status.

Short, chubby, bespectacled, and balding with thin gray hair at the sides, Dr. Herlong immediately conjured an image of a mild-mannered mad scientist.

Since Al and Jack were a little early, Dr. Herlong was running a little late, leaving the two detectives to digest their lunches in the padded chairs outside the coroner's actual office. Al looked around after a secretary had shown them to their seats.

"I think I miss the old place," he said. "I like my morgues to look like morgues."

Jack nodded. The old coroner's office had a dank, Dickensian air to it, from its cramped rooms to the small, ancient amphitheater where cadavers were occasionally dissected in front of an audience. The new office had a much more clinical feel to it.

Jack was about to comment when Dr. Herlong swept into the room and ushered them into his office. He had a casual, calm look on his face as he walked behind his desk, which was stacked high with files. Jack pitied the secretary who had to sort it all out. Luckily, the doctor seemed to know where everything was.

"Detective Sladky, Sergeant Brickman," Dr. Herlong said as he extended his hand across the desktop. Since he was so short, both he and the detectives had to lean forward quite a bit to make physical contact. He smiled as he shook their hands.

"Still bait fishing, Al?" the doctor asked as he eased into his chair.

"Every chance I get, which ain't much these days," Sladky replied.

"Someday, I'm going to get you to start fly fishing," Dr. Herlong said. "You know, it really is a gentleman's sport."

"Doc, first, I'm no gentleman. And I got two problems with fly fishing: One, I ain't standin' in three feet of water, freezin' my valuables off so I can catch some trout. We're supposed to be smarter than the fish."

Jack and the doctor laughed.

"And two, I just can't tie those little knots. I mean, for chrissake, look at those things."

Al finished with a wave towards a glass case displaying assorted flies on the wall behind the physician.

"Sadly, the nimble fingers of a surgeon are not useful in too many other hobbies," Dr. Herlong said with grin. "I am lucky enough to enjoy one of them. If I ever decide to become a card cheat, oh the damage I could do!"

Jack again marveled at how Sladky seemed to know everybody in Cleveland. Of course, Dr. Herlong had long been a fixture at the coroner's office, and Al and he had consulted on a number of cases over the years. And Dr. Herlong *still* wasn't the best source Al had the office.

The diminutive doctor looked over at Brickman.

"And you, Jack. How's the short game?" he asked.

"Same as always," Jack said. "Awful." Jack was a hacker.

"I'll have to get you out to Canterbury some day," Dr. Herlong said.

"Any time, doctor," Jack replied.

"Cheryl tells me you two are on the Timmons case," the doctor said as he dug through one of the piles on his desk.

"Your secretary was right," Al said.

"She's been here longer than anybody can remember," Dr. Herlong said. "The next time she gets something wrong will be the first time. And we are supposed to refer to her as my executive assistant now, detective."

"These times, they are a changin'" Sladky said.

"Indeed," Dr. Herlong said as he continued his excavation. Finally, he pulled out a file.

"Ah, here it is, Jameel Timmons." The doctor looked at them over his glasses. "Do you want the medical version or the short version?"

Al pointed his thumb at Brickman.

"Doc, the kid could probably decipher the medical junk, but I gotta have it simple," he said.

They all knew that wasn't true, but the doctor proceeded with the layman's version anyway.

"Mr. Timmons died as a result of a single stab wound to the base of the brain. The knife was inserted from the rear in such a manner that it severed the top of the spinal cord. The knife was then twisted to complete the severing of the cord and further damage the brain stem. A second knife wound on the inside of the left leg severed the femoral artery. From what we could determine, the heart had nearly stopped beating by the time the second cut was made, rendering it somewhat superfluous.

"The knife blade was triangular in shape, with a single edge and an angular point, like a chisel. From metal fragments we found when it hit the bone, the blade was treated to give it a black coating."

The doctor looked up from his notes at the detectives.

"This was unusual," he said. "That's a Japanese style of fighting knife. Supposed to be better for piercing bone and armor, I guess. It's called a *tanto*."

"Like in The Lone Ranger?" Al asked.

"Just sounds the same," Dr. Herlong replied. "I had to look it up. Continuing, we also found some slight bruising on the right side of the deceased's face and jaw. Slight because the force was inflicted just prior to the first stab wound. My best guess is that the victim was approached from behind by one unknown assailant. The assailant grabbed the victim around the neck with his left hand and drove the knife into the base of the skull with his right. Still holding onto the victim, the suspect pulled the knife out from the base of the skull and pulled it from front to rear across the inside of the left thigh."

"What about hair, fibers or scrapings" Jack asked.

"Our technicians were unable to get any usable hair from the scene," the doctor said. "At any rate, it is difficult to retrieve hair samples from an open crime scene, as you well know. No scrapings, so he didn't fight back. I don't think he saw this coming. Whoever did this did it so fast that the victim didn't even have a chance to try and pry the arm from around his neck."

Jack nodded.

"We did get some cloth strands that did not match the victim's clothes. Again, we have no way of estimating their evidentiary value at this point. He may have just brushed up against somebody at bus stop for all we know. We'll log them just the same."

"Opinions, doc?" Al asked.

"Probably the same as yours, at this point," Dr. Herlong said. "You are dealing with somebody who knows what they are doing. My guess would be ex-military, judging from the placement of the wounds. And from their strength. This is somebody who has excellent upper body strength, I'm basing that mainly on the grab, not the stab wound. And this is somebody who wanted the job done right, otherwise why risk the femoral cut? That makes it messy."

Jack suddenly remembered something Lumika Murphy had mentioned during their brief interview.

"What about old wounds, doctor? We were told he might have been at the receiving end of a bad beating while he was locked up the last time."

"As a matter of fact, there was evidence of some previous injuries," Dr. Herlong said. "Three recently healed broken ribs, and a broken cheek bone, probably occurred at about the same time. Also, a broken left wrist. That one, at least, looked like a doctor had set it. The others healed sloppy, like he just ignored them. Not much you could do for the ribs, but the face might have healed faster had it been set right."

"That tracks with our information," Brickman said. "He probably didn't want to bring too much attention to the beating in jail. The broken wrist he could explain away, but the guards probably would have started asking questions if he had shown up at the infirmary with too many wounds."

"Why would he care?" Dr. Herlong asked.

"Prison culture," Jack began. "If he knew he had the beating coming, and if he thought it might take care of some unfinished business, he might just take it and let it go. Plus, he might need the people who smacked him around for protection later. And nobody likes a snitch."

"You got the pictures, doc?" Sladky asked.

Dr. Herlong paged through the file and came up empty.

"I had them down in the lab. Must have left them there," he said apologetically. "The victim is still here too, if you'd like to take look."

Neither Jack nor Al relished the thought of heading to the morgue, where the body would be stored, but both were too professional not to at least take a closer look at the fatal injuries, and the bruising that had not been visible in the darkened lot. There was no pressing need for them to examine the body – the coroner's report was substantially more conclusive than their observations would be – but it wouldn't hurt, either.

"Lead the way," Jack said.

The detectives followed the short doctor as they threaded their way through the offices into the lab area of the building. A team of technicians was in the process of cutting open a man's chest as the trio passed the main operating room. The stench that poured into the hallway as the main body cavity was sawed open was horrible, and Jack felt his stomach turn slightly. It was always the smell that got to him. He glanced over at Al and noticed a disinterested look on his partner's broad face. It was Al's way of not looking too closely at the work in progress. Al wasn't squeamish. He just knew what to ignore.

They paused as Dr. Herlong stopped to talk to the lead examiner, and Jack watched as the team sawed through the corpse's rib cage and pulled it free. Jack could tell from the bright red blotches that the man had probably died from carbon monoxide poisoning.

"Suicide?" Brickman asked the doctor as he rejoined them on the way to the morgue.

"Good eye," Dr. Herlong said. "We think so. He left a note, and they found him in his garage with the car running. Of course, we won't know for sure for a while yet."

Dr. Herlong led them down the hall to the room that served as the actual morgue. The entire building was not, as is commonly believed, the morgue. In fact, the morgue itself was a surprisingly small room, considering the number of "clients" the facility saw on a regular basis.

As Dr. Herlong opened the heavy insulated door to the room, Jack could see several bodies laying atop gurneys spaced around the room. Apparently, there wasn't enough drawer space to accommodate the overflow. Blue-green sheets and shiny metal surfaces caught the glow of fluorescent lights, creating a feeling of unease.

"Busy day?" Jack asked the coroner.

"Not particularly. Oh, you mean these. They're just waiting to go – either to the lab or the morticians. That one is yours," Dr. Herlong said, pointing toward a gurney in the corner.

The detectives followed the coroner past several corpses. Their faces and bodies were hidden by sheets, but their feet still stuck out from under the covering, each with tags tied to their toes, designating their status. Even in death, there was a pecking order. Jack found himself wondering if there wasn't a better way to do it, maybe with barcodes and scanners or something. There probably was, but Jack could see Dr. Herlong wanting to stick to proven methods. Walking towards the back of the room, Jack was also struck by the wholly inappropriate observation that a lot of dead people probably could have used a pedicure in their final days.

As they gathered around Jameel Timmons, Jack noticed Al maneuvering carefully past a large corpse on the gurney next to them. Al, Jack knew, wasn't fainthearted as much as he was practical. Dry cleaning wasn't cheap, and Sladky had admonished Jack dozens of times, "Don't brush against a stiff – you'll never get the stink out."

Dr. Herlong pulled the sheet back and gave the detectives what Jack hoped would be their final look at the man.

Timmon's skin had lightened some, and Jack could immediately see where the forensic team had done their cutting. A network of stitches crossed Timmons' chest and the back of his head where they had put him back together after the autopsy. Jack supposed it must be relatively stress free for a doctor to reassemble a dead person. It's not as if it really matters if you got everything back in exactly the right place.

The doctor had been right about the bruising. In the shameless glare of the overhead tubes, Jack could see the vague outline of a handprint on the right side of the face and neck. He pointed it out to Al, who grunted in acknowledgement.

Dr. Herlong pulled a pair of rubber gloves from the pocket of his lab coat and put them on. With surprising gentleness, he rolled Timmons' head over so the detectives could see the entrance wound at the base of the skull.

"As I said earlier, detectives, note the shape of the blade," he said. "Also, notice the tearing of the skin in the area of the wound, most likely caused by the suspect twisting the knife in an attempt to cause further damage. Quite unnecessary in this case, but we are dealing with a thorough individual here."

Dr. Herlong lay the head back down on the cold steel surface and moved down to the legs. He bent the leg up and held it in position for them to see.

"Again, like I said, one fast, deep cut made with a very sharp knife," he said.

"Seen enough?" Dr. Herlong asked as he straightened the leg.

"Soon as I walked in the door," Sladky said. "Next time, the photos will be enough."

"Not getting soft in your old age, are you Al?" Dr. Herlong said as he re-covered Jameel Timmons. He then pulled the gloves off his hands with a snap and pitched them into a "biohazard only" can near the door.

"Nope, just getting smarter," he said as they headed back into the hallway.

The trio nearly ran into a lab tech who was holding a file folder.

"Looking for these, doctor?" he asked. "You left them in the lab."

"Thanks a million, Don," Dr. Herlong said as he took the file and started paging through it. "We were just on our way down to get it so I can get these detectives back on the street."

"Yeah, ten minutes sooner and you could have saved us a trip to the meat locker," Sladky said.

The tech laughed, a sound completely out of place in the present surroundings.

"You get used to it," he said.

"God, I hope not," Al replied.

"If you detectives can spare the doctor for a minute, I could use a hand with something," the tech said.

"I believe we were done, weren't we gentlemen?" Dr. Herlong asked.

Jack held up the file, now complete with photographs.

"I think we have everything we need, doctor," he said. "If we have any more questions, we'll be sure to call you."

"Fine, fine," the coroner said. "Keep working on that short game, Jack."

"As soon as I find the time, doctor."

"Make the time," Dr. Herlong said with smile. "You can find your way out, right?"

"No problem," Al said. "Thanks for the time."

Dr. Herlong nodded and headed off down the hall with the lab tech, who looked over his shoulder at Sladky and winked as he followed a pace behind the coroner. Al gave a half salute and turned to Brickman.

"How about some fresh air, kid?" he asked.

"Absolutely," Jack said, and they turned and headed past the main examining room just as the bone saw came back to life. As they exited the lab area, they could hear the high-speed blade whine as it started to dig into the skull of the apparent suicide victim. They worked their way through the corridors and past the main reception desk where they signed out and turned in their visitor badges. Within minutes, they were on the street, breathing the comparatively fresh air of springtime in Cleveland.

Jack inhaled deeply as he sucked the outside air into his lungs. It was still cool out, but the lower temperature helped add to the cleansing feeling he got as they walked back to the car, though the air was still tainted with the smell of death. The smell seemed to have lodged in his nostrils and throat. He knew from experience it would be there a while.

"So," Al asked, "Did we learn anything today?"

"Yes," Jack replied. "Always call first and make sure the photos are with the files. Otherwise, have a light lunch."

"I mean, besides that," Al said.

"I'm sticking with my original guess," Brickman said. "Our bad guy is someone with training and experience. Notice how there weren't any test cuts?"

Al nodded. Test cuts were common in stabbings. Usually, a person didn't know how hard to cut in order to break the skin or penetrate the bone. Especially when the suspect was a woman or a kid, you could expect to find superficial wounds or shallow cuts in clothing that showed tentative exploratory slashing. Not so with the Timmons suspect.

Jack continued.

"This is definitely a guy with training," he said. "Maybe military, maybe prison. Hell, he could even just be a martial arts guy. I know the Filipinos are big into knife and stick fighting."

"Seems like a reach to me," Al said as they neared the car.

"Probably," Jack conceded. "And I've still got a feeling this was personal, not professional."

"Well, maybe when The Padre runs down Andre Clark, we'll get some answers."

"I'd settle for a hint," Jack said as he unlocked the car and slid behind the wheel.

"Where to?" he asked.

Sladky checked his watch.

"Let's take a run over to mom's on Buckeye," he said. "She might be ready to talk to us."

"Or not," Jack said. "She might be a little gun-shy after the story in *The Press*."

"We won't know until we ask," the older man replied, digging through his notebook for the address. Once he found it, they were on their way to talk to a grieving mother who probably had no interest in talking to them.

Jack pulled the Ford into a vacant spot on Buckeye Road near Patrice Campbell's address. The neighborhood was full of run-down two-story homes, many of which had been converted into multi-family dwellings. Thirty or forty years ago, the neighborhood had been almost completely Polish and Hungarian immigrants. Slowly, that had changed. Poverty and drugs had taken their toll on this neighborhood, just as they had on too many throughout the city. A few homes showed some sense of civic pride, with well-maintained exteriors and manicured lawns. Most, though, just looked tired.

Jack adjusted his coat as they walked towards Patrice Campbell's house. The house wasn't in as bad shape as some of the others, and it was better than most of them. The exterior was a deep brown with yellow trim. It was a traditional two-story affair, with the large front porch typical of the both the area and the era in which it was built. From the porch, two teenaged girls sat on cheap plastic lawn chairs and warily watched their approach. As they mounted the steps, one of the girls got up and walked through the wrought iron security door into the house. The remaining girl stared blankly at them. Jack nodded in her direction and rang the doorbell. Not surprisingly, a middle-aged woman appeared at the door almost instantly, no doubt warned by the teen who had disappeared.

"Ms. Campbell?" Jack asked, careful to annunciate the "z" sound at the end of "Ms."

"Yes," she said.

Jack and Al produced their badges and IDs.

"Ma'am," Jack said. "I'm Sergeant Brickman and this is Detective Sladky. We're with the Cleveland Police Department. I realize this is a difficult time, but we'd like to ask you a few questions about Jameel if you feel you are up to it."

Jack was deferential and emphatic, careful to use the victim's name to show he saw him as person, not just a body.

Patrice Campbell sighed. In her dark mourning clothes, with her lined face framed by black hair turning too soon to gray, the effect was total. Her eyes were bloodshot, but not watery. She had probably long since cried herself out.

"Please come in," she said, although it was clearly taking all her effort to hold herself together. She moved with quiet dignity as she ushered them into the living room Two other middle-aged women sat on stiff backed chairs in one corner of the room. The teen lookout was nowhere in sight, although Jack could hear faint voices coming from the kitchen and a stereo playing quietly someplace upstairs. The house seemed neat enough, even if the furniture looked old and the carpet was more than a little worn. It gave all the appearances of a family trying to

43

make do with what they had. Jack wondered how Jameel had fit into the equation. Most likely, he hadn't.

"Eleanor, Stella, would you excuse us, please?"

The two matrons rose quickly, with the look of people who cared enough to sit and talk with a grieving mother, but who still felt uncomfortable enough to take the first escape route that presented itself. Jack didn't blame them. He didn't want to be here either.

One of the women, the more heavyset of the pair, eyed the detectives cautiously.

"You sure you gonna be all right, Pat?" she asked protectively.

Campbell took a measured look at Jack and Al.

"I'll be fine," she said. With that, the two ladies adjusted their dresses and purses and, in turn, embraced Patrice Campbell on their way out the door.

"You hang in there, girl," the thinner woman said as she left. Campbell managed a weak smile as the ladies exited. She seated herself on a worn chair.

"Please, sit down," she said, motioning toward an equally distressed loveseat under a picture window.

"Thank you," Jack said as he sat down. Al remained standing. He managed a sheepish grin.

"I'm sorry, ma'am, my back is hurting something fierce," he said. "I'd feel better standing if that's OK."

"Sitting usually helps my back," Campbell said, "But I'm on my feet all the time at work. You probably drive a lot and sit behind a desk."

"More than I'd like to," Al said.

Jack knew Al's back was fine. But his little white lie had killed a few birds with one stone. First, it gave him an excuse to stay on his feet on the outside chance there was some kind of trouble. He didn't expect any, but then again, you rarely did until it was too late. Second, Al had capitalized on Patrice Campbell's empathy. The detective had created the image of just another member of the working class, which didn't hurt when you were talking to someone who cleaned office buildings for a living. And finally, it established Jack as the point man in the interview, consigning Al to the role of sympathetic bystander. Contact and cover.

"We're sorry to intrude, Ms. Campbell," Jack said. "The last thing we want to do is make this harder on you than it already is."

"Yes."

"But you know the sooner we ask the questions, the sooner we can find who did this to your son."

Patrice Campbell clasped her hands and leaned towards Jack.

"I know that's your job," she said. "I know you have to be here. But that doesn't make it hurt any less, you know. Plus, I've got family here." She nodded towards the kitchen.

"If we could wait, we would," Jack said. "Every day that goes by could put Jameel's killer even farther away."

"Fine," Patrice said. "Ask your questions, then."

"When did you last speak to your son, Ms. Campbell?" Jack asked.

"I'd guess it was about three weeks ago, maybe a little more."

"Did he come by, or did you talk on the phone?"

"He came by. It was about dinner time on Sunday. He didn't stay though." She still looked hurt by that. Jack knew his own mother took it personally if you didn't have a plate when you visited. Thug or not, Patrice Campbell was still trying to be a mother to her son.

"How did he seem to you? Did he seem worried or scared?"

"No," Patrice said. "Same ol' Jameel, same ol' big smile" She managed another hint of a grin, and tears seemed on the verge to well up from some hidden reserve.

"I know my son was wrapped up in some bad stuff, detective," she said. "I always tried to stand by him when he got in trouble, but I know you don't go to jail for nothing these days, either. And the last time he was in jail was hard on him."

"Why? What happened?" Jack asked.

Patrice shook her head.

"He wouldn't tell me," she said. "But I visited him once and he was just all beat up. Said it was no big deal, but he looked a little scared, you know? Never did tell me what it was about, but he was like that. Kept things from me."

Jack figured that was a more telling description of Jameel's relationship with his mother. Despite what she wanted to believe about her son, Brickman was getting a picture of a self-centered, secretive young man who knew how to pull the charm-school act on his mother. It was probably good enough to get an occasional place to crash or bail money. If Jameel had ever gotten hit with a murder rap, Jack would have bet the farm that mom would have rushed out and mortgaged the house for bond and legal fees if Jameel had flashed that "big ol' smile."

"Was there anything in particular he talked about? Maybe a friend or something?"

"All he wanted to talk about, like usual, was his boy," she said. "You know, I've never even met my grandson? Probably never will now."

Jack was seriously starting to wonder if this interview had been worth the effort. It seemed like it was just too soon to be asking Patrice Campbell questions about her son. She was clearly still in denial mode, and was focusing on her son's memory as if he had been a Boy Scout and not a hood. Jack couldn't begrudge her wanting a nice picture to hang in her mind, but it wasn't helping his investigation much.

So, with the odor of her dead son's corpse still lingering in his nostrils, Brickman offered what he hoped was an encouraging smile.

"You never know," he said, "Things have a way of working out sometimes."

"I certainly hope so."

"Did you know any of your son's friends?" Jack asked, trying to redirect the interview.

"Not lately, no," she said. "I knew some of them back in the day, like when he was in school. Nobody in that new crowd."

"Did Jameel ever talk about anybody wanting to hurt him?" Jack asked.

"No," Patrice said. "But like I said, he didn't talk much about that stuff with me." She looked nervously toward the kitchen. "I hate to rush you, but I do have family to see to. Do you have any more questions for me?"

"Do you know where you son was living?" Jack asked.

"Oh, I have an address somewhere," Campbell said. "Jameel asked me to send him his mail. He still has stuff there."

Patrice stood up and walked to the kitchen. The detectives could hear some talking, but it was hushed. Death and the police had a way of keeping people's voices down.

Patrice returned quickly, with a slip of paper in her hand.

"I hope this helps," she said as she handed it to Jack. Brickman glanced down at the address. He knew better than to take it without looking. Many people had poor penmanship. It was easier to ask the person to translate their writing when they were standing in front of you than it was to make a phone call later. Patrice Campbell, Jack was glad to see, had good, clear longhand.

Jack carefully folded the piece of paper and put it in his pocket, along with his notebook, pausing to pull out a business card. He stood up and extended the card to Patrice Campbell.

"If you happen to think of anything else, or you have any questions, please call me," Brickman said.

"Thank you, I will," she said. "Did I help at all?"

Jack smiled and lied.

"Yes, you did," he said. "We'll be in touch."

"Take care of yourself, Ms. Campbell," Sladky said, breaking his silent vigil.

Jack's last glimpse of Patrice Campbell was of a tired, sad woman, trying to hold herself together, forcing another weak smile.

Al and Jack didn't say a word until they were in the car. Sladky turned to Jack, who was driving again.

"Well, that was productive," he said.

"Did you expect anything different?"

"Nah, but what you gonna do? You gotta ask."

"Where to now? Do you want to check out the address?"

Sladky shook his head.

"Might as well head in," he said. "We're going to need a warrant for Timmons' place anyway and no way we're getting that on a Friday afternoon. I'll leave a message for Ramirez, let him have some guys check on it. Plus, he can page me if he gets Clark over the weekend. Otherwise, I say pick this up next week."

"Good enough," Jack said. He would have preferred to keep working the case, but they didn't have much beyond Clark.

"Swing by Cousin's on your way in though," Sladky said. "I need to make a stop."

Jack headed the Ford towards Euclid Avenue where he eventually double parked in front of Cousin's Cigar Shop while Al ran into the store. Well, Al didn't actually run in, but he did walk quickly. Jack ignored a few angry beeps he heard while waiting for Al to emerge from the store. In a couple minutes, his partner hopped back into the passenger seat with a small brown paper bag.

"Hey, junior," he said as they headed back toward the office, "What would you say to a cold beer?"

"I'd say 'hello, beautiful,'" Jack responded.

The detectives wasted little time once they got back to the office. Jack left a short email for McNamara, who was out again, and typed a brief supplement to the report. Al made two phone calls, one to The Padre, who had nothing new to report except a possible lead on Andre Clark.

On the way to the garage, they bickered about where to go. In the end, Jack won out with his choice of Edison's, a nice neighborhood bar in Tremont. It was more of Jack's kind of place than Al's, who favored the east side haunts close to his home. On the plus side, it was likely to be quiet at this time of day.

By mutual agreement, Jack dropped his car, and gun, at home and Al assumed chauffeur duties. Even with the brief detour, they were seated at Edison's and lifting frosty pints to their lips within thirty minutes of leaving the office. Both cops drained about half their glasses in the first pull.

"Now that's the way to start a weekend," Sladky said. "Especially after a crappy day like today."

"Yeah," Jack said. "You'd think we'd catch a break sooner or later with this one."

"Ah, it's early yet. Something tells me we ain't gonna put this one away any time soon."

"Based on your experience or intuition?" Jack asked after taking another long swallow of beer.

"Little of both," Al replied, "But mainly just a hunch."

"Well, you've got the figure for it if you want to start going with gut feelings."

Al put his hands on his ample belly and assumed a look of mock surprise.

"This?" he asked. "I need this for ballast when I go fishing. Plus, it's my secret weapon for dealing with bad guys."

"Oh, really?"

"Yeah. Don't tell me you never heard of the Fat Man Flop."

"They must have skipped that in the academy."

"Muscle is overrated," Al said. "Mostly, you just have to outweigh them. Oh, and get on top. That helps."

"Don't tell that to my wife."

Al laughed and drained his glass. He signaled the bartender for another round. There were only four or five other people in the bar, and the bartender was also waiting on tables, at least until the wait staff came in for the evening rush.

"Same thing, guys?" he asked as he came over to the booth.

"Yeah, why not, Pete?" Jack said.

"You guys want to see menus?" he asked as he brought their new beers to the table. "Or would you rather just soak up the ambience?"

"I'm good with the liquid diet for now, " Jack said. Al nodded his assent as he embraced the fresh beer.

After Pete returned to his post behind the bar and resumed his daily battle with the crossword puzzle, Jack took a napkin from the stainless-steel holder and blew.

"I can never get that morgue smell out of my nose," Jack said.

"Yeah, it kind of lingers," Al said.

The older man dug into his jacket pocket and produced the brown bag from Cousin's. He extracted two cigars.

"Here, stunt your growth," he said as he offered one to Jack.

48

Brickman took the cigar and examined the label. He wasn't a huge smoker, but in the course of his partnership with Sladky, he had learned to appreciate the occasional stogie. And these were Partagas, a brand Jack knew occupied the higher end of the price spectrum. Seven bucks for a cigar seemed like a lot of money to Jack, but since he didn't smoke them every day, he figured he could afford the good stuff. Not that it mattered today, since Sladky was buying.

Al handed a cheap plastic cutter over after he had lit his own cigar. A quick snip later and Jack was puffing away, knowing as he did so that he would catch a little hell for it when Karen got home from work. Smoking was not high on her list of favorites. He only smoked on the golf course, at poker games, or after a trip to the morgue. Or a particularly malodorous crime scene. Cigar smoke was one of the few things that masked the smell of death.

Jack took another sip of beer. He glanced over at the pool table where a young couple was playing a game of eight ball. The girl, a tiny blonde with short hair, scrunched up her nose in displeasure at the smell of their smoke, but said nothing. Hell, Jack thought, half the people in every bar he'd ever been to smoked cigarettes. It wouldn't be fair to discriminate against one type of smoke. Besides, he was almost halfway through his second beer, and well into not giving a damn about what a young stranger thought.

The pace of their drinking dropped off considerably as they sat and talked, but the partners managed to put away a couple more pints before Al checked his watch and declared it was time to head home. They paid up and left, Jack waving to a couple guys he knew from the neighborhood.

"See ya Monday, junior," Al said as he dropped Jack off at home. "I'll give ya a call if The Padre comes through with something."

"Right," Jack said, half hoping that Ramirez wouldn't call. He was planning to enjoy his weekend.

"Thanks for the stogie."

Al laughed.

"Always happy to corrupt an impressionable youth," he called as he backed out of the driveway.

Jack wasted no time changing into a pair of jeans and a sweatshirt. A quick search of the fridge yielded some Italian sausage that Karen liked. His wife was not much of a meat eater, which made cooking for her a risky proposition. He managed to dig some peppers and mushrooms out of the vegetable bin, and found some buns that were reasonably fresh.

Jack cracked open a fresh Great Lakes Elliot Ness Amber Lager and started slicing up the vegetables, stopping to run out and light the grill that held a place of honor on the rear deck throughout the year. Jack grilled out in all but the most inclement weather.

He checked his watch and opened a bottle of merlot for Karen. Brickman grabbed a portable radio, his beer, and the food. He set the plates aside and tuned in to the Indians pre-game show and sat back in a low Adirondack chair. His timing was nearly perfect. The grill was ready just as Karen's Toyota pulled into the garage.

Karen Brickman, formerly O'Neil, got out of her car and paused to grab her briefcase from the back seat. She was wearing a dark business suit that highlighted her figure. Karen was a petite woman, with short dark hair and green eyes that spoke volumes about her Celtic heritage. She was the kind of girl who, back in her school days, would have been unfailingly described as "perky." Jacked preferred to think of her as lively or energetic. Either way, she had a smile that still made him feel special every time he saw it. And she was smiling now.

"Well, hello, stranger," she said.

"Hello, yourself," Jack replied as she came over and bent down to kiss him.

"Ugh," she said. "Let me guess – you and Al went out after work."

"Right the first time," Jack said. "It was one of those days."

A look of concern flickered across Karen's face.

"That bad?"

"Nothing dangerous," Jack said, anxious to reassure his wife. "Just a case that seems to be going nowhere fast."

Her smile reappeared.

"Well, we've got the whole weekend to forget about it, don't we?" She glanced over at the sausages and vegetables. "I guess you're cooking tonight?"

"Unless you'd rather go out."

"Are you kidding? I've been dying to get out of these clothes all day."

"I can help with that."

"Easy, sailor," Karen said, laughing. "At least buy a lady dinner first."

"I opened a bottle of wine, if you want a glass," he said.

"Great! Let me throw on some jeans and I'll meet you right back here," she said. "Can I bring you a glass?"

Jack held up his two-thirds empty beer bottle.

"Another one of these, please," he said. "Never change horses in the middle of a race."

Once Karen disappeared inside the house, Jack stood and started putting food on the grill. As he forked the sausages over the hot surface, Jack Brickman smiled. He had a nice home, a gorgeous wife, the beginnings of a good buzz, and two days off to enjoy them all. As he sat back down, their cat, Smalls, came prancing along the top of the fence, meowing until she vaulted onto the deck. She hopped up into Jack's lap, where she was treated to a vigorous scratching behind the ears. She purred loudly.

50

"All in all," he thought, *"I've got it pretty good."*

CHAPTER 10

The Padre didn't come through over the weekend.

Monday morning found Al and Jack once again kicking their heels in one of the seemingly infinite waiting areas tied to the legal system. Their subpoenas had been for nine o'clock, which they both knew was a joke. Even the judges rarely got in before ten. Still, on the off chance that a jurist did actually get to his chambers on time, the detectives made it a point to be where they were supposed to be when they were supposed to be there. Judges wielded godlike powers. Luckily, they had been able to commandeer an unused deliberation room which offered them a place to spread out their files, read the paper, or catch a few minutes of shut eye while they waited. That didn't happen as much to Jack now, but it was a common occurrence back when he had been on the midnight shift. In fact, it was common to see three or four guys in blue polyester pants with their heads at odd angles, snoring away in the institutionally uncomfortable chairs. Night shifts were brutal.

Jack knew they were working on a plea agreement in the Hawkins case. Ernie Hawkins held up a convenience store on the near West Side. The clerk had made the fatal mistake of trying to wrestle the gun away from Hawkins. During the struggle, the gun had gone off, killing the clerk. Now, Jack knew that guns didn't just "go off." Unless the weapon was poorly designed or defective, somebody had to have their finger on the trigger for it to fire. And it had to be pointed in the right direction to kill somebody. When Jack and Al had finally caught up with Hawkins, he confessed to the robbery, but swore he never intended to shoot the clerk, which created the conditions for the plea bargain.

Jack and Al had already switched newspapers, with the younger detective getting his first crack at *The Press*, and Sladky opening *The Plain Dealer*. Brickman had just finished the front section when his pager started vibrating. He checked the number and didn't recognize it, although he could tell by the prefix that it was a CPD extension. He was about to find a phone when he saw Al reach for his own pager. He glanced at the display. Al, who had a better memory for numbers, recognized the source of the call.

"It's The Padre," he said. "You too?"

"Probably," Jack said. "You want to call him, or should I?"

"Go ahead," Al said, "I'm just getting to the funnies."

Jack headed down the hall to the clerk's office and dialed up The Padre.

"Ramirez," the voice said.

"Lieutenant, this is Jack Brickman," he said. "You paged?"

"Hey, Jack, how's it going? Yeah, I paged you and Al both. We grabbed Andre Clark this morning."

"Great," Jack said. "What did you get him on?"

"It's weak," Ramirez admitted. "His probation agreement says he's not supposed to hang out with any of his old gang, which is almost impossible since they're mostly from his neighborhood. One of our units saw him having breakfast at a diner with a couple of his homies. They grabbed him up right away."

"Did you talk to him yet?"

"Yeah," Ramirez said. "Thought you might want first crack at him, but he seemed to be in a talkative mood. You know how that goes. Gotta take advantage when they're talking. Anyway, sorry to tell you this, Jack, but I don't think he's your guy."

"What? Why?"

"First, he seemed really surprised by Timmons being dead," Ramirez said. "He seemed happy about it though, or at least as happy as he gets. Second, when I pressed him about the trouble between them, he admitted right away that he had put the beat-down on Timmons when he was in prison. As far as he was concerned, debts were paid. He said that if he had wanted J-Time dead, he'd be dead. To quote Andre: 'When I got a holler with someone, I settle up quick."

"I'll buy it so far, but I know you aren't taking him at his word," Jack said.

"Hell, no," Ramirez replied. "The real kicker is the call I got after we picked him up. Seems there's a joint DEA-FBI task force working Andre Clark, among others, as a RICO case. Nice of them to let me know," he added sarcastically.

"Anyway," he continued, "they've had him up on surveillance for a couple of weeks. Not even a hint of a hit on Timmons."

"Racketeering, huh?" Jack said. "Mighty big pole for such a little fish."

"Don't knock it," The Padre said. "That's how they broke the back of Larry Hoover and the Gangster Disciples. 'Bout time the Feds got creative."

"So, I guess I can cross Andre off the list of likely suspects," Jack said.

"I'd say so," Ramirez replied. "You can always sweat him later, but I think he's a longshot."

Jack closed his eyes and pinched the top of his nose in frustration. He took a deep breath.

"OK, Padre," he said. "Where do we go from here?"

"I can run with it a little, see what shakes out," Ramirez said. "Can't make any promises, but something could turn up with some of the other players."

"Thanks," Jack said. "We'll stay in touch."

By the time Jack sat down and briefed Sladky about the call, the assistant prosecutor came in and told them that the judge had decided that it was time for lunch. So, they went to lunch like everybody else. And when they came back, they waited.

Brickman and Sladky waited the rest of Monday and most of Tuesday for Ernie Hawkins and his public defender to take the deal.

They used the next day and a half to update paperwork and track down some weak leads, mainly calling or visiting known associates of Jameel Timmons. As far as the detectives could tell, he had been keeping a very low profile since his release from prison. He certainly hadn't spent much time looking up old friends. It was not very productive period of time for the detectives. Detective work is mainly a grind, and they checked boxes for the rest of the week. Jack was a little frustrated but used to it by now. He was tired by the time Friday rolled around. He was hoping the weekend would give him a chance to reset. He was going to be disappointed.

CHAPTER 11

Jack was just pulling into his driveway on Saturday night when his pager went off. He stopped short of the garage and checked the number. It was the office. Jack cursed quietly but without much sincerity. He was on call, so the page wasn't exactly unexpected. It came with the job, and Brickman knew that, but he had been looking forward to a good night's sleep after a dry night out celebrating the end of Police Memorial Week. With any luck, it wouldn't be anything out of the ordinary, since he would be working it alone. They called in one detective for overtime cases, and Sladky was out of the rotation this weekend.

The lights were still on, so Jack guessed, rightly, that Karen must still be awake. As he unlocked the door, he could hear the muffled tones of the television from the living room.

"Jack?" Karen called from the other room.

"Yeah, it's me," he responded.

"How was the Tattoo?" she asked, referring to the night's event.

"Great," he said, "better than last year. Hang on a minute, I gotta make a call."

Jack picked up the kitchen phone and dialed the number. He got the desk sergeant at the Third District, on the East Side.

"Sergeant Kovatch," a gruff, tired voice said.

"Sarge, this is Detective Brickman, the on-call floater," Jack said. "I just got a page."

"Yeah, Brickman, here's what we got. Guys on the street say it's a DOA. They're saying somebody damn near cut this guy's head off."

"What?"

"Yeah, I know it sounds weird, but that's what they're saying. Real mess, I guess."

Brickman recovered a little and reached for the small notebook and pen in his shirt pocket.

"What, was it like a domestic or something?"

"Nope, near as we can tell, nobody has a freakin' clue what happened," Kovatch said. "We got guys askin' around, but nothing firm yet. Figure you bein' the detective and all, you could tell us, maybe."

Jack ignored the last comment. He was used to it.

"Just give me the location, sergeant, and let your guys know I'm on my way."

Brickman scribbled down the address on Empire Avenue. He knew it was a side street off the winding Martin Luther King Blvd. The detective looked at his watch.

"I'll be there in fifteen, twenty minutes, tops," Jack said.

"I can hardly wait," Kovatch said before hanging up.

Brickman went into the living room where Karen was curled up on the couch, dressed in flannel pajama bottoms and an old T-shirt. There were some files from her office scattered around her on the floor near the couch. She was watching some old movie on cable and had obviously just been killing time waiting for him to get home. She smiled when she saw Jack, but that smile quickly faded when she saw the look on his face.

"Sorry," Jack said. "I just got buzzed. I have to go in."

"Is it bad?" she asked.

"Won't know 'til I get there," he said. "I'm sorry, thought we'd get a chance to hang out a little."

"It's OK," Karen said. "I'm tired anyway. Just be safe."

"I will. Always." Jack said. "Love you."

"Love you, too," Karen replied.

Brickman locked the door again and was back in his car in minutes. He was thankful he had resisted the temptation to have a beer, despite many offers. Once he told the other cops he was on call, they immediately understood. If Jack had been a different kind of cop, or this had been twenty years ago, he probably would have partaken of a cold one or two. But he took being on call seriously. He carried the pager religiously and tried to stay within the city limits. At two thousand officers, the department was finally up to its full strength, so they were fairly well staffed. It was rare that Jack got called in, but as tonight proved, it didn't pay to take chances.

Jack would concede that he probably drank more than he should, but he also knew that conceding that point meant he had a realistic view of his habits and vices. He also knew that alcohol abuse, always a stereotype of police officers, still plagued law enforcement. That, he knew, was changing some. Gone were the days when every corner call box had a bottle inside so cops walking the beat could "keep warm" on their rounds, and most neighborhood bars had served up a special "coffee" to their local constables. Gone too were the days when the press and other cops would look the other way when alcohol-related incidents occurred.

It still took a major screw-up for such incidents to make the news, but, unfortunately, they had always seemed a part of the police culture. Even Elliot Ness, longtime safety director for post-Prohibition Cleveland, had hamstrung his political career by leaving the scene of an automobile accident while allegedly under the influence of alcohol. Jack had always found that historical tidbit extremely ironic, and extremely unfortunate since Ness had been such a tireless and innovative crime fighter. He had even started the Cleveland police academy as part of an effort to stamp out corruption on the force.

As Brickman exited the freeway and headed south on MLK, he found himself thinking about another of Ness' failures, the Kingsbury Run murders. The killings, also known as the Torso Murders, and occasionally the Jackass Hill Murders, had thwarted CPD and Ness. Several corpses – Jack forgot how many – had turned up around the city completely dismembered. Some body parts were found drifting in Lake Erie, while others turned up in a variety of other places. Cleveland lore held that the bodies had been cut up with surgical precision, although he had read many accounts that disputed that theory. Still, it was also part of Cleveland legend that the perpetrator had been a wealthy socialite, possibly a medical student or med school dropout whose rich family had whisked him away to a private sanitarium when they discovered his crimes.

At the time, the newspapers had pegged the killings on the work of a maniac or pervert, terms they actually used in headlines in the old days. The journalists of the day widely speculated that the grisly crimes were the work of a bum living in one of the many shantytowns that had sprung up around the city during the Depression. That speculation fueled public fervor over the hobo villages. That fervor, coupled with CPD's growing frustration at its own inability to arrest the culprit, eventually led Ness to make another questionable decision. He had finally ordered his officers to clear out the shantytowns, an order they conducted *in extremis*. They burned the makeshift huts to the ground and rounded up the residents, dishing out severe beatings with little or no provocation. Ness and CPD were crucified in the press, despite the media's earlier cries for action. They never solved the Torso Murders.

And here he was, decades later, driving towards another gruesome murder. Despite what the sergeant had told him over the phone, Jack doubted that he would really be looking at an actual beheading. Even cops, he knew, could tend to exaggerate. It was likely to be unpleasant, though.

Brickman turned onto Empire, and slowed down, threading his way through parked cars and onlookers. There were still multiple marked units on the scene, as well as the trace evidence van from the coroner's office. Jack was glad to see that they had taped off a large perimeter. If the murder had been another stabbing, it was unlikely that the crime itself had been confined to a small area, the Timmons scene notwithstanding. Jameel's near instant death was unique – stabbing victims usually managed to run or crawl several feet before collapsing. Even mortally wounded victims occasionally managed to make several blocks before finally hitting the ground.

Jack parked in the middle of the street. It was already blocked off by police cars and crime scene tape, so it didn't really matter if he was disrupting traffic. He had driven straight from home to save time, so he didn't have the luxury of putting the emergency strobe lights on. As he got out of the car, he wondered if he shouldn't buy an old-fashioned "gumball" light for future use. At least he could deduct the mileage on his taxes.

The neighborhood had seen better days. It was a fairly short block, with about twenty homes on each side of the street. Of those, at least half were burned out or boarded up. Jack surmised that the drug trade had decimated the neighborhood.

The crime scene appeared to be centered in the small front yard of a home that seemed more or less intact. At least it had windows and a front door, although it looked like it was about to be condemned, too. Jack approached a young, uniformed officer who was manning the tape barrier they had stretched out around the scene and flashed his badge to identify himself. Jack noticed that the rookie seemed a little uneasy.

"First time?" Jack thought.

"Who's in charge?" he asked.

The cop, a skinny Black kid named Larkin, looked around before pointing to a uniformed officer with sergeant's stripes on his sleeves, standing in one corner of the cordons.

"That's him, Sgt. Wiersboski," he said, although he was tentative, as if he wasn't sure of the pronunciation.

"Is it safe to come in?" Jack asked.

"Uh, I think so…what do you mean?"

"Did the lab techs start processing yet?" Jack was actually a bit surprised they had beat him to the scene.

Larkin hesitated before answering.

"Yes, they're over there," he said, gesturing toward the body.

"Where did they start? Did they walk in from perimeter?"

A light came on in the rookie's brain.

"Oh, yeah," he said. "Yeah, detective, they walked it and moved in already. I don't think they found anything except close to the body."

"You sure?"

"Yes, sir. Watched them do it."

"OK," Jack said. "They're going to be a while. I'm coming in. Make sure you log it."

"Yes, sir."

You didn't hear "sir" much on the street, so the kid must have been fresh out of the academy. Jack slipped under the tape and approached the sergeant. Wiersboski was talking to a couple of older officers, neither of whom Jack recognized.

"Sergeant Wiersboski?" Jack asked.

The sergeant, a slightly disheveled looking man with a receding hairline, turned and faced Brickman. Despite the man's appearance, Jack got the vibe that he was probably a good street cop. Sometimes, you can just tell.

"You the detective?" he asked, sizing up Jack with his eyes.

"Yeah, Sergeant Brickman, working with the floaters out of headquarters. I was on call. Sorry it took so long to get here."

Wiersboski checked his watch.

"Actually, you got here quicker than Kovatch said you would," he said. "Old bastard will have to find something else to bitch about tonight."

"Wow, he sounded like the cheerful type on the phone," Jack said.

Wiersboski laughed, joined by his officers, who obviously knew the desk sergeant well enough to appreciate Jack's sarcasm.

"What do you expect?" one of the cops said. "Guy's ROD, just putting in his time. He's pissed they put him back on midnights to finish his twenty-five."

ROD, Jack knew, was police jargon for "Retired On Duty."

Down to business.

"So, what do you have for me?" Jack asked.

"DOA's name is Karnelle Lane, also known as 'Beezer,'" the sergeant said. He didn't wait for Jack to ask the next question, instead he held up his hands out with the palms turned upward. "Don't ask me why. I guess it's a gang thing. I can never figure this stuff out."

Wiersboski continued as Jack took notes.

"Anyway, we know he's been running around with some local guys lately, doing some dealing. We've popped him a couple times for possession, but he had a taste for some violent stuff, too. Word is, he liked pulling rip-offs."

"What kind?"

"You know, little stuff like sticking a gun in some guy's face when he pulls up to buy crack. Supposedly only rich white guys, guys who aren't going to run and tell the cops they got jacked buying drugs. We had a sting op going a couple of months ago, but he wouldn't take the bait."

"This payback?" Jack asked.

"If it was, the guy must have been really pissed off," Wiersboski said. "Somebody really did a number on Lane this time."

"He get ripped off, too?"

"We haven't checked yet," the sergeant said. "In this neighborhood, probably, but we didn't want to start going through his pockets until after the techs got in there. EMS ain't been in, either."

"Nobody tried first aid?" Jack asked.

Wiersboski laughed again, mirthlessly.

"You kidding? Hell, even my rookie knew this guy was DOA. Larkin already puked once, poor kid."

"It happens," Jack said, remembering several times when he'd lost his dinner.

"Shit, I'm the North Coast hurling champ," the sergeant said. "Least the kid had the sense to hold it in until he got clear of the crime scene. I don't think I did that my first time. He's only about two weeks out of the academy."

"Anything from the canvass?"

"Nothing yet," Wiersboski said. "I've got everybody I can spare knocking on doors and working the crowd, but nobody saw anything. At least they're not saying if they did."

"OK," Jack said. "Let me know if that changes."

"Right," the sergeant said. "Techies are still working the scene. Said they'll wave us over when we can come in closer."

Jack looked over and recognized the two trace evidence experts immediately. One was Heath Moore, a short, thin, manic guy with thick glasses. He was the kind of person you automatically thought of when you heard the word "geek." That impression wouldn't last long, though. Moore was one of the best trace evidence technicians in the state. If he had an equal, it was the stout, rather plain looking woman working next to him, Therese Vidalia. Brickman immediately counted himself twice blessed. Moore and Vidalia were not usually teamed up. Contaminated evidence was suddenly removed from his list of concerns.

Just then, another young officer, this one a blond guy, made his way through the small crowd of people, holding a cardboard carryout tray of coffee in front of him. He brought it straight to the older officer talking to Jack and the shift sergeant. The older cop, probably the kid's field training officer, took a step back under the "Police Line, Do Not Cross" tape to accept it.

"Thanks for not contaminating my crime scene," Jack said.

"We try," Wiersboski said.

"Here you go," the young officer said as he reached the foursome.

Wiersboski and the older officers each took a lidded Styrofoam cup. The older cop, Finelli, by his nametag, took the last cup and offered it to Brickman.

"Jack, right? You want a cup?" he said. "Looks like they're going to be a while."

Brickman nodded toward the young officer, obviously a rookie like Larkin.

"What about you? I'm not going to take yours," Jack said. He had no interest in being party to a hazing ritual.

The new cop looked genuinely surprised by the gesture. He was still new enough to hold detectives, especially sergeants, in high regard. Jack wondered how long that would last.

"Mine and Larkin's is in the car, sergeant," he said. "I got an extra and couldn't carry them all."

"Signs of hope, at last," Finelli said, taking a sip of his coffee as the novice officer disappeared into the group of people on the edge of the crime scene.

They waited over an hour before the technicians were ready for them. Jack tried working the crowd a little, but it had thinned out rapidly. There wasn't much to see, and it was getting chilly. Plus, the neighborhood wasn't well populated. Two television camera operators showed up and deployed tripods in the distance. There were no reporters in attendance, so Jack figured they must just be getting background footage to go with a voiceover when CPD released more information about the crime. Several photographers from the papers showed up, but they didn't last long either. They were too far away to get any really good shots, and the privacy barriers the technicians had put up blocked most of the scene. Anyway, neither *The Press* nor *The Plain Dealer* would run graphic pictures of murder or accident victims. They still had a code.

Nobody seemed to know where Lane had been living, and none of the spectators knew if he had any relatives in the area. The general consensus was that he had not. Tracking down someone to notify of his demise would have to wait. Pending that, they couldn't even release the name to the media, although they certainly already knew it by now. Everybody, it seemed, had known who "Beezer" was and where he plied his trade.

"I better go take a look and talk to the techs," Jack said.

"Holler if you need something," one of the cops said as Brickman moved away.

As he walked toward the center of the crime scene, Jack tried to get a feel for the area. It was hard, since the location was now flooded with the flashing lights from patrol units as well as the brilliant white light from cruiser spotlights and the floodlights from the side of the mobile crime scene truck the coroner's office had sent over. The truck was a state-of-the-art acquisition that resembled a rescue squad. In fact, they shared the same basic foundation, although more of the crime scene truck's interior was occupied by equipment since it didn't transport bodies – that task went to somebody else.

There were cars parked on the north side of the street. From what he could see, the body was on the tree lawn of the south side. There were a few large trees around, but not much else. The streetlights, of course, were out. It was a fairly quiet, deserted street. Overall, not a bad place to sling rock. Cars could drive up and make purchases quickly, and the dealer could see if any patrol cars were nearby with a quick glance in any direction.

They had obviously finished much of their investigation since they had started to examine the body itself. There was usually plenty of evidence on a murder victim, including hair, scrapings, cloth fibers, and blood. In some cases, they might find foreign semen, urine, or feces. Mud, chemicals or tar on shoes could be vital later on, since they could tell you where the victim had been. Thorough technicians took everything, including dozens of photographs and measurements. They would figure out what it all meant later, or in some cases, let somebody else figure it out. Most found it made their jobs easier to concentrate on gathering evidence, not interpreting it. They worked quickly because every minute it took to collect evidence meant more chances it would be contaminated. Jack found himself thinking about the Timmons scene again. They hadn't found much there.

"Here and now, Jack," he told himself.

Jack approached the pair of technicians cautiously, pulling on a pair of rubber gloves as he went.

"Hey, Heath, Therese, how's it going?" he asked.

Both techs looked over their shoulders at him. They had to look up because they were kneeling next to the body.

"Sgt. Brickman, hey," Moore said. "Glad you got this one. Looks like a good one."

Next to him, Vidalia sighed.

"He says it's good, I say it's a big mess," she said. "No Al tonight, Jack?"

"He's home in bed, probably," Jack said. "I was on call, he wasn't."

"Lucky for Al," Vidalia said. "You must not be living right."

"My wife sure wouldn't argue with you," Brickman said. "What have you got so far?"

"So far? Not much beyond what you see," Moore said. "I hate these outdoor scenes."

Jack looked at the body that had been Karnelle Lane. The uniformed cops had been right. Lane had been nearly decapitated. Veins, muscles, and bone had been sliced through, leaving only a flap of skin connecting the head to the body. Karnelle Lane was flat on his back, his shaved head nearly resting on his right shoulder, his lifeless eyes already milky and staring. On his face, frozen forever, Jack supposed, was a look of shock and surprise.

"Wonderful," he said quietly.

"Yeah, ain't it pretty," Moore asked, his speech quick. "Near as we can tell, the neck wound was the fatal one...we got huge arterial sprays out to ten feet, but it decreased rapidly. Doesn't seem to be anything else except for a contusion on the right wrist. Looks like he was wearing a bracelet or something and the suspect tore it off him, either in the struggle or after it. There are about ten rocks of crack in the pockets, and $214 in cash."

To Jack, it didn't make any sense. Why would you rip a guy off for a piece of jewelry cut his head off and then stop without taking the cash and drugs. Stolen jewelry usually got pennies on the dollar if you could find a buyer. Even pawn shops had been avoiding jewelry lately.

"Any guess on the weapon?" he asked.

This time, Vidalia answered.

"Well, you know we don't like to guess," she said. "But I think we're safe in saying it was some type of edged weapon, like a machete or something, although that's a little flimsy to do this kind of cutting. You can rule out an axe...the blade on most axes wouldn't be wide enough to sever the whole neck, unless of course it was an executioner's axe or something from *Braveheart.* You'd probably just end up breaking the victim's neck with something you picked up at Home Depot, not slicing it like this.

"I wish I could tell you more, Jack, but I just don't know. On the surface, I can tell you that this guy made a pretty clean cut, but Dr. Herlong is going to have to do the rest."

Brickman squatted down and looked again at the victim. He was reminded again of Jameel Timmons. Lane, like Timmons, was black and young, early twenties. He was wearing a long-sleeved jacket, so it was impossible to see if he was sporting any prison-style tattoos. Jack guessed he probably was. And there was no denying the thoroughness of the attack, or the apparent skill of the attacker. Edged weapon attacks tended to be sloppy, and now, in the span of less that two weeks, he was investigating two murders with similar details. Jack found himself wondering if there was a connection or if this was just a new way of settling scores on the street. Mexican gangs, maybe? The cartels were this vicious.

He paused and looked around, taking a more objective look at the area, looking with "soft eyes." Like the Timmons murder scene, the area was lightly traveled but still populated. It was a good, quiet spot for a killing, but certainly not an ideal one, since a car or neighbor passing could easily have wandered by while the murder was taking place. Although robbery may have been a motive, Jack wasn't ready to take that as gospel truth yet. Based on the fact that only one item had been taken, it was possible that this crime, too, had been committed for personal reasons rather than profit. Unless of course, Lane had been wearing some priceless artifact on his right wrist, something Jack seriously doubted.

Jack stood up straight and stretched his lower back muscles. As he did so, a hunch surfaced somewhere inside his head. Therese Vidalia stood up next to him.

"I know that look, Jack" she said. "You've got something, don't you?"

"Maybe," he said. "Just a feeling."

"Care to share?" she asked.

"Not yet," he said. "I don't want you guys fudging your research to fit my theory."

"Like we'd do that," Moore said, sounding defensive.

"Not on purpose, no," Jack conceded.

"Anyway, you said 'feeling,' not theory," Vidalia said.

Jack shrugged.

"Well, you've got to start somewhere," he said. "Any chance of moving this one to the head of the line?"

It was Therese's turn to shrug.

"It's been a busy weekend," she said. "Only two other homicides, and both of those were from the suburbs. Lots of natural deaths, though, but nothing the family doctors wanted to sign off on, so we get them. We'll be lucky if Herlong sees this guy before Tuesday."

Moore chimed in, curious.

"What gives, Jack?" he asked. "It's not like you to ask for special treatment, especially when the cause of death is pretty obvious."

"Yeah, I know," Jack said. He did not elaborate.

"OK, Jack," Vidalia said, "Since you hardly ever bitch, we'll see what we can do, but we can't make any promises."

"Thanks," Jack said. He turned and walked back toward the edge of the crime scene. As he did so, he saw the coroner's van back up to the tape barrier. Two overall-clad workers exited the cab and opened up its rear doors. Jack watched absently as they swung open double doors and pulled a gurney out. Instead of EKG machines and drug bags that would be sitting on the stretcher if it were coming out of an EMS rig, the coroner's "meat wagon" gurney only carried a black body bag. Now that Heath and Therese were finished, the plain white van would carry the body of Karnelle Lane downtown for Dr. Herlong's careful attention.

The few cops staffing the perimeter saw the truck pull away and figured they were just about finished protecting the scene. Once the body was gone, they were going back on the road, patrolling, and answering calls. It was well past three, so there were probably several calls holding for the patrol officers. There always were. Nobody else was around. The novelty of the murder had worn off. The beat cops were looking bored and restless, eager to rip down the yellow crime-scene tape. In a less accessible area, they would seal the scene and post an officer there indefinitely. That wasn't practical on a public street, its low traffic pattern notwithstanding.

Brickman was still gathering his thoughts as he again approached Sgt. Wiersboski and his patrol officers. Wiersboski looked like he was ready to pack it in, too.

"So, what do you think, detective," he said.

"I think he's dead," Jack replied.

"God, you're good...we'd have never figured that out."

"It's a gift," Jack said. "Sarge, when your guys get done with the initial reports, get them to me ASAP, OK?"

"Sure," Wiersboski said. "I'll fax over everything as soon as they're done. Should be in your box before the shift ends. Are you working tomorrow? It's Sunday, you know."

"My boss is going to have a heart attack when he sees the overtime slip as it is," Jack said. "But I want to make sure I get them first thing Monday when I come in."

"OK," he said. "Let us know if you need anything else. I'll be in tomorrow at midnight."

"Great, thanks."

Jack headed back to his car. He slid in behind the wheel and started the tedious task of turning it around on the narrow street. Jack conducted the activity absently, on autopilot, not really paying too much attention to what he was doing. Instead, he was focusing on the latest murder and the gnawing feeling that the two were somehow connected.

After extricating the Ford from the side street, he headed back to MLK. Jack concentrated not on the similarities of the two cases, but on the differences. If Al were sitting next to him, that's exactly what the older detective would be doing, and Jack needed somebody to play that foil. This was one of the rare instances when Jack's education and experience worked against him. If he weren't careful, he would be guilty of doing exactly what he had wanted to avoid with the lab technicians – making the facts fit theory instead of the other way around. And that was important.

On the surface, there were more differences than similarities. The murder weapons had obviously been different, since there was no way a knife had killed Karnelle Lane. The method of killing itself had differed greatly. Of course, the most convincing difference was that the Lane killing, at least in part, had been a robbery and the Timmons murder had not, as far as they knew. If it was in fact the same suspect, or even the same crew, the MO differed greatly. That would be unusual. Why change something if it worked? There had been no sign that the Timmons murder had not gone according to plan. This was not, after all, improvisational theater.

Jack was hesitant to start crying "psycho" to his bosses. It was unlikely they would agree with his intuition at this stage of the investigation, and his bosses, even Mac, were likely to dismiss his hunch as wishful thinking by a detective who had earned both his reputation and his master's degree by specializing in behavioral science and aberrant behavior. It would take more than a hunch to point the investigation in the direction of a single actor. Even Jack wanted more proof.

Traffic was understandably light at this time of the morning, and Jack found few obstacles in his way as he headed toward the office. If it had been anything but a murder, Mac wouldn't expect the report to be finished and on his desk by Monday morning. But it was a murder, and a fairly horrific one at that. Jack's latest case, even standing on its own merits, would likely garner plenty of attention both within the department and in the media. It wasn't every day that somebody had his head cut off. Well, almost cut off, anyway. Regardless, there were going to be plenty of people interested in his report, so he had better get something on paper right away. He wondered how Wilson Young or whoever was managing media at this time of night would handle the press release for the Lane murder. By the time Jack parked, he had produced a few slick phrases for the release, along with a couple of catchy headlines they could spoon feed to the newspapers. Brickman found himself laughing at his own jokes, a sure sign of fatigue.

After running the gauntlet of night guards and secured elevators, Jack found himself alone in the office. He briefly considered making a pot of coffee and quickly dismissed the idea. With some luck and no interruptions, Jack was hoping he would be home in a couple of hours, and he didn't want to completely screw up his sleep cycle. His estimate turned out to be just a little optimistic. Downloading Karnelle Lane's computer jacket, writing up his preliminary report and emailing a synopsis to the PIO office took Jack a little longer than expected. He was on his way home just under ten minutes after finishing.

Nowhere in the reports did he mention his hunch.

CHAPTER 12

Jack slept past noon on Sunday, thankful he had left a note on the bathroom mirror for Karen begging off Mass due to his late night. The house was quiet, so his wife must have gone to nearby St. Ignatius on her own.

He made a pot of coffee, ate a ham sandwich, and flipped idly through the newspapers. There was nothing about last night's murder. The killing had obviously come after the print deadline. Well, they would catch up with the television stations today. When he was done reading, he grabbed another cup of coffee and headed to his home office. Out of habit, he flipped on the TV and muted the sound.

Brickman checked his watch and hesitated briefly before picking up the phone. He had Sladky's home phone number on speed dial, though he hated to call his partner on a Sunday. He needed to bring Sladky up to speed on the Lane murder, and Al never liked to be blindsided on a Monday morning. Besides, Brickman wanted the veteran to think about the case. His insight and experience would be invaluable. And he might be able to steer Jack in a new direction. Sladky would likely have little patience for his one-killer theory if it were without merit.

The phone rang once before one of Al's sons picked it up.

"Hello, Sladky residence," the young voice said.

"Hi, Matt," Jack said, hoping he guessed right. "It's Jack Brickman. Is your dad around?"

"Yeah, hang on," he said. "Dad, it's Mr. Brickman on the phone." Matt Sladky was obviously holding his hand over the speaker part of the phone, but it was still loud as he yelled for his father. Jack wondered if that was a trait all teens shared. It seemed to be. Still, Jack appreciated the "Mr." He had told Al's sons they could call him Jack, but Al had obviously vetoed that.

If Al was bothered by the call, his voice didn't show it.

"What's up, kid?" he asked when he took the phone.

"I got called in on a new one for the slice-and-dice category," Jack said. "Street-level dealer got his head cut off last night, more or less."

"Postmortem?" Al asked.

"Nope, looks like the cause of death."

"No kidding? That's a first for me. Had a couple who got cut up after, you know, to get rid of the body easier, but never had a live one. Execution?"

"Not as far as I can tell," Jack said. "If it was, it was in a public place. Street."

"Gimme what you got," Al said.

Jack ran down the facts of the case for his partner. Al was a good listener and rarely interrupted. There wasn't much to tell him at this point, but he rattled it off anyway.

"That's not much of a start," Al said. "Any gang ties?"

"Marginal," Jack said. He hesitated before continuing.

"Al, Therese Vidalia said the cut looked really clean. Ring any bells?"

"Jack, you thinking this is the same guy?" Al asked. "That's leaping ahead a bit, isn't it? Sounds like you been reading your own thesis again."

Jack knew that was coming. He wouldn't have expected anything less from his partner.

"I'm not saying it is, and I'm not saying it isn't," Jack said. "I just think it's a direction we might want to consider."

"Kid, I been workin' the streets a helluva long time, and I never, not one time, ever came across a professional killer, or a serial killer, especially not one who uses knives and swords."

"Maybe it's something new," Jack ventured, "Maybe it's somebody trying to scare the crap out of everybody else. Or maybe it's got nothing to do with business."

"OK," Al said, "Maybe it is a new kind of intimidation thing. If it is, though, that sounds more like a West Coast or East Coast kind of thing. Like maybe Asian gangs. I heard they like that kind of crap. But if you're telling me it's the same guy, well, I want to see a little more before I go barkin' up that tree."

"I asked them to light a fire under Doc Herlong," Jack said. "If we get lucky, maybe we'll have more info tomorrow."

"Lunch at Slyman's says this is just a coincidence," Al said. "I respect your hunches, junior, but let's wait and see before we start crying wolf. Appreciate the call, though."

"Hey, I like to keep my partner up to date," Jack said. "Day shift tomorrow, remember."

"Thanks for the reminder," Al said, and hung up.

Jack had gotten what he needed from his partner: A bit of cold reality splashed in his face. Brickman would have to work to bring Al, or anyone else for that matter, around to his way of thinking. And that was assuming Jack himself continued along the same lines of thinking. He was too good a cop to ignore the facts, and if the facts flew in the face of his hunch, then so be it.

Al was right to try to rein him in a little, though. He was just trying to keep the younger detective from violating a cardinal rule of investigation: Don't make the case into something it's not.

Jack leaned back and put his feet up on his desk, taking his coffee mug in both hands and looking idly at the television. He wasn't thinking about what was on the screen, though. He was still thinking about Timmons and Lane. Jack wouldn't have any more information on the latest murder until tomorrow, but that didn't mean he couldn't do a little digging on his own.

He fired up his laptop and started searching various websites for recent unresolved murders with similar MOs. This was known as "open source" research. He started the search broad, at the nationwide level. The first search told him that the term stabbing was far too general, as hundreds of stories from news sources popped up on the screen. If it did turn out to be the same killer, somebody else might have to take the time to rack down the details on each of the crimes, but it would take an incredible number of man-hours.

Brickman narrowed it to "beheading." In the past twelve months, there was only one, and that was a bizarre farming accident in Montana. He changed the search parameters and found three more stories detailing bodies found dismembered post-mortem. At least that told Jack that this wasn't a unique trend in the crime world.

He was about to start checking some other websites when he heard Karen's car pull up in the driveway. Shortly after that, he heard the back door open and the sound of bags being put down on the countertop, followed immediately by the sound of a cat food can being opened. Jack wondered if Smalls food bill was higher than his own. Jack logged off and wandered into the kitchen.

"Hey," he said.

"Hey, yourself," Karen said. "I didn't know if you'd be up, so I ran to the store. I didn't want to wake you."

"Thanks," he said. "I slept pretty good."

"Just remember it's your turn to do the shopping next. When did you get home?" Karen asked as she started unpacking groceries and stowing them around the kitchen.

"About four, I think," he said.

"The news was talking about somebody getting their head cut off. Was that you?"

"Three cheers for radio," Jack thought. He preferred not to share too many specifics with Karen. He was getting paid to see the ugly side of the world. That didn't mean she had to see it, too.

"Yeah," he answered. "I really earned my overtime pay last night."

"Catch the guy yet?"

"Nope," Jack said. "I need a little time to get my mojo working."

Jack was purposely trying to keep the exchange lighthearted. He didn't want to have the same conversations at home he was likely to have at work.

"I'm sure you'll get him," she said.

"I wish I was," Jack thought.

CHAPTER 13

Page B1, *The North Coast Press*

May 22

By Cliff O'Brien

CLEVELAND - Police are investigating a bizarre and brutal murder that occurred on the city's east side late Saturday night.

Police spokesperson Wilson Young confirmed that Karnelle Lane, 26, was found dead at approximately 11 p.m. Young stated that Lane had died of stab wounds, but would not elaborate, referring further questions to the coroner's office.

Witnesses at the grisly murder scene on Empire Avenue were more forthcoming, however. One man, who did not wish to be identified, said that Lane appeared to have been decapitated.

"I know the cops aren't going to tell you, but I saw it," he said. "I got about as close as you could get, and I saw it. You don't mistake something like that."

According to the man, who said he lived in the neighborhood, said the victim didn't live nearby, but he worked there, allegedly plying the drug trade to drive-up customers.

"We called the police a bunch of times about these guys," he said. "They'd come by and round up a couple of these thugs and they'd be back in a week or two. This used to be a good neighborhood, until they started selling that crack."

Young would not confirm the witness' statements, although he did characterize the crime as "particularly gruesome." The police spokesperson did confirm that the department had targeted the area for increased drug interdiction efforts.

"When we get complaints from the people of this city, we try to act on those complaints," he said. "I wish we had a budget that let us put a cop on every corner. But we don't. No city does."

Young emphasized that this type of violent crime can be expected where the drug trade flourishes.

"It's no secret that drugs and violence go hand in hand," Young said. "I believe this underscores the need for more community involvement in our fight against drugs. Nobody should have to see this kind of thing on their street."

Little information was available concerning the victim, Karnelle Lane. Young would only state that Lane did have a criminal record and that his next of kin, an uncle in the Youngstown area, had been notified.

This was the city's second stabbing death in less than two weeks.

Leo Nelson poked his head into Cliff's cubicle just as he put the down the paper after giving the story a second read. He was in earlier than usual today. He had several interviews set up for a couple different stories, none of which were pressing. Still, most people worked during the day, so he occasionally had to adjust his schedule accordingly.

"I see somebody called you about Saturday's murder," Nelson said, nodding at the paper.

"Yeah," Cliff answered. "One of the interns on scanner duty called and left me a voice mail. I had to follow-up on Sunday, though."

"Oh," Nelson said. "How come we didn't get it for Sunday?"

"Christ, Leo," Cliff said, a little annoyed. "Give me a break. The first call didn't even come in until after the print deadline. Especially for a Sunday."

The Sunday edition, which was heavy in features and advertisements, was assembled well in advance of the usual deadline. Plus, because more people got the paper on Sunday than on any other day of the week, the delivery trucks had more stops to make. They only waited for a few breaking stories to fill in the front page, and even that space was severely limited.

"Easy, Cliff, easy," Leo said. "Yeah, you're right. Guess I'm just getting a little greedy."

"Anyway, nobody else had it either," O'Brien continued. "Besides, it's not like I would have gotten anything from the cops that soon anyway. They still have to clear everything with the PIO."

Leo held up his hands in surrender.

"OK, OK," he said. "You win, I'm sorry. Man, you're really not a morning person, are you?"

"You should know that by now, Leo," Cliff said smiling a little. "I dread the buzzing of the alarm clock. That's why I don't work for a living."

"That's a pretty weird story, though," Leo said. "You've covered the police beat for a while. You ever handle anything like this before?"

"No," Cliff said. "I covered a pretty bad child mutilation case when I was in Cincy, but they arrested the kid's babysitter on the spot."

"Second stabbing in a couple weeks," Leo said. "You going to connect them?"

"Not yet," he said. "Not sure the dots line up. The only similarity right now is that both victims were young Black men, killed by edged weapons. None of the cops I talked to mentioned any connections, not that they would of course, but I don't see anything worth another story yet."

"The TV news is going to be all over it," Nelson said. "They'll be calling it an epidemic or something."

Cliff grinned and leaned back in his chair.

"Yeah, they will," he said. "And they'll probably be wrong, too. And after they get it wrong, they'll never mention it again."

"Hey, we're in the only business that publicizes its own mistakes," Leo said. "Now, what do you have coming up this week?"

CHAPTER 14

Jack Brickman was in the office early on Monday, too.

Not only was he in earlier than usual, but he had also come bearing a peace offering for his partner in the form of a half-dozen doughnuts and a thermos of fancy coffee. Well, the coffee was expensive at any rate, although it wasn't flavored since Al would never drink anything as nouveau as hazelnut or Irish crème. As Jack poured himself a mug full of the dark brew, he admitted "peace offering" might be too strong a term for the breakfast treats. A more accurate term might be "greasing the wheels." He had done a lot of thinking and web searching on Sunday, and he wanted a receptive audience when he ran it by Sladky.

Jack was searching CPD's computer files and the case folders of Jameel Timmons and Karnelle Lane. He was in the middle of Lane's CCH when Al Sladky came through the door. He was already holding a paper cup of coffee, but he polished it off and pitched it into the trash can before hanging up his jacket and sitting down across from Jack.

"Mornin' kid," he said.

Jack pushed the bag of doughnuts and the coffee across the desk toward Al.

"Morning, Al," he said. "Help yourself."

Sladky raised a bushy eyebrow and pulled the bag over the metal surface. A grin broke out on his face as he peered into the paper sack. He put two doughnuts on a manila folder in front of him and checked his coffee mug to see if it was clean. It apparently passed inspection. He poured himself a cup. Sladky sipped it through a mouthful of doughnut. He swallowed and looked at his partner, a jelly doughnut poised halfway to his mouth.

"OK, Jack," he said. "You got me all buttered up. What's on your mind?"

Brickman feigned surprise.

"Al, can't a guy just do something nice for his partner once in a while?"

"Kid, I can smell a con job a mile away," he said as he munched on what was probably his second breakfast of the day. "Why don't you just lay it out?"

"Take a look at this first," Jack said as he handed the Lane file and his initial report on the murder to his partner.

Al took the file and started reading. Lane's CCH, Jack had discovered, was quite lengthy, although not as long as Jameel Timmons. The CPD file on Lane told a more interesting tale, because it listed Lane as a suspect in a half-dozen serious crimes but for which he was never charged. The young man had been a slippery customer. Unlike Timmons, he had only been marginally connected to gangs, so he was more or less an independent hustler.

While Al read, Jack continued searching CPD's database for similar crimes, constantly broadening and narrowing the search parameters, as well as going farther and farther back in time. There were, he was learning, a surprising number of stabbings in Cleveland. As far as he could tell, though, few were committed randomly or by strangers, and those were usually components of armed robberies. Even fistfights that had turned into knife fights seemed to have generally occurred between known associates.

Brickman leaned back in his chair and rubbed his eyes. He had not slept well last night...he rarely did when he was on a case. He had gotten to work a little earlier than required for day shift in an attempt to get better access to the computer files before the clerks and other cops started tying up the system with their daily chores. The electronic pathways got crowded in a hurry on Monday mornings.

Sladky closed the file and looked at Jack.

"Look," he said. "I know what your gut's telling you. Mine ain't telling me anything like that, but I ain't gonna say there's no common themes here. With Timmons we got a pissed off guy who knows how to use a knife, a guy who wanted the job done right the first time. And we got that confirmed by the coroner. With this Lane guy, you got the same kinda thorough work, but 'til Doc Herlong throws his two cents in, we got no idea if the second killer knew what he was doing or not."

Al took a swig of coffee and refilled his mug before continuing.

"Now, Therese Vidalia's opinion notwithstanding, we don't even know for sure if it was one clean cut or not," Sladky said. "Knowin' Therese, probably it was, but still maybe we're lookin' at some broad who got ticked off at Lane and grabbed a meat cleaver. I seen some freaky stuff in my time that made first timers look like stone-cold pros, like one guy on Clifton shot another guy clean through the heart, some neighborhood gripe or something. Anyway, after they measured it out, the guys were fifty-three feet apart and the shooter only fired one shot. Everybody's sayin' how they think the shooter was a gun nut or a Green Beret or something."

"I did the interview," Al said. "Turns out, the guy had only shot like ten rounds through the gun when he bought it, not even a whole box of ammo. And the guy had pretty crappy eyesight. But he sure got the job done in style."

"So, you're saying I'm jumping to conclusions," Jack said.

Al shook his head.

"No, I'm just sayin', lots of times, you start lookin' at one thing and it makes sense, but then something else comes along and points you in another direction. Like lookin' for a fastball and hittin' a changeup out of the park. You gotta go with what you get."

Jack smiled at the baseball analogy.

"OK," he said. "So, I guess we play this one close to the vest for a little while longer. With any luck, Herlong will have the autopsy done before lunch, and we can brief Mac then."

While they waited for the call from the coroner, Jack and Al kept themselves busy working the phones on the Lane and Timmons cases and on a few less serious crimes they had on their desks. Detectives rarely worked on only one case. Primarily, their calls were to other cops, and some were just returning voice mails they had received over the weekend.

One message in particular that had caught Jack's attention was from Sgt. Wiersboski. The shift sergeant sounded particularly tired on the phone, understandably since it was probably at the end of his midnight shift when he called.

"Brickman," the recording said. "Wiersboski. We worked that murder the other night. Listen, I was talking to my guys, and they said they were wondering if anybody found Lane's gun. They're telling me that Lane always carried a little piece of crap gun, like a .380 or something he used to jack people once in a while, you know, when the right target came looking to buy rock. Anyway, we didn't find it, and word was he was never without it. It was supposed to be stainless steel or chrome, or something shiny. Just thought you'd want to know. Might have been part of the robbery. Give me a call."

Jack paged through his notes and the report on the Lane Murder. He didn't remember anybody saying anything about finding a gun, and that was certainly something that would have stuck in his mind. The possible existence of the gun might be a factor that could either help or hinder the investigation. On one hand, a stolen gun could help them, mainly because it could be traced. Of course, tracing the gun would hinge on whether or not the gun had been bought through legal means (doubtful), or if it had been bought secondhand or stolen (likely.) Unless a search of Lane's residence turned up a receipt or something that showed a serial number, they would have a tough time tracking the gun to its source. It would take some effort, and the ATF could work some magic. Jack still filed it under "longshot."

The major worry was that the missing gun had been knocked loose in the scuffle and had gone unnoticed by the first responding units. Worse yet, it could have been picked up by one of the bystanders who had come to gawk at the crime scene. Jack did not like the possibility that some young kid was wandering around with a cheap, loaded handgun in his backpack.

Still, the missing gun gave them a possible lead. It also gave them a possible motive beyond robbery. Maybe one of Lane's victims had decided to come back and deliver a little street justice. Jack briefly entertained the possibility that some crackhead had cut off Karnelle's head during a drug-induced rage. He didn't think it was likely. Cocaine addicts were always looking for cash or property that could be easily fenced. And although crack addicts could be very violent, they were generally not in the best physical condition. Based on his assumption that only a desperately strung-out crackhead would have attempted a rip-off, he sincerely doubted that any possessed the skill or strength to deliver a killing blow like that one Karnelle Lane had been dealt. And it was highly unlikely they would have left the crack cocaine and cash in Lane's pockets. With the crack in hand, it was doubtful they would have even noticed the existence of a gun or the jewelry.

Jack relayed the latest information to Al, who immediately used it as ammunition to shoot down Jack's one-killer theory.

"See, it was probably just a rip-off," he said.

"You really believe that, Al? When was the last time somebody got their head cut off in a robbery?"

"We covered that," Sladky said. "Never. But, hell, a crackhead can do just about anything when he's jonesing."

"I'm not going to argue that point with you," Jack said. "But I'm not ready to throw in the towel, at least until I hear from the coroner."

As if on cue, Jack's phone rang. On the other, Dr. Herlong greeted him cheerfully. Jack wondered how he did it.

"Good morning, Jack," he said. "I must say I'm surprised to find you at your desk so early. I always envision you and Al as night people, prowling the alleyways of the city under the cover of darkness."

Jack laughed.

"Doc, detectives lurk, maybe even skulk, but we never prowl," he said. "I'm assuming Therese Vidalia got my request to you?"

"Yes," the coroner said. "Like her, I was a little surprised at the request, but when I considered the source, well, I decided to move Mr. Lane to the head of the line, so to speak. Anyway, it's probably no surprise, but the cause of death was of course the massive wound to the neck. The assailant was really swinging for the fences. Just a little more follow through and he would have made a clear cut all the way through. As it was, he only left the dermal layers on the left side of the neck intact."

"How clean of a cut are we talking about, doctor?" Jack asked. "I mean, how hard is it to do something like that?"

"Well, surgically, we would probably use a saw for something like this. Although removing the head, even in an autopsy, is an exceedingly rare procedure," he said. "In a historical sense, executioners used swords or axes, and later the guillotine. I don't know the physics, but it would be a combination of strength and technique. I believe the efficiency of the blow was increased by the overall weight of the instrument. The condemned were almost universally in a prone position, with the executioner positioned above and usually behind them. Gravity would do much of the work."

"You seem to know an awful lot about the subject," Jack commented.

"Occupational hazard," Dr. Herlong said. "I sometimes wonder what a psychiatrist would say if he saw my book collection. Executions offered some of the first opportunities for early scientists to study death and anatomy without fear of public outrage, so I suppose I do know quite a bit about the topic. And don't even get me started on the Romans."

"What kind of weapon was it?"

"Definitely a long single-edged weapon with a straight edge," Dr. Herlong said.

"Like a machete, maybe?"

"Not a chance," the coroner replied. "Unless it was a high-quality bolo or sugar cane knife, and you are not likely to find either around here. Plus, they have a slightly curved edge. A machete is too thin. No, to do something like this, you would need a relatively thick blade."

"And this one was?"

"Yes, thick and sharp. But probably more interesting to you boys is the metallurgy," Dr. Herlong said.

"Something unique," Jack asked hopefully.

"No unfortunately not," the coroner said. "Based on the chips we removed from the spine, the metal itself was just simple 440 stainless steel. But it had the same black coating as the blade used in the Simmons murder, which was obviously why you wanted the report so fast."

"Bingo," Jack thought.

"Was it the same blade?" he asked.

"Same type of metal, yes. Same weapon, no," Dr. Herlong said. Jack's enthusiasm dropped just a notch. "Based on the angle and distance of the attack in the Timmons murder, there is no doubt that it was done with a much shorter weapon. And the Lane murder was definitely done with a longer weapon, most likely a sword of some type. They are NOT interchangeable, although they shared some similarities as well."

"Such as?"

"The taper of the blades is remarkably similar. We find the fine edge on both widened immediately. I don't know what the name of the sword is, but I'd say we are probably looking at a version of the *tanto* blade, which may or may not mean the new weapon also has Japanese or at least Eastern origins."

"Is something like that rare?" Jack asked.

"I wouldn't know, really," Dr. Herlong said. "We certainly aren't talking about high quality blades here. In fact, the sword was fairly brittle. There must certainly be a fairly good chunk missing from it, based on what we found in the deceased."

"Anything you can tell me about the killer?"

"He was right-handed, or at least he swung from his right side," Dr. Herlong said. "The cut was almost perfectly horizontal, so that means he was probably about the same height as Lane. I say probably because it's possible he could use the blade well enough to make a level cut, despite any difference in height. If he were shorter than six feet, I'd expect to see a slight upward slope in the cut, vice versa if he were taller."

Brickman suddenly remembered the other injury Vidalia had mentioned, the ligature marks around Lane's right wrist.

"Doctor, Therese said something about a bracelet or something being torn off his wrist," Jack said. "Any chance of getting a better description of that based on the wounds?"

He could hear Dr. Herlong flipping through pages. He must have been on a speakerphone.

"All I can determine is that the links were on the large side for jewelry." he said. "They were quarter inch, and we took imprints. I can't even tell you what kind of clasp held it on, sorry."

"That's OK, doctor," Jack said. "I'm trying to track that down through other sources. Anything else of interest?"

"Nothing surprising," Dr. Herlong said. "He had the pharmacology you would expect from a man in his occupation and social position. He had cocaine, THC and alcohol in his system, not massive amounts but enough that it might have affected him. Oh, and he had hepatitis C. Tested clean for HIV, though."

"Well, those were his occupational hazards," Jack said. "Can you fax me a copy of the report right way?"

"Absolutely, Jack," he said. "And I'll have a messenger bring the copies of the photos over as soon as I can. Should I assume we'll be talking about this again?"

"I would have to say yes," Jack said. "I'll be in touch, thanks."

"Glad to help," Dr. Herlong said, and hung up.

Sladky, who had been watching and listening as Jack talked to the coroner, could tell by the look on his face that he had heard something worthwhile.

"I ain't seen you this interested in something since the Tribe signed Sabathia," he said. "What gives?"

Jack told his partner what the coroner had just told him. Al had been able to pick up the gist of the conversation from Jack's responses, and from reading Jack's scribbled notes upside down from across the desk. To his credit, Al took the information in stride. They weren't at the point yet where he would have to concede defeat, but Jack's theory was slowly starting to fall into place.

Jack picked up the phone and called Wiersboski's district. He doubted the sergeant would be in, since he obviously worked the midnight shift, but he might get lucky and connect with one of the detectives who worked the precinct. The desk sergeant, thankfully not Kovatch, directed his call to a detective Jack didn't know, Drew Kirby.

"Detective Kirby, this is Sergeant Brickman from downtown," he said.

"Morning, sarge," Kirby said. "Wiersboski told me you caught the Lane murder. Thought you might be calling. Figured I'd be bagging and tagging Karnelle one of these days. Guess I picked the wrong weekend to skip town, otherwise I'd have been called in, too."

"You don't exactly sound surprised that Kane bought it?" Jack said.

"Beezer? Hell no," Kirby said. "We came close to busting him on a buncha cases, including a couple with gun specs. Just couldn't make any of them stick. He was nailing people driving up to buy crack. Who's going to report that to the cops?"

"Yeah, that's what Wiersboski was saying Sunday morning, too," Jack said. "How much do you know about Lane?"

"Plenty," Kirby replied. "What do you need?"

"Well, from what Wiersboski said, Lane's gun was missing, either stolen or picked up afterward," Jack said. "We got a good description on that, so we're keeping our eyes out for it. We're also trying to find his bracelet. I was wondering if you could describe it."

"Bracelet? Man, that doesn't ring any bells," Kirby said. "I don't remember Beezer being big into bling. Let me see if I can pull the property sheets from the last time he was brought in here – maybe they got a description of it when they booked him in. I'll call you back. Shouldn't take too long."

"Thanks, Drew," Jack said. He hung up the phone and told Al they'd have to wait a little to add the bracelet to the missing property portion of the report.

Jack leaned back in his chair and closed his eyes. Based on the information they had, Jack was already trying to produce some kind of profile of the killer. In his mind, he was already thinking of it as "killer," singular. It was a challenging task at this stage of the game, especially considering the limited knowledge they had about the killer. Another issue that was handicapping Jack was his lack of knowledge about the methods the killer had used. From what Dr. Herlong had said about both murders, he knew that the killer had to have some strength and training. How much, exactly, was something Jack needed to know if he was going to get an accurate picture of the killer. The more skill and strength, the more motivated and dedicated the murderer was likely to be. Plus, it would shrink the pool of suspects.

He decided that a good place to start asking questions was the same place he usually started. Jack looked over at Al, who didn't remotely resemble the image of an ace detective with a big doughnut crumb on his chin. Brickman handed a coarse napkin over to Sladky, who took it absently and wiped his face. Appearances were deceiving.

"Al," he said, "Do you have any idea how hard it is to cut a guy like this?"

"That rhetorical?"

"No."

Al shrugged.

"Honestly, I don't know," Sladky said. "I been thinkin' about it since you gave me the heads up. I know on TV, they make it look easy, but hell, I seen enough corpses to know that bodies can be pretty damn tough. Chances are the blade's gonna break before the bone, least at the same time. How strong you gotta be, or how good a blade you gotta have, I don't know."

"I suppose the Corps doesn't cover sword fighting," Jack said.

Al shook his head.

"Nearest we ever got was bayonet stuff, and even that I think they just taught because they had too," Sladky said. "It ain't often you hear the order to fix bayonets nowadays. Mostly guys would only put them on their rifles to pry open cases. Makes a helluva crowbar. Just don't let your sergeant catch you."

"Well, what's the purpose of the bayonet, anyway?"

"To kill, sir, to kill!" Al answered smartly. "Sorry, I just fell back into boot-camp mode. You could slash with it some, but mainly you'd stab. Same with the knife. Even if you were going for the neck, you wouldn't want to try to cut the whole head off, you'd just go for the throat or something. But why go through the trouble? Unless you got a serious case of the machos, a gun works better. That's what the Marines said, anyway. Guys who liked bayonet training just liked showing how tough they were."

Jack mulled it over. His partner was right. It was possible that the suspect had been unable to obtain a firearm through legal channels, and that had forced his choice of weapons. Possible, but unlikely, but since all it really took to get a gun was money and patience. Still, if the killer had no contacts in the illegal arms trade, the hurdles were more formidable than the anti-gun faction would have the public believe. In the State of Ohio, a felony conviction or history of mental problems, drug, or alcohol abuse, would have precluded him from buying a gun legally. For that matter, a misdemeanor conviction for domestic violence would have raised red flags.

Assuming that the suspect could get a gun, why would he choose an edged weapon, which was more difficult to use and presented both higher probabilities of failure and vast potential for forensic evidence? An edged weapon requires proximity and generally produced unpredictable wound effects. The suspect was likely to be splattered, if not covered, with blood evidence. Therese Vidalia and her comrades had made a science out of reconstructing crime scenes based almost solely on blood splatter patterns. So why risk it unless you had to?

"Unless," Jack thought, *"the killer **had** to use a blade. Was this a compulsion? A fetish?"*

Jack was about to pose another question to Al when Lt. McNamara came through the door, his arms, as usual, laden with files and paperwork.

"Hey, Jack, Al, morning," he said as he shuffled to his office. He had to flop his burden down onto a file cabinet just outside his office door to free up a hand so he could dig into his pocket for the key to the door. Jack had often wondered why Mac didn't invest in a briefcase. Even a shopping bag would have been a giant leap forward in personal organization.

Their boss finally crossed the threshold of his office, after which they heard the telltale thump of files hitting the desktop. Mac reappeared quickly, an empty coffee cup in his hand. He grabbed a paper towel off the dispenser near the coffee machine and disappeared into the hallway, headed for the drinking fountain. When he came back, he was vigorously rubbing the towel over the mug. He stopped short when he noticed the coffee pot was empty. Jack raised the insulated carafe on his desk.

"We've got some left, L.T.," he said.

"Thanks, Jack," he said, taking the proffered container. He sipped the brew and closed his eyes in appreciation.

"Now that's the way to start the day," he said.

"You look like your day started a long time ago," Jack said.

"Feels like it," he said. "New homicide division head wanted to have a sit-down with everybody. Guy's an early riser, so the meeting started at seven."

"Anybody tell him the shift starts at eight?" Sladky asked.

"He musta forgot it during his rise to the top," Mac replied. "Guy makes crappy coffee, too. Least he coulda done was order out for bagels or something. Hey, you guys catch the news this morning? Somebody on the East Side got decapitated. Wonder what poor sucker had to work that crime scene." Mac obviously hadn't checked his email yet.

Jack slowly raised his hand.

"I forgot you were on call," Mac said. "You must have done something really bad in a past life, Jack. You seem to get all the weird ones."

"This one might be weirder than you think," Jack said.

"Here we go," said Sladky, rolling his eyes.

Mac looked puzzled.

"You want to tell me, or should I just read the report?" he said as he sipped his coffee.

"The live version's always better," Jack said.

He launched into a detailed account of the Lane murder. They didn't bother adjourning to Mac's office since Al and Jack were the only detectives in. Anyway, it was easier this way since they didn't have to heave files off the extra chairs in the boss' lair. Jack hesitated before expounded on his one-killer theory, but after speaking to the coroner, he had a little more confidence that he was on the right track. Plus, proving or disproving his hunch was going to take many man-hours, and they would need Mac on board to give them a little clout. At least for the immediate future.

It took a while to bring Mac up to speed, since he took the time to spell out all the details that had helped him develop his theory. If he had any hope of convincing his boss, he had to paint a fairly vivid picture. By the time he was done, Mac was just finishing off the last of his coffee. To Jack's pleasant surprise, his boss seemed somewhat receptive to the theory.

"I gotta tell you, Jack, if this was coming from somebody else, I might be more skeptical," Mac said. "I know some guys would say you're just trying to prove that your education is valuable, but I'm not one of them. I know you let the facts speak for themselves. Plus, I've never known you to bullshit me."

He looked at Sladky.

"You buying any of this, Al?"

"Enough to keep me interested, but not so much that I ain't gonna keep lookin' in other places," Sladky said. "But I'm with you. If Jack were some rookie, I'd say he'd been watchin' too much TV. Lots of his hunches have panned out."

"Thanks," Jack said. "I'm going to take back some of things I've said about you."

"As of right now, you two are on the Lane and Timmons killings full time," Mac said. "Hand off everything else you have open. I'll take care of the assignments." There would be some grumbling from other detectives.

"Keep the possible connection quiet," Mac continued. I don't want this getting out prematurely. Keep Jack honest, Al. No leaps of faith just yet, OK?"

"Right."

"Where were you planning to start?"

"I need to take a look at the coroner's computer files, see if we have any other possibles," Jack said. "Our files are good, but this guy could have been working in other cities, too. Herlong would have better access to them than we would. I could send out a teletype, but if you want it quiet, that might raise too many eyebrows.

Mac nodded. They often used LEADS, the Law Enforcement Automated Data System, to link crimes or seek assistance. The system was generally used to run license plates and check criminal histories, but since just about every police department in the state had a terminal, it was a great way to distribute and gather information.

"Good enough," Mac said. "What else?"

"I need to do a little research, find out what kind of training somebody would have to have to kill like this," Jack said. "We might be dealing with a lucky amateur, but this guy's got something going for him besides a good breakfast."

Mac thought about that for a moment.

"You guys know Sam Rausch?" he asked.

"The SWAT guy?" Al said. "Yeah, I ran into him a couple of times. I shoulda thought of him right away. Sure, he's the perfect guy to ask. You worked with him when you did that negotiating gig, didn't you Jack?"

Brickman shook his head.

"He was just coming off a knee injury then," Jack said. "They had him teaching in the academy while he rehabbed. I only met him once or twice, though I heard all the stories. The SWAT guys think he walks on water."

"The Living Legend?" Mac said. "Hell, yes. All the medals and bullshit aside, he's a lot smarter than most people think, and both the press and the mayor's office love him. He's right downstairs, too."

"We'll give him a try," Jack said. "Thanks, Mac."

"That's what I'm here for," Mac said as he headed to his office.

Jack picked up the phone and dialed the coroner's office. He got right through to Dr. Herlong, who agreed to let them browse their computer files. Brickman still didn't expound on his reasons, but Herlong had heard enough to convince him that this wasn't just a random fishing expedition.

"I'll tell Cheryl to be ready for you," Dr. Herlong said. "I can't promise I'll be around, but they'll be able to find me if they need me."

Jack hung up just as Al was putting his phone back in the cradle.

"We're in luck," he said. "Rausch is in, and he can sit down with us right away."

"Great," Jack said, and grabbed his notebook.

Jack was intrigued by the chance to work with Lt. Sam Rausch. When Brickman had worked with the SWAT unit as a hostage negotiator, Rausch had been recovering from injuries sustained dragging one of his guys out of the line of fire in a standoff that had gone bad. The team member had been one of the entry officers and had weighed about 260. Rausch had torn the medial crucian ligament of his left leg in the process. He had also earned his third Medal of Valor for the rescue. It was his second "injured on duty" award, too. Rausch took little satisfaction in either award, though he accepted them with grace. He blamed himself even though the situation had deteriorated too quickly for him to have made a difference. The suspect hadn't survived.

Rausch had been something of a legend in the department for years. When he turned eight, his parents had enrolled him in a karate class at the local YMCA, and he had taken to it immediately. By the time he had graduated from high school, he had earned his second-degree black belt in Shotokan karate and was working towards a black belt in jujitsu. He had also gotten a taste for adventure and joined the United States Army. Even the Army had been impressed with his martial proficiency, and after the grueling Ranger certification, he had been assigned as a hand-to-hand combat instructor.

After his honorable discharge, Rausch returned to Cleveland and joined the force. It hadn't taken him long to earn a reputation as a tough and cool operator, clawing his way up through the ranks to eventually command what had become one of the premier SWAT units in the country. But although he was well-known in law enforcement circles, Rausch hadn't been widely known to the public, except as a martial arts instructor. That had all changed one day when Sam Rausch had some banking to do.

On a clear autumn Saturday morning, Sam Rausch had wanted to deposit the student fees from his modest martial arts dojo in Parma. He had just left the school, and as he had a strict rule barring firearms from the school grounds, even for cops, he was unarmed and dressed casually in a warmup suit. As luck would have it, Sam did his banking at the main branch of Key Bank in downtown Cleveland so he was standing in line waiting his turn just like everyone else when three masked gunmen decided it would be a good time to hold up the bank.

As brave as Rausch was, he followed the advice he would have given any cop put in the same situation – keep your eyes open, your mouth shut and your head down. A rookie with a cowboy attitude and a gun might have immediately tried to shoot it out or take control of the situation. Unarmed and alone, Sam hit the ground along with everybody else and stayed there, trying to get a good look at the robbers without drawing attention to himself.

The robbers seemed scared and nervous. They had handled the lone security guard easily enough, but they didn't seem to have much of a plan. While one watched the door, the other two argued over whether they wanted the cashiers to turn over their cash drawers or whether they wanted access to the main vault. By the time they had sorted out what they wanted, it was too late. Somebody had hit the silent hold-up alarm and the lookout suddenly yelled that the cops were already outside. That had been a mistake on the employee's part, since most bank policies state they don't want anybody hitting the alarm until after the robbers have left the building. That was done specifically to avoid the hostage situation that had just evolved. Ironically, the banks wanted the same thing the crooks wanted – to get the robbers out without bloodshed.

But now here they were, running an operation for which they had obviously not prepared.

To their credit, the crooks had learned enough from TV to stay away from the windows and gather all the hostages to the center of the floor. The lookout guy kept the other two criminals apprised of the situation, including the arrival of the SWAT team and the hostage negotiators. As he lay on the floor with his hands over his head, Sam had wondered who was commanding the team in his absence, and whether or not they had paged him. Luckily, he had left his pager in the car. If they followed procedure, and they were too well-trained not to, they would start running the license plates of the cars parked around the bank. Eventually, they would figure out he was inside. His biggest worry was that they would start searching the customers or robbing them and find out he was a cop. If they did find his badge and ID, he figured one of two things would happen: Either they would kill him outright or he would become a huge bargaining chip.

Moving so slowly that even the bank's security cameras had a tough time following it, Sam had managed to move his badge holder from his pocket and slide it under a nearby desk. After that, he concentrated on doing the world's best imitation of a rock.

The crooks weren't well armed from what he could tell. Not that it mattered since a bad gun beat out no gun every time. Still, all he could see were handguns – two semiautos and one revolver. Sam's practiced eye had told him that none of the criminals seemed to know much about pistolcraft, but again, how good did you have to be to execute somebody?

Rausch could tell the negotiations weren't going well. For one thing, the leader of the trio, a short guy wearing an old army coat, kept asking for outrageous items, like Lear jets and helicopters. He had obviously seen too many movies. Regardless, he became increasingly agitated as the day wore on. Same guessed that he was probably overdue for a fix of his favorite drug. From his twitchy mannerism, Rausch assumed it was meth.

Whatever his personal issues were, they were clearly not helping the situation. Approximately two hours into the standoff, the leader decided to pistol-whip the bank's manager for some reason. Sam had felt his body tense and then he forced himself to relax his muscles. Acting now would only make things worse.

Unfortunately for the middle-aged man who had incurred the crook's anger, things were about to get much worse.

The leader decided that they had waited long enough for the cops to deliver, and that they had to show them they were serious. They clearly had no idea what the SWAT response to an execution would be, but Sam knew. He had quite literally written a book on the subject. He had overheard the trio discussing why they needed to kill the manager, but he was still almost in shock when they marched him over to the front door and told him to kneel down. The leader, who was apparently going to be the shooter, stayed clear of the doorway, and, so he thought, out of harm's way. The other two moved around the lobby to cover the remaining hostages.

The leader called up the hostage negotiator on the cell phone the team had thrown in. He put the phone down and shouted so they could hear him.

"Since you fuckers ain't gonna pay us our props, I gotta make you know we're for real. On the count of five, I'm gonna blow this motherfucker's head off."

With that, he pointed his revolver at the manager's head and started his countdown, his voice shrill and nervous. On "three," the man had thumbed back the hammer on the gun. On "two," Sam Rausch had acted.

One of the gunmen had unwittingly moved too close to the prone cop. Sam's timing had been almost perfect since the nearby crook's attention had been focused on his comrade. He obviously had wanted to see what happened when a motherfucker's head got blown off.

From flat on his stomach, Rausch executed a textbook leg sweep that brought the gunman down on his back right next to Sam. He pivoted in place and delivered two elbow strikes, one to the solar plexus and one to the throat, either one of which would probably be lethal. Somewhere in the process, the crook's gun had popped out of his hand. Sam had snagged it neatly out of the air. He instinctively racked the slide back on the semiautomatic just in case there hadn't been a round in the chamber. Out of the corner of his eye, he was vaguely aware of the front window of the bank shattering and a misty pink cloud filling the air near where the leader had stood. The third gunman had seen none of that, since he was trying to draw a bead on Sam, who had rolled to his right.

Later, Rausch would remember hoping that the gun would fire and that it would shoot straight as he pulled the trigger and hammered out a triple-tap that drilled the criminal through the head with the first shot and through the center of the chest with the next two. He had never been a fan of Taurus pistols, but he judged this one's performance as acceptable.

Sam dropped the gun to the ground just as the first flash-bang concussion grenades went off inside the bank. In the din that followed, he recognized some of the voices of the SWAT team members as they stormed the building.

It took a while to get things sorted out. They were aided by a state-of-the-art digital color camera system that recorded the entire incident from start to finish in high definition. Afterwards, Sam sat in on the debriefing and was able to fill in the parts he had missed.

He had been right in assuming they would realize he was in the bank. That had actually made little difference in their tactical planning since they expected a cop of his experience to sit tight and let them call the shots. The team's incident commander, Greg Giles, had known that the leader of the crew, Ramone Swanson, was a paroled murderer with nothing to lose. In fact, the bank robbery appeared to be part of a killing spree. As soon as they matched the plate of the driverless suspect vehicle to Swanson, cops swarmed his apartment, only to find the body of his hooker girlfriend mutilated in a filthy bathtub. Based on those facts, Giles had given the green light to his snipers as soon as Swanson had put the bank manager in the execution pose.

Unknown to most civilians, police snipers operate under fairly strict rules of engagement. In the worst command-and-control setups, the snipers had to wait for specific authorization from the incident commanders. That was bad because it created a delay that often cost the sharpshooters a critical shot. It took too long for the brain to register an auditory command and translate it to a physical response. Even with the feather-light triggers of their precision rifles, the delay was usually costly.

Under green-light conditions, however, the shooters could take the snot as soon as the target came into view. The main concern at the Key Bank holdup had initially been the thickness of the laminated ballistic glass, which could deflect a crucial shot. Giles had solved that dilemma by approving the use of the unit's big gun, literally. Firing a projectile that weighed over an ounce, the Barrett .50-caliber sniper rifle was capable of penetrating just about anything on a city block. Some journalists and civic leaders would later decry the use of the Barrett as excessive force. A review board would eventually disagree, calling the decision "an appropriate use of available equipment." They did, however, quietly encourage the SWAT team to deploy their .308s and .30-06s in all except the most desperate situations. Sam said he would take that under advisement.

Lars Hendriksen, the best sniper on the team, had made the fatal shot from 44 yards way. He later said that he had just drawn a bead on the last gunman when Rausch had dropped him first. He complained in his southern Ohio accent that he had been robbed of a great chance to use the Barrett twice. Snipers, Rausch knew, were a different breed.

Although the incident transformed Rausch into a local celebrity, it was the existence of the crystal-clear video and audio recordings from the bank's security systems that had catapulted him into the national spotlight. National media could not get enough of the vivid footage.

In addition to receiving CPD's Medal of Honor and a multitude of awards from civic groups across the region, Rausch had received laurels from the state attorney general's office. He had also been featured on several national TV shows, including *20/20, Nightline* and *America's Most Wanted*. Eventually, he had been named the nation's Top Cop and had received the award from the President of the United States himself.

Rausch had taken the kudos in stride, but he had been eager to escape the limelight and get back to doing what he loved best, which was commanding what he felt was the best SWAT team in the country. Eventually, they had let him get back to work, and things had slowly gotten back to normal, although it was rumored that Rausch hadn't needed to buy a beer for himself since the holdup, and that he was never turned down for a loan from Key Bank.

Brickman was lost in thought as they rode the elevator to the sub-basement of the Justice Center, trying to remember what else he had heard about Rausch. They said he was a pretty easygoing guy. Still, Jack found himself wondering what kind of emotional baggage came with killing another person with your bare hands. It was almost a foregone conclusion among the uninformed that taking a life would turn a cop into a drunk or a recluse. Jack knew that was garbage. There would have to be some scars, he knew, but it was possible for a mature, well-balanced adult to take a critical incident and put it in perspective. Eventually.

Since the recent renovations to the Justice Center, CPD's SWAT team had been based one floor above the basement garage in one of three sub-levels. It was a cheerless, windowless group of offices, briefing rooms, and locker rooms. But what it lacked in charm, the area more than made up for in intensity. When you walked past the security doors and the armed officer, the air was charged, electric.

The first room you came to was the main briefing room, which was full of wide tables and comfortable chairs. Along the walls were dry erase boards, although they were now hidden behind shutters. The shutters made things much easier to conceal current operations when the team was out. Secured or not, you never knew who might wander in at the wrong time. The room was not as spartan as you might expect, but SWAT briefings could be long, and the members carried heavy equipment. They needed a place for team leaders to check gear before they stampeded down the stairs into the waiting vehicles. For full deployments, they could call on "Mother," an armored car that carried a wide variety of equipment and firepower, but for the most part they preferred the maneuverability and low profile of the dark Ford vans with heavily tinted windows.

Beyond the briefing room was an armory secured with a massive vault-like door complete with digital lock. From snipers to the entry teams, nobody liked people messing with their weapons.

Somewhere in the cluster of rooms was also a locker room and a weight room for the exclusive use of the team. Some patrol officers bitched about the special privileges the SWAT team enjoyed, but frankly, they had really hustled for the donations that had made the fitness room a reality. Their modern weaponry and equipment had also been the product of extensive begging and grant proposals. As a premiere, elite unit, the SWAT team had many supporters.

Th SWAT area was empty when Jack and Al arrived. It was only about ten, which was either early or late of SWAT operations. When they planned a raid, they usually tried to hit the target late at night, when criminal activity was at its peak, or incredibly early in the morning, when the bad guys' energy was at its lowest. If it was a very high-risk operation or the target was elusive, they liked to hit just before dawn on Sundays or even holidays. Many crooks still went home to mom for Christmas and Easter. Cops had been serving warrants on holidays for years, and the bad guys still couldn't shake old habits.

Sam Rausch was sitting at a desk in his office. The door was open, but Jack knocked anyway. Sam looked up from the book of tactical plots on his desk. Jack knew they hadn't surprised the lieutenant, but he still had the feeling that Rausch would have been hard to sneak up on anyway.

"Come on in guys," he said.

"We're not interrupting anything, are we?" Jack asked.

"Not at all," Sam said as he rose to shake hands. "Just trying to catch up on a little research."

"Long time no see," Al said.

"Too long, Al," Sam said. "Seems like we used to cross paths more often."

"Mainly at The Zone Car," Al said, "But I've been floating a while now. Tough to get in a routine."

"You're Brickman, right?" he said as he shook Jack's hand. It was like iron.

"Guilty as charged," Jack said.

"Sorry I missed working with you when you were negotiating. Giles said you did a great job for us."

"The feeling's mutual," Brickman said. "Nice to work with guys who have their shit together."

"Actually, they told me that you were too good," Rausch said. "You didn't let them play with their toys."

"Hey, I was just trying to keep costs down. Ammo is expensive."

Rausch laughed.

"We appreciate it," he said.

Jack could see why Rausch was universally liked and respected. For a guy with such a serious job, he seemed relaxed. You noticed immediately that he didn't want for self-confidence, but he wasn't cocky, either.

Physically, Rausch was definitely not what you would expect from the stories. For starters, he wasn't a tall person. He stood about five seven and was a wiry 165 pounds. At first glance, the lieutenant was not an imposing person. If you saw him on the street or in a restaurant, you'd probably assume he was something harmless, like a pharmacist or an accountant. But when he moved, he did so with the confident cat-like grace you would expect in a dancer or a boxer. A person looking carefully might notice the rippling muscles of his forearms, corded from years of clenching and unclenching fists or applying chokeholds. Or they might notice the callused palms or knuckles, sure signs of a serious martial artist. Jack wondered if the three now-dead bank robbers had ever given Rausch a second glance. Probably not.

Rausch matched both his Germanic surname and his military background. His hair, which had turned mostly gray, was cut short. A pair of clear brown eyes looked out past a nose that had been broken more than once. That, paired with a smile that never seemed to completely fade, gave Rausch the look of a man who knew something that you didn't.

Which, Jack mused, was exactly why they were sitting in this cramped office on a Monday morning.

"You were a little vague on the phone, Al" Rausch said. "But it sounded like you wanted some information on swords and knives. My guess is you guys caught the Empire beheading."

"Good news travels fast," Al said. "Yeah. Well, actually, he caught it. I'm just along for the ride."

"I was on call over the weekend," Jack explained. "But, yes, we're looking for some background on swordplay, and some help with another case, too."

"Sure," Rausch said. "Just don't call it 'swordplay.' I'm no purist, but the Japanese would never forgive you for the term. Once the sword is drawn, the fight is on. There's no play involved."

"I thought you dealt mainly in the empty-handed styles," Jack said.

"That and guns, yes," Rausch said, "But I've been studying weapons, *kobudo*, for a while, too. They say you can never truly understand weaponless fighting until you understand fighting with weapons. Has to do with distance and timing if you want the long lecture."

"Maybe later," Jack said, his confidence boosted by Rausch's obvious in-depth knowledge of the topic. "Right now, we're curious about the beheading. How hard is it to pull something like that off?"

"That depends on a number of factors, I suppose," Rausch said. "Can you fill in the blanks? The rumor mill might be fast, but it's a little short on specifics."

Jack launched into a narrative of the Empire Avenue murder. When he was done, Rausch had a thoughtful look on his face.

"In a fluid situation like that, you would have to be very good with a sword to make a cut that clean," he said. "You would have to be in relatively decent shape, although there are plenty of martial artists running around with potbellies. Good technique goes a long way, especially with edged weapons."

"How so?" Al asked.

"Well, it's not like a club or something where the amount of damage relies almost exclusively on momentum and strength," Rausch said. "Generally, you let the blade do the work for you. With a traditional samurai sword, like a *katana*, you actually pull towards you as you cut. It's almost like a saw."

"But this guy used a straight blade," Jack said. "Or at least that's what Dr. Herlong said. Didn't the samurai use curved blades?"

"Yes," Rausch said. "They had to since they fought from horseback much of the time. They needed a sword that was flexible enough to withstand the momentum of the horse plus the impact of the swing."

"I thought those things were like indestructible," Al said.

"Not quite," Rausch said. "The cutting edge of the blade, or *ha*, was exceptionally strong and razor sharp. Even that would break though if the whole blade were rigid. The key to the *katana's* resilience is in the *shinogi-ji*, or "upper outside" of the blade. That's the unsharpened edge on the inside of the curve. It's actually made of a softer metal that lets the blade flex as the blow is struck."

"Would you find that on a straight blade?" Jack asked.

Rausch shrugged.

"I don't know," he said. "In any case, you'd be talking about an heirloom piece or a custom-made reproduction. Even in Japan, they're expensive and hard to find. In the U.S., there's only one outfit that I know of that make swords the traditional way, and their cheapest model is about a thousand bucks. And all I've seen them advertise is curved blades."

"So, are these things hard to get?"

Rausch laughed.

"Not if you're looking for a cheap one," he said.

He turned to one of his bookcases and rummaged through a pile of magazines. When he turned his chair back to the desk, he had several catalogs in his hands. He tossed most of them onto the desktop and flipped through one until he came to the page he was seeking. He folded the catalog over itself and handed the booklet to Jack.

"And that's just one of them," he said.

Brickman looked down at a page full of samurai swords with different colored hilts and sheaths, of different lengths with different markings. He flipped the page and found even more.

The product descriptions held vivid phrases such as "razor sharp" and "fully functional." The prices, Jack noticed, were not very high. In fact, you could get a nice-looking katana and something called a companion sword for less than a hundred dollars, plus shipping and handling, of course. Jack was just a little discouraged. He had been unrealistically hoping that swords would be harder to find, and easier to trace. He paged through to the end of the catalog and handed it back to Rausch.

"Who buys this crap anyway?" Jack asked.

"I do," Rausch said, smiling. "OK, not a lot of it, but the cheap blades work just fine for demonstrations, and it's not a big deal if you screw up the edge."

Jack suddenly realized something.

"I didn't see any straight blades in there," he said. "And I don't see any with black blades, either."

Rausch leaned forward and sorted through the remaining catalogs on his desk. He picked one and tossed it into Jack's lap.

"Try that," Rausch said.

Jack started paging through the full-color advertisements. He stopped when he came to a page full of black bladed knives and swords in which was apparently the stealth portion of the catalog. At the top of the page was the *tanto* Dr. Herlong had mentioned. A little lower on the page was a sword Jack would call a no-frills model. It had the same chisel pointed end the *tanto* had, although the handle was nothing more than a black cord wrapped around the hilt. The entire length of the blade was flat black except for the very edge, which gleamed brightly. According to the product description, the sword was thirty-six inches long, with a blade of twenty-eight inches.

Jack passed the catalog over to Al, pointing out the sword.

"Yeah," Sladky said, "That could be it."

Al passed the catalog back to Rausch. Sam leaned in and looked at it, nodding.

"The *ninjato?*" he asked. "Sure, that matches what Herlong said, I guess."

"OK," Brickman said. "How hard would it be to do the job with that?"

"With the right training, not much harder," Rausch said. "Normally, you would stab with it. The point is designed to penetrate armor, but the edge is still good enough to make the cut."

Sladky interrupted.

"I thought you said curved was better."

"So you are paying attention," Rausch said. "Yes, for the most part, they are. But they were developed when metallurgy was still advancing, and the samurai swords of feudal Japan were the smart bombs of their day. But hell, a good kitchen knife of today would have been a miracle two hundred years ago. Making a cut with a ninjato would need a little more muscle, a little more technique."

"Where could you go to learn to do that?" Jack asked.

"I could teach you," Rausch said. "*Kenjitsu* and *iaido* get more popular all the time. Barring that, those catalogs are full of videos and books that'll teach you how to swing a sword or throw a punch. Nothing beats hands-on, though."

"Is that shit even legal?" Al asked.

Rausch leaned forward on his desk and crossed his arms, resting on his elbows. He looked at Al.

"Are books about boxing legal, Al? How about wrestling? Or shooting?" Rausch asked. "Those are all martial arts."

Al retreated.

"Don't get me wrong, lieutenant, I'm just tryin to get my head wrapped around what we're dealing with. I'm just a dumb Slovak from the village."

Rausch leaned back, his gaze softer.

"I know that's not true," he said. "Look, there's always been a market for this stuff. The knife culture draws all kinds of people, from bikers to hunters to preppers. And martial arts have been big for a long time, too."

Jack redirected the conversation.

"What you're telling me is this guy could have learned this from a book?"

"Possibly, but not likely," Rausch said. "Yeah, there's a lot of self-training involved, but I still think you'd have to study with somebody at some point. When's the last time you heard of a golfer making par without playing eighteen holes once a week or a guy hitting home runs without ever facing a real pitcher? At some point, you've got to work against real people, or in real conditions."

"So, we got a guy with a knife fetish running around," Jack offered.

Rausch's answer was surprising.

"Maybe, maybe not," he said. "You mentioned Lane's bracelet was stolen, but you don't have a description of it and you say nobody remembers him wearing one. So why do you think he had one?"

"Oh, that," Jack said. "His right wrist was torn by the chain of the bracelet when it was yanked off him. The links were driven into his skin."

"And don't forget his pistola," Al said. "They never found his gun, either."

Rausch picked up one of the magazines and thumbed through it. He stopped in the middle of the booklet and handed it to Jack.

"Could it have been something like this?" Rausch asked.

Jack looked at a page of strange implements. At the top was a device with two octagonal weights connected by a black chain.

"Sure," Jack said. "I'd have to check the size of the links, but it could be. What is it?

"It's called a *manriki,*" Rausch said. "The real name is *manrikikusari,* which means '10,000 power chain,' apparently because of its effectiveness and versatility. Another name for them is *kusarifundo.* It's a favorite of the ninja. You could use it to choke somebody, but generally it was used to disarm."

"Disarm?" Jack asked. "How?"

"Well, from what I understand, you hold on to one end and swing it," Rausch said. "When the other end wraps around the wrist, or weapon, you pull and the weapon pops free. Hopefully. The ninja used to use all sorts of weapons connected by ropes and chains. I know they had one with a stick on one end and a sickle on the other."

Rausch paused, deep in thought.

"Listen," he said. "It seems like you guys are after one bad guy in this, but…I don't know…you might be looking at a pair of killers."

"How do ya figure?" Sladky asked.

"We're talking about two very different weapons here, with two completely different approaches," Rausch said. "I'm not saying it isn't possible that one person did this, but I'd be very impressed if it was. Even on my best day, I don't think I could pull something like this off."

"Why?" Jack asked.

"Without looking at the crime scene or the files, to me it plays out something like this: The victim – Lane, right? – is out on the street, taking care of business, when out of nowhere comes the killer. Lane sounds like a squirrelly guy, so as soon as he senses something is up, he comes out with his gun. The killer whips out the *manriki* and separates Lane from his weapon and follows up with a nearly perfect cut to the neck. If it was one guy, he'd have to have swung the *manriki* with his left hand, hold onto it and still manage to deliver the fatal blow. So, unless there's something you're not telling me, it's more likely it was two bad guys."

Jack disagreed, but he had come here seeking information. It wouldn't make sense to ignore Rausch's opinion just because it didn't mirror his own.

"OK," Jack said. "Just for the sake of argument, let's say it was one guy. From what you're saying, he'd have to be nearly perfect to pull it off. Could he learn that from books and videos?"

"It would be tougher," Rausch said. "There was a guy in the Dayton area who specialized in *ninjitsu*, probably a couple more on the west coast. It was popular for a while, but interest kind of fell off. Not much call for professional assassins these days. People want a martial art they can use. Anyway, yeah, you could learn it well enough to get by, I suppose, but without real opponents to practice with, it would be awful tough to get the timing down."

"You seem to know plenty about it," Sladky said.

Rausch shrugged indifferently.

"Not really," he said. "Oh, I read a lot, but to be honest, I always thought the whole *ninja* craze was kind of hokey and exaggerated."

"Didn't you do a lot of creeping around in the Rangers?" Al asked. "I thought this'd be right up your alley."

"Some of it might have filtered down," Rausch said. "Different eras, different weapons, different tactics."

Jack decided to do a little fishing.

"What about knife work?" he asked.

"That I know a little better," Rausch said. "I spent a lot of time learning how to use one and teaching other guys how to use one. Good for taking out sentries and stuff. We weren't too big on suppressed weapons yet back in my day."

The lieutenant looked at Jack and switched his gaze to Al.

"You guys after something else? I thought you said it was definitely a sword that killed Lane. If it was a knife, it would have to be damn big."

Jack took a deep breath and decided to go all in.

"Actually, we're looking into another murder, a stabbing," he said. "We could use some background on that, too, if you've got the time."

"I already said I'm not busy, so let's have it," Rausch said.

Jack gave the lieutenant a full description of the Jameel Timmons murder. He didn't mention their other leads, or the fact that they had struck out so far in that case.

"I guess we're asking the same question," Jack concluded. "How good would you have to be to kill somebody that fast with a knife?"

Rausch answered the question immediately. He was clearly in his element and enjoying the discussion.

"That's a fairly basic technique," he said. "In fact, if memory serves me, I think they teach that, or something like it, in the Army's basic hand-to-hand course. The follow-up, though, now that's something the average person probably wouldn't know. The femoral artery is a favorite secondary target in a lot of knife-fighting styles, so that doesn't really narrow it down."

"What about skill level?" Jack asked.

"Less than the Lane murder," Rausch said. He saw the expectant look on the detective's face and continued. "The big difference is stability. He came up behind the guy and wrapped him up with his left arm, right? So the base of the skull isn't moving when he stabs. Lane? He was probably doing a lot of moving, especially if he saw the blade coming."

"So, if the killer could disarm a guy with a chain and cut his head off, he could probably sneak up behind somebody and stab him a couple times just as easily?" Jack asked.

"Or killers, plural," Rausch corrected. "Unless you're telling me you think it's the same guy who did both the murders."

"Just speculating for now," Brickman said.

"Look, I may not be a detective, but I can tell where you're going with this," Rausch said. "Just spare me the cloak and dagger act, OK? I understand that you don't want to go floating wild theories in the rumor mill, but anything you say to me goes no further than this office."

"It's not a question of trust, Sam," Jack said, eager to keep Rausch as an ally. "Right now, we just don't have anything beyond similar MO. I'm trying to firm that up a little by talking to you, but I'd be a lot more comfortable if we had some forensic evidence linking the killings and that's something we don't have."

"Hell, even I ain't buyin' it yet," Al said.

"Fair enough," Rausch said, placated. "Anyway, for the knife work, that's about the same as the sword stuff. You could pick that up from books and movies, but maybe your guy learned that somewhere else. Maybe military, maybe prison. Who knows? There are martial arts systems that do plenty of knife fighting, but they aren't very common around here."

"What kind of physical shape are we talking about?" Brickman asked.

"From what you're saying, he'd have to be pretty strong, not necessarily big, but good arms and hands," Rausch said. He paused momentarily, then continued. "Funny though. If it is the same person, and it's only one person, then he's working backwards."

"Huh?" Al said.

"When we teach *kobudo*, weapons, we usually start with the *bo*," Rausch said. "That's a wooden staff, Al, about five feet long. The *bo* has the longest reach of the non-missile weapons, so beginners start with it because it keeps them farthest away from the opponent. As they get better, then we move to the shorter weapons."

"And more dangerous ones," Jack added.

"Not necessarily," Rausch said. "Sure, a blade is dangerous, but it really only has one dangerous part – two if you count the point, I suppose. Every part of the staff is dangerous. You can jab, swing, block, and even trap with the whole thing. Think about a nightstick, Jack. Does it matter which part you hit somebody with?"

"I hadn't thought about that, but no, I guess it doesn't," Brickman said.

"Of course, that's just the way we teach it," Rausch said. "I'm sure some places go right to the shorter weapons. I just think it would be awful tough to learn that way."

"You mean this guy is comfortable working in close," Jack said.

"Personally, I'd go with the 'big stick' approach," Al said. "But I guess that might be a little hard to hide under your jacket."

"It might be a little easier to explain, though," Rausch said. "When was the last time a guy got arrested for CCW with a piece of wood?"

"Good point," Al said.

"I think that gives us a better picture of what we're dealing with," Jack said, handing the catalogs back to Rausch. "Thanks for the help."

Rausch held up his hands.

"Keep them," he said. "I'm on every mailing list in the world."

He scribbled numbers on a Post-it note and handed it to Jack.

"That's my pager and cell phone," Rausch said. "If you need anything else, let me know."

"I'm sure we'll be calling," Jack said.

"Thanks, Sam," Al said.

The detectives headed out of the lieutenant's office back through the ready room. Two SWAT troopers were on their way in, obviously headed to the weight room judging by their apparel. Jack happened to know both of them, so he paused long enough to ask the obligatory "how you doing" before joining Al in the stairwell.

"Well, that was worth the trip," Jack said.

"Told you that guy knows his stuff," Al said.

"Does that mean you're on board?"

"Let's just say I'm starting up the gangplank," the older man said. "I still want to see what Herlong's got."

Jack, however, was not to be disheartened.

"Nothing like winning a bet from you," he said. "I can taste the corned beef already."

CHAPTER 15

Lt. McNamara's decision to put Brickman and Sladky on the Timmons and Lane murders exclusively turned out to be a smart move.

From Rausch's office, the duo had driven straight to the coroner's office where Dr. Herlong's secretary had set up two computer terminals in an empty conference room and put an intern at their disposal to pull files and run errands. Even with the help, the detectives ended up burning the rest of Monday and most of Tuesday delving into the paper and electronic files the coroner had provided. To make matters more challenging, Herlong had taken the liberty of contacting his counterparts in all the surrounding counties, exploring homicides with similar fact patterns. And he had reached out to Toledo, Akron, and Youngstown, too. Jack and Al suddenly found themselves nearly overwhelmed with paperwork. Because the other coroners had decided to just send over all their homicide files, solved and unsolved, breaking away to catch a new case would have been nearly impossible.

On Tuesday, Al had sent the intern out to grab them some fast food for lunch. The intern's name was Paul Madsen, and he seemed like a good kid. Herlong said he knew when to shut up and when to listen, and that was good enough for the detectives. Madsen had graduated from Penn State with a degree in biology, and was doing an internship with the coroner's office to fill time before starting medical school. The young man was smart and energetic, obviously glad to a have a break from whatever it was he did for the coroner.

As the three of them sat munching take-out burgers, Jack sifted idly through the files and printouts they had singled out as possible crimes committed by their suspect. It had been a long process, but Jack felt they had narrowed it down enough to really start looking closely at the remaining files. He had started the search broadly, just as he had with CPD's computer files, but on late Monday, Al had thrown a new wrinkle in the project when he came across a case from Elyria that had almost no visible connection to theirs.

"Jack," he had said, "You remember what Rausch was saying about starting with a longer weapon, and working closer?"

"Sure," Jack said.

"I'm just throwing this out there, but what weapon gives you the longest reach?"

Jack had thought briefly. It didn't come right away, but his hand brushed against his sidearm as he shifted his weight in the chair. Then it dawned on him.

"A gun, I'd say."

"Right," Al said. "Take a look at this."

The file Al passed over was from an unsolved murder that had occurred over a year ago in a public housing complex in Lorain County. According to the synopsis, an unknown suspect had entered the victim's apartment with no signs of forced entry and shot the victim, Karl Dawkins, four times with a .22-caliber pistol. Forensics had placed the shooting distance at fifteen to twenty feet. The shots had been very accurate, with two each to the head and chest. Those to the chest had been less than two inches apart. One had hit the heart dead-on.

The bullets, as often happened with the small, high-velocity .22, had been extensively damaged by their trip through the bone and tissue of Dawkins. The fragments were almost useless as far as ballistics were concerned. They were able to tell the brand and type of bullet, but beyond that, they had nothing. There had been no empty shell casings at the scene, robbing the police of another piece of potentially vital evidence. The brass often yielded fingerprints, left as the rounds were loaded into the gun. It could be difficult to lift them due to the burnt powder residue and the violent energies the firing process produced. Barring prints, spent shell casings displayed firing pin indentations and extraction scratches which could conclusively link the brass to the murder weapon. In the least, the unique impression left by the firing pin striking the primer, or in this case, the rim, could help them identify the brand of weapon.

Jack and Al had tossed around a few theories about the murder weapon. Initially, they assumed the gun in question had been a revolver, which would explain the lack of shell casings left on the scene. As he read the accompanying police file, however, he noticed that no shots had been reported. The victim had been found two days after the killing when a neighbor complained about the smell.

The fact that no one had reported hearing shots fired meant one of two things. Like many low-income buildings, apathy was the rule. It was possible, and even probable, that the shots had been heard but not reported. Many people apparently felt that if it wasn't happening to them, it just didn't matter.

The other possibility, one Jack was almost unwilling to entertain, was the possibility of a silenced or "sound suppressed" weapon. Despite what Hollywood would have the public believe, silencers were not abundant among criminals. Suppressors were strictly regulated by the BATF. A gun charge alone may or may not attract the attention of the federal government. An illegal suppressor certainly would get them on the agency's radar, and most criminals didn't find it worth the risk.

Still, Jack knew that such modifications could be made to a gun. He had paged through enough catalogs and been on enough mailing lists to have seen the books that promised to tell you how to make your .22 "whisper quiet." Of course, none of the publications advocated the modifications; they apparently just wanted you to know how it could be done. The First and Second Amendments aside, Jack had often wondered how such publications remained legal.

In the end, Jack and Al had decided that if the gun had indeed been suppressed, then it had probably been a semiautomatic. A revolver was almost impossible to silence because of the gap between the chambers and the forcing cone that ensured the bullet entered the barrel properly aligned. The gap allowed plenty of gases to escape, along with a plenty of noise. It was a remote possibility that the killer had used a single shot pistol, like the Thompson Contender, but both the number of shots and their placement made that highly unlikely. It was doubtful the shooter would have been able to eject and reload fast enough to incapacitate Dawkins before he escaped, attacked, or yelled for help. Same with a two-shot derringer.

Dawkins had gone down quickly, almost instantly, and that had meant heavy damage delivered very rapidly. And that meant a semiautomatic. Either the shooter had figured out a way to catch the brass as it ejected from the pistol, or he had stopped to pick up his empties.

The problem was, as far as Jack was concerned, it didn't quite fit with the other killings. Dawkins had been killed in his own apartment, not a public place. According to the Elyria Police Department file on Dawkins, he had been a low-level drug dealer who, like Timmons and Lane, had done time for several minor crimes. Dawkins had been Black, and he had started his criminal career as a juvenile. His CCH showed he had been convicted in both Lorain and Cuyahoga counties on various charges. He had also once been a gang affiliate, but he had never been a full-fledged member.

Victimology aside, the methodology had a familiar ring to it. Al had reiterated his initial theory that a first-time killer was certainly more likely to use a gun than anything else because it greatly reduced the risk of injury to the shooter. Jack had solved the disagreement by calling Rausch.

"That was fast," Sam said when he answered.

"Hey, we work quick," Jack said. "We're over at Herlong's office digging through some files and found something interesting, maybe something you can help us with."

"Fire away," Rausch said.

"You said a beginner would probably want to start farther away with weapons," Jack said. "What about guns? Would that fit anywhere in the mix?"

"Sure," Rausch replied. "If we're talking about somebody who has a thing for ninja weapons, well, they were big into bows and missile weapons like *shuriken* – throwing stars – but they were also way ahead of the rest of Japan in using guns. Granted, guns and the related tech weren't very advanced in the feudal period of Japan, but I think they had some crude, last ditch matchlocks. It kind of defeats their purpose since a gun makes a lot of noise, but they did use them."

"Think that would appeal to a modern ninja?" Jack asked.

"From what I hear, that psych stuff is more your bag," Sam replied. "I'd say if you were into creeping around and whacking people, there's a definite advantage to keeping it quiet."

"Great," Jack said. "Thanks."

"So, what'd he say?" Al asked when Jack hung up the phone.

"He says it's possible," Jack replied. "Apparently, the ninjas weren't averse to using guns."

Paul Madsen, who had been sitting quietly in the room at the time, ventured a question.

"Did I hear right?" he asked. "Are you guys looking for a ninja?"

"No," the detectives replied in unison.

Madsen smiled.

"OK," he said. "I knew I didn't hear that right, so I'll just forget I didn't hear it."

"Dr. Herlong was right about you," Al said.

"I'll take that as a compliment," Madsen replied.

With the possibility that their killer had at one time used a gun, Jack and Al were forced to start their search over. Eventually, they found a case that was hauntingly similar to the Dawkins murder. This one though, had occurred in Painesville, a city with more than a few rough spots in the heart of Lake County. It was far east of Cleveland, and in a different orbit completely from Elyria, which was well west of Cleveland. Despite the difference in geography, the cases were very similar.

Carlos Rice had also been murdered in a public housing complex, shot to death about three months before Dawkins. The murder weapon had also been a .22, and the victim had been shot three times in the head, again from approximately fifteen feet away. And again, neighbors had heard no gunshots, and there had been no signs of forced entry. The Lake County Crime Lab had recovered no spent shells, and the bullets had fragmented into unrecognizable and unusable pieces. But even that had proved helpful.

"They get a bullet type from Elyria?" Al asked as he read the Rice file.

Jack flipped through the report from Lorain County.

"CCI Stinger," Jack said. The Stinger was a round used for hunting small game, with a hexagonal hole in the tip that ensured expansion upon impact. It was advertised as "hyper-velocity" ammunition. Despite its small size, it was a very nasty little bullet.

"Same in Painesville," Al said, adding yet another link to the chain connecting the cases.

A review of Rice's criminal pedigree was strikingly similar to Dawkins', as were his race and age. Al and Jack immediately started burning up the phone lines to Elyria and Painesville, trying to track down the investigating detectives on the respective cases. After a frustrating round of phone tag, they finally made contact. By that time, it was nearing the end of the shift for both cities detectives, so they promised to fax over their complete reports and follow-up via phone on Tuesday.

"You think we're grasping at straws?" Jack asked Al after they had spoken to their counterparts to the east and west.

"Maybe," Sladky replied. "If nothing else, we might have linked two murders that have nothing to do with our guy. That could be the foot in the door Elyria and Painesville need. 'Course, that doesn't help us."

They had worked late, continuing to sift through the remaining cases. Luckily, most murders were relatively straightforward, with plenty of suspects to go around. Murder, as a rule, was a crime perpetrated by someone known to the victim. Still, the coroners had answered Herlong's request with enthusiasm, so Jack and Al had plenty of paperwork to scan. Primarily, it was unsolved cases with no suspects. There were a few apparently unrelated cases, however, that had found their way into the mix.

Even after calling it quits for the night, one case in particular had continued to gnaw at Jack's intuition. That case, strangely enough, had been one processed by Dr. Herlong's staff. Why the coroner had included it in the files, Jack would never know. Maybe Dr. Herlong had a hunch, too.

When they returned to the coroner's office on Tuesday, Jack, with a good night's sleep behind him, was rested and eager to get back to work. The first case file he picked up was the one that had plagued his thoughts through the previous evening.

The case was from Shaker Heights, a near suburb of Cleveland known for its old-money aristocracy and a growing mix of races and ethnicity. The homes in Shaker Heights ranged from mansions to bungalows. Despite a relatively large number of apartments and its proximity to Cleveland, the city had somehow managed to retain its image as a good place to live, if you could afford the taxes, which were exorbitant.

It was in one of those apartment buildings, a huge older building just off Shaker Square, that Charlie Clayton had met an untimely end. Well, untimely if he had been anything but a low-level thug with a lengthy CCH. Jack didn't know what the life expectancy of a drug dealer was, but it sure couldn't have been much past the age of thirty.

Clayton had been twenty-four years old last November when the crime occurred. Like Rice and Dawkins, he had been home alone in his apartment when he had been murdered. Unlike the others, however, he had not lived in a low-income residence, nor had he been shot. Clayton had been beaten to death with a hammer and stabbed with an ice pick. They also had a suspect, Jerome Lang, his one-time roommate and occasional business partner. There had been no signs of forced entry, and Lang, it was believed, still had a key. Shaker Heights PD also had information that Lang and Clayton had been feuding about something for a while. They had issued a warrant for Lang, who had suddenly vanished.

According to the autopsy report, the attack had apparently taken Clayton by surprise. There had been a noticeable lack of defensive wounds on Clayton, which was surprising considering he had seemed to be in good physical condition. They had found that several bones in the back of the victim's right hand had been broken sometime during the struggle, but that was it. There was no way of knowing from his file if Clayton had been good with his fists or not, but Jack assumed that he had some self-defense acumen. It was rare for a predator not to have at least minimal fighting skills. It was, after all, often part of doing business.

The coroner's report pointed to an attack that had been explosive and devastating. That made it possible that Clayton had been too stunned to mount much of a defense. The corner had been unable to determine which weapon had struck the fatal blow because they had apparently

104

been delivered in such rapid succession. Judging from the circular impression driven into the victim's left temple, a common claw hammer had delivered a knockout blow. Another swing with the hammer had broken two ribs on the right side of his abdomen. A third had been swung like an uppercut into the bottom of the jaw.

In the forensic re-creation of the incident, the killer had pressed the attack as Clayton staggered backward. The follow-up had been with a long, pointed instrument, most likely an icepick. That had penetrated the chest cavity near the heart. A second stab had actually pierced that organ while a third had been driven through the right eye, deep into the brain. The follow-up attacks had been superfluous, since two of the three hammer blows would most likely have done the job.

As Jack read and reread the report, he noted one aspect in particular that had been unusual. The autopsy showed another wound that had been made by the icepick. It was quite shallow and had barely penetrated the skin. Brickman and Sladky agreed that it appeared to be a test cut. A person who either doesn't want to stab somebody or doesn't know how hard to cut will often display a reluctance or inability to deeply penetrate the skin. It was quite common in juvenile crimes and cases of domestic violence. Typically, once the first shallow cuts are made, the attack becomes more forceful as the attacker gathers confidence and his anxiety level increases. Once the adrenaline takes over, the wounds tend to get deeper and the assault more frenzied.

In the Clayton case, the test-cut theory would have been solid if it didn't contradict the other evidence. From all indications, the hammer had been used first with devastating effect. There had been no hesitation on behalf of the killer when swinging the impact weapon. Why would the killer suddenly get squeamish and hesitate with the icepick? Jack knew that it was highly unlikely that somebody in the middle of a savage attack would have been able to regulate his pace.

The angle of the shallow wound was also different from the deeper injuries, another piece of information that might or might not mean something. In a struggle, strange things could happen. Still, what really stood out to Jack was the placement of the shallow wound. It had been almost exactly two inches away from the deep wound to the heart. Jack had seen too many reports not to be surprised by round numbers. Forensic statistics were precise and so they rarely landed exactly on one inch or one foot. The technicians appeared to have an affinity for decimal points.

And then there was the question of how the attack had been carried out. The assault had started in a narrow hallway between the living room and dining room and bedroom. Clayton had been driven towards the living room by the attacker. That didn't give the killer much room to swing a hammer. The confines of the hallway also made it nearly impossible for two people to have carried out the attack, as Sam had suggested. So, did that mean the killer had carried a hammer in his right hand and an icepick in his left? If it had, then they were once again dealing with a highly skilled person.

"And who learns to fight with a hammer?" Jack wondered.

As they were finishing their greasy lunch, Jack brought the case up to Sladky.

"Al, does that make sense to you?" he asked.

"What do you mean?" Al replied, wiping his hands on a napkin.

"Well," he began, "We've seen a lot of cases like this, right?"

"*I've* seen a lot of cases like this, yeah," Sladky said, smiling. "I don't know if your tab qualifies as 'a lot,' but I'm willing to give in on that point."

"Thanks," Jack said. "Seriously, though, how does this play out to you?"

"Way I see it," Al said, "Lang, or whoever, has a beef with Clayton over something. He's still got a key if it's Lang, so he just lets himself in while Clayton's out and waits in the bedroom. He waits until he hears Clayton come in and then, wham, it's Bob Villa time."

"You don't think it could be somebody Clayton let in?" Jack asked.

Sladky shook his head.

"Nah," he said. "Say it was, say it was even Lang for whatever reason. Clayton lets him in, maybe he gives him some song and dance about having left something in his bedroom he wants to get. So he goes in the room and comes out with a hammer and pick. He'd have to had it stuffed in his coat or something. You think Clayton is going to miss that? I don't think so. You've seen his CCH. Guy had some street smarts."

"What about two guys?" Jack asked.

"Ah, yes, the old bum's rush," Al said. "Nope, and you probably know why already but I'll spell it out for ya'. Hallway's too narrow. No way you'd get two people side by side in it. They'd be tripping over each other."

"Not much space to swing a hammer, either," Brickman added.

"Where there's a will…" Al said.

"They never found the murder weapons," Jack said. "Are we sure we're making the right assumptions?"

"Huh?"

"I spent a little time last night going through those catalogs Rausch gave us," Jack said. "I even did a little surfing online. You'd be surprised at the weird weapons that are out there."

"So, you think one of these weird weapons got used on Clayton?" Al asked. "You sure you're not just trying to make the facts fit your theory?"

"I think they do already," Jack said. "I just need a little bit more to firm it up."

"You going to bug Rausch again?" Al asked.

Jack was already dialing the number.

"He said to call anytime, right?"

There was no answer on Rausch's cell phone and Jack got kicked into his voice mail. He left a brief message and the extension of the conference room. Al and Madsen were out somewhere in the halls of the coroner's office trying to track down some fresh coffee when Rausch called back. In the background, Jack could hear the shop popping of gunfire. Jack guessed the SWAT team was out at CPD's range near West 85th and Denison. Rausch confirmed Jack's guess.

"Sorry, I didn't get the call," Rausch said. "We were just running through the shoot house when you called. I just happened to pick up the phone during a break."

"When I was with the team, those guys practically lived in that house," Jack said.

"We have to call it training, but it's really just an excuse to make some noise," Rausch said.

"I knew it," Jack said. "All those psychiatrists were right about guns being phallic extensions."

"How did the team ever understand what you were saying?" Rausch said, laughing. "We like single syllables down on the farm."

"I forgot," Jack said. "Hey, the reason I'm calling is I have another question for you."

"Shoot," Rausch said.

Jack detailed the Clayton murder for Rausch, who didn't answer immediately after Jack had finished. When he spoke, his tone was thoughtful.

"That's interesting," he said. "Yeah, I might have an idea about that. You guys are still at the coroner's office, right?"

"Yes."

"I'm leaving here now," Rausch said. "I've got to make a quick stop, but I think I can be there in half an hour, if you guys are still going to be around."

"Far as I know, yeah," Jack said. "Unless something comes up, we still have some files to go through and I want to talk to Dr. Herlong about something."

"OK," the lieutenant said. "Just call me if you have to leave in a hurry. Otherwise, I'll see you in a bit."

Jack hung up just as Madsen and Sladky came back in. The intern was holding two cups of coffee, Al had one. The two had somehow gotten into a heated discussion about who had the better chance of winning the Big Ten in football. Madsen, of course, was backing Penn State while Sladky was praising the Buckeyes. Brickman, thankfully, was not forced to weigh in on behalf of the Wolverines or World War III might have broken out. At any rate, football season was still a spring and summer away. Even for a diehard alum like Jack, it was a little early to start worrying about the gridiron. He still had a whole season of baseball ahead before then.

"Put your money where your mouth is, kid," Al said.

By the time they noticed Jack, they had already bet a case of beer, "the good stuff," on the outcome of the OSU-Penn State game in the fall. Al gave him a business card with his home phone number scrawled on the back, along with the bet just in case the soon-to-be med student had a short memory.

"If you're done with your illegal bookmaking, is there any chance we could get back to the case?" Jack asked.

"The only case your partner's got to worry about is the one he's going to owe me," Madsen said.

"I thought Doc Herlong said you were the quiet type," Sladky growled.

"Not on important matters," he said, smiling.

"What's up?" Al asked Jack.

"Rausch is on his way over," Jack said. "Should be here soon."

"He have any ideas?"

"Yes, but he didn't go into detail," Brickman said. "It sounded like he wanted to show us something."

They dispatched Madsen to the lobby to wait for Rausch and bring him in. In the meantime, they started sorting the unrelated files and stuffing them back into boxes. Herlong had said to leave the files and he would take care of returning them. Jack wondered if Madsen would be going on a road trip soon with a van full of boxes in the near future. By the time Rausch arrived, they were left with three piles of papers, one each for the cases that might be related.

Madsen shortly entered the conference room with the lieutenant in tow. Rausch looked a little grimy around the edges and was still dressed in his black BDU's. The uniform worked for Rausch. It made him look tougher, if that was possible, but it was more than that. He looked perfectly at home in the dark military apparel. Maybe it was the relaxed grin on his face that made him look more dangerous. That subtle ferocity was all the more impressive when you considered his stature. Well, Audie Murphy had been much shorter than Rausch, and he had been pretty tough, too.

Strapped to his right thigh in a tactical holster was a single-action pistol based on the Colt 1911 frame. The gun was in fact a .45-caliber semiautomatic that was almost a carbon copy of the venerable former military sidearm. Rausch's pistol, however, was made by Springfield and was the "loaded" Tactical Response Pistol. The "loaded" label meant the guns came with an impressive array of features – ambidextrous safety, rails for a tactical light, Tritium night sights and a ten-round magazine. It was definitely not your father's .45.

All of the SWAT team members carried the pistol. They were the only officers in the city permitted to carry a duty weapon other than the Glock nine millimeters.

"Hey, guys," he said as he walked in.

"Afternoon, Sam," Al said. "See you're still lugging that hog leg around."

"Jealous?"

"Hell, yes," Sladky said. "One thing I miss about the Corps is my old .45. Dang, they were nice."

"You should give this one a try some time," Sam said. "You wouldn't even recognize it."

"Love to," Al said. "When?"

"Sooner rather than later, I hope," Rausch said. "Hey, Jack, how's it going?"

"I'm wearing out the seat of my pants and my eyeballs, but otherwise OK," he said. Thanks for coming over."

"I probably could have explained it over the phone, but I thought it might be easier if I just showed you," Rausch said. He nodded toward Madsen, who had returned to one of the conference table chairs. "He OK?"

"Doc Herlong says so," Jack said. "So far, he's been very helpful."

"'Cept for the Penn State thing," Al said.

"Pardon me?" Rausch said.

"Never mind."

The lieutenant had been carrying a slim black bag in his left hand. He laid the case down on the table and unzipped it. When it folded open, Jack, Al, and Madsen leaned in for a closer look. Inside the felt-lined case were two black metal instruments that resembled giant forks, except they only had three tines and the center tine was at least twice as long as the handle. The handles were wrapped in black leather and had heavy pommels.

"What are they?" Jack asked. "I've seen these before, haven't I?"

"They're called *sai*," Sam replied. "You may have seen them in the movies, but probably not. They're not that popular of a weapon. If you know Greek letters, the psi looks a lot like these. I don't know if the similarity in names is a coincidence or not. That symbol sometimes shows up in gang signs, too."

"What do you do with them?" Al asked.

"Funny you should ask."

Rausch picked up the weapons, one in each hand. At first, he held them by the handle with a thumb hooked through the tines. Then he took a step back and flipped them around so the longest tines lay on his forearms, with the grip and pommel pointing away from his body. The index fingers now lay along the grip, pointed toward the pommel. Rausch flipped the *sai* forward and back in a smooth, seamless movement. He had obviously been practicing for a while. When he reversed the grip, he started to explain the weapons.

"Generally, you'd hold the long end against the forearm, like this," he said. "You would use them to block with."

In a blur of movements that Jack had trouble following, Rausch demonstrated a series of blocks.

"You could also use them to trap with," Rausch said. He reversed his grip on the weapons again and drove them over his head, crossing the tines as he did so. He then sharply turned them towards the ground.

"Theoretically, they're supposed to be good for blocking and trapping swords, though I personally don't like the odds," Rausch said.

"Who comes up with this stuff?" Sladky asked.

"Weapons of necessity, Al," Rausch said. "The *sai* have their origins primarily in Okinawa. They may have evolved from Chinese spears, which were originally used to prop open shutters on temples. Regardless, the *sai* were mainly used as defense against swordsmen. Swords were outlawed for commoners from time to time. Coincidentally, they're commonly considered a policeman's tool, since you could trap and control."

"I'm guessing they weren't just defensive weapons," Brickman said.

"Good guess," Rausch said. "Most people assume the tapered ends are actually blades, like knives…"

"That's what I thought when I saw them in those catalogs," Jack interrupted.

Rausch, who had spent years teaching kids karate, barely noticed the interruption.

"Common mistake," Rausch said. "Anyway, they're not. The ends are pointed though. You use them as stabbing weapons almost exclusively. The taper just about ensures deep penetration."

The lieutenant punctuated the statement by executing a series of thrusts that seemed to come from all directions, including straight down. There were even some double strikes, from what Jack could interpret.

"You could also use the long ends as striking tools, though it's a little harder to get any power out of it," Rausch said. He demonstrated by again reversing the sai in his hands. He flipped them, one at a time, forward and back in a downward motion Jack instantly related to the towel-snapping fights kids sometimes get into in locker rooms. What power there was obviously came from the whipping action

"Finally, you could attack with the pommel," Rausch continued. "Really, you're using the same stroke as a punch, so if you can hit hard, you could do a hell of a lot of damage with these things. You're concentrating all the power of a punch into a piece of metal about the diameter of a quarter. Or a hammer head."

Rausch demonstrated several more techniques, this time with the tines again laying along his forearms. He then launched into a series of movements that connected all the blocks, strikes, and traps he had just shown them. When he finished, there was just a hint of breathlessness in his voice.

"There's also some historical evidence that the really, really, good practitioners could also throw the *sai*," Rausch said. "According to some books, they would carry a third *sai* in their belts and throw one to pin a guy's foot to the ground. I've never seen anybody carry more than two, but it is another option. Anyway, these could be what you're dealing with."

"Can I take a look at those things? Al asked.

"Be my guest," Rausch said. He handed one to Jack and one to Al.

Brickman took the weapon gently. He was surprised at its heft. It was much heavier than it looked. As he examined it more closely, its weight made sense. The *sai* was basically just one piece of steel, which probably made it hard to break. Jack made a careful inspection of the tines flanking the center spike. They, too, were pointed, though they angled out slightly. In his mind's eye, Jack could see the sai being driven into Clayton's chest, deep enough for one of the flanking tines to have caused the "test wound." He felt a stir of excitement.

"I'm looking at the murder weapon, aren't I?" he thought. And, more important, it gave Jack a solid piece of evidence linking at least three of the five murders.

"So, what's the verdict?" Sladky asked Brickman.

"As far as I'm concerned, it's the same guy," Jack said. "OK, it's a little early to link the shootings, but Clayton, Timmons, and Lane – definitely."

Sladky took a moment to digest the statement. He glanced down at the yellow legal pad he had been using to take notes since he got to the coroner's office. Al flipped slowly through the pages, pausing occasionally to circle something. Jack, who was accustomed to Sladky's cautious decision-making process, was waiting in silence. Finally, the older man looked up.

"Yeah, I think you're right," he said. He looked over at Rausch. "You got any comment?"

"I haven't been holed up in here for two days like you, but I think it's a definite probability," he said. "You're either dealing with one very skilled individual or several. I'd say the odds against finding more than one person with these kinds of abilities and getting them to work together is highly unlikely."

Madsen, who had been watching the discussion intently, asked the obvious question.

"So, is this like a serial killer?"

Jack, who had been so far reluctant to say the "S-word" aloud, nodded.

"It depends on what definition you're using," he said. "But yes, we're looking at a serial killer. Technically, the last two murders were close enough together that you could almost call him a spree killer. The one in November makes it a serial, and that's not counting the two shootings."

"Wow."

"I don't think I have to tell you to keep this quiet, do I?" Jack asked. "I'd hate to have to charge you with interfering with an investigation."

"Hell, no," Madsen said. "Doc Herlong went out on a limb to get me into Case's med school. No way I'm going to screw that up. Plus, I think your partner would love an excuse to throw me in jail."

"OK," Al said. "Now what?"

"First, we get a hold of Painesville and Elyria and give them the heads up," Jack said. "Things are going to get very busy for them in the near future. Next, we need Dr. Herlong to go over all these cases right away. There wasn't any trace evidence of note, but maybe something will match on a second pass."

"Paul, could you track down the doc?" Al said. "We're going to need to light a fire under these other medical examiners."

Madsen was up and moving before Sladky finished the sentence. That left Rausch the only one with nothing to do.

"What about me?" he said.

Jack thought a moment.

"How free are you in the near future.?"

"Never can tell when something is going to pop off," he said honestly. "Most of our raids are planned, but I'm behind my desk way more than I'd like to be."

"We're probably going to need your help again with this, Sam," Jack said. "Right now, I think we're good, but keep in touch, OK?"

"Sure," Rausch said, collecting the sai and zipping them carefully back into their case.

"And thanks, Sam," he said. "We'd have never come this far this fast without you."

"Ah, you could have dug this stuff up on the Internet," Rausch said. "But you're welcome."

"See ya', Sam," Al said, covering the mouthpiece of the phone with his hand.

Rausch nodded in Al's direction on his way out of the room.

When he had left, Al looked over at Jack.

"Now what?" he asked. "NOSCU?"

"Yeah," Jack said. "I think it's time to release the hounds."

Brickman picked up the phone and dialed Lt. McNamara's office. Mac picked up on the second ring. He listened without interrupting as Jack described the three new cases and spelled out why he felt they were linked. When Brickman had finished, the only question he had was whether or not Al agreed with his assessment. After Jack assured him that Sladky was on board, Mac rattled off a few orders and gave him permission to make even more calls.

"You know the protocol better than I do, Jack, so do what you gotta do," Mac said. "Just make sure you get it written up right away when you get back to the office. I need your paperwork ASAP, so make sure I get the whole report and a synopsis. Upstairs needs to know, too."

Brickman immediately called the Cleveland office of the FBI, now located in a pristine new building overlooking the waterfront and Burke Lakefront Airport. His call rang directly to the desk of Assistant Special Agent In Charge Ken Bright. Bright had been a guest instructor in Quantico when Jack had attended the FBI's National Academy. The two had hit it off immediately, their friendship cemented by their shared hometown. Since then, their paths had rarely crossed on official business, although Bright had been instrumental in helping to develop the contingency plan he was now activating.

"Ken, it's Jack Brickman," he said.

"Hey, Jack, what's new?" Bright asked. "Any kids yet?"

"No, we're still negotiating," Jack said.

"Start while you're young," Bright said. "Is this a social call, or do you need something official?"

"Funny you should ask," Jack said. "I think we've got an active serial killer working the North Coast."

Bright's tone changed instantly, from light and bantering to all business. Like most career cops, the Federal agent knew when to turn it on and when to turn it off.

"I'm listening."

Unlike McNamara, Bright interrupted Jack constantly. One thing Jack and Bright shared was a master's in psychology, though Bright also held a juris doctorate, a document common in the FBI. He had spent time with the behavioral science department at FBI headquarters, a section that had earned a well-deserved reputation as THE authority on serial crimes. Bright had done well in the unit, although his tenure there had been brief. He had taken the Cleveland assignment to be closer to his parents and with the understanding that he would be next in line to head the office.

"OK, Jack," he said. "I agree with your assessment. This definitely sounds like one person, but to be honest, I just don't see the connecting forensics evidence. Certainly, that will be forthcoming. Motive needs some firming up. If it is one guy, what's he getting out of it? You start a profile yet?"

"Haven't had the chance, no," Jack said. "Just some ideas."

"I'll assume that's next," Bright replied. "I'll try to throw something together, too. Officially, though, there's nothing here that falls into the Bureau's authority."

"Understood," Despite the public's perception to the contrary, a serial crime rarely fell under the purview of the FBI. Although they often lent forensic expertise and support to ongoing investigations, unless they involved crossing state lines, the Bureau was powerless to act. Jack had known that when he called. He was after something else from Ken Bright.

"Ken, I'd like to activate NOSCU, and I just wanted your support," Jack said.

"I figured that's where you were heading with this," Bright replied. "Yeah, of course. I think it's an easy decision. I'll start making the calls. Keep me posted, and thanks for the call."

When Jack hung up, he gave Al a thumbs up and dialed another number he knew by heart. It was long distance, and he hoped Doc Herlong wouldn't mind paying the toll. Someone on the other end picked up after several rings.

"Ohio Attorney General's Office," a pleasant female voice answered.

"George Sellers, please."

"Who shall I say is calling?"

"Jack Brickman, Cleveland Police," he said.

"Please wait while I direct your call."

Jack's wait was short.

"Jack, what's the good word? Haven't heard from you in a while," Sellers said.

"We've been a little busy lately, George, that's why I'm calling."

"Sounds serious, Jack, what's going on?"

"I'd like to activate the Northern Ohio Serial Crimes Unit, George. Here's why," Jack said, and once again ran down the facts of the assorted cases. The more he told the story, the more concise he became, and the more it helped him organize the facts of the case in his head. It was getting to the point where he rarely needed to consult his notes. He hoped he spelled it out clearly enough. Of all the people Jack needed on board, it was Sellers who would make the final decision on NOSCU, since the Attorney General's office would fund and oversee the project.

Like Bright, Sellers asked many questions, though he tended to ramble. It was by far the longest conversation he'd had about the case, and it was the only one he was nervous about. He was going to need help on this case, and NOSCU was the only way to get it. His anxiety turned out to be misplaced.

"I'm going to give the order, Jack," Sellers finally decided. "Fax or Fed Ex your reports to my office right away, since I'm going to need that for the bean counters and the AG. It's going to take a couple of days to get everything going, but as of right now, NOSCU is up and running. Stay in touch."

Jack felt his apprehension dissolve, replaced by a combination of relief and the hope that he would be up to the task ahead. Well, thanks to the attorney general's office, he'd be collaborating with a team of the best cops in the business. And he would need them.

Jack scribbled down Sellers' fax number and hung up the phone. Sladky, too, had finished his calls.

"Well?" he asked.

"It's a go."

CHAPTER 16

Cliff O'Brien was just starting a several part feature story on whether or not organized crime was dead and buried in Cleveland. It was a story he had been developing, off and on, for the better part of the year. It had been slow going since reliable sources were hard to find. The cops and the FBI had provided him with some information, but he had really wanted something from the other side, and organized crime's reputation for silence had proven to be well-earned. Still, it had finally come together. All that was left now was to write it up if Leo Nelson would just give him the free time in which to do so.

Cliff's fingers had barely hit the keyboard when Leo poked his head into the cubicle.

"You got anything else on that beheading?" Nelson asked. "TV's been playing it up, and Joel asked me if we had something in the works on it."

By "Joel," Leo meant Joel Dye, the paper's managing editor. And by "we," he obviously meant Cliff.

"Nothing," Cliff said. "I've checked some sources, but so far nobody's got anything on it. TV is just playing it for shock value…they haven't had anything new, either. I know, I've been watching."

"Well, somebody upstairs thinks it's big news," Leo said. "If you get a chance, see if you can dig a little deeper."

"I'll try, boss, but I was just starting the mob piece," Cliff said, gesturing to his computer screen. "I don't know how long it's going to take to write up. I'll keep on it, but I don't think I can dig until next week. Unless you want me to start chasing rumors."

"No," Nelson said. "I'd rather have it right than have it first. Just don't let it go too long, OK? This would be a nice one to get a scoop on."

"You're preaching to the choir, Leo," Cliff replied. "Nothing like a little bloodshed to get readers interested."

"You sound like a ghoul," Nelson said.

"Only in a professional sense," Cliff said. "Anyway, I'd like to get back to work, if that's all right with you."

"Sure, sure," Nelson said, walking away.

Before Cliff started typing again, he jotted a reminder on his desktop calendar to call Jack Brickman. The detective might be able to give him something on or off the record about the Lane murder. Then he started writing again in earnest. His last thought as he dove into the organized crime story was that the beheading probably wouldn't end up being that big of a story. Of course, he had no way of knowing that it already was.

CHAPTER 17

Jack Brickman had worked late into the night on Tuesday, typing, faxing, and organizing reports. Luckily, Al Sladky had been around to help him, otherwise it would have been an even longer night. The work was necessary, however, now that he had been able to successfully activate NOSCU.

NOSCU, the Northern Ohio Serial Crimes Unit, was part of a contingency plan dreamt up in large part by Jack Brickman himself. While attending the FBI's National Academy, he had the good fortune to meet George Sellers, who had been attending the school on behalf of the Ohio attorney general's office. It was rare that a non-police officer was permitted to attend the academy. The exception had been made for Sellers because the attorney general had been able to convince the FBI that it was vital for the state's highest law enforcement organization to keep abreast of the latest training in the field.

It had been during a class detailing serial crimes, taught by Ken Bright, that Jack and George had hatched the idea for NOSCU. Well, not just NOSCU, but temporary serial crimes units throughout the state of Ohio. Bright had spent several days discussing the Green River murders in the Sea-Tac area of Washington State that had stumped law enforcement for decades. All types of problems, from command crises to personnel changes, had plagued the Green River Task Force. Brickman and Sellers had agreed that the task force had been thrown together too quickly and without the right people. They were good cops and seasoned investigators for the most part, but they were dealing with a new kind of crime.

Jack had reasoned that the best chance for successfully catching a serial criminal rested with a hand-picked team of specialists from, and this was vital, several different jurisdictions. Serial crimes were rarely restricted to one city, or even one county. Brickman occasionally wondered whether a regional task force was big enough to manage serial crimes. Lately, there seemed to have been a trend toward serial killers that stalked their prey along entire interstate routes. Well, if it were across state lines, that would fall squarely on the broad shoulders of the FBI. If it were within Ohio, Jack supposed they'd just have to activate several SCU's. He didn't envy Sellers the task of pushing that past the bean counters.

They had gotten their heads together with Bright, who immediately recognized the merit of the idea, though he felt that a standing serial crimes unit made more sense. He was willing to scale the idea down in the face of bureaucratic opposition. So, between the three of them, they had written up a proposal, including funding, and submitted it to the state. From there, it had been kicked up to the U.S. Attorney's Office, which had OK'd the whole package, including the funding plan.

So, though it was a state-sanctioned program, the bulk of the financial support would be coming from the Federal government. NOSCU members would never have to worry about getting paid for working overtime. While they would submit their overtime slips to their respective departments, those departments would be reimbursed by the State of Ohio, which in turn would be reimbursed by the United States government. Nothing ran without money.

It would be the first time any of the SCUs had been activated, so it remained to be seen if the arrangement would work. On paper, it was an open-ended arrangement. The only way to gauge success or failure meant catching the bad guy. A superior performance would be clear-cut. A failure would be harder to define, though Jack suspected that the longer they tracked the killer, the less successful NOSCU would be considered. And if the killer started racking up a body count while NOSCU was on the case, it would certainly be considered a hit against them. Given the killer's apparently increasing pace, Jack found himself wondering if he might even strike again before the team was even assembled.

The concept of the team was simple – they would work on this case exclusively until it was solved. No distractions, no interference. It was just a question of getting the team together.

Luckily for Jack, Sellers and Bright had done most of the recruiting in the months since the whole NOSCU concept had been approved. Upon activation of the team, they had burned up the phone lines contacting the chosen ones. Official letters would be arriving by messenger immediately, advising both cops and their respective departments of the new duty. Jack hoped they wouldn't leave holes that were too hard to fill when they left for God only knew how long.

Right now, the biggest worry on Jack's mind, and the one that had bothered him since NOSCU's inception, was whether or not they could keep it quiet. Cops in general were horrible gossips, and even worse when it came to wild speculation. The cops coming in to work on the team would definitely be missed. No amount of secrecy would keep the activation of NOSCU from getting out eventually. He hoped they would have at least a couple of weeks before the story broke in the press. The last thing he wanted at the beginning of a serial crime investigation was pressure from a panicked public.

It fell to Jack and Al to pack up all the evidence and files they had and get them ready for delivery to NOSCU's new digs. They would personally be riding shotgun in the delivery van for the short ride to their new and hopefully temporary home. Dr. Herlong had again loaned them Paul Madsen to assist in the organization of the files and assorted paperwork.

When Madsen had returned to the conference room with the medical examiner, Dr. Herlong had not been in the best mood. His demeanor did not improve when he heard that in all likelihood, his staff had dropped the ball in identifying the murder weapon in the Clayton case. He commented that the staff had almost endless resources and reference guides and that somebody should have made the connection. Jack had calmed Dr. Herlong down by suggesting that it was only human nature not to look past the obvious. Besides, there was no proof that Rausch had been right yet, and there wouldn't be until they re-examined the wounds and found a match.

Jack spent most of Wednesday answering phone calls from team members. Most of them he knew professionally, some personally. There were a couple that he knew only by reputation. Bright had recruited them, so Jack was certain they would be top-notch. Jack would not be heading the unit. That would fall to a representative from the attorney general's office. By rank and experience, Jack would be one of the more senior cops present. And by virtue of his work in identifying the case as a serial crime, he would also enjoy some status as lead investigator. Ken Bright would be on board as liaison to the Federal government since the FBI had no official stake in the investigation.

Before calling NOSCU's boss, a lawyer from the AG's office named Calvin Stoddard, Jack ran a couple of ideas past Mac, who gave them both the OK. Two of the Cleveland detectives slated to join the team had to decline for medical reasons. He called Stoddard. Jack had to identify himself to Stoddard, who sounded just as harried as the detectives. He had only spoken to Stoddard once before, and that had been brief. The lawyer had a good reputation, though Jack would have been more comfortable with a commissioned officer heading the team. Stoddard was said to be a no-nonsense kind of guy who knew how to get things done.

Jack explained his problem briefly.

"Yes," Stoddard said. "I received notice today about that. I was planning to activate the second tier unless you have another idea."

The second tier was another pool of officers that could be activated if the scope of the investigation grew. Stoddard could also pick from the second tier to fill vacancies in the active team.

"Actually, I do," Jack said. "Two detectives who were scratched from the team came from CPD. I'd like to fill their spots with two CPD officers if that's OK."

"Anybody in particular?"

"My current partner, Al Sladky," Jack said. "He knows the cases so far, helped connect them. Plus, he's been around the block a few times. He's got twenty-two years on and he knows the streets and other cops all over the area. I think he'd be a real asset."

Stoddard didn't answer immediately. He seemed to be weighing the suggestion carefully.

"OK," he said. "I assume you cleared it with your boss already?"

"Just did," Jack said.

"Who else?"

"Sam Rausch."

"The SWAT guy?" he asked. Apparently, the lieutenant's reputation extended far beyond CPD.

"Right," Jack said. "We had to consult him when we were working on plans for NOSCU, since the framework did specify tactical support. Plus, given the MO, I'd say we're going to need to pick his brain frequently. He's a subject matter expert."

"I don't know," Stoddard said. "He's a supervisor, right? Think he'll have any problems taking orders?"

"That's a strange question," Jack thought, but didn't say.

"Not at all," he said. "In fact, we probably wouldn't even be having this conversation if Sam hadn't been around."

"Any investigative work in the past?"

"Not that I know of, but I'd say he's plenty smart enough, seems to be a good observer, eye for detail," Jack said. He wondered what the opposition was to Rausch. Maybe Stoddard was just trying to make sure he didn't waste a spot on a mindless grunt.

"I'd like him on board," Jack said.

"George and Ken Bright both said I should trust your instincts, detective, so I will," Stoddard said. "Was there anything else?"

"Not right now," Jack said.

"Good," he said. "Then I'll see you Monday. Nine sharp."

Jack didn't bother telling Stoddard that he would probably be there before seven since he wanted ample time to prepare his presentation for the team. Stoddard sounded like he was wound a little tight. Jack wondered if that was going to end up being in the plus or minus column when everything was said and done.

The news that he would get to continue on the case definitely came as a relief to Al. He confessed to Jack that he had been hoping his partner would find a way to keep him around. Jack also suspected that a real mystery appealed to Sladky. Brickman found himself breathing a little easier, too, knowing that he would have a familiar face around him for the near future.

Rausch, too, seemed glad to be included on the team. At first, he sounded mildly reluctant to leave his duties with the SWAT team, but Jack assured him that he would have plenty of time to keep tabs on his interim replacement. Plus, NOSCU had been designed with a full-time tactical support so Rausch would still be in constant contact with at least part of his team.

The only other immediate concern was convincing Shaker Heights PD that they had to re-open the Clayton murder investigation and probably eliminate Jerome Lang as a suspect. Police in general did not like to be told that they were wrong, and homicide detectives in particular rarely admitted mistakes. Granted, by the time an indictment was issued in a murder case, you could bet good money the cops had the right guy. Investigators as a rule were meticulous in the work that led them to bring charges against a suspect. Murder cases are the most scrutinized crimes facing the justice system, so it was extremely rare that a warrant was issued for the wrong person. Contrary to what Hollywood and media would have the public believe, and erroneous conviction for murder was an anomaly indeed.

Luckily, the lead detective on the Clayton murder was somebody Jack knew personally. More important, he had also been tapped to serve on NOSCU. It had been Friday before he had been able to contact the detective, Stan Lombardo. He took the news like the professional he was.

"Clayton, huh?" he asked. "I don't know, Jack, I mean everything fits with Lang. Motive, means, method, everything. Plus, he disappeared right around the time of the murder. I'm not saying I'm one-hundred percent sure he's the guy, but I was sure enough to issue the warrant for him. We've got plenty of probable cause. I'd feel better if we could find him. I think he'd confess if we got him. But you don't think he's the guy, do you?"

"We looked at it again, and some of the stuff doesn't fit," Jack said. "We focused on the method of attack, and we have an expert who thinks the murder weapon was something called a *sai*. That sort of helps our theory."

"What's a *sai*?" Lombardo asked.

Jack explained as best he could over the phone. By the time he was done, it sounded like Stan had gotten the picture.

"Well, if that's the murder weapon, that doesn't fit Lang," he admitted. "As far as we know, and we know a lot about Jerome Lang, he was never into karate or anything like that. OK, Jack, I guess we'll look at this on Monday. And I'm not from Missouri, but you're still going to have to show me."

"I think we will," Jack said. "Either way, a little extra attention might help confirm Lang is the killer. We're going to have plenty of good people looking at all these cases."

"Some guys may take offense to that statement, but I'd rather be proven wrong now than in the middle of a trial," Lombardo said. "Or when a guy's on death row. Hell, I'm just glad to be part of the team. I'll bring everything I've got on Clayton. And Lang."

"Great. Thanks, Stan."

The rest of Friday was spent packing up files and transporting them to the new office. Jack spent the weekend on the phone and in his office at home. He felt he was ready by the time he went to bed on Sunday night. Still, he did not sleep well.

CHAPTER 18

One of the more recent additions to the Cleveland skyline is a white, slim building poking up between the Terminal Tower and the Cuyahoga River, just east of the Flats. It has a unique look that is partly necessitated by the narrow strip of land it occupies on Canal Road. The side of the building facing the river is curved while the remaining sides are straight, connecting at angles that lend the building more than a passing resemblance to a 27-story slice of pie. The average Clevelander or commuter would probably be hard pressed to name the building, or guess its purpose. Most would probably assume it was new office space for business expansion. They would be wrong. The building is in fact the Carl B. Stokes United States Court House, home of the U.S. Marshals, the U.S. District Court, and the temporary home of the Northern Ohio Serial Crimes Unit.

Like every bureaucracy, the Federal government always seems to be short of space. The new courthouse was designed to alleviate the cramped conditions of the old building. It was really much more space than they needed, but it was felt the courts would grow into it. So, by happy accident, and due to the money trail from NOSCU back to the U.S. government, the serial crimes team had a home in a brand-new building in a spacious suite of offices.

Jack and Al had gotten their first look at their new accommodations when they had helped deliver the case files to the fourteenth floor after picking up keys from a suspicious Federal Protective Services officer. Calvin Stoddard had obviously been busy since the suite looked ready for business. Stoddard had apparently also made sure they spelled his name right when they put it on the door to his office, an expansive room overlooking Collision Bend. Though his name was not on the door, Ken Bright apparently rated his own office with "FBI Liaison" listed on the plastic name plate.

"Hey, check this out," Al said, pointing to another door off the main room. The placard said "Team Leader."

"Is that you?" he asked.

"I'm guessing it is," Jack said. He had been both pleased and a little embarrassed. He had not expected his own office, although he was well aware of his status as lead investigator. Jack had wondered how Al would take it. He was relieved to see Al staking his claim on a desk near Jack's door, which seemed a little juvenile considering the size and vacancy of the office.

But that had been on Friday. On Monday, the office was filling up faster than Jack had expected. He had planned to greet each cop personally as they entered the office, but that plan had quickly deteriorated. He got sucked into several long conversations with officers he knew. In the meantime, other investigators came through the door and hooked up with cops they knew. Most were early. That was impressive considering the distance some of them had to travel to get downtown. Jack could feel excited undertones as the cops reacquainted themselves, and speculated about the case. With the help of Al, he was able to usher them all into a large conference room about five minutes before nine.

The room was off the main bullpen area of the suite. It was large enough to accommodate a conference table with twelve chairs. That left eight team members in chairs spaced along the walls. Calvin Stoddard entered the room promptly at nine.

"Good morning," he said. "Welcome to the Northern Ohio Serial Crimes Unit. My name is Calvin Stoddard. I represent the Ohio Attorney General's Office and I will be overseeing the investigation. You were picked for this assignment because of your experience and skill, and also in part because of where you work. NOSCU was designed to cover plenty of ground, and you will see why very shortly. I just want to take this time to assure you that the Attorney General is behind this project one hundred percent. Anything you need and don't have, ask me. For the most part, I'll be handling the bureaucracy and trying to stay out of your way." That elicited a chuckle.

Stoddard had an oddly formal way of speaking. Jack supposed it was from too many years of law school and trying to impress judges and juries. And even though the stocky, balding man was smiling, Jack thought he could detect the same tension he had heard over the phone. Maybe it was just pre-game jitters.

"Many of you know each other already," Stoddard said. "However, for those of you who do not know him, I would like to introduce FBI Assistant Special Agent in Charge Ken Bright of the Cleveland office."

Bright, impeccably dressed as always, stood up halfway and nodded to the group.

"Agent Bright will be acting as liaison to the Federal government," Stoddard said. "As it stands, this case has no Federal statute implications. However, the FBI has kindly loaned us Agent Bright to assist the team. The FBI has also placed their entire forensic and evidentiary facilities at our disposal on a priority basis.

"As for NOSCU itself, your team leader will be Detective Sergeant Jack Brickman of the Cleveland Police Department."

Brickman stood up.

"Good morning," he said. "We have a lot to get through today, but I think it is important to thank you for being here. I know some of you are leaving open investigations to join NOSCU. Unfortunately, the need here is very real. People, we have an active serial killer working the North Coast. He's killed at least three times and possibly as many as five. That's the first thing we're going to work on. Everything I know about psychology and everything I've learned on the street tells me that he's not done yet. Not by a longshot."

"I hate to put anybody on the spot, but since we come from several different jurisdictions, I'd like each of you to tell us who you are and where you come from," Jack said. It was an exercise universally hated by cops, mainly because they'd all had to do it countless times before at lectures and seminars Brickman had almost decided against the practice, but had changed his mind at the last minute. These officers would be working closely together for the foreseeable future. He needed them to function as a team.

As they had gone around the room, Jack realized that many of the officers already knew each other. As detectives and investigators, they relied more on different jurisdictions than the average patrol officer. They were a little CPD heavy, with eight officers including Rausch, Brickman and Sladky. When they finished, Jack passed out case folders to each investigator.

"In your folders, you have the complete files on each of the five murder cases we're going to be looking at," he said. "For now, the Dawkins and the Rice cases are separate from the others, but we expect that to change."

"Now, exactly what are we dealing with?"

Jack flicked on a projector that was built into the ceiling and walked the team through the Lane, Clayton, and Timmons murders with a PowerPoint presentation. He gave as many details as he could, outlining forensic evidence as well as field interviews. The presentation took well over ninety minutes. Cops like to ask questions.

When he had finished, Stan Lombardo took over and gave an in-depth lecture on the Clayton murder. He did not hide the fact that they had issued a warrant for Clayton's roommate. Shaker Heights, apparently, was still waiting for Dr. Herlong to confirm what Jack and Al suspected about the killer's weapon of choice. Lombardo did concede that the type of attack that had taken place on Clayton had never seemed to fit Lang's personality.

"Lang was always a slippery kind of guy," he said. "We could never pin him to any kind of violence. If things got tough for him, he usually just split. Never figured him for any muscle work. Even if he had, my bet is he would have gone for a gun."

After Lombardo finished, Jack turned the floor over to Elyria PD Det. Andy Fulmer. Fulmer, as luck would have it, had actually worked the Dawkins murder. He was obviously well-versed in the facts of the case since he rarely consulted his notes. Fulmer was young, much younger than Jack, but he seemed to know much about conducting an investigation. More importantly, he knew what he *didn't* know.

"This one felt like a hit right from the start," he said. "We knew Dawkins was dealing, mostly pot, maybe a little Ecstasy from time to time, but we never figured him for the kind of score that would get you this kind of attention from a professional shooter. Dawkins was always a little paranoid, so it's still hard for me to believe he just forgot to lock his door. It was a third-story apartment, so the only ways I can figure it is somebody had a key, somebody picked the lock, or he let somebody in."

"What about the super?" asked Bryce Cramer, a CPD detective.

Fulmer shook his head.

"Said he never gave out a copy," Fulmer said. "He passed a polygraph, which he didn't have to take. I guess it's possible somebody swiped the keys from him, but he swears that's impossible. Now, a good lock picker would fit if this were a professional, but there weren't any unusual scratches on the lock. Besides, why go through the trouble of picking the lock anyway? Dawkins lived in a public housing apartment. Somebody is likely to catch you picking a lock. Kicking the door is a little noisier, but it's a hell of a lot quicker.

"And I think we can all agree the shot placement was damn good," Fulmer said. "So, our investigation has always been focused on a drug tie-in."

Fulmer paused.

"There's one thing that doesn't fit though," he said.

"What's that?" Sladky asked.

"Well, I don't know how much it means, but whoever the shooter was pissed his pants while he was there," Fulmer said. "That sure doesn't sound like a pro to me."

Brickman suddenly remembered that the Lorain County Coroner's report had in fact noted that they had found urine other than Dawkins' at the scene. They had found traces of it in the vinyl floor of the kitchen where they believed the shooter was standing. Even more had been found on some paper towels in a small wastebasket under the sink.

"He took the time to clean it up, though, didn't he Andy?" Jack asked.

"You read the file," Fulmer said. "Yeah, he did. And that's another thing we couldn't figure out. I mean, there's blood all over the place, right? This guy probably got some on himself, but they didn't find any evidence that he tried to clean that up. So why bother to clean up the urine other than to hide DNA and what are the odds he's going to know we can pull it from urine? From everything I saw, this job was well planned and executed. Why would our guy waste all that time cleaning up?"

Jack immediately got an idea of why the killer might take the time to clean up after himself. And it didn't have anything to do with evidence.

"Pseudosexual response," he said absently. Ken Bright nodded. Some of the investigators in the room stared blankly at him. In most of the others, however, he could almost see the light bulbs switching on. He decided to elaborate.

"Look, let's say your shooter is our guy. The time frame was months before the Rice murder, so that makes Dawkins his first kill."

"That we know of," Bryce Cramer said.

"Right," Jack said. "Anyway, if our guy is a sociopath or a thrill killer, then he's probably getting some of kind of charge doing this. It would fit the standard profile of a serial killer to have some sort of sexual hang-up, from aberrant fantasies to complete dysfunction. It's common for the killer to leave urine or feces at the crime scene. They can't get off in the normal way, so urination or defecation is their way of expressing sexual excitement."

"You see that a lot in arson cases, right?" Lombardo asked.

"So they say, Stan," Jack replied. "We don't investigate arson...that's up to the FD...but fire and sex are very closely linked for some people."

Jack continued.

"Of course, it's possible that he just got really excited," he said. "I think that makes this his first kill, or at least his first kill as an assassin."

"OK," Fulmer said. "I'll buy that. But why clean it up? And if it is a sexual response, if he's getting so sexually excited he gets off in the only way he can, why haven't we seen it in any of the other murders? That seems to me like it would be a signature."

"Good point," Jack conceded. "Ken, you have any ideas?"

"Off the top of my head, I'd say he's probably embarrassed," Bright said.

"Who wouldn't be?" Sladky said.

"It's different for him, Al," Bright continued. "You've got to look at it from his point of view. He's created this image of himself as a stone-cold killer, right? He sneaks into Dawkins' apartment and executes him like a real pro. But either he loses control because of arousal or because of fear and excitement and now he doesn't feel like such a tough guy anymore. And for some reason, that's important to him. Take it a step further, too. He knows damn well that information is never going to be leaked to the public. . .no pun intended. . .so why clean it up?"

"So we don't think any less of him," Fulmer said.

"Bingo," Bright said. "To him, we are either adversaries or allies, depending on whether he sees himself as a villain or a vigilante. Either way, our perception is important to him. He wants our respect."

"What else can you tell us about this guy, Ken?" a detective from Lake County asked. "Have you got a profile on him yet?"

Bright shook his head.

"We're still working on that," he said. "We'll know more as we go. Right now we need a solid link between Dawkins and Rice and the rest of them. Jack and I will be working on that throughout the investigation. Honestly, we're just speculating on the information at hand. That speculation is based on some pretty solid research though."

Jack jumped into the conversation again.

"This is exactly what we need if we're going to catch this guy," he said. "We're all used to looking at certain types of evidence, like prints and DNA. It's probably going to be the little things that put the case together. Nothing, and I mean nothing, is too small a detail."

"Yeah, but we missed some big things already," Fulmer said. "Somebody should have connected the dots between us and Painesville right away. I mean, DNA and all that fancy stuff aside, they're almost identical."

Ed Payne, the Lake County Sheriff's Office detective who had spoken earlier, bristled a little at what he felt was a backhanded attack on his region, though Painesville PD, not the SO, had done the investigation.

"Are you saying we dropped the ball?" Payne asked. "Painesville put out the teletypes when it happened. I remember because I helped with the case. Maybe you guys just didn't bother to read them."

"Christ, I hope this doesn't start the whole East versus West Civil War," Jack thought.

Brickman was about to jump in when Andy Fulmer responded.

"Maybe you're right," he said. "Maybe we just forgot we got teletypes. And maybe you didn't catch the ones we put out looking for similar cases."

"So, this is just a case of 'Oh, well, we goofed'?" Payne asked.

"I'm willing to admit somebody on our end fouled up," Fulmer said. "But I'm not going to take all the blame."

Jack finally stepped in.

"Look," he said. "We don't have time to start the blame game. We're going to go back to every single one of these cases, tear them down and build them back up from scratch. . .piece by piece. If NOSCU is going to work, we've got to check our egos at the door. I'm personally responsible for two of these cases, and I'll bet even money that I missed some things, too."

"As his partner, I'd like to advise you all to take that bet," Sladky said.

Sladky's attempt at humor managed to break the tension of the room. A few of the detectives chuckled. Most at least smiled, Even Payne and Fulmer seemed mollified.

"OK," Payne said. "Yeah, nobody's perfect. I guess we're lucky to be getting a second crack at this one anyway."

"Good point, Ed," Fulmer said. He added a subtle nod in Payne's direction, his way of apologizing. Cops generally are not big in the hugs and kisses department. Jack knew that Payne and Fulmer would probably approach each other later and smooth things out on their own. Even if they didn't, they were unlikely to cross paths very often during the course of this investigation. Although NOSCU was headquartered in Cleveland, logistics and common sense would keep both the Dawkins and Rice investigations based in their respective regions. The investigators could cover more ground without having to commute to the United States Court House every day.

"Do we have any description at all on the killer?" Cramer asked.

"From the DNA we have from the Dawkins case, all we know for sure is that we're looking for a white male," Jack said. "The Lake County crime lab is still going over all the fibers and hair samples they took from Rice's apartment."

"How come they didn't do that already?" asked Terri Rome , one of two female cops on the team. Rome was a CPD detective who specialized in sex crimes.

"Too expensive," Ed Payne said. "Rice wasn't exactly the world's best housekeeper, and the crime-scene techs collected something over twenty different hair strands, not to mention dozens of different fibers from carpet and car floor mats. They collected everything of course, but they were waiting for a suspect before they started analyzing the DNA."

"I know that seems a little backwards," Payne continued, "but the DNA database isn't anywhere near the size of the latent print inventory. It just isn't cost effective for us to run each and every hair strand without a suspect. Sorry, but it's a dollar issue."

"That's another thing NOSCU can help with," Stoddard added. "I have no idea when we'll get the results, but with any luck we'll match up in about ten days or so."

"Are we operating under the assumption that this is the same guy?" Cramer asked.

Jack shook his head.

"Not until we have it confirmed," he said. "I don't want any assumptions. It's too easy to miss things that way. I'd rather you just went in cold, like these murders just happened and you're the first guy on the scene."

"OK," Cramer said.

Jack could tell everybody was eager to get started, but he had one more person to introduce, and some specific assignments to hand out.

"For those of you who don't know him, I'd like you to meet Lieutenant Sam Rausch," Jack said. "Sam's commanding CPD's SWAT team right now, and he'll be providing tactical support for NOSCU throughout the investigation. As a bonus, Sam's an expert on martial arts, so he'll be helping out with the investigation, too. The lieutenant was the first guy to get us pointed in the right direction on this, so we're lucky to have him. Sam."

Rausch stood up.

"I'll keep this short," he said. "First of all, let me give you the rundown on the tactical support. NOSCU will have a twelve-man response team on-call 24-7. I had to cut them loose from our SWAT team, but Jack wants to be able to move on to the suspect right away if we get the chance. I agree. I'd hate to let anybody slip through while we waited for a response team to wander in. Depending on where the investigation leads, members of NOSCU's response team will be available to shadow you in the field. Just as a precaution, of course. But don't hesitate to ask."

"Jack, Al and I are all under the impression that the suspect, for whatever reason, has styled himself after some sort of modern *ninja*," Rausch said. "Anybody who's caught a late-night karate-fest on the TV probably has some idea of what a *ninja* does. The simplest way to describe him is that he's an assassin. Historically speaking, the *ninja* would hire out to the highest bidder, though occasionally they were trained within a clan and served out of loyalty.

Jack tells me the evidence doesn't support the mercenary theory, so we probably have somebody here who has a very specific agenda."

"OK," asked Terri Rome, "TV aside, what can we expect from this guy?"

"Well, from what Jack and Al have already seen, our guy is obviously very good with edged weapons," Rausch said. "He can also shoot. Better than most cops. But based on the other evidence, he's in excellent physical shape. My guess is he works out a lot, but I wouldn't expect him to be bulky like a weightlifter. Picture somebody really cut, like Bruce Lee."

"As far as what a ninja could do, they obviously specialized in killing," Rausch said. "They were also experts in using disguises, spying, climbing and improvising weapons from common tools. You sometimes hear *ninja* referred to as 'shadow warriors.' I'd expect our suspect to follow that path. I'm sure he prefers sneaking around to a head-on confrontation. I've brought some books with me if anybody wants to borrow them. I've been brushing up myself, and I think it's worth the time."

"Anything else, Sam?" Brickman asked.

"Just one," he said. "I don't have the investigation experience that a lot of you have, but I guess I've got some street experience. The biggest thing I'm worried about is keeping you guys safe. I guess I don't want you sitting down to an interview with the *ninja* and not knowing it's the guy until it's too late to call in the troops. I know shooting isn't a big part of your jobs right now, but I'd feel a lot better if you all spent some extra time at the range. For those of you who are going to be working out of this office, the marshals said we could use the range downstairs, and I should be available for some one-on-one sessions if you want."

"Good point, lieutenant," Jack said. "Might be a good way to blow off some steam, too."

Rausch's statement had been a good safety reminder for the team. By addressing basic officer safety issues, Sam helped bring everybody back to reality. In the excitement of finding the killer, Jack could see how members of his team might get so caught up in the investigation that they would ignore their own safety. It was always a possibility, especially with goal-oriented professionals. Rausch had also christened the killer, who went from *ninja* to *The Ninja*.

It was past eleven by the time the meeting was finished. Jack concluded the session by handing out assignments. Their assignments were more or less based on geography. Three officers, including Andy Fulmer, were sent to Elyria. Another trio, led by Ed Payne, would be revisiting the Dawkins murder in Painesville. Bryce Cramer, Terri Rome, three CPD officers and two investigators from the Cuyahoga County Sheriff's Office would be taking another look at the Timmons and Lane killings while Al, Jack and Stan Lombardo would be focusing on the Clayton murder. Ken Bright would be spending a lot of time at NOSCU's headquarters along with Calvin Stoddard, whose primary role was legal oversight and budgeting. The rest of the team would man the phones and help piece it all together.

Manning the phones at this stage in the game would probably not be an overwhelming responsibility. Later, when the story broke out in the media, and it certainly would at some point, fielding tips would probably become a full-time job. Jack already had a contingency plan to call in more help once tip lines activated. With the proliferation of e-mail, Jack even had one of his investigators developing a simple web page to gather the inevitable electronic tips. Brickman had been a cop long enough to know that tips rarely panned out. He also knew that on the rare occasions when the tips were for real, it was like striking gold. In a case like this, though, he expected an even higher number of cranks and pranks.

After dismissing the team, Brickman, Sladky, Rausch and Lombardo were about to head out to take another look at the Shaker Hts. crime scene when Stoddard intercepted them.

"Jack," he said, "I need to speak to you."

"Sure," Jack replied. He nodded to the others. "You guys go ahead. I'll meet you there."

"Did you want Vidalia and Moore to meet us?" Sladky asked.

"Only if they're not busy, Al," Brickman replied. "I know they're assigned to us, but let's not burn them out too early. Besides, I already have them sifting through the trace evidence from all five crime scenes."

"I'll just give them the heads up, see what they want to do," Al said.

"Good."

Stoddard lead Jack into his office and asked the detective to close the door behind him.

"*Uh oh*," thought Jack.

The older man settled in behind his large desk and gestured for Jack to take a seat in one of the chairs positioned in front of him. Jack noticed Stoddard's office was considerably larger than his, with room enough for a small conference table and several large filing cabinets. Behind the attorney on a series of shelves were dozens of law books.

"How do you feel the morning went, Jack?" Stoddard asked.

Jack took a moment to think over his answer. While thinking about his response, out of the corner of his eye, he caught a huge ore ship moving up the Cuyahoga River to parts unknown. He quickly returned his gaze to Stoddard.

"I think it was a good start," Jack said.

"Elaborate."

"Well, the team seemed to gel fairly quickly," Brickman said. "Granted, a lot of them already know each other, but they seemed to be on the same page already. I think the heads up gave them a chance to start focusing on the crimes already. You don't usually get that chance. In the bureau, you never know what the next phone call is going to bring, so you have to be ready for anything."

Stoddard nodded. Apparently, he wanted Jack to continue.

"Anyway," he continued, "I think we've got the right people on the right jobs. That's going to be a big plus."

"So, you don't see any problems?" Stoddard asked.

"Honestly? No."

"What about the friction between Detective Payne and Detective Fulmer?" Stoddard said. "Does that not present a problem for us?"

"That?" Jack asked, surprised. "As far as I can see, they're both past that already. Cops have big egos, Calvin. Toes get stepped on sometimes. But these guys are the cream of the crop. Part of the reason they got picked for the team was because of how well they work with others."

"I want you to keep an eye on it regardless," Stoddard said.

Jack felt his blood start to stir.

"What the hell is this?" he thought, *"I am supposed to be a den mother?"*

"There's nothing to keep an eye on, Calvin," he said. "Trust me."

"Perhaps," Stoddard said. "And what about Lieutenant Rausch?"

"What about him?" Jack asked.

"From what you told me, I expected hm to contribute more to the meeting," the lawyer said. "And I surely didn't expect that part at the end. I thought we were relying on his team for tactical support."

"I may be out of line, Mr. Stoddard," Jack said, now thoroughly ticked off, "but Sam Rausch has already contributed as much to this investigation as anybody else, including me. And as for reminding the team that they're cops, well, you heard me. I always think it's a good idea to stress officer safety. This is not just an academic exercise. Even if they don't run into The Ninja, they're still going to be getting into some pretty shitty places, and that means keeping on their toes."

Stoddard apparently sensed that he had ruffled Jack's feathers. However, he showed no inclination to back down.

"Just so we are clear on one thing, sergeant," he said. "George Sellers and Ken Bright apparently think the world of you. As far as they're concerned, you are some sort of magician. As far as *I* am concerned, that remains to be proven, although I will concede you appear to be headed in the right direction. My point as far as Lt. Rausch is concerned, however, is that this is an investigation. I do not wish to see it turn into a seek-and-destroy mission. NOSCU does not exist in a vacuum, Jack. There are many important eyes up on us."

"I know that" Jack said. "Hell, we all know that. And it's just going to get worse once the media gets a wind of this. But those concerns are secondary to catching The Ninja. You worry about the big wigs if you want to. Maybe I'll even worry about them a little. But the team should never even have to think about politics."

"It's not politics I'm talking about," Stoddard said. "It's about support, funding, and cooperation. Remember, this concept is experimental. If we don't do everything just right, it may destroy the whole program."

Jack took a deep breath.

"Calvin," he said. "If it doesn't work, maybe the program should be disabled. I helped come up with the idea, and believe me, my ego isn't so big that I'd choose to stick with failure instead of finding something that works."

"Please don't misunderstand me, Jack," Stoddard said. "I trust you to make the right calls. I suppose I'm just a little nervous about NOSCU."

"So am I," Jack conceded. "I want a home run with this team, too. But we've got a long way to go, Calvin. I don't think we need to worry about problems that aren't there. As they come up, we can knock 'em down together."

"Perhaps," Stoddard said. "Regardless, I certainly did not intend to offend you, nor did I mean to keep you from your field work."

"OK," Jack said. "I'll keep you in the loop, but don't expect too much on the first day."

"Understood," Stoddard said. "Thank you, sergeant."

The attorney had already started shuffling through a stack of papers on his desk before Jack had reached the door. The detective found himself wondering exactly what was going on behind those thick glasses. He hoped this was just a slight personality clash and not the beginning of a downhill slide in their professional relationship. Stoddard must be competent. Why else would Sellers have assigned him to the team? Brickman had to fight down the urge to run to his office and call George Sellers. Stoddard really hadn't done anything wrong, and Jack was no snitch.

Brickman forced a smile at Stoddard's secretary, Lenore Patterson, who was busy at her desk. It was amazing how much paperwork NOSCU had already accumulated.

Jack was on his way out the door when he literally bumped into Ken Bright.

"Where you headed, Jack?" he asked.

"I'm meeting Al at the Shaker Heights crime scene," Brickman replied. "I should have gone with them, but Calvin wanted to have a sit-down first."

Bright raised an eyebrow.

"And how did that go?" he asked.

"I'll tell you later," Jack said.

"I'm free now," Bright said. "Would you mind some company?"

"The more the merrier, they say."

Unlike most government offices, NOSCU actually had an office assistant who doubled as receptionist and switchboard operator. Natalie Price was in her mid-twenties and on a loan from CPD's secretarial pool. She seemed competent, and had a dazzling smile that sharply contrasted her dark skin. Jack and Ken had already signed out on the dry-erase board in the main bullpen that showed who was where, but they let Natalie know where they were heading anyway. She sent them on their way with a big smile and cheerful "good luck." As they headed toward the parking garage, Jack absently wondered if a few weeks of answering phones in an ongoing investigation of a serial killer would dampen her enthusiasm. His own eagerness had certainly been reined in by his meeting with Stoddard.

Ken Bright offered to drive to the crime scene and Jack didn't object. The FBI agent wasted no time in bringing up the topic of their boss.

"So, what did you think of ol' Calvin," he asked.

"Wound a little tight, isn't he?"

Ken laughed.

"A bit, I guess," he said. "He's got a good reputation, though. Apparently, he worked a lot with the Ohio Highway Patrol, helping with their major investigations, etcetera. Did some work on internal stuff, too, like the review of the Lucasville riots."

Jack nodded. Lucasville was an Ohio maximum security prison that had erupted a few years ago resulting in the deaths of several corrections officers and dozens of injuries to inmates. OHP's Special Response Team had been brought in to help quell the riot. The incident had inevitably spurred an endless number of lawsuits from the rioters themselves. The attorney general's office had had their hands full for months sorting out what had happened at the prison.

That bit of information boosted the detective's confidence. When you mentioned the Ohio Highway Patrol in law enforcement circles, two images invariably came to mind. One of the spit-and-polished, chickenshit troopers who took great pleasure in issuing traffic citations to anybody and everybody, including cops. The other image was that of serious professionals whose training in survival tactics, driving and shooting was unrivaled. When they put that Smokey the Bear hat on your head and the flying wheel patch on your shoulder, it said a lot about your skill, dedication, and training. Political though OHP might be, it was a no-nonsense outfit from top to bottom.

"So then why the nervous act?" Jack asked. "It's like he's got to prove he's the boss or something. He doesn't have to prove it. He's writing the checks."

"He's always been a little pompous, or at least he comes across that way sometimes," Ken said "I've worked with him a couple of times and he seems OK to me. Maybe he's just marking his territory."

"Shit, Ken, you know I hate office politics. That's why I don't want to be a lieutenant."

"Bull," Bright said. "You're an overachiever, Jack. You want to call the shots just like the rest of us. Anyway, Stoddard's a bureaucrat at heart. Heads roll all the time over big investigations that don't produce. I know. I've seen it happen."

"Maybe that's it, then," Jack said. "But that still doesn't explain why he doesn't like Rausch. Sam usually doesn't rub people the wrong way."

"Could be the old scholar versus the warrior thing," Bright said. "Maybe he doesn't think a Neanderthal like Rausch belongs with all of us heavy thinkers."

Bright's tone turned more serious.

"Give it time, Jack," he said. "Remember, this is new for everybody. We've all got something to prove."

"OK"

During the rest of the drive to Shaker Heights, Ken and Jack caught up on gossip and family matters. They didn't have much time to talk, since Ken drove a lot faster than Jack would have liked and Shaker Heights wasn't all that far away from downtown.

Clayton had been murdered in a five-story apartment building off of North Moreland Drive, just a stone's throw from Shaker Square. Clayton's apartment had been at the rear of the building, on the fourth floor. Bright parked the car on the street in front of the building and they began circling the building on foot. Training and experience had taught them both to start at the edge of the wide perimeter and work their way in. And it never hurt to take a good look around, either.

As they rounded the corner, they were surprised by the scene that greeted them. Poking his bald head out of the fourth-floor window of what had undoubtedly been Charlie Clayton's apartment was Stan Lombardo. He was talking loudly to Sam Rausch. Who was dangling in a rappelling harness between the roof and the fourth floor. Steadying the rope at the roofline was Al Sladky.

"What are you doing?" Jack shouted up to the odd trio.

Rausch yelled down to Brickman and Bright, but most of the words were lost in the wind. May in Cleveland is generally a blustery affair. Rausch tried again with no luck. After a short pause, the lieutenant yelled something else, but all Jack caught was ". . .be right down." Sam made a rapid descent down the rope and hit the ground as gently as if he had just stepped out of bed. He signaled up to Al, who began pulling the ropes back in.

"I'm impressed, Sam," Bright said. "But what's with the high-wire act?"

Rausch was smiling broadly.

"Give your partner the credit, Jack," he said. "He must have been listening this morning, because he suggested we check out the roof almost as soon as we got here."

"The roof?" Jack asked.

"Yeah," Rausch replied. "Up 'til now, we've been assuming that the suspect entered through the door, right? Either with a key or because Clayton didn't bother to lock it. Nobody every thought about the window because it was locked when Shaker Heights showed up. Plus, there's no fire escape and no trees or poles you could use to climb up to the window. But Al started thinking, 'What about climbing down instead of up?' Oh, here he is. . .I'll let him tell you."

Sladky came walking up to them, a coil of rope wrapped over his shoulder. Apparently, he had been in a hurry since he was still breathing heavily. He handed the rope to Sam.

"Didn't want you to lose this," he said.

"So, tell us about your theory, Al," Jack said.

"Damn," Sladky said. "Did he steal my thunder?"

"Just whetted their appetite," Rausch said. "You tell the rest."

"I just got to thinkin', this guy thinks he's a *ninja*, right?" Al said. "So, he's not going to do anything the way we'd do it. He's gonna do it the hard way. Plus, Sam said these guys were good at climbing. Once we got here, I started lookin' around. Obviously, there's no way he coulda climbed up a tree or something, right? So, I started thinkin', in Cleveland, people are always finding a way to get on the roofs of these buildings to beat the heat or watch the stars or get laid or whatever, so how about if The Ninja goes up on the roof and climbs down from the top. Sure as shit, the lock on the door to the roof is busted. Looks like it has been for a while. Stan said they didn't find a rope, and I couldn't figure out why a guy would go risk going back up to untie the rope and bring it with him. That's why Sam decided to do some climbing."

"I drove, so I had some rappelling gear in my car," Sam said, shrugging.

"Boy Scout?" Bright asked.

"Close," Sam said. "Anyway, Al's right. We've been thinking about how *we* would do it, not how *he* would do it. Once he brought up climbing, I remembered the *shuko*."

"What?" Jack asked.

"*Shuko*," Sam replied. "They're like claws the *ninja* strapped to their hands and feet. They were perfect for climbing trees and the rough walls of castles. You couldn't climb a sheer surface. . .the claws don't dig in that way. . .but if there's a big enough seam, it would be no trouble. Take a look at these walls."

Jack and Ken both examined the side of the building. It was old, made of common red brick that had weathered the years quite well. The mortar, however, had seen better days. In fact, it was sorely in need of work. The white material had significantly worn down, leaving at least a quarter of an inch gap from the surface of the bricks to the remaining mortar.

"Some mason didn't do a very good job," Jack observed.

"Right," Sam said. "And it's like that all the way from the top. And that's not all. There are several sets of deep gouges in the brick, in sets of four, spaced exactly the same distance apart. They aren't exactly brand new, but my guess is they haven't been there that long, either."

"We better get Moore and Vidalia down here," Bright said.

"Already called 'em," Al said. "They're on their way. Woulda called you two, but I figured one of ya would show up sooner or later."

"How are they going to get up there?" Bright asked.

"Good question," Jack said. "I know they've got some ladders on their rig, but none of them will reach that high. And I doubt they can rappel."

"Already thought of that," said Stan Lombardo, who apparently had gotten restless waiting in the empty apartment once occupied by Charlie Clayton. "I called our service department. They're on their way over with a cherry picker. Should be tall enough to reach. And it's got a double bucket."

"Did they give you any trouble?" Jack asked.

Lombardo laughed.

"Hell, no," he said. "Those guys work their asses off, but man do they love a break from the routine. They were just pruning trees anyway. Lots of branches down with the wind and all."

Brickman pulled out his cell phone and paged through the LCD phonebook. In turn, he was able to contact Fulmer and Payne and tell them to focus on the rooftops and windows. He didn't have to bother the Cleveland contingents, since Lane and Timmons had been killed on the ground. When he finished, he asked Stan Lombardo if he could look around the apartment. It was vacant now, but maybe he'd be able to get a better feel for the murder by having a look around. Ken Bright followed him in while Sam and Al waited to guide the Shaker Heights service department and the coroner's technicians when they arrived.

"Not a bad break, eh Jack?" Bright said as they followed Lombardo up the stairs.

"I'll take it," Brickman said. "It's better than a lead-off double."

Jack was in good spirits, but he was still a little worried about linking the Elyria and Painesville murders. He tried to put it out of his mind. Payne, Fulmer, and their teams had good reputations. Brickman felt he had put a good team on the field. Now it was a question of letting them do their jobs.

Black and White, Blue and Gold

139

CHAPTER 19

Cliff O'Brien had been very busy since he started to piece together his story on organized crime.

The series of articles ended up running a week later than he had planned, much to the dismay of Leo Nelson. Not that it had been completely Cliff's fault, since several breaking news stories had competed for his attention. The stories included a suburban city councilman being arrested and charged in a hit-skip, drunk driving accident that had left two people injured and a particularly bloody and public occurrence of domestic violence that had taken place in a shopping mall on the city's East Side. Like most of the other stories Cliff worked on, he liked to look beneath the surface and do the kind of background investigation that the television stations rarely had time to conduct.

So, exhibiting uncharacteristic behavior, O'Brien didn't get around to calling Det. Brickman about the beheading follow-up until more than two weeks after Leo Nelson had reminded him about the case. It would have made little difference to O'Brien or Nelson if he had made the call, since the reporter had been working non-stop following leads and writing articles. Occasionally, in the feast-or-famine world of journalism, some stories just had to wait.

Fortunately for Cliff, he happened to see the reminder scrawled on his notepad before the case had gotten too stale. If Jack were willing to talk to him about it, which he occasionally was, he might still be able to find an angle that would freshen up the story enough to get readers interested in it again. Not that it would take much. A beheading still pretty much sold itself.

So, late Thursday morning, O'Brien picked up his phone and dialed Jack Brickman's number at CPD. It rang three times and Cliff was waiting to get kicked into the voice mail system when somebody whose voice he didn't recognize picked up the line.

"Detective Harris," he said. "What can I do for you?"

"This is Cliff O'Brien. I was trying to reach Sergeant Brickman."

"What's this about?"

"It's regarding the Lane murder from a couple weeks ago," Cliff said.

"Well, the sergeant is working out of another office now," Harris said. "But he's still working the Lane case, so I'm sure he'll want to talk to you. Hang on."

Harris apparently covered the mouthpiece with his hand, but Cliff could still hear him clearly yelling across the room.

"Tony, what's Jack's new number?"

There was a pause and Harris came back on the line.

"You ready?" he asked. Cliff said he was and scribbled down the new number. There was no extension, which was a little strange. The number also did not have a familiar prefix. Cliff thanked Harris and hung up.

Harris' well-meaning cooperation would turn out to be the single act that leaked the story to the media. In his defense, with Al and Jack out of the office, the rest of the floaters were very busy, so it was hard to keep track of who was who. And they had never been told not to give out Jack's new work number. Brickman still checked his voicemail every day, but Carmen had just happened to pick it up before the automated system routed the call. Harris would also later swear that he thought O'Brien was a cop. Cliff, of course, had not identified himself as a reporter, but he had never pretended to be a cop either.

Needless to say, Cliff was very curious about Brickman's new assignment. The reporter was on good terms with the detective. He would even go so far as to categorize their relationship as a working friendship, though he would be reluctant to go much farther than that. Still, he was surprised Brickman hadn't given him the heads up on the new post. Generally, a sudden switch in assignments was either something very good or something very bad. Jack didn't seem like the type of guy who made major-league mistakes, so maybe it was promotion or something.

O'Brien dialed the new number. His call was answered on the first ring.

"NOSCU," a female voice said. "How can I help you?"

"NOSCU?" Cliff thought, *"Now why does that ring a bell?"*

"I'm trying to reach Detective Brickman," Cliff said.

"I'm sorry, Sergeant Brickman is out of the office. Would you like his voicemail?"

"Sure."

Cliff waited a moment until he heard Jack Brickman's recorded voice asking him to leave a brief message and phone number. When it had concluded, O'Brien did as asked and hung up.

Cliff sat back in his chair and started wracking his brain, trying to remember what NOSCU was. He came up blank. Obviously, it was some kind of special assignment, but what? The reporter was not content to wait until Brickman returned his call. He got up and wandered over to the vending machines and bought himself a Coke and a candy bar. Once back at his desk, he started digging through the vast computer archives of *The North Coast Press*.

His search did not take as long as he had anticipated, although he fouled himself up by initially spelling NOSCU with a "Q" instead of an "SCU." Even after he got it right, he was surprised that the search came up empty. No stranger to computer research, Cliff played around with the search parameters until he shorted it to "SCU." That search hit the paydirt. It wasn't much, but it was all the springboard Cliff needed.

The computer search had yielded one short, rather anemic press release that had run in *The Press* last spring. The article detailed a cooperative contingency plan between federal, state, and local law enforcement agencies that would allow the activation of special Serial Crimes

Units, or SCUs, that would permit legal local jurisdictions to pool their manpower and brainpower to investigate serial crimes.

"Bingo," Cliff thought, *"Jack's working a big one."*

Cliff pulled a new notepad from his desk drawer and jotted some notes from the computer screen. It would have probably been easier to hit the print button and pick up the hard copy from the printer stand in the corner of the office, but O'Brien was so focused he never thought of it. After transcribing the particulars, he started trying to figure out what trail the detective might be on.

It seemed pretty obvious that the Lane beheading had had something to do with it, since Detective Harris had immediately given Cliff NOSCU's number when he mentioned the case. The Timmons murder also came to mind, since that had been the last big murder Jack had worked on. Cliff's own words came back to him and he remembered the coroner's report that had labeled the Timmons murder more or less an expert job. So, were the two related?

Cliff dug up his notes on the two stories to refresh memories. After staring at them and trying to speculate for about twenty minutes, he finally threw his pen down in frustration. Sure, the cases could be related, but for all he knew, Brickman was working a decades-old series of rapes. He could speculate all he wanted, but he needed some hard facts to put together. Cliff punched the numbers on the desktop phone that would automatically forward any calls to his cell phone. He grabbed a notebook, car keys and a jacket. It was time to hit the streets. If Brickman called, fine. If not, Cliff wanted something on the record ASAP. He had a feeling this story was not going to stay under wraps for long.

CHAPTER 20

Jack Brickman had been a cop long enough not to get too carried away with an early break in a case. Still, it had been hard for him not to get excited by Al Sladky's discovery at the Shaker Heights crime scene.

The east and west contingents of NOSCU, tipped off by Brickman, had determined that The Ninja had in fact entered the Dawkins and Rice murder scenes via the window. In both cases, the windows had been resecured by the suspect after he had entered. There had been no signs of forced entry at either crime scene, so it was likely that the windows had been unlocked. Likely, but not certain, since both apartments had very old windows, with poor insulation and worn-out clasps. A thin metal tool could easily have been slid through a gap and used to raise the latch, and it was doubtful that such a tool would have left any telltale scratches.

At both scenes, they had found almost identical scratches on the exterior surfaces of the buildings. In Elyria, however, they had also found deep marks on a telephone pole near Rice's apartment window. Access to the roof had been all but impossible because the only way up was through a small hatch, secured with a heavy-duty padlock in a locked utility closet. Andy Fulmer believed The Ninja had used the pole to climb up to, rather than down to, Rice's apartment. The Lorain County crime lab had come to the same conclusion. Vidalia and Moore had concurred.

So, on day one, NOSCU had successfully linked three murders. The scratches alone, of course, would never be enough to score a conviction. But with the careful forensic analysis, including metal scrapings and precise measurements, it could be a vital part of the case. Therese Vidalia and Heath Moore had painstakingly photographed, marked, and measured each series of scratches. If possible, they had been even more meticulous than usual. Both experts seemed to relish the fact they could spend as much time as they wanted working the crime scene. Not having to watch the clock or worry about new assignments meant they could afford to be painfully thorough. It was a luxury they apparently intended to exploit to the fullest.

Once they had determined exactly what they were dealing with, Moore and Vidalia had scoured catalogs and martial arts magazines, ordering every variation of *shuko* they could find. The experts were still working out of the coroner's office, so Jack only knew what they were up to by their occasional phone calls and the receipts that crossed his desk on their way to final approval from Calvin Stoddard. Brickman barely glanced at the bills. As long as they had been issued a blank check from the state, he was not about to start nitpicking over expenditures, especially from Moore and Vidalia.

Therese had explained that the only way they could find an exact match was to make their own measurements on a wide variety of *shuko*. For evidentiary and investigative purposes, they could not rely on catalog descriptions.

In addition to analyzing the latest developments, the forensic technicians had also been scouring the trace evidence in all five cases. They had been in constant contact with their counterparts in Lake and Lorain counties since NOSCU had been activated. They were both perfectionists and Jack hoped they were being diplomatic in their dealings with the other experts. So far, there had been no signs of friction. Unfortunately, there had been little new progress either.

The investigators too, had bogged down a little after Sladky's discovery. For the most part, they had fallen back on one of the most time consuming, boring, and frustrating techniques of investigation – good, old-fashioned legwork.

They almost completely ignored notes from prior canvasses of the crime scenes. They had literally started from scratch, interviewing and re-interviewing anybody and everybody connected by association or location to the crimes or the victims. Nothing was blown off. If nobody was home when the detectives came calling, they wrote down the address and tried again. And they kept trying until they made contact.

The interviews themselves changed, too. The investigators were no longer content to let a potential witness off the hook just because they didn't want to talk to the police. Even a bad memory was no longer a valid excuse. The cops pushed as hard as they could with the public, going right up the limits of the law. They were insistent and persistent, occasionally bordering on rudeness. A few complaints came to Jack's attention, none of which held any merit as far as he was concerned. In a perfect world, cops could always be pleasant and polite. The fact they were trying to snare a serial killer before he struck again painfully illustrated that this was not a perfect world.

Still, for all their efforts, NOSCU was coming up empty.

Strangely, Jack was not worried. Despite initial optimism, he had not expected the case to solve itself. He was a realist and he knew they were dealing with a highly motivated, careful, and cunning killer. Careful, but not perfect.

Jack and Ken Bright had been focusing primarily on the developing a profile of the killer, based on what they knew about The Ninja. Profiles were not foolproof, nor were they always accurate. A careful study of the methodology and motivation of the killer would at least point them in a specific direction. They knew how The Ninja was killing. He had made his penchant for traditional martial arts weapons very clear, at least in the last three murders. Unfortunately, that told them little about why he was killing. Jack and Ken had gone back and forth about the methodology since NOSCU's inception. They knew The Ninja was trying to say something, but what was it?

One problem they had was The Ninja's switch from a gun to more traditional weapons. That had been an odd jump, especially since he had been so successful with the pistol. It was rare that a serial killer changed his pattern so drastically. If he had missed with the pistol, sure, it made sense to try something else. In general, though, a criminal would rarely go from a higher level of force to a lower one. Many inexperienced robbers and rapists had been thwarted because they had attempted to use only brute force to achieve their goals. Once they got out of prison or had been injured, they learned to arm themselves better. As a rule, cops assumed that the presence of weapons meant they were dealing with a repeat offender.

"Maybe it's a macho thing," Brickman had ventured one day while he and Bright had hashed it out in Jack's office. "Maybe he's overcompensating for some gay or feminine leanings."

"Possible," Bright said. "But do you really think that's the motivator? Repressed homosexuality?"

"Probably not," Jack conceded. "I'd say it's probably more along the lines that he doesn't want to be the sissy boy. To me, this looks like the bullied turning into the bully."

"Revenge?"

"It fits," Jack said, "Look, just for grins, let's say The Ninja started off as the typical weak, awkward kid. Maybe he's got older brothers or a father who are always on his back about being a wimp. Or let's say he's getting picked on by the neighborhood bullies. Eventually, he gets into karate or weightlifting or whatever and that seems to solve the problem. But it doesn't make the memories go away."

"So, he goes back and finds the bullies and settles up?" Bright asked. "We know that didn't happen because there's absolutely no connection between the victims."

"So I noticed," Jack said. "My guess is most of his trouble happened when he was young. Chances are, his family probably moved to a different area at about the same time he started shaping up, probably when he's ten or so. I'd look for him to be too young to remember the names clear enough to go back and get the bullies. He probably moved far away, too. Otherwise, he might have made more of an effort to find his original tormentors."

"That's assuming his family wasn't to blame," Bright said. "I almost have to assume that The Ninja had a dysfunctional family growing up."

"I'd say that's a given," Brickman said. "I just wonder how dysfunctional."

"If you think he got into karate young, maybe he was looking for a father figure," Bright said.

"How do you figure?"

"Look," Bright said. "As far as I know, most karate teachers are men, right? If Rausch is right, and he thinks this guy has to have been training for a long time, maybe he stuck with it because he was getting something there he wasn't getting at home."

"That's assuming he actually went to a martial arts school," Jack said. "Sam also says it's possible to learn that stuff pretty much on your own. And besides, lessons cost money. If we're talking about a single-parent home, how much extra money do you think is floating around for luxuries like karate lessons?"

"Do you really think he started that young?" Bright asked. "What about the ex-military angle? If he's really trying to overcompensate, what better way to do it than to get dressed up and play soldier? That would have given him both the discipline and the foundation to get started as The Ninja. And this guy obviously did some planning and some reconnaissance. They stress that a lot in the military, you know."

"How well do you think he'd function in the army, Ken?"

"It depends," the FBI agent said. "From what we've seen, based on the timing and planning of the murders, this guy has plenty of self-discipline. He's probably really good at following the rules. A guy like that would thrive in the military. The problem is though, our guy obviously is pissed off at someone or something, and he had the initiative to do something about it. That kind of pent-up anger is eventually going to boil over. I'll bet that when we do get this guy, we're going to find out that he had one or two big fights in the military, if he was actually in the military. Maybe it was something serious enough to get him dishonorably discharged."

Ken smiled.

"Then again, it's possible he never served."

Jack nodded. In spite of their combined experience and their specific knowledge of serial crimes and profiling, they were operating in somewhat of an information vacuum. The only real signature The Ninja was leaving was his choice of weaponry and predisposition for stealthy attacks. Based on established psychological data, they could take what they had and try to extrapolate the killer's motivation and hazard a guess on where he might strike next, but quite frankly, they were still just guessing.

"So, we're back at square one," Jack said. "We're definitely in a holding pattern."

"Until he hits again?" Jack asked.

"Or until we get a smoking gun from the techies or the team," Bright offered.

"How far along are you on your profile, Ken?"

"I'm done," Bright replied. "How about you?"

"I just finished a couple days ago," Brickman said. "I keep going back and tweaking from time to time."

"You feel good about it? Then leave it be."

"Well, since you put it that way, I'd say its time to compare notes."

Jack pulled open the center drawer of his desk, dug out a folder and handed it to Bright. The FBI agent sorted through some papers on the small table next to the office chair and traded them with Jack. The two investigators read in silence for about fifteen minutes. Jack finished first and leaned back in his chair and closed his eyes. After a few more minutes, he grabbed his mug and headed out to the wet bar where NOSCU kept their coffee.

Bryce Cramer and Terri Rome were both working the phones in the bullpen, and they both nodded to him as he walked by back to his office. The whole team had been working long hours and fatigue was starting to show in subtle ways. Cramer, for example, had developed a habit of doodling abstract figures on a yellow legal pad. Rome, who had been a casual smoker three weeks ago, was making at least two pilgrimages every hour to the designated smoking area at the front of the building. Morale continued to be high, but Jack wondered how long that would last. Working non-stop on one investigation had plenty of pluses, but it could also be frustrating, especially when they had so far come up empty. Stoddard seemed oblivious to that fact, holing up in his office for most of the workday. Apparently, he had decided to let Jack do the hands-on work with the team, which was fine to an extent, but Jack had a lot of work to do, too.

By the time he had returned to his office, Ken Bright had finished reading the profile.

"So, what do you think?" Jack asked as he sat down.

"Pretty solid, considering," Bright replied. "If I didn't know better, I'd say you were looking over my shoulder when I wrote mine."

"I noticed that," Jack said. "I guess that means we're either both right or both wrong."

Bright laughed.

"Yeah, I thought of that, too," Bright said. "I just didn't want to jinx us. When do you want to spring this on the troops."

Jack checked his calendar. It was Thursday afternoon, and although they might be able to get everybody together on Friday, the beginning of next week would probably be a lot easier to arrange.

"How about Monday?" he said. "We could set up a teleconference with Payne and Fulmer pretty easily. Plus, we can get everybody together again, see how things are shaping up."

"Energize the team?" Bright said. "Sure, sounds like a plan. Should we talk to the boss, first?"

"Yeah, I guess we'd better brief him," Jack said. "I'm sure he's going to want to see what we've got."

"OK."

"Let me check my voicemail and I'll meet you in Stoddard's office."

As Bright left his office, Jack punched numbers into his speakerphone. There were three messages. One was from Andy Fulmer, and one was from Al Sladky. They didn't have anything new - they were both just basically checking in. The third message was not wholly unexpected. Jack listened to it twice before he gathered up his notes and headed to Stoddard's office.

By the time he had walked down the hall, Bright was already seated in Calvin Stoddard's office. Stoddard was looking harried and gaunt. He was down to his shirtsleeves, his tie was undone and his desk was covered in paperwork, most of which appeared to be about the budget, Jack could only speculate how much of Stoddard's apparent stress was self-imposed and how much was coming from outside sources. George Sellers didn't seem like a slave driver, and he had only checked in with Jack twice so far. If Stoddard had been hoping for a quick arrest, he had been disappointed.

148

"Ken tells me you two have solidified your profile," Stoddard said.

"As best we can, yes," Jack said.

"I know it's a good tool, Jack, but how do you feel it's going to help the investigation?"

"It gives us a direction, Calvin," Jack said, spelling out what he had thought should be obvious. "The formula is pretty simple. If we can figure out why it's being done and how it's being done, we can figure out who's doing it."

"It's that simple?"

"In theory, yes," Jack said. "Ken's had a lot more experience with this than I have, at least on the street. Most of my background in profiling is academic, although I've done plenty in connection to the homicides I've worked. Quite frankly, I usually work it backwards since we usually have a suspect in mind for the average homicide."

"Profiling isn't voodoo, Calvin," Jack continued. "Research and experience have set some standardized characteristics, but we're still just basically looking at the known facts and extrapolating. You take what you know and build from there. And yes, there is a little educational guesswork involved."

"Well, tell me what you have developed."

Jack and Ken read their respective profiles to Stoddard, who jotted several notes. He did not ask as many questions as Brickman had anticipated, so he was apparently buying it.

"When does the team receive this information?" he asked when they had finished.

"We'd like to schedule a team meeting for Monday morning," Jack said. "That will give Ken and I a chance to condense our reports into one file and summarize it for them."

"Set it up, then," Stoddard said. "Now, where does this investigation stand?"

"Well, you've been getting the daily reports so you know we haven't had much new information lately," he said. "We're still waiting on some of the forensic data, but right now the team is basically backfilling."

"Backfilling?"

Ken Bright jumped in to explain.

"They're kind of doing what Jack said before," he said. "They're shoring up the details, making sure we have plenty of evidence to link the suspect to all the crimes – after we get a suspect."

"Does that mean the investigation is stalled? It sounds as though you have conceded the win already."

"Not at all," Jack said. "The evidence hasn't changed, nor has the course of the investigation. We just haven't found anything that points to one specific person. I guess the easiest way to explain is that we're more or less focusing on the prosecution of The Ninja rather than on identifying him."

"And if he kills again while your team is doing this 'backfilling?'"

Jack shrugged.

"Then we hit the ground running on a fresh crime scene," he said. "That sounds bad, I know. But now we know what we're looking for, and that gives us an edge."

"Barring another murder," Stoddard said, his voice rising slightly, "Do you have a plan?"

"We're still working the victimology, but once we establish a better pattern, that might give us a foot in the door."

"I hope you are right, sergeant, I truly do," Stoddard said. "Very well. Brief the team on Monday. I'll be here, of course."

Ken Bright started to get out of his chair when Jack spoke.

"There's one more thing," he said.

"Yes?"

Jack took a deep breath before starting.

"The media might be on to this," he said.

"Wonderful," Ken said.

"How?" Stoddard asked.

"I don't know," Jack said. "I just checked my voicemail. There's a message from a reporter named Cliff O'Brien - he writes for *The North Coast Press* – and he's looking for information about NOSCU and the last two Ninja murders."

"How specific was his information?"

"He didn't sound like he was fishing, so my bet is he managed to piece it together from the nature of the Timmons and Lane killings."

"Can we stall him?"

"I don't think so," Jack said. "I know O'Brien. He's a good reporter, very thorough. And he's got a lot of contacts. He's got a solid reputation with cops, so chances are he's going to be able to at least confirm the shuffling we did to staff NOSCU. I can ask him to sit on it, but I'm pretty sure he won't. It's a big scoop if he gets it first, and judging by the lack of television cameras around here, I'd say he's the only one who has it."

"So you would rather not ask him to hold it?"

Jack shook his head.

"Honestly, no," Jack said. "He's cooperated in the past, and we may need a friend in the press before we wrap this up. I don't have to call him back, but that's your decision. Either way, we're going to have to go public. The sooner we hold a press briefing, the better chance we have to put the right spin on it. Especially considering the lack of progress."

Stoddard nodded and looked over at Ken Bright.

"Comments?"

"Jack's probably right," Bright said. "We knew this was coming sooner or later. I think we were lucky to keep it quiet as long as we did. You never know – this could work out in our favor. We might actually get a good tip out of it."

"Highly unlikely," Stoddard said. "Jack, go ahead and call him back. You do not have to stall him, but don't volunteer too much. You two are going to have to sit down and come up with a press kit and a briefing plan."

"When do you want that?" Jack asked.

"Just get it ready," Stoddard said. "I want to hold a press conference within six hours of when the story breaks, regardless of who breaks it first. I don't see any pressing need to do the media's work for them, so we might as well enjoy the calm before the storm."

"I'll get on that right away, Calvin," Bright said as he got up and headed for the door. Jack started to follow when Stoddard stopped him.

"Close the door and sit down, Jack," he said.

Jack did as he was told and waited.

"I'll make this short sergeant," Stoddard said. "I would be lying if I said I was happy about the media tumbling to this investigation so fast."

"I think we made out OK," Jack said. "We got a solid three weeks jump on them. That should give us a chance to eliminate a lot of bogus tips."

"Always the optimist, eh Jack? I suppose that is helpful. I just hope I don't find out later that you tipped this O'Brien yourself, since you seem to know him."

If Stoddard had rubbed Brickman the wrong way in the past three weeks, he was thoroughly pissing him off now. It took every ounce of control the detective could muster to keep his voice down. Still, the edge in his words was unmistakable.

"Look," Jack said. "I don't know what your problem is, and I don't care. If you don't like the way I'm running this investigation, fine, replace me. You've got all the right in the world to call me on the carpet about the quality of the job I'm doing, but there's no way I'm going to sit here and let you question my integrity. Maybe things aren't going as smoothly as you wanted. Too bad. Murder investigations can be like that, but I guess you don't have the experience to know."

Stoddard's face turned red and he started to speak, but Brickman cut him off.

151

"This is a team, Stoddard. That means everybody has a job to do. I'm doing mine. You do yours. Write the checks and stay out of our way."

"Easy for you to say, Brickman," Stoddard said. "You don't have the attorney general and the mayor calling you every day, looking for an arrest."

"You can't handle it, fine," Jack said. "I'll talk to them. But you better learn to deal with it, Calvin, because once the media gets ahold of this, it's going to be a lot worse."

With that, the detective left his boss' office, still trying to figure out exactly what had just happened.

CHAPTER 21

For Page Al, *The North Coast Press*

June 15

By Cliff O'Brien

CLEVELAND - A serial killer is preying on the North Coast.

In an unprecedented move, federal, state, and local law enforcement officials have activated a special task force to investigate at least five murders believed to have been committed by one suspect.

The Northern Ohio Serial Crimes Unit, also known as NOSCU, was activated approximately three weeks ago in response to a series of murders with similar traits. The last murder was the beheading death of Karnelle Lane on May 19.

According to sources in the law enforcement community, NOSCU is also investigating at least two other recent deaths in the greater Cleveland area, including the stabbing and beating death of Charles Clayton in Shaker Heights late last year and the more recent murder of Jameel Timmons in Cleveland. (See related story.) Sources were unable to elaborate on two other murders which may or may not be connected to the Clayton, Timmons, and Lane murders. However, investigators are said to have reopened two fatal shooting cases, one each in Lake and Lorain counties.

At this point in the investigation, it is unclear what led to the activation of NOSCU, or what led authorities to link the crimes together. One Cleveland Police Department source, who did not wish to be identified, said the only connections he could see in the cases he had heard about were that all the victims had been Black males and all had had criminal records of varying degrees.

"It's weird," he said. "As far as I know, all these guys were killed in different ways. Two of them were shot. That doesn't sound like any serial killer I ever heard of."

The officer, who admitted that he is not close to the case, said that he first learned about the activation of NOSCU by what he called a "brain drain."

"All of a sudden, the best detectives started getting reassigned," he said. "We all knew something was up, but they tried to keep it quiet."

In police circles, rumors travel fast, and the killer, christened "The Ninja" by some officers, has managed to stay several steps ahead of authorities.

"I heard they bogged down already," said another.

According to other sources, approximately two dozen investigators from departments across the North Coast area, stretching from Lake to Lorain counties, have been assigned to NOSCU. The unit, which was established through a special grant from the Federal government, is under the supervision of Calvin Stoddard, an attorney with the Ohio attorney general's office. The lead investigator is veteran CPD homicide Detective Sgt. Jack Brickman.

Brickman was understandably tight-lipped about the investigation; however, he did confirm that NOSCU had been activated and that the team was pursuing leads on several cases that appear to be connected.

"We are currently investigating a series of related murders that appear to have been committed by the same person," Brickman said.

When asked why the public had not been informed about the activation of NOSCU and the presence of a serial killer in the area, Brickman stated that those decisions were made in an effort to improve the efficiency of the investigation.

"In the three weeks since NOSCU's activation, we have been able to reopen several investigations with minimal interference from the media," Brickman said. "That's allowed us to work with unbiased and untainted potential witnesses."

Brickman said that, while the public can be a vital asset in an investigation, bad tips can hinder an investigation as much as good ones can help.

"That three-week period has given the team an excellent window to focus on specific leads and evidence," Brickman said.

The detective denied rumors that that investigation had stalled.

*"I've got the best cops in the area working on this case,"
he said. "We've already made a lot of progress, and I expect
that to continue. It's just going to take time."*

*Brickman would not elaborate on the methods used by the
killer, nor would he speculate on a possible motive for the
killings, deferring to a press conference slated for 4 p.m.
today.*

Cliff was sitting in his cubicle with his feet up, reading the story and sipping a cup of coffee. He was in early again Friday. Frankly, he was a little wired. He had burned up the phone lines during the previous day, trying to get somebody to confirm the story. Nobody had wanted to go on the record, which was understandable considering the police had strict rules about speaking to the media. Eventually, however, he had been able to piece together the story by promising anonymity. It was not something he liked to do, since he felt it detracted from the story's credibility, but it was a tactic he was forced to use from time to time.

The real coup, of course, had been getting Jack Brickman to go on the record. Cliff could only assume he had gotten permission to talk from Calvin Stoddard, whoever the hell that was. Regardless of who Stoddard was, Cliff was pretty sure it was Jack who was really running the show, and that would make it even more interesting.

O'Brien had been basking in the glow of a real, honest-to-goodness, make-E.W. Scripps-proud, bona-fide scoop. With the ravenous electronic media constantly circling, looking for a quick meal of breaking news standing by with instantaneous access to the public, it was getting rare that print journalists broke a story first. Cliff took pride in his thorough investigative pieces, but, man, was it nice to beat the TV stations to the punch.

The story had run with a short sidebar detailing the Clayton, Timmons and Lane murders. Cliff had been unable to identify the victims in the Lake and Lorain county murders. He knew some cops out in those areas, but none well enough that they were willing to bypass departmental channels to talk to him. He had called as many departments as he could, but nobody was talking, although the Lake County Sheriff's office did confirm that they had assigned at least one detective to NOSCU. He had been working non-stop since he found out the team had been activated.

Even so, he had almost had to sit on the story. Brickman hadn't called him back right away, and Leo Nelson had not wanted to run the story without a named source. So, Cliff had continued making calls while he waited for the detective to call him back. By the time he called, O'Brien had nearly exhausted his considerable list of sources. Leo had practically looked over Cliff's shoulder while he hammered at the keyboard. As it did for many writers, the back-seat driver actually slowed him down. In the end, he had to send his editor back to his own office. Leo's anxiety clearly showed how badly he, too, wanted the scoop.

O'Brien had been rewarded with an exclusive, and the knowledge that the Associated Press had also picked up the story and was distributing it across the country under his byline.

Cliff had bought the first round at Griff's after work. Everybody knew he had hit a big story, but to their credit, they kept the specifics quiet, since the bar was haven for all kinds of journalists. Cliff was in great spirits, basking in the glow of knowing something that nobody else did. He just sat at the bar and smiled, almost giddy with anticipation. It took almost all his restraint not to close the bar. The reporter wanted his head clear for the day ahead. He consoled himself with the fact that he was not scheduled to work at all over the weekend and would be able to really indulge once the press conference was over and his subsequent story was filed.

Doreen Ellis was one of the first reporters in that morning. She had worked an early shift on Thursday and hadn't seen the story until the paper hit the street on Friday morning. She had a folded copy of *The North Coast Press* in her hand and she used it to point at Cliff as she rounded the cubicle wall.

"You *are* the man, Cliff O'Brien," she said, smiling broadly. "Nobody, and I mean nobody, has this story. Are you sure you didn't just make it up?"

"You wish," Cliff said. "TV and radio don't have it yet?"

"Well, yes," Doreen said, "but they're quoting your story so it looks like you caught everybody napping. Nice work."

"Did they mention me by name, or just the paper?" Cliff asked.

"Cliff!" Doreen exclaimed in mock surprise. "You mean you have an ego after all? I'm shocked and stunned."

"Just kidding, Dor," O'Brien said.

Doreen Ellis gave him a long look.

"You know, Cliff, when somebody has to say 'just kidding,' they're usually not," she said.

"Wise words," O'Brien said. "Where did you hear that?"

"From you," she said. "The TV stations must be frantic."

"God, I hope so," Cliff said.

"Congrats again," Doreen said, as she circled towards her own cubicle. "Great scoop."

"*Yes, it was*," Cliff thought. He finally put the paper down and started making another round of phone calls. He wanted to do as much as he could from his desk, since many of his sources would have to be contacted in person. His intent was to get as much background as he could before the press conference at four. Now that the lead investigator had gone on the record, some of his other sources might be willing to give him more information. He was experienced enough to know he couldn't rely on a press conference alone for a good story.

CHAPTER 22

Unlike Cliff O'Brien, NOSCU had a very busy weekend, due in large part to the instant media blitz about The Ninja. Jack had had the foresight to call in another six members of NOSCU to handle the phoned, faxed, and e-mailed onslaught of tips and questions.

The questions were relatively easy to answer since nobody except Brickman and Stoddard were authorized to speak to the press. It has been made perfectly clear to everybody on the team, including Natalie Price, that leaks to the media would result in immediate termination and possible criminal charges. Even Jack did not have carte blanche when it came to talking to the media, but as lead investigator, he was afforded plenty of latitude.

The tips were another matter. Cases like this one drew the nutcases and whack jobs like a magnet, each one with their own theory or suspect. The people handling phones had been selected primarily for their ability to sift through the callers for a worthwhile bit of information. It was really a matter of prioritizing. Later, when the good leads had dried up, the team might go back and look at some of the less promising tips and so on down the list until even the wildest conspiracy theories were checked out.

Jack had also approached Stoddard about bringing in another six investigators to follow up the incoming tips. Stoddard had approved two, citing the cost and the relative lack of activity by the first team. They had been basically covering old ground for the last two weeks, and Calvin felt they could start tracking down some of the new information. In the end, Jack had agreed after obtaining a pledge that the remaining four would be activated as soon as the need surfaced. Tactically, he supposed it made sense, since it would let him call in reinforcements later. That might be a good morale booster if things got really bogged down, plus it would let him tap into fresh brainpower later. If he brought them on board now, they might end up just as fatigued as everybody else as the investigation progressed.

The phones had been ringing almost non-stop since the press conference on Friday. That had only increased after the news at five and six, as the local stations dutifully displayed the tipline phone numbers on their crawls. Luckily, the phone banks were in a separate room dedicated to that purpose. It kept the rest of NOSCU's office relatively quiet, although everybody could hear the phones ringing when the operators entered and exited the room, which was often. Jack had encouraged them to take frequent breaks.

The press conference had gone better than Jack had anticipated. Along with Ken Bright, they had come up with a cautious informational packet for the media, confirming what Cliff O'Brien's story had already said. They did not identify Rice and Dawkins as possible victims because they had not yet positively linked them to the other three. All they had told the press was that they were investigating possible connections to "other crimes" in Lake and Lorain counties, creating a vacuum that encouraged speculation, most of it wrong.

Initially, Stoddard had done most of the talking. To Jack, it was amazing how the attorney seemed to change as soon as he was in front of the cameras. He was smooth, relaxed, and professional. Brickman was forced to admit to himself that Stoddard was probably hard to beat once he got in front of a jury. Things had apparently blown over between them for now, and Stoddard seemed to have adopted an air of cordiality toward the detective. But the tension was still there, lingering below the surface. Jack could sense that Calvin was still anxious, and he doubted that anxiety was going to dissipate under the onslaught of media attention.

The press briefing had been short. When Stoddard had run into trouble about the specifics of the investigation, he had turned the podium over to Jack, who answered as many questions as he could – very carefully. He was uncomfortably aware of his appearance, and he did his best to sound confident without being cocky. He wanted the public to feel that something productive was being done with their tax dollars.

Most of the questions were about things he had answers for, but could not release. A couple of them were quite probing, though those tended to be from the print journalists. As expected, Cliff O'Brien had already started looking for more specific information about the methods of killing and why they thought the murders were linked. He had even asked if they had prepared a profile of the killer yet. Brickman had to stonewall him, but he respected the effort nonetheless. From his position at the podium, Jack could plainly see the jealousy in the eyes of the other journalists when Cliff asked his questions. That was understandable. It was a competition, after all, and nobody liked to lose.

Other reporters had asked some rather inane questions, one wanting to know why the FBI wasn't running the investigation. Jack patiently explained that the case did not fall under their jurisdiction. The reporter either just wanted Jack to explain it to the public or didn't know better herself. Jack figured it was the latter, and put the blame on Hollywood.

Of course, the TV cameras were the worst. They never seemed satisfied. After the press conference, Jack had to quickly navigate through a maze of bright lights and microphones just to reach the secured elevators for the trip back up to the NOSCU offices. When he finally left the office for the night, he had been doubly thankful for the covered, secured parking lot in the basement of the building. There was no place for the TV crews to ambush him as he headed home.

Jack had turned in early that night, holding Karen close as they lay in bed together. She had been chatty, since Jack had been working longer hours than even she was used to. Jack had done his best to stay awake through the small talk, but he eventually had just dozed off. He hadn't set the alarm, so he woke up later than usual, but at least he woke up refreshed. Karen had taken a little while to warm up to him again, and that only after he made her café latte with the gourmet coffee machine they had splurged on a while back. That seemed to take the edge off, but she was still clearly concerned about the toll the investigation was taking on their marriage.

Twelve-hour days were fast becoming the norm for Jack, though he was occasionally able to slip away and meet her for lunch or dinner. Even those encounters tended to be a little rushed since Brickman's cell phone seemed to ring constantly. Karen was surprised that, in an investigation that seemed to be making such little headway, they needed to talk to her husband so often.

Jack seemed to be handling the stress well, but she was worried about his eating habits and lack of exercise. She knew he was eating much more fast food than he should be, and workouts had become a distant memory. By the time he came home from work, he was usually exhausted, though she had been able to coax him into walking around the block a few times. The only fringe benefit was that his hectic schedule and perpetual on-call status had practically eliminated his alcohol consumption. Not that she felt he had a problem, but he did get carried away from time to time. He wanted to be fresh, alert, and sober if he needed to rush to a fresh crime scene.

On Saturday morning, Karen put her foot down.

"Jack," she said. "I know they need you at the office, but what about us? I'm trying to be patient, but we're like two things that go bump and pass each other in the night. Can't you take a day off?"

Jack's first instinct had been to object. He had warned Karen that he would be working long hours until the case was over, and he was being well compensated for his time. But after he thought about it for a moment, he realized that she was right. He was in danger of becoming too immersed in the case. He needed to step back and get a little perspective.

Jack called the office and talked to Al Sladky, who just happened to be in. He told Al he planned to take the weekend off, though he would probably work from home a little on Sunday to finalize the profile for the meeting with the team on Monday.

"Sure, sure," Al said. "Leave the grunts to do the dirty work."

Brickman ignored the comment, which he was certain his partner did not mean.

"Anything new?" Jack asked.

"Nah," Al said. "I just checked with the phone guys and nobody's got anything hot. Most of it is just pure BS."

"You going to be in long?"

"I don't think so," Sladky replied. "I'm going to talk to the first responders from Shaker Heights, see if they might have missed anything. I know Lombardo talked to them already, but I just wanna run something by them."

"OK," Jack said. "Just make sure everybody knows how to reach me."

"Right. Have fun."

"I'm sure going to try," Jack said.

So, while NOSCU stayed busy tracking down wild tips and returning phone calls, Jack Brickman took a little time to get reacquainted with his wife. He had to remind himself to take a look at the overtime sheets and see if anybody on the team needed to be reined in. Unfortunately, a dedicated cop could almost literally work himself to death when he got on a good case.

For the most part, Jack was able to relax as he and Karen did a little shopping, went to visit her parents in Chagrin Falls, and had a late dinner at The Great Lakes Brewing Company, which was a challenge of Jack because he had to resist some of the best beer offerings in the city. They talked and held hands, and did all of those little things that remind people why they got married in the first place. It was a welcome change from the hectic routine his life had become in the last three weeks.

On Sunday, they found time to visit Jack's parents, who still lived in a small bungalow in Bay Village where Jack had grown up. Ed Brickman was a newly retired crew supervisor for CEI. Mary Brickman was a retired schoolteacher who still worked part-time at St. Raphael's Catholic Church. While many of their friends had moved south when they hit retirement age, Jack's folks had stayed put. Cleveland was their home. It was where their kids and grandkids lived. Why should they move away just when they had time to enjoy family?

Ed Brickman, an avid fisherman and notorious tinkerer, kept himself busy volunteering around the parish, doing odd jobs and minor electrical repairs for some of the elderly members of the church community. Not that he was a saint. He had liked to raise a little hell back in his younger days, and could still put away impressive amounts of beer, but married life had mellowed him considerably. As a man who had been lucky enough to get a good job right out of high school, he had carefully managed their finances and managed to put Jack and his brother though college. Jack's scholarships had mercifully lessened that financial burden.

Jack had been lucky enough to find a wife who got along well with his mother. It really wasn't surprising, however, considering that just about everybody got along well with Mary Brickman. She was just one of those people that you liked right away. As soon as they arrived at the elder Brickmans' home, Jack's wife and his mother set up shop in the kitchen, catching up on gossip and finding out what was new with Jack's brother and nephews. Jack headed outside to the small deck where his father was preparing to cook on the grill. His preparations consisted of lighting the grill and sitting back on an Adirondack chair with a cold beer, listening to the Tribe on the radio while waiting for Mary to tell him to put the steaks on.

Ed Brickman stood up as Jack walked onto the deck. They shook hands, Jack almost wincing as they did. His father, who had manhandled his share of tools over the years, had powerful hands and forearms. At sixty-three, he was still a fit man. Ed held up a beer and a Coke from the cooler.

"You on call?" he asked.

"Unfortunately, yeah," Jack said.

Ed tossed him the Coke and cracked open the beer for himself.

They caught up on current events, like the Indians' latest winning streak and how his car was running. Inevitably, their discussion turned to The Ninja, since it was no secret that Jack was running the case.

"Is this guy really that good, Jack?" Ed asked, taking a long sip.

"So far, yeah," Jack replied. "I feel like we're right on the verge of breaking this thing open, but I don't know. He hasn't left much of a trail. He's careful and he must be taking a lot of time setting up these hits, because nobody's seen a thing. It's like he's just sitting there, watching. When the time's right, boom, he moves right in and does it."

Ed Brickman nodded.

"When I was in Korea, that's the kind of stuff the snipers would pull," he said. "They'd just set up on a target, get the routine down and wait. They didn't like to waste a shot. 'Course the Koreans would pull the same thing, except they would sneak up and kill guys with a knife, a lot of times right after they changed the guard. Thank God I never went to the front. What a mess."

Ed had been drafted in the Army during the Korean War. He had been lucky enough to serve as a driver for the commander of a quartermaster division. He didn't talk about it much because there wasn't that much to tell. But he had answered his country's call and done what they had asked him to do. If they had wanted him to pick up a rifle and fight, Ed said he'd have done that, too. They just never asked.

"The paper says you're looking for a white guy, right?" he asked.

Jack nodded.

"Yeah."

"That's gutsy," Ed said. "I've worked in a lot of neighborhoods, some good and some not so good. Some black and some white. There were days I'd look around and the only white faces I'd see would be on my crew. I'd think he'd stand out a little."

"Me too, dad," Jack said, reaching into the cooler for a second soda. "You ever get nervous working in the rough neighborhoods?"

"Nah," Ed said. "Oh, every once and while, one of our guys might get held up on pay day or something, but you learn not to carry anything except lunch money. Mainly, people left us alone. We were there to help them so we usually got a free pass. So, how long is this thing going to take to wrap up anyway?"

"That, dad, is the million-dollar question," Jack said. "Soon, I hope. I think Karen misses me a little."

"You'll get him, Jack," Ed said. Their wives stepped out onto the deck and talked turned to other topics. Jack sat down to dinner and let himself enjoy a leisurely evening with his family.

Unfortunately, as he lay in bed waiting for sleep, he started thinking about the case again. He had two main worries. One was the slowness of the lab results. He felt that once the lab matched up the DNA, he would have a better chance of seeing a pattern. The second was that The Ninja would kill again. Soon.

CHAPTER 23

Everybody was prompt for the Monday morning meeting.

Once they had settled in around the conference table with the ever-present coffee mugs in front of them, Jack called the meeting to order.

"OK," he said. "Let's get started."

Ken Bright opened up a large box of files and started passing them out to the team.

"For those of you joining us in our radio audience, Sergeant Brickman is handing out some suspicious looking folders," Al Sladky said.

"Sorry," Jack said. "I'm new at teleconferencing. Andy, Ed, you should have a stack of files at your offices. Go ahead and pass them out."

When everybody had a file in front of them, Jack started his presentation in earnest.

"You all have the full profile in front of you, so I'm just going to hit the high points," Jack said. "Ken and I spent a lot of time on this, although it probably looks a little flimsy to you. Unfortunately, The Ninja is unique, so we had to stretch a little to connect all the dots. First, what do we think we know?

"The Ninja is a white male. We put his age at 25 to 34. We know he is in excellent physical condition, and a male in that age range could still get into peak condition without killing himself. Much older than that and it would be a little harder, as we all know. We could have placed his age lower, but the kind of patience that he has shown clearly points to an older man. With a younger killer, I think his work would have been a little sloppier and the killings would have been closer together. Plus, it took him a while to produce the *ninjitsu* angle. He probably had training in martial arts, but may or may not have kept up with it.

"We can rule out any sort of physical defects that would affect his ability to climb and fight. But The Ninja has plenty of anger that has probably been building for a long time. Ken thinks it probably stems from a distinguishing feature that might have got him bullied as a child, possibly a speech impediment or facial deformity. Those may help explain why he likes sneaking around, and could explain why he identifies with the *ninja*, who traditionally hid their faces.

"Socioeconomically, The Ninja most likely lives alone and either rents or owns his own home. We're betting he owns a house, mainly because it gives him the most freedom to come and go at all hours without attracting attention. Plus, we know he has an intense physical conditioning regimen. For his specific training, he needs privacy since a guy practicing with swords and chains is likely to attract attention at the local health club."

"I can vouch for that," Sam Rausch said.

"Right, Sam," Jack continued. "The Ninja probably works a part-time job somewhere since a full-time job would also hinder his activities. So, he also probably has a good supply of money or has access to it. He probably works in a capacity where he doesn't have a lot of public contact, based on Ken's theories about a facial or vocal defects. Possibly, he lives in a house he inherited from his parents, since it's unlikely his mother or father are living."

"How do you figure that?" Sladky asked.

"Guilt," Ken Bright said. "Even if his parents were SOBs, and they probably were, The Ninja wouldn't want to get caught being bad, especially if he thinks everybody else is picking on him. That parental approval is very important to a lot of serial killers for some reason."

"In The Ninja's case," Jack said, "If you take in Ken's theory about him being bullied as a kid, he probably had a strong attachment to his mother, so strong in fact that he chose to target men rather than women. That says something about him. It's possible that his mother was abused by his father, though that is just fishing. It wouldn't surprise me if his mother died shortly before the first murder, since a major stressor like that can often be the trigger that gets these guys started.

"We still haven't figured out what's driving this guy. That's the weakest part of the profile. Ken is leaning more towards revenge for being picked on when he was little, since the thugs who are getting knocked off probably most remind The Ninja of the bullies who knocked him around while he was growing up. Personally, I think he's got a misplaced sense of vigilante justice since he has exclusively targeted criminals. Until he shows us something else, that's academic. Sorry

"Lastly, we're betting he lives in Cleveland, or at least the immediate area. Generally, we would have expected him to first kill in the area where felt the most comfortable. I'm throwing that assumption out the window, since his first and second kills were so far from each other. It's likely that he pulled those two jobs just to see if he could do it. Working closer to home cuts down on the chances of him getting caught, since he's that much closer to his base. He needs to get to and from these crime scenes. The shorter the trip, the less likely it is to get randomly stopped. And let me correct myself. These are the only killings we know about. Based on his methods, which has shown no hesitation, we're fairly certain he has killed before this. It may have just been animals, but there is a definite possibility that he practiced a little before he became The Ninja.

"So where does that leave us?" Jack asked rhetorically. "The first thing I'm asking you to do is going to take plenty of legwork, but it might be worth it. Ken and I hashed it out, and we both agree that we're highly unlikely to catch The Ninja in the act."

"Or going to or from the crime scene," Ken Bright chimed in.

"Why not?" Terri Rome asked.

"He's too careful," Bright said. "He might be a little pumped up right after he kills, but we can't assume he's going to be out of control, at least not to the point where he's going to be cruising down the road covered in blood, wearing a hood, and dangling a sword out of the window."

"We might get lucky, though," Rome said. "It's happened before."

"Timothy McVeigh comes to mind," Bryce Cramer said. Heads nodded in agreement. The worst mass murderer in American history had been caught because a sharp-eyed state trooper had noticed the license plates on McVeigh's car were handmade. Upon stopping the Oklahoma City bomber, the cop had also noticed the telltale bulge of a shoulder holster and Glock under the terrorist's jacket.

"Yeah, we might catch a break, Bryce," Jack said. "I'm just not willing to sit by and wait for us to get lucky. One of the first things we did when we set up shop here was to send out teletypes to all area police departments, asking them to give special attention to white males showing up in low-income, predominantly Black neighborhoods. The description we sent out, of course, is fairly vague, so I'm not holding my breath. At least it gives us more eyes and ears out where we need them the most.

"Anyway, we're getting paid the big bucks to think ahead, and I'd rather not let The Ninja call the shots. What I want you to do is start reviewing all the FI cards you can get your hands on."

An "FI" card was a field interrogation card. Every department had them, though many gave them different names, such as "field contact" cards or "field interview" cards. Regardless, they could be great tools in investigations if street cops bothered to do them. The concept of the FI card was basically to keep a record of suspicious persons or anything out of the ordinary. They were a great way to keep track of who had been in certain areas at certain times. It was a good tool because it meant the police could chronicle the comings and goings of people without arresting them. You still needed at least an articulable suspicion to make the contact though.

"I want you to start near the crime scenes and work outwards," Jack said. "And work backwards chronologically."

"How far back?" asked the digitized voice of Andy Fulmer over the speakerphone.

"For now, let's go back eighteen months from the date of the murder," Brickman said. "If nothing turns up from that, then we'll talk about going further back. And I want a master list compiled, including names, physicals, and license plates. We're going to pile them all together and see if we get any duplicate names."

FI card results were not part of the LEADS database.

Calvin Stoddard interrupted.

"What do you hope to find, sergeant?" he asked. A few of the cops in the room shot stunned looks at Stoddard but quickly got their poker faces on while Jack explained.

"The Ninja has obviously had his victims under surveillance," Jack said. "That's going to be the time when he's most exposed, especially since he's a white guy operating in mainly Black areas. A white guy in a minority high-crime area is going to attract attention. Cops are going to wonder what he's doing there, and they're going to assume he's there to buy drugs or looking for a date."

"A date?" Stoddard asked.

"Like a blow job, Calvin," Terri Rome said. "You know, from a hooker."

To her credit, Terri managed to deliver the line with a straight face. She also managed to say it without a trace of condescension. Stoddard turned bright red.

"Carry on, Jack," he said.

Jack did, though he had to admit he enjoyed seeing Stoddard flustered. His lack of street knowledge only reinforced Jack's feeling that a cop should be leading the team.

"Right," Jack said. "Anyway, since The Ninja isn't buying drugs or looking for sex, he probably was never arrested."

"That makes sense," Cramer said. "If he checked out, they'd have no reason to arrest him, so no arrest record."

"Correct," Jack said. "So, with any luck, the blue suits did what they're supposed to do and at least documented the contact."

"How about trespassing, stuff like that?" Al asked. "Seems like if he's walking around, surveilling and whatnot, he might've gotten picked up for peeping or something."

Jack had meant to bring that up, but was glad his partner had mentioned it. Al had already solidified his reputation on the team, but it never hurt to pump up your stock a little.

"Al's right," he said. "Let's take a look at any arrest records for voyeurism or trespassing. Use the same parameters as the FI cards."

Jack looked around at the team.

"Anything else?" he asked.

Bryce Cramer raised his hand.

"What is it, Bryce?"

"Well, with all due respect to you and Ken, Jack," he said. "Are you sure these aren't hate crimes? I mean, I know you've spent a lot of time on the profile, but is it possible we're overlooking the obvious?"

"The profile isn't carved in stone, Bryce," Jack said. "But right now, I'm standing by it. Ken's handled some hate crimes, so maybe he can explain it better."

Ken cleared his throat.

"I agree with Jack," he said. "I won't go as far as to say that race has absolutely no role in the victim selection, but it's probably more of a footnote than anything else. And there has been no indication that an anti-Black bias was the motivating factor in any of the killings. If The Ninja were killing African Americans just for the sake of killing African Americans, he would have let us know by now. Why send a message without signing it?"

"True," Jack said. "I'm fairly confident that once we get this guy, we're not going to find he was a racist. At least not based on what we have so far."

"If you two say so," Bryce said. "But how long do you think it's going to be before the public starts asking the question?"

"I don't know," Brickman admitted. "All I can say is we're not going to let public opinion run this investigation."

"I'm not saying we should," Bryce said. "I'm just saying we should keep it in mind. Hell, maybe I'm just being too sensitive. It just hits a little close to home."

Jack understood Cramer's message immediately. As one of three African Americans on the team, maybe he felt the race issue more acutely than the rest of the team.

"OK, Bryce," he said. "Point taken. That may be an angle that comes up later. Everybody, let's not be quick to dismiss a racial motive. Follow the evidence. The Ninja's been quiet for a while, and I don't think he's shown us all the cards he's holding."

Ed Payne's voice came in over the speakerphone, changing the topic.

"Jack, what about forensics?" he asked. "Did we match up yet?"

Jack shook his head no and then remembered that Payne couldn't see him.

"Sorry, Ed, no," he said. "I've been on the phone every day trying to light a fire under the lab, and they keep telling me it's coming any day now."

"Keep us posted," Payne said.

"I will," Jack said. "That's about all I have today. Ken and I, and probably Al and Sam, will be going over the victimology again. Everybody's field notes look pretty good, so that will be a big help. You're all doing a great job. Hang in there. I'm only worried about one thing, though."

Looks of concern and annoyance crossed the faces of the team members he could see.

"Make sure you all take a day or two off from time to time," he said. "The time will come when we need you to work around the clock, and I want everybody ready to go when that time comes. I know the hours you're logging because I see your overtime slips before they go to Calvin. And I know most of you are working even more hours than you're reporting. So, relax a little. That's an order."

The meeting took a few minutes to break up. As always, everybody seemed to want to talk to Jack, bounce ideas off him and let him know what they were doing. The team members were busy, including Therese Vidalia, Heath Moore, and Sam Rausch.

Moore and Vidalia had gone over the forensic data from the five crime scenes so many times they could recite statistics verbatim from memory. Once that was done, they hunkered down behind their desks and started creating computer simulations of the crimes and three-dimensional layouts of the crime scenes. It was a painstakingly slow process since the computer imaging had to be precise enough to introduce as evidence in a courtroom. Luckily, both technicians were adept computer operators. Vidalia, in fact, had been instrumental in developing the very software they were using.

The two technicians showed no signs of the fatigue that seemed to be affecting the rest of the team. By their nature, both were perfectionists. The job demanded it. Because they rarely were given the time to do such thorough support work, they were both reveling in the unlimited time and resources they had been given for The Ninja murders. Granted, it was not a simple task since they were reconstructing five different murder scenes. That task, however, had been reduced somewhat by the fact that the Lorain and Lake county crime scene labs had done extremely thorough jobs at the Rice and Dawkins murder scenes.

Working backwards from a multitude of measurements, including blood splatters and pooling, wound channels, ballistics, and the body itself, they were able to generate computer videos of the murders that were chilling to watch, even if the depictions of the participants did resemble little more than mannequins. The computer-generated figures were completely articulated and precisely mirrored the physical dimensions of the victims, so the on-screen movements and reactions were as life-like as they could make them. Not surprisingly, the re-creations showed the crimes had occurred almost exactly how the detectives and the coroner had described them. Jack and Al took pride in that.

Anybody who was in the office when the sequences were complete was treated to a screening in the conference room, with the PowerPoint projector offering a nearly true-to-scale reenactment of the killing. Typical of the dark humor of homicide investigators, Heath Moore had initially clothed the computer killer in a black *ninja* uniform and added sound effects. Calvin Stoddard had found it distasteful and immediately asked Moore to "clean it up." He did, but Jack was fairly sure there was more than one copy of the original floating around the office.

The Charlie Clayton murder re-creation was particularly brutal to watch, mainly because the killing took the longest to accomplish. Seeing the digitized victim recoiling and retreating from The Ninja while being wounded and spilling computerized blood was more than a little disturbing. Stan Lombardo had watched it several times, perhaps finally convincing himself that he had been wrong.

Sam Rausch had done his best to keep contributing to the team. He had fielded many questions about the martial arts in general and *ninjitsu* in particular. The lieutenant had also accompanied a number of investigators into the field when nobody else was available. As a rule, it was not safe for a cop to venture out alone, especially into some of the neighborhoods where the investigation led. All of NOSCU's detectives were experienced street cops, so while they weren't necessarily anxious about heading out alone, the reassuring presence of a living legend didn't hurt, either.

Rausch also managed to find time to check on his SWAT team and check the status of the 12-person tactical response unit that had been assigned to NOSCU. They had been shuffling people in and out of the unit to keep them fresh, but there had been more down time than they would have liked. Like the elite professionals they were, they filled that time with training, bitching, and sleeping. Sam had been giving them regular briefings about the capabilities of The Ninja and possible scenarios they might face if and when they found the killer. The SWAT team had responded by reconfiguring their live-fire exercises to deal specifically with close-quarters encounters of an armed, highly skilled opponent.

The prospect of dealing with a skilled swordsman did change their tactics a little. Since they had plenty of time to work through the problem, the team members had been able to produce a plan that better addressed the arm's length confrontation they were likely to experience with The Ninja. It had really been a question of swapping weapons operators around. Two of the MP-5 9mm submachine gun operators, mainstays of any good SWAT unit, had been exchanged with two officers armed with specially modified Benelli semiautomatic shotguns with 14-inch barrels to lead the tactical stick.

The two additional shotguns, which were usually loaded with special breaching rounds to blow hinges and deadbolts out of doorframes, had their payloads changed to address the need to stop a swordsman in his tracks. They now carried #4 buckshot in 3-inch Magnum shells. There had been considerable debate about the loads, with about half the team pressing for the heavier 00 buck. The 00 buckshot spat pellets which were about .32 caliber, while the lighter #4 fired a slightly wider pattern of .25-caliber pellets. In the end, the shotgun operators themselves made the decision, and they felt that the smaller pellets gave them a slightly larger margin for error.

The margin probably wouldn't be needed. The shotgunners were by definition the best of the best. It still took skill and training, though. Contrary to widespread belief, you had to actually aim a shotgun, regardless of how short the barrel was. The pattern only spread about one inch in diameter for every three feet of travel from the barrel, so accuracy was paramount. Even if the suspect were wearing body armor, the sheer force of the blast, with a couple dozen high-velocity metal balls slamming into a concentrated area, would almost certainly stop anybody where they stood. The same could not be said about the light 115-grain jacketed slugs delivered by the MP-5s. Hollow-point ammunition might even out that equation, but Heckler & Koch specifically prohibited the use of anything but jacketed rounds in their automatic weapons. Anything else might jeopardize reliability.

Rausch had also made good on his offer to help team members with their sidearm proficiency. He was a regular sight at the range located in the basement of the courthouse. Some of the U.S. Marshals had initially balked at letting anybody else use their range, but they had changed their tune once Sam had shown up. They had immediately welcomed him into the fold, inevitably trying to pick his brain on a variety of topics, from weapons to tactics. Even some of their firearms instructors had sought him out for private sessions, which he was happy to conduct when he had the time. His first priority, of course, was NOSCU, but it never hurt to cement interjurisdictional bonds.

Jack had joined Sam twice a week since the team had been activated. The sessions had been fairly brief, but they had been worth the time. Sam was a patient coach and Jack was a good student and a natural athlete with immense potential. Sam, of course, saw plenty of room for improvement.

One of the first things he did was to get Jack firing faster.

"Look," he said. "There's nothing wrong with a nine-millimeter. It wouldn't be my first, or even my second choice, but that's what you've got so that's what you've got to work with. First of all, you've got to think past that 'tac-tac' stuff they taught you in the academy. You probably won't drop somebody with two jacketed rounds. Realistically, you need to shoot until the target goes down, but you don't want to just empty your magazine at a bad guy, especially if you're only carrying one spare magazine on your belt. Plus, you don't want to have to worry about reloading in the middle of a firefight. That's going to take a few seconds even if you're good and that's way too long when somebody is shooting at you.

"What I like is two very fast strings of three rounds each," he continued, then illustrated. "Pop-pop-pop. Pop-pop-pop. I especially like that for our .45s since I can get three strings of three out of a mag. That leaves one in the chamber for a combat reload."

For Jack, it was a definite change from the way he had been taught to shoot. Unlike some firearms instructors, who acted as if the cost of ammunition was coming out of their own pockets, Sam Rausch seemed to take unholy glee in blowing through as many rounds as possible. To him the equation was simple – all the bullets in the world weren't worth one cop's life.

Even Al Sladky had come down to practice a couple times. Despite his age, Al could still shoot decently, and he shared Rausch's exuberance for volume of fire. Al had been in two shootings in his lengthy career. He had missed the suspect with two rounds in his first shooting, which had occurred less than eighteen months out of the academy He had come through that one unhurt, and the suspect, who was at least as scared as Al, had dropped his gun while running away. After that encounter, Al realized he needed to upgrade his skills.

In the second shootout, Al had been able to quickly pick up his sights, contrary to the "point shooting" craze of those days. He emptied his revolver so fast that one person within earshot later told the newspaper that the police had used a machine gun on the suspect. Al hadn't, of course, but three out of the six shots he fired at the armed robbery suspect had hit the man, killing him. Sladky's hit-to-miss ratio had been higher than the national average for police-involved shootings, so the practice must have paid off. He was still good enough to be dangerous, even with the newfangled semiautomatic.

Al had taken great pleasure in "test driving" Sam Rausch's .45. When he handed it back to the lieutenant after firing a few magazines worth of ammo, he had a huge grin on his face.

"Nice," was all he said.

Rausch himself did not shoot much, at least not in front of the other NOSCU members. Jack suspected that he didn't want to embarrass anybody or discourage them from practicing. Plus, he was a humble being. Sladky finally managed to goad him into it by calling into question the skill and honor of the U.S. Army Rangers. Well, Sam had to defend the black berets. It was lucky for Al that he hadn't wagered lunch on the match. At fifty feet, Rausch quickly and effortlessly punched out the X-ring in the center of a police silhouette target. They couldn't find all ten bullet holes because the group was so tight, but Al and Jack were both willing to give Sam the benefit of the doubt. It was highly unlikely that he had thrown a flier off the paper. Just to prove a point, though, Sam slapped another magazine in the pistol and cut a necklace of bullet holes between the head and torso of the target. He followed that up with a series of three-round strings fired as fast as he could pull the trigger. Each of those groups ended up as a shamrock on the cardboard.

"Of course, " Sam said when he had finished, "it's not that easy when they're moving and shooting back at you and you're moving and shooting, too. But it doesn't hurt to practice, either."

So far, the people of NOSCU had been getting along well enough with each other. As often happens within groups, different cliques had formed. Jack, despite his leadership role, spent most of his time with Ken Bright, Sam Rausch, and, to his dismay, Calvin Stoddard.

Al Sladky spent much of his time in the field, mostly talking to other cops. He had a knack for talking to them so casually that they rarely knew they were actually being interviewed. Sladky had taken it upon himself to personally speak to every officer who had played even the smallest role in any of the murder investigations to find out if they had failed to report some miniscule fact about the case. When that was finished, he had gone out and talked to the beat cops and detectives who worked in the area of the crimes.

That double checking had taken time since many of the officers worked rotating shifts and had rotating days off. Plus, Al had to sell himself a little to Elyria and Painesville cops, who didn't know him the way the Cleveland-area cops did. He had found out a few things, gotten a few new observations, but nothing earth shattering. Al was able to report to Jack and Luis Ramirez that the killings absolutely were not related to any gang feuds. The Padre was happy to get that confirmation. He already had enough on his plate.

Regardless, when Al was in the office, he didn't wander too far from Jack. The veteran detective was another source of support for Jack. Despite his laid-back manner, Sladky was a tireless worker who never quit. And he never let Jack forget just who the senior partner was. If nothing else, it was good for Brickman to see a familiar face around the office. By necessity, he had quickly forged good working relationships with the people of NOSCU, but he considered Al a close friend, someone he could trust. And that was priceless.

By the time the team had been sent on their way, Jack found Al, Sam, and Ken clustered around his office, already looking through the files they had on the victims. The stack had rapidly grown as the detectives tried to gather information about the dead men. Considering their lack of progress with the investigation, finding something, anything, linking the victims seemed like the next logical step.

"Dig in, junior," Al said, handing Jack a file.

"Thanks for nothing, Al," he said, sitting down behind his desk. He took a moment before opening the manila folder.

"The answer is in here somewhere," he thought, and began to read.

CHAPTER 24

Bryce Cramer's comments about public opinion turned out to be prophetic.

Fueled by constant media attention, the public's thirst for information about The Ninja and the ongoing investigation became insatiable. Television crews ran around interviewing people on the street, getting their reactions to the killings. The local news stations also started trotting out an eclectic list of self-styled experts on serial crimes. Some of them actually were experts, but lacking the inside information available to NOSCU, they couldn't do much more than hazard educated guesses. The one advantage they had over the team was that there was no penalty for wild guesses. They could sit back and spin theories at their leisure. If they were wrong, it cost them nothing.

To NOSCU, of course, a bad guess could waste vital time since it could send the investigation in the wrong direction. The media, on the other hand, rarely suffered for their mistakes. Jack and the rest of NOSCU were too busy to pay much attention to what the media was saying, though Jack did catch an interesting interview with a local author who had written a number of books about Cleveland crime and other tragedies. Being a fan of the genre, he had been intrigued by the writer's take on the case since one of his books had expended a lot of ink on the Torso Murders.

Much of what appeared on TV and in the papers, however, dealt little with the facts of The Ninja murders. The media, it seemed, was more interested in stirring up controversy.

The first rumblings about the race issue had started almost as soon as the initial news stories about The Ninja had been broken. In the beginning, the fact that all the victims were Black was just a footnote. That had changed when the media had gotten wind of the fact that the police were looking for a white suspect. The task force had not released that information to the public, primarily because they could offer littler more than The Ninja's race and gender as a description. Jack and Ken Bright had both felt that they were better off waiting until they had something more definitive, like a sketch or hair color, before going public. Somebody, probably a cop, had mentioned that the suspect was white to somebody who had gotten the information to the media.

Since then, several community leaders and politicians had taken up the issue, demanding to know why young Black men were being massacred in the city and why the police weren't doing anything about it.

Another issue that had cropped up was the debate over whether The Ninja was a good guy or a bad guy. Some people seemed to identify with the killer, since he had so far only targeted people with criminal records involved in the drug trade. Some people liked the idea of lone vigilante, doing what the courts and the police could not or would not do.

The scrutiny Jack Brickman had expected and Calvin Stoddard had feared was on its way.

CHAPTER 25

For Page A1, *The North Coast Press*

June 20

By Cliff O'Brien

CLEVELAND - As the Northern Ohio Serial Crimes Unit and other police agencies continue to hunt for the elusive killer known in some circles as "The Ninja," some area residents have started saying they aren't sure how much effort should be made to find him.

Carl DePesto, a butcher from Cleveland Heights, said he can't figure out why police are even bothering to look.

"Yeah, I know people got killed, but so what?" he said. "The paper says all the dead guys were ex-cons, drug dealers. When they find that Ninja guy, they ought to give him a medal."

DePesto said he wasn't worried about an increase in violent crime.

"Increase?" he said, "I bet crime goes down. It probably will, since five bad guys got killed. I mean, I feel bad for their families and all, but I bet these other guys out there dealing their crack are scared stiff. Ain't that a good thing?"

Other area residents echoed DePesto's sentiment.

Millicent Carver, of Shaker Heights, said she thought the murders would make people think twice about breaking the law.

"When I was growing up, the streets were a lot safer," she said. "You could walk to the corner store without being bothered. Then things got bad. Maybe it's high time the crooks got a little taste of their own medicine."

Carver too, said that although she worried about her safety from other criminals, the man known as "The Ninja" didn't scare her at all.

"If he wants to go get these rascals off the street, I say go get 'em," she said. "I've never had so much as a parking ticket in all my years, so I suppose I'm safe."

Rev. Sean McMurray, pastor of St. Timothy's Catholic Church in Garfield Heights, said that while he understands the frustration some people feel over rampant crime, he does not feel that more violence is the answer.

"There are those who are quick to espouse the 'eye for an eye' philosophy," he said. "My parishioners unfortunately know the face of violent crime well, and some of them have expressed satisfaction over the recent developments. But I would caution them and ask them to remember the families of these victims."

And The Ninja is certainly no hero to local law enforcement.

"Much as we might wish otherwise, there is no place for vigilante justice," said Cleveland Police Chief James DiSanto. "We might be frustrated with crime, or with the justice system, but we do have police and laws in place to deal with criminals. Citizens need to let us do our job. Helping us do even better."

DiSanto cautioned the public not to start considering The Ninja a folk hero.

"This guy is not Robin Hood," he said. "We are dealing with a murderer, pure and simple, regardless of what nickname somebody gave him. NOSCU and CPD are doing everything we can to get him in custody."

NOSCU and the police department are not without their critics, however. Some community activists have openly questioned whether the special task force has really been maximizing its efforts to catch the killer.

Rev. Clinton Thomas, widely considered the foremost leader of Cleveland's African American community, said he feels the attacks are racially motivated, despite what NOSCU has said.

"All the police see is another dead Black boy," Thomas said. "I see five lives, troubled perhaps, but still full of promise. Most of these victims had no family, so we, as a community, will grieve for them.

"The police don't want to call these murders crimes of hate, but I do. It is easier for them to turn a blind eye to the plight of our community, just as they have for the last four hundred years."

Thomas said that the activation of the serial crimes unit was a step in the right direction, but it was a step that took far too long.

"Where was the special task force when the first boy was murdered?" he said. "Or the second? How many children must die before our leaders take notice?"

Det. Sgt. Jack Brickman, NOSCU's lead investigator, was unavailable for comment.

CHAPTER 26

From *The North Coast Press*

Page E-1

By Mike Pendleton

I've been writing a column in this town for a long time. I'd be lying if I said I've seen everything, but I thought I had come pretty close.

Like most of you, I've been following "The Ninja" investigation since the beginning. I know it's real life and not just a story in the paper, but I have to admit, I'm hooked.

The story's got it all - gruesome murders, disreputable victims, dedicated cops, and a mysterious, skillful villain lurking in the shadows. The radio thrillers of my parents' day couldn't do it any better.

But what I really think has struck a chord with the people of the North Coast is that The Ninja, (I'll call him that even though the police don't want us to), has done what the courts and the police and the federal government have never been able to do - he's put fear into the hearts of criminals and hope into the hearts of decent people.

Somewhere along the line, vigilante has become a bad word. I wonder why that is? I've been thinking about the days when even Ohio was considered the frontier. When the bad guys came rolling into town, the townspeople didn't wait for the magistrate or the sheriff or the marshal to take care of business. They formed up a posse and handled it themselves. Later, as we became "civilized," that changed. We hired police and sheriffs and asked them to handle the problem for us. And then we cut them off at the knees with lawsuits when they try to do their jobs. That's one reason crime is flourishing.

I think the cops do a pretty good job. But not everybody thinks that. A lot of people are frustrated. It was just a matter of time before somebody decided to take matters into their own hands. Frankly, I'm surprised it took this long.

Now, I know you're sitting there with your morning coffee, reading this, and saying "Gee, Mike, how can you say that? Are you really glad people are being killed?" Glad is probably not the right word. I'm not sad about it, I can tell you that. Especially since The Ninja is getting results.

I was talking to a cop I know – we can call him Officer Bill. Bill confided in me that they've seen a huge decline in street level dealing since The Ninja story broke. He says they're like little kids, looking over their shoulders and checking under the bed for the bogeyman. Except this bogeyman has a sharp sword and is not a figment of the imagination. Officer Bill says he's not implying that the dealers are gone – they're just scared.

Pleasant turn of events, isn't it?

Cliff O'Brien read and reread the column. He was not happy. He folded the copy of the paper up and walked over to Leo Nelson's office. Leo was editing something on his computer screen. He looked up as Cliff entered.

"Don't you knock?" he asked.

"Yeah," Cliff said, rapping his knuckles on the doorframe. He held up the paper with the column facing his editor. "What's this all about?"

Nelson barely glanced at the copy.

"Looks like a column by Mike Pendleton," he said. "What's the problem?"

"Damn it, Leo, he's practically nominating The Ninja for sainthood," Cliff said. "You know the cops are trying to downplay the vigilante angle. They really think it could hurt the investigation if people start treating this guy like a folk hero."

"Is that per your buddy Jack?" Leo said. "You know, you are supposed to be objective."

"Supposed to be?" Cliff asked. "You know damn well I'm as objective as anybody else. And my work proves it. But Leo, come on, you know how vital my sources are. Some of them are a little sensitive. Do you think they're going to want to talk to me if they think we're propping up a murder suspect as the best thing since Robin Hood?"

"Hey, Cliff, it's your job to schmooze your sources, not Pendleton's," Leo said. "I see your point, and I guess I agree. But nobody tells Pendleton what to write. He's the 800-pound gorilla of this town and we were lucky to sign him. Plus, it's an opinion piece. He's got the right to express his, even if you and your cops don't like it."

"OK, Leo, OK," Cliff said. "But you better remember something. The Black community is getting up a full head of steam about The Ninja murders. How many readers do you think Pendleton's piece is going to cost us?"

Nelson shrugged.

"I don't know, Cliff" he said. "And those aren't my concerns. I just make sure we get the facts straight and the names spelled right."

"Don't you think that's a little short-sighted, Leo?"

"Maybe," he said. "But it keeps me busy. Just do the best you can, Cliff. Your Ninja stories are playing well upstairs. If Pendleton's columns start to hamstring you, maybe we can have a sit-down with him later."

"OK," Cliff said, a little placated. "I just hope my sources will keep talking to me."

CHAPTER 27

One of the reasons that Jack Brickman was unavailable for comment was that, after a frustrating delay, the crime lab had finally matched up DNA samples from the Painesville and Elyria crime scenes. The conclusive connection had been delivered to NOSCU on Tuesday by the lab's director, who had apologized repeatedly about the delay. They had had a lot of samples to examine, he said, and it had taken longer than they had expected.

Regardless, they had already conclusively determined that the *shuko* used at the Dawkins and Rice crime scenes had been identical in shape, size, and material as those used at the Clayton murder in Shaker Heights. They had managed to retrieve several samples of miniscule metal scrapings from all three crime scenes. Once they had the *shuko*, it would be a simple matter to demonstrate that the scrapings had come from them exclusively.

The news was a considerable morale booster for the team since it tied all five crimes together and put them all on the same page. Jack knew that Ed Payne and Andy Fulmer had been working their parts of the case almost as separate crimes. The definite connection brought them much closer to the rest of the team.

Unfortunately, outside of re-energizing the team, the new evidence really had little effect on the course of the investigation. The core of NOSCU had been operating under the assumption that all five murders were connected from the beginning, so all it meant to them was that they had gotten at least one thing right so far.

Stoddard decided against holding another press conference, and instead decided to issue a press release. NOSCU braced for another onslaught of "helpful" tips.

Some of the team were sitting around the office, sifting through files, and taking phone calls. Jack and Ken Bright had just finished fine-tuning the press release. It could be a painstaking process since they had to inform the public without tipping their hand to the killer. Luckily, Bright had been keeping an updated file of press releases on his computer. As new information came in, he just added it to the mix. Bright was probably the fastest typist on the team and had a great command of the English language, so he could generate printable pieces at an amazing rate. Jack was thankful for that since it freed up his time considerably.

Not that he had much to do at the moment. They had gone over the victim profiles again and again with few results. Yes, there were plenty of surface similarities. All of the victims had criminal records, all were Black, all were males and all were in approximately the same age group. But the similarities had stopped there. NOSCU had gone over everything, from prison to school records. They had even subpoenaed the sealed juvenile records of the victims looking for links. Every time they thought they had the connection, they would find an anomaly, something that didn't fit the pattern. It was frustrating.

Jack found himself sitting in his office staring idly at a shelf that had become a weird menagerie of ninja action figures. Somebody had started bringing them in and putting them on his desk. Jack thought it was funny and carved out a niche on a bookshelf for them . He wasn't sure why he thought they were funny. Maybe it was because they pissed off Stoddard.

Despite the encouraging news about the DNA evidence, Jack was a little burnt out. He missed working the street, getting his shoes dirty and asking questions. He thought he was probably doing a good job leading the investigation and managing the team, but he felt a little isolated spending most of his time at the office. He put his feet down and wandered out into the bullpen to see what was going on.

Bryce Cramer, Terri Rome, Sam Rausch, and Al Sladky were sitting around, talking about something in the newspaper.

"Look, I ain't saying he's right, I'm just sayin' I can see how people might agree with him," Al Sladky said.

"Who?" Jack asked.

"Mike Pendleton," Cramer said. "Did you see his column today?"

"Yeah," Jack said. "I read him every day."

"So, what did you think?"

Jack shrugged.

"Al's probably right," he said. "Most people only know what they see on TV or read in the papers. They think the drug dealers are running the streets. We know better, but how are you going to explain that to a housewife from the suburbs? Their perception might be that The Ninja is doing a better job than we are."

"He's sure rackin' up an impressive body count," Sladky said.

"Sure he is, Al," Cramer said. "But do you think people would be cheering him on if the murders were happening in Gates Mills or Parma? Or Slavic Village?"

"Do you think we're sandbagging because the victims are Black, Bryce?" Al asked, clearly offended.

"I know we're not, Al," he said. "I'm here every day too, remember. I'm just saying that nobody is completely color blind, as much as we try to be."

"Like it or not, race is always going to be an issue," Terri Rome said. "At least to somebody."

"I don't know," Sladky said. "I only see blue and those who are not."

"I think everybody's got a good point," said Sam Rausch, the consummate peacemaker. "I don't know how much of it is racial, but I can see how cops might identify with The Ninja, too. He's getting away with something a lot of us have probably wished we could have done at one time or another."

"You think that feeling will last?" Jack asked.

"Until some cop or some civilian gets in his way, yeah, I do."

The discussion would have continued except that Calvin Stoddard wandered into the bullpen and asked Jack into his office. It took the better part of an hour for him to convince the attorney that bull sessions were an important part of the investigation and not necessarily a waste of time. Jack didn't like being lectured, but since he had little else to do, he just sat there and took it. His mind wandered a little, and he found himself half hoping The Ninja would hit again. At least that would get him out of the office for a while.

CHAPTER 28

It was July before The Ninja stuck again.

Based on the short time span between the Timmons and Lane murders, Jack would have bet money that the killer would have accelerated his pace rather than slowed it down. The violent behavior of serial killers usually snowballed into killing sprees as their lust for mayhem increased. In a way, it was almost as if they were addicted to the killing the way an alcoholic or drug abuser was. Eventually, one kill just wasn't enough to get satisfaction. Ted Bundy, one of the most notorious serial killers in American history had finally exploded and murdered four co-eds in one night at their Florida sorority house. Those killings had earned him the death penalty.

The Ninja's restraint was impressive. His lack of activity had universally brought NOSCU to the realization that their quarry was even more dangerous than they had initially thought. The Ninja was patient and cautious. That patience made him far less likely to make a mistake. Jack and Ken Bright both thought it was possible that the publicity about NOSCU had made The Ninja even more careful. Al Sladky had disagreed.

"What, you think this guy is sitting around, reading your press clippings?" he had chided them.

Whatever the killer's agenda, he seemed more than happy to keep it and his schedule to himself. In the weeks before his sixth kill, NOSCU had examined and re-examined every scrap of information they had on the case. Even Jack was sick and tired of looking at the same files over and over again.

The media, however, did not seem to share his frustration. Most of the TV stations and local newspapers had kept up a steady barrage of commentary, stories, and pseudo-stories about The Ninja and NOSCU's apparent inability to track him down. The public, for the most part, remained divided over whether The Ninja was a good guy or a bad guy. Still, for all the buzz the story had generated, the media blitz had finally started to wane when The Ninja hit again.

Jack was in his office at home, balancing his checkbook and going through his E-mail while Karen was curled up on a recliner in the same room, plowing through her summer reading, shooing away Smalls who seemed to think that a paperback was a great place to stand. Jack's cell phone rang just before 11 p.m. It was Natalie Price who had volunteered to work the weekend shift at the NOSCU office.

"Jack?" she said. "This is Natalie, from the office. There was another murder. They think it's The Ninja."

"When and where?"

"I just received the call," she said. "Sounds like CPD was on scene about twenty minutes ago. It's over by Denison."

Jack scribbled down the address.

"Get the team moving," he said. "I'll be leaving from home."

"Do you want the Lorain and Lake teams, too?" she asked.

"Yeah," he said "Send everybody, but start with Vidalia and Moore. I want them moving right away. Leave two people on the phones. Let their relief sleep in. We're going to need them fresh. And make sure you call Stoddard, let him know what's going on."

"OK"

Karen had already marked her place in the book and put it down.

"You going out?" she asked.

"Yeah," Jack replied. "Looks like our guy hit again."

"I'll make some coffee," Karen said. "You'll probably need it."

Jack hurried upstairs to change . He considered running a razor over his face, but decided not to waste the time. He did slip out of his worn out blue jeans and put on a pair of khakis and a polo shirt. By the time he strapped his sidearm onto his belt, Karen had already brewed the coffee and poured it into a travel mug. She also handed him a recycled plastic grocery bag he would later find out held a couple of Clif bars and a roast beef sandwich. They hugged and kissed at the door.

"Be careful," she said. "Call before you come home, OK?"

"I will," Jack said. "Make sure you lock up."

Brickman was eager to get to the crime scene and he had to force himself to exercise caution backing out of their narrow driveway. More than one side mirror had fallen victim to a rapid egress since Jack had bought the home. Once on the road, Jack drove as fast as he could without taking stupid chances. He had a red dashboard light he could have plugged into the cigarette lighter, but his car had no siren. He did not like his chances without one even at this time of night. And if he got into an accident, he wasn't going to be able to help anybody for a while.

As he headed to the crime scene, he sipped the coffee, more out of habit than out of need for caffeine. Jack's blood was pumping enough already. Still, the stimulant would help him stay alert when the adrenaline jolt was gone. He was pleased to note that Karen had guessed right and not added sugar to the brew. The bitter taste, for some reason, helped him focus.

Try as he might, the detective could not fight the urge to start forming mental images about the crime scene he was heading towards. Theoretically, he should be going into this with no preconceived ideas. Being intimately familiar with The Ninja, however, made that nearly impossible. There was always the possibility that this was going to be a false alarm, but Jack doubted that. The city's homicide detectives had been thoroughly briefed on the victim profiles and the Ninja's methods. The orders had come down from the highest levels of command – "When in doubt, call NOSCU out."

There were other concerns, of course. Since the story had hit the papers, Jack had been painfully aware that The Ninja murders could spark one or more copycat killings. They had been careful enough, or so he thought, in shielding the details from the press that copycat killing would be quickly identified.

This latest killing, Jack hoped, would let NOSCU start fresh, with the best forensic experts and detectives the North Coast had to offer. With a little luck, they might be on the verge of a breakthrough. That such a breakthrough might come at the expense of somebody's life was not lost on Jack. He intended to make the most of it.

Jack pulled his car right up to the perimeter of the crime scene. It looked remarkably similar to the Empire Avenue crime scene where Kamelle Lane had died. It had the same rundown houses with the same, small, neglected lawns. A casual glance up and down the street told Jack that several houses had obviously been condemned or boarded up as nuisances. Most of the streetlights, he noticed, were either burned out or smashed out.

Jack got out of his car and opened the trunk. He pulled out a blue windbreaker with "Police" emblazoned in reflective letters across the back and over one breast. The windbreakers had been supplied by NOSCU. Initially, Jack had wanted them to say "NOSCU," but he had decided against it. It might boost team spirit, but it was likely to ruffle some feathers with the street cops. Plus, the news media would know they were on scene soon enough. There was no reason to advertise the fact.

A small crowd had started forming around the crime scene. Stragglers seemed to be drifting in from throughout the neighborhood. Kids zipped by on their bikes, obviously going to tell their friends about the entertainment. Judging by their clothes, demeanor and bad teeth, Jack assumed the onlookers were on the low end of the earning curve. They were also exclusively white.

"I hope they didn't drag me out here for nothing," Jack thought.

Brickman identified himself to a cop working the perimeter tape.

"What can I do to help, sergeant?" the cop asked. He looked like he had been around a while.

"First, move the perimeter back another fifty feet," Jack said. The rest of my team is on its way, and they know what to do. Just make sure everybody gets signed in and out, and for God's sake, keep the media out."

The cop smiled.

"With pleasure," he said. "The DB boys are over there."

Jack surveyed the area as he headed over to where the plainclothes men were gathered. The body appeared to be at the edge of a vacant lot, sandwiched between two alleys. It was overgrown and strewn with garbage and rubble. At one time, there may have been a house standing there, though there was no evidence of a basement. It had either been on a slab or the lot had simply become a dumping ground for construction debris and neighborhood junk. The house closest to the body appeared to have been abandoned and boarded up. From what Jack could see, the alleys that bordered the lot actually cut through to the next cross streets.

"Hey, Joe, long time no see," he said. "What's new?"

"Different day, same shit," the detective said. "Cept for this mess, of course." He motioned to another detective. "This is my partner, Carl Beech." Jack and Carl shook hands.

Joe Palmer had started in the department at about the same time as Jack. They had worked together a couple times when they were both still in uniform. Palmer had become a detective just after Brickman, but hadn't done very well on the promotional exams. The last time they had talked, Palmer had been looking forward to the next test.

"What do you have?" Brickman asked.

"We have a deceased white male, 23 YOA, name of Robert Dupree," Palmer said, reading off his notebook.

"White male?" Jack asked, surprised.

"Yeah, white male. Take a look yourself," Palmer said, nodding toward where the body was slumped face-first on the ground about ten feet away.

"No thanks," Brickman said.

Palmer raised an eyebrow.

"You getting squeamish, Jack?" he asked. Beech had a grin on his face, too.

"No," Jack said. "I want my forensics people to get this scene as fresh as possible. I've got Therese Vidalia and Heath Moore on the way right now."

"So that's where they went," Beech said. "I've been wondering about that."

"Who's been in contact with the body?" Brickman asked.

"The first guy on scene checked for vitals, I think, and I got his wallet out," Palmer said. "That's how we made the ID. Plus I did a quick wound check. That's why we called you in."

"How'd he die?"

"Well, near as we can tell, looks like somebody wrapped a chain around his neck and dragged him over there and strangled him with it," Beech said.

"A chain?" Jack asked, already starting to wonder if he had called in the troops too soon.

"Yeah," Palmer said. "He's got a tank top on, so you can see the link marks real clear. Plus, there's the pepper."

"Pepper?"

"The blue suit noticed the smell first, couldn't quite put his finger on it at first," Palmer explained. "When his nose started running and his eyes started watering, he figured it out."

"Did somebody hit him with OC to set him up?"

Palmer shrugged.

"It's possible, I guess," he said. "But this isn't spray. It's like a really fine powder. Whatever it is, it burns like hell. The cop, Sturgis, must have got some on his hands and touched his face. He's over there with a Sudecon, trying to clean up." Sudecon was a chemically impregnated towelette that was supposed to neutralize the effects of pepper spray. Sometimes it helped.

"So, you think this is one of yours?" Palmer asked.

"I don't know," Brickman said. "It doesn't fit exactly."

"The teletypes say we're supposed to be on the lookout for anything out of the ordinary, especially if it deals with clean hits on street level dealers," Palmer said. "I know this guy ain't Black, but it sure seems out of the ordinary to me. Not, of course, that any part of this job is ordinary."

Jack nodded.

"Well, Joe, we're sure going to respect your hunch," he said. "Even if it isn't our guy, we'll take it from here."

"I'd thought we'd hang out a while, if that's OK with you," Palmer said.

"Sure," Jack said.

Just then, Vidalia and Moore pulled up in the forensics van. They looked ready to go.

The rest of the team started trickling in as Jack debriefed the technicians. They immediately got samples of hair from the detectives and the uniformed cop who had gotten to the scene first. They also measured and photographed the officers' feet and made them stand on a piece of material that looked like aluminum foil. Somehow, when hooked up to an electrical source the material gave them exact duplicate of the sole of their shoes. Jack knew they were creating elimination sets that would allow them to dismiss certain hairs and prints as soon as they were developed.

Therese had been particularly thorough when questioned Sturgis.

"When you checked for a pulse, did you have rubber gloves on?" she asked. "I don't care if you didn't, even though you should wear them, but I need to know now. I don't want to waste time processing your fingerprints."

"I wore them," the cop said, his eyes still watering . "I put 'em on even before we pulled up. The call we got was for a man down, possible DOA. I always glove up right away. I don't want to catch anything."

"Good for you," Vidalia said. "How about your partner?"

"He stayed with the car, called it in," Sturgis said.

"Do you remember where you walked, officer?"

"Yeah, I can show you, if you want," Sturgis said.

"Just point it out."

After they had gotten what they wanted from the police, Vidalia and Moore started the agonizingly slow crime scene analysis. They worked from the outside in, first photographing the scene from as many angles as possible, then scouring every inch of the ground surrounding the body, measuring, and gathering as they went. They were always careful, of course, but tonight they seemed even more meticulous than ever. The importance of their work was never more obvious.

Stan Lombardo, Al Sladky, Terri Rome, and Bryce Cramer arrived in short order. Jack put them to work immediately canvassing the crowd of onlookers. Everybody wanted to talk, but nobody had actually seen or heard anything. The investigators did their best to separate potential witnesses from the rest of the crowd and question them quietly. Considering the growing excitement of the crowd, they did an excellent job. They had made great progress by the time the furthest team members had arrived on scene. The latecomers started the tedious task of knocking on doors.

Jack had focused on getting more information about the victim, Robert Dupree, from the cops on the scene. What he found out certainly fit The Ninja's taste in victims, all except for Dupree's race of course. Dupree, according to the local boys, had been a street level dealer. Like all the other victims, Dupree too had done time as an adult and a juvenile. The most serious offense was eighteen months for aggravated assault.

From what the detectives were able to tell Jack, the latest victim lived alone in a crappy third-floor studio apartment above a duplex. They knew that because Palmer himself had served a warrant for probation violation at the address. As far as anybody knew, Dupree had no relatives in the area, and no close ties with his neighbors.

Brickman quickly tired of watching the technicians work. He dutifully jotted down the limited information Palmer and Beech could offer. Jack left the two detectives to keep an eye on things and latched on to Al Sladky.

"You want to go knock on some doors?" Jack asked.

"For old times' sake? Sure, why not?" Sladky replied.

The rest of NOSCU had fanned out along the street, knocking on every door they could and carefully recording addresses where nobody was home, or at least where nobody answered. The number of security bars on front doors and peepholes in interior doors told them all plenty about what kind of neighborhood this was. It was common to knock on a door and have to convince the residents they were cops, even badges and ID's didn't always do the job. When the door did open, they were usually met with a combination of ignorance, apathy, and animosity. Once in a while, though, you came across somebody who, despite their own shortcomings, seemed to actually care.

One such person was Aggie Marsters, a single mother of two who lived diagonally across the street from the crime scene.

Marsters and her kids lived on the second floor of a duplex that had been converted from a single-family home. It was not as bad as some homes Jack had been in during his career, but it was depressing, nonetheless. The wallpaper in the hallway was peeling, apparently from some old water damage, and the carpet was worn down past the padding in some places. There were no cockroaches in sight, which Brickman thought was a good sign. He had been in places so infested that he had tucked his pants into the tops of his shoes. In places like that, you had to be careful not to brush up against the walls and you sure as hell didn't sit down.

Aggie Marsters was probably in her late twenties, but she looked at least ten years older. A cigarette hung out of her mouth. She had on a waitress' uniform, so she had either just gotten off work or she had just been too tired to take the polyester outfit off. And she did look tired. Jack was suddenly reminded of Jameel Timmons' mother. Marsters had the same hard-working, disillusioned aura about her.

Jack and Al identified themselves and asked her the obvious questions. Her answers was surprising in its earnestness.

"Dupree?" she said. "Yeah, I know who that son of a bitch is. Always out in the lot dealing that shit. Used to throw my boys a buck or two from time to time, for pop or whatever. They thought he was cool, but I know what he was up to. Just trying to get them working , if you know what I mean. I told him if he ever talked to them again, I'd string him up by the balls. He'd just call me a bitch when I walked by, but he got the picture. Thank God the kids figured out what an asshole he is."

"I guess somebody shared your opinion," Sladky said. "Mr. Dupree was murdered tonight."

"No shit?" Marsters said. "Right across the street? There goes the neighborhood, I guess, but good fucking riddance if you ask me."

It always bothered Jack when parents used bad language in front of their kids, and judging by the sporadic laughter from inside the apartment, the kids were still awake. Over Aggie's shoulder, he could see the corner of what appeared to be a fairly large television set. It amazed the detective that regardless of income, the poor always seemed to find a way to get a big screen TV. Somehow, that had become a necessity.

"Did you happen to see anything?" Jack asked.

"Nah," she said. "I sacked out right after work. Long day, you know."

Judging by the smell of alcohol on her breath, she had had a little help "sacking out."

"Did you see Dupree outside when you got home?"

"Yeah," she said. "I just got off the bus, and asshole was out there. Gave me the usual greeting and went back to doing whatever it is he does. That was probably about nine."

"How old are your kids?" Al asked.

"Twelve and nine," she said. "Both boys."

"Do you think they saw anything? You got a pretty good view of the murder scene, I suppose."

"Them two? Hell, I couldn't pry 'em away from the TV before," she said, "I sure couldn't do it now."

"Why?" Jack asked. "Something good on?"

"Probably not," she said. "But it don't matter. We been gettin' free HBO and Cinemax for a week now. Figure it's some kind of promotion or something, but they haven't budged since they found out."

Jack produced a business card and handed it to Marsters.

"If you think of anything that could help us out, maybe a new face in the neighborhood or something, give me a call."

"Sure," Marsters said. "I guess the guy who killed Dupree should go to jail, but for my money, you'd be better off givin' him a medal."

Jack gave the woman a neutral nod. Sladky was a little less reserved. He smiled before they turned and walked down the street.

"Do you ever get sick of never having a witness?" Brickman asked the older detective when they were outside.

"After all these years?" Al replied. "Hell, I'm used to it. I assume we're *not* going to have a witness. It makes for a lot fewer disappointments in life."

As they started to head to the next house, Jack noticed Sam Rausch had arrived on scene. He was glad to have him there, though he wasn't sure how much help the SWAT commander would be. He seemed to have good intuition, but going door to door was a little out of his area of expertise. Brickman found himself wondering if he shouldn't have had Natalie let Sam sleep in instead of calling him to the scene. Well, it certainly wasn't the first time the lieutenant had been called out in the middle of the night and it was just as certainly wouldn't be the last time, either.

"You mind taking the next one by yourself, Al?" Jack asked his partner. "I want to talk to Sam a minute."

"I think I can handle it, junior."

Sam Rausch was talking to Palmer and Beech when Jack walked up.

"Morning, Sam," he said. "Glad you made it."

"Sorry it took so long," Rausch said. "We hit a meth dealer on Clifton earlier tonight, and we were still cleaning it up when the call came in."

"I thought you were letting your sergeants run the show while you're with us."

"I am, I am," Rausch said. "We got word that these guys were well-armed and fanatics, so I wanted to be there, just in case. Plus, we heard there was a lot of cash and drugs at the house and it was moving fast. That's why we hit them so early."

Jack nodded. The SWAT team generally liked to hit drug houses and dealers between three and six in the morning, when the suspects' reactions would be at their slowest.

"Well?" he asked.

Rausch smiled, a wicked little grin.

"For once, the informant was right," he said. "We got over $30,000 in cash and a cartload of drugs. Plus, the main man himself. There was no lab there, thank God, but the narcs are sweating him for the location now."

Jack nodded in the direction of the deceased.

"Any thoughts, Sam?" he asked.

"From what these guys are telling me, I'd guess it was our guy," Rausch said. "The MO sure fits, although this guy was obviously white."

"What about the cause of death? Strangulation seems a little sloppy compared to the kind of work we've seen so far."

"If we're working under the assumption that The Ninja thinks of himself as a *ninja*, then the method itself really doesn't matter," Sam said. "In fact, his ability to change tactics like this makes it pretty obvious to me that he wants to be seen as a master assassin. Remember, historically the *ninja* could use a wide variety of weapons, usually manufactured just for them but often improvised on the spot."

"Any idea on the weapon here?"

Rausch shrugged.

"Take your pick," he said. "It's like I said in the beginning – chains and flexible weapons were favorites for these guys. It's probably just a version of the *manriki* he used to Empire."

"What about the pepper?" Jack asked. "These guys are saying Dupree's face is full of something ground very fine and very hot. Does that fit?"

"Sure," Rausch said. "Everybody, us cops included, think that pepper spray was a modern invention. I know the first time somebody threw it all together in its current form was in 1976 or thereabouts. But there are written records of pepper being used in warfare thousands of years ago. I know the Chinese used to make grenades made out of burning leaves wrapped around pepper. Mainly, it was to irritate the enemy, not necessarily incapacitate them. Any edge you can get, I suppose."

Detective Palmer looked at Sam, then Jack, with raised eyebrows.

"Does he always talk like this?" he asked. "He sounds like a college professor."

Rausch laughed.

"Sorry for the long version," he said. "It's not often I get to discuss relevant history in the line of duty. Usually, I just bore my students and my kids."

"So how about the *ninjas*?" Jack asked, getting the lieutenant back on track.

"Did they use this kind of stuff? Yeah, they did," he said. "In fact they used that kind of stuff a lot, from smoke bombs to stink bombs. It falls under the art of invisibility tactics. They liked good distraction techniques. I'm just wondering how The Ninja scored a direct hit with whatever it is he used."

"How so?" Detective Beech asked.

"Well, somehow he had to get the pepper on – what's his name, Dupree? – on Dupree's face. They're saying there was quite a bit of it on the victim. How did it get there? When we use OC, it's in a liquid base with some kind of propellant. It's easy to spray it say ten, twelve feet. There was no liquid residue, which you would find with a commercial product. That means it was delivered dry. And to do that, you'd have to be damn close."

"Any ideas?" Jack asked.

"A few," Rausch said, "In the old days, they'd just put it in the end of a bamboo tube and blow it at their target. I'd think walking up on a street dealer with something like that in your hands would tend to put him on the edge."

"So, whatever he used, he got close enough to use it." Jack said, restating the obvious.

"Right," Rausch said. "Don't sound so surprised Jack. It's not like this guy is creeping around in public wearing a complete *ninja* outfit from cowl to *tabi* boots. He's going to do whatever he can to blend in, especially now since we're on to him. And if we're on to him, you know darn well the dealers are, too. Druggies may not be smart, but they're cunning. Most of them have very good survival instincts."

Jack was about to comment when Heath Moore walked over to them. In his hands he held a clear plastic evidence bag. He handed it to the detective.

"Thought you might want a look at this," Moore said. "Found it under the victim."

Jack held the baggie up to the light. Inside the bag was a twenty-dollar bill, half folded onto some weird shape. He borrowed a flashlight from Palmer and examined the item more closely. He could see a very fine powder on the surface of the greenback.

"What's on it, Heath?" Brickman asked as he handed the packet to Sam Rausch. Palmer and Beech craned their necks to get a better look.

"Without the lab work, I can't be sure," Moore replied.

"Care to guess?"

"Sure," the technician replied. "It looks a lot like the same stuff that's all over the victim's face."

"Pepper?"

"I think so," Moore said.

"It probably is, Jack," Rausch said. "I'd bet the farm on it."

"Why you so sure?" Palmer asked.

"It's origami," Rausch said.

"Why you so sure?" Palmer asked.

"It's origami," Rausch said. "I'm no expert, but I've seen enough stuff to know what it looks like. My kids like to mess around with it sometimes when they're bored."

"So?" Jack asked.

"Look at how this is folded," Rausch said. "If we opened it all the way, my bet is it would look like a tube. Look, let's say The Ninja walks up to Dupree to make a buy, or at least that's what he wants Dupree to think. No dealer is going to give up the drugs without seeing the cash first. Dupree probably asks to see the cash and The Ninja shows him the twenty, all folded up. When Dupree leans in for a closer look, roof, The Ninja blows all this powder into Dupree's face and follows up with the *manriki*."

As Rausch explained his theory, he illustrated it with his hands. In his mind, Brickman could clearly picture the murder. The theory made sense. He was reasonably sure the forensic evidence would confirm it.

"How about the cause of death?" Beech asked. "Strangled?"

Moore shook his head.

"No," he said. "It looked that way at first, but when we moved him, you could tell right away his neck was broken. Can't be sure yet, though. For all we know, that was postmortem. I don't think so, but Doc Herlong is going to have to make the call."

"You guys call him yet?" Jack asked. "I know he wanted to be notified right away."

Moore shook his head.

"We're going to be a couple more hours here at least," he said. "By the time we get this guy loaded up and carted back to the morgue, it'll probably be close to the time Doc Herlong gets up anyways. He's an early riser, but we figured we'd let him get a full night's sleep and call him when we're through."

"Anything we can do to help?" Brickman asked.

"Just keep the crime scene secure and the civilians out of our hair and we should be fine," Moore said, heading back to where Therese Vidalia still worked. Jack wondered what else they would turn up at the crime scene.

As Jack watched the technicians work, he noticed a couple TV news vans on the perimeter of the crime scene. There were no reporters on them, just the camera operators. Apparently, they didn't like to send out the on-air talent for something as mundane as a single homicide. Jack wondered if that attitude would be different if they knew this was a Ninja murder. He imagined they would have been swamped with media if they had known. Somebody was doing a good job keeping it quiet.

Slowly, the team started drifting in from the canvass. The looks on their faces told Jack the whole story. They had struck out again.

"It's like all the rest," Bryce Cramer said. "Nobody saw a thing; nobody heard a thing."

"Does anybody ever see anything?" Terri Rome asked rhetorically. "Look at all these people standing around. You'd figure somebody was outside on a night like this. Most of them don't have air conditioners. Usually that means a lot of people on the front porch, trying to catch a breeze."

Jack agreed. Even this early in the morning, the night air was hot. He looked around at the dwindling crowd. They looked sweaty and bored now, ready to call it quits for the night. Judging by the attitude of this team, they were about done, too.

As they checked in with him, Jack sent them back to the office to type up their notes and try to piece together what had happened. He called Natalie Price and asked her to post a notice for a 10 a.m. meeting Tuesday. By then, he hoped to have Doc Herlong's findings as well as the photos and sketches from Vidalia and Moore. With a little luck, maybe they'd catch a break this time.

Jack was on his way back to the office when he suddenly realized that Calvin Stoddard had never shown up at the crime scene.

"I wonder what that means?" he thought as he pulled into the parking garage.

CHAPTER 29

From *The North Coast Press*

Page A-1

July 9

By Cliff O'Brien

CLEVELAND — The elusive serial killer police have dubbed "The Ninja" struck for the sixth time on Saturday.

The latest victim, identified by police as Robert Dupree, 23, of Cleveland, was killed late Saturday night in the area of Denison Avenue. Police would not elaborate on the cause of death, deferring questions to the Cuyahoga County Coroner's office.

According to witnesses at the scene, Dupree did not appear to have been the victim of a stabbing. The last three victims of "The Ninja" died due to stab wounds. In another departure from his pattern, Dupree was white.

Despite these differences, sources close to the investigation confirmed that the Northern Ohio Serial Crimes Unit was activated Saturday night and have evidence linking Dupree's murder to the other crimes. The source would not specify what clues led NOSCU to make the connection to "The Ninja" on the fear that such details might jeopardize the investigation.

Residents of the area said the police practically invaded their neighborhood after Cleveland detectives arrived on scene.

"There were, like, a couple of couples standing around when my kid came up and told me what was going on," said Vince Pallagis, who lives near the crime scene. "Then it went nuts. Cops started showing up one after another for like an hour. I think they knocked on every door on the street at least twice. I wish they paid that much attention to us all the time. Maybe stuff like this wouldn't happen if they did."

NOSCU's lead investigator, CPD Det. Sgt. Jack Brickman on Sunday confirmed that NOSCU had been called to the scene and that they had taken over Dupree's murder as part of "The Ninja's" killing spree.

"I give a lot of credit to the first detectives on the scene," Brickman said. "If they had been less alert, they might have missed the clues that linked this murder to our suspect."

When asked about the changes in "The Ninja's" pattern, Brickman would not speculate on what caused the apparent shift.

"That type of information is at the heart of the investigation," he said. "It wouldn't be responsible for me to float theories in the press until we've had time to sort out exactly what happened.

Brickman deferred further questions until a press conference could be held later this week.

Rev. Clinton Thomas said he was not sure if the murder of a white man lessened his concerns for people of color in the Cleveland area.

"So now this so-called ninja killed a white man," Thomas said. "Does that change anything? And how do we really know if this poor victim was killed by the same person? All we know is what the police and their special unit tell us. Who is policing the police?"

Thomas did concede that it was possible that race hadn't been the motive for the previous murders. But he said he still felt that the police shouldn't just ignore the issue.

"I may not be a cop," he said. "But I know as well as anybody the injustices delivered upon the heads of proud Black men and women in this country even in so-called modern times. We're still the oppressed, whether it's by racists or criminals."

CHAPTER 30

From *The North Coast Press*

Page E-1

July 10

By Mike Pendleton

How do you score a game with three teams in it? In Cleveland, I guess it should look something like this: Ninja 6, Bad Guys 0, Cops 0.

Yes, if you've been following The Ninja case, you know that the killer/vigilante has struck for the sixth time. (I added the "/" myself. I think the people of this city should have a choice in this matter, despite what the police would have us believe.)

The latest victim was a guy named Robert Dupree. The cops say he was kind of a jack of all trades in the low end of the crime business. Theft, assaults, drugs – Dupree was an equal opportunity low-life who finally managed to get himself eliminated from the food chain. And the eternal question remains: So what?

Since I started putting my two cents in about The Ninja, all of my mailboxes, (voice, E, and snail), have been full. I've been keeping an informal tab on the yeas and nays on The Ninja issue, and as of my last guestimate, the yeas have it by a five-to-one margin. Almost everybody, it seems, is fed up with crime and criminals. Welcome to the party, pals.

I've always thought of myself as a law-and-order kind of guy. I don't like it when the cops get the blame for everything. Like when a bank robber is running from the police and broadsides a minivan full of kids. The cops get crucified. Why is that? The criminal was the guy who caused the problem, not the cops. Like I've said a million times in my past columns, it's because the cities that employ the cops have deep pockets and the crooks don't.

There are some people in our community who seem to think the cops are looking the other way because most of the victims of The Ninja were Black. I hope the latest killing changes that feeling. As far as I can see, The Ninja is just anti-scumbag, not anti-Black.

Anyway, I'm not afraid to throw a few stones at the cops, either. And while I think this Ninja character has the right idea, I've been wondering how he managed to pull off his sixth kill right under the noses of the people hunting him. How exactly does that happen?

They've got this team of whiz kids over at the Stokes building who are supposed to be the best investigators on the North Coast. So, what are they doing? I mean, it sounds like a great idea – throw together a bunch of good cops from different cities and turn them loose on major crime. I like to call it a think tank with guns. And it seems like a solid move on paper. So far, I'm not sure we're getting our money's worth out of NOSCU.

In NOSCU's defense, maybe I'm just spoiled. I'm a huge fan of cop shows. Heck, on some nights they catch two or three bad guys in an hour, plus they find time for back stories and occasional partial nudity. Maybe in our society of instant gratification, I just expect the same thing of NOSCU. The crime solving, I mean, not the nudity.

I've got a buddy. He's a retired FBI agent. He told me the other day that NOSCU was probably glad to get a fresh murder, especially since this is the first time they know what they're looking for. I guess only time will tell if NOSCU is up to the task.

I'm still torn though. I'd like to see the cops and NOSCU rack up a win on this one. If there is any consolation, it's that one win is all the cops need – game over. I'm just not sure how soon I want them to get in the "W" column.

Cliff O'Brien could feel his blood boiling well before he finished Pendleton's column. When he was done, he folded it up, kicked himself away from his desk and literally stomped towards the elevator. He was as mad as he ever got. Luckily, he had to wait a little while for the elevator to arrive. That gave him some time to do a little deep breathing before he started kicking the walls and knocking things over.

When the elevator door opened, he nearly toppled a reporter with an armload of files as she exited. He stabbed the button for the sixth floor, where Mike Pendleton enjoyed the rarest luxuries – his own office.

O'Brien ignored the receptionist's attempt to see if he had an appointment. He just flashed his employee ID and kept walking towards Pendleton's lair. The door was slightly ajar when he came to it. He rapped, once, sharply, on the glass and barged in. Pendleton was typing something into his computer when Cliff entered. Pendleton was a gray-haired man with broad features who looked like he escaped from a caricature gallery, leaving an empty space in the space marked "Crusty Old Journalist." He looked surprised.

"Cliff, right?" he asked, though they had met several times before. "Hey, great work on The Ninja story. I love it."

That just about did it for Cliff.

"Great work?" O'Brien said. "It's hard work, damn hard work. And this kind of bullshit makes it even harder."

Cliff tossed the paper onto Pendleton's desk. It was just the editorial section, so it didn't have the weight to do any real damage on the columnist's desktop, though it did manage to wobble a can of Coke when it hit. Cliff found himself wishing it had been Sunday, which had the heaviest paper of the week. Much more dramatic.

To his credit, Mike Pendleton did not get angry. Despite his crusty appearance, he was a quiet guy. He did his talking in newsprint.

"I call it like I see it, Cliff," he said. "That is a luxury I think I've earned."

"Dammit, Mike, that is a luxury that makes cops stop returning my phone calls," Cliff said. "I need friendly sources to keep the stories coming."

"What's the problem, Cliff? Am I that far off base?"

"Yes," O'Brien said. "I know these guys, Mike. You call NOSCU's office at eleven at night and you're likely to get Jack Brickman himself picking up the phone. Call back the next day at eight and he's in already. They want this guy, and they're doing everything they can to make it happen."

"Maybe, maybe," Pendleton said. " And maybe they're just not up to the job. I know some people feel like the FBI should be in charge, not some city detective. And I didn't really blast the cops – I just put a thought out there. It's not a thought people aren't already thinking."

Cliff mulled that over a moment. Maybe Pendleton was partially right.

"OK," Cliff said. "It makes my job tougher, but maybe you have a point. I can mend the fences, I guess, but it just seems like a waste of time. Plus, you're painting The Ninja like he's Robin Hood or something. That's not helping, either."

"Helping?" Pendleton asked. "I write a lot of columns with good human angles, O'Brien. I help out in ways you can't. But I'm a commentator, too. No offense, but you get paid to report the facts. I get paid to comment on what you report. And if I think The Ninja is somebody with the right idea and the wrong method, I'm going to say so. Without apology. You're tight with the cops, right? Don't let it cloud your thinking. If you could listen in when it's just cops talking, you'd probably hear them saying the same things I am."

Cliff started to respond and then closed his mouth.

"Damn it," he thought. *"He's probably right."*

Pendleton's relaxed manner had calmed him down considerably since he had entered the office.

"OK, Mike," he said. "I guess you get the big bucks to say what's on your mind. I'm probably wasting my breath, but could you take it easy on the cops, especially NOSCU? They're doing the best they can with what they've got."

"You're right," Pendleton said, a smug grin on his face. "You are wasting your breath. But I'll promise you this: When they do something right, I'll make sure to bang the drum."

"Fair enough," Cliff said, and turned to leave. Pendleton stopped him.

"And O'Brien?" he said. "Next time, try counting to ten. And make an appointment."

Cliff wasn't sure if he should be angry or embarrassed. He solved the dilemma by closing the door gently behind him. He was not looking forward to his next conversation with Jack Brickman.

CHAPTER 31

By Tuesday morning, Jack was eager to get the review meeting with NOSCU underway. The previous two days had not been the most pleasant.

Sunday had gone well enough. The team had drifted back to the office once they had finished at the Dupree murder scene, welcomed with fresh coffee and bagels, courtesy of Jack Brickman. It was a small thing, but it seemed to go over well with the team. Cops loved free food. Admittedly, Jack's motive had been twofold. While he was a nice guy at heart and did, in fact, care about his team's physical well-being, he was also concerned about productivity. It was around 5 a.m. when they started to clear the crime scene, and Jack knew everybody's adrenaline would start wearing off by the time they got back to the office. The food and coffee seemed to boost everyone's energy levels somewhat, and the team dove into the task of organizing and transcribing notes with purpose.

By the time they started leaving the office in twos and threes, it was close to eleven. Jack left it up to the individuals whether or not they wanted to re-canvass the crime scene later in the day once they had grabbed a few hours' sleep at home. His one caveat had been that they check in at the office to sign out on the dry erase "Big Board" Jack had requisitioned to keep track of his team. It had been noon before Jack himself had gotten home. By then, he was thoroughly exhausted.

Karen had met him at the door. He gave her a snapshot review of the latest events at the kitchen table, but his head was starting to nod as he spoke to her. Jack went upstairs, secured his pistol, and stripped off his street clothes before collapsing into bed. He had been vaguely aware of Karen tucking him in under the blankets.

Had he been awake, he would have seen the look of concern on his wife's face as she turned off the light and carefully shut the bedroom door. Karen had accepted Jack's job when she had said "I do." She knew what he was doing, especially now, was important. She did her best to support him, but lately she had been asking herself if the sacrifices her husband made were worth it, worth the extra burden they put on her and the family they hoped to have some day. She knew she was being a little selfish, but she had gotten married to Jack so she could spend her days and nights with the man she loved, not the half-dead zombie who had been shuffling in and out of the house over the past weeks. He was excited about what he was doing, that much was clear, but Karen found herself asking if there wasn't something better out there for a guy as smart as her husband.

Oblivious to his wife's growing concerns, Jack had slept like the dead for a couple of hours until he was suddenly jolted out of bed by the ringing of his cell phone, which he had left on, clipped to his belt. It rang several times before he sifted through the tangle of clothes at the side of the bed and found the device. When he answered, it was Calvin Stoddard.

"Sergeant Brickman, this is Calvin Stoddard," he said unnecessarily since Jack recognized his voice immediately.

"Uh huh," Jack mumbled, still trying to wake up.

"I understand The Ninja killed again last night," Stoddard said.

"That's right, yeah," Jack said.

"I have to say, I'm not happy."

"That makes two of us," Jack thought.

"Well, we didn't think he had just gone away, Calvin," Jack said, his head clearing. "In a way, this helps us. Gives us more information, new evidence."

"So, with all the time, money, and manpower NOSCU has used up, we still let somebody else die," Stoddard said. "That seems a high price to pay to prove your theory and your profile."

"That's not the way it is and you know it," Jack said, his voice rising. "We've got a better chance at shutting this guy down as a team that any single department, and that includes the FBI. Even Ken Bright thinks so."

"Some people think otherwise," Stoddard said. "Regardless, I am also annoyed that I was not contacted when you were. That, as I understand it, was the protocol."

"Ruffled feathers?" Jack thought. *"Give me a break."*

Brickman forced himself to calm down before answering.

"Natalie Price called you at home and paged you," the detective said. "Short of sending a car to your house, I don't know what else we could have done."

"Not that I need to answer to you, sergeant, but I had turned the ringer off on my phone to get a good night's sleep. You are not the only one working long hours. And my pager was on vibrate, so I didn't get the call until this afternoon. Next time, I expect to be notified immediately. If that means sending a car to my home, then you are to do so. Are we clear on that?"

"Crystal," Jack said.

"I will be in early tomorrow morning," Stoddard said. "I expect a full briefing."

Jack said, "OK" but the attorney never heard the response. He hung up before Brickman could get the word out. Jack would have slammed the phone done, but it was his phone. Why be pissed off and have to beg for a replacement phone from Stoddard? Jack lay in bed and tossed fitfully for a few minutes before falling back to sleep. Sometimes, he was just too tired to give a damn. He decided to start giving a damn again after he slept a little more.

When Jack did wake up, he still felt groggy. His bedside clock told him it was 5 p.m. From experience, he knew that was about all the sleep he was going to get . He wandered downstairs to find a note from Karen that she had gone to her parents' house for the day, presumably so he could sleep. He poured a glass of iced tea and headed to his first-floor office. He flipped on the TV in time to catch the Tribe polishing off the Kansas City Royals with some tenth-inning heroics. So much was going on that baseball had become an afterthought. That was a rare circumstance for Jack.

Brickman shuffled through some old papers before making the inevitable call to the office. The phone was answered by Janice, one of the other receptionists at NOSCU. Jack had either forgotten her last name or had never bothered to learn it, which was also slightly out of character.

"Hey, Janice," he said. "This is Jack. Is anybody in?"

"Yes, detective, there are several officers in the office," she replied. "Who were you looking for?"

"Al Sladky, if he's there," Jack said.

"He is," she said. "I'll put you through."

Al picked up on the second ring.

"Hey, junior, I was wondering if you were going to grace us with your presence," he said.

"I was planning on coming down after dinner," Jack said.

"Don't bother," Sladky said. "There's nothing for you to do yet."

"Really?"

"Yeah. Bryce and Terri Rome have been and gone. Trying to hit some of the addresses we missed last night. Rausch checked in. So did Fulmer and Payne. Lombardo's still out doing some interviews. He took one of the SWAT guys with him. Nobody else was around."

"Any word from Doc Herlong?" Jack asked.

"Just to let us know he had already finished the autopsy," Sladky said. "Vidalia's going to walk the full report over tomorrow morning."

"And that's it?"

"Yeah, 'less you count the phone guys," Al said. "They're going full tilt. You made the right call not bringing them in last night. Looks like they got a busy coupla days ahead. Oh, and Ken Bright called about a half hour ago. Said he just got back to town and found out. Said to call him if you need anything, otherwise he'd see ya tomorrow."

"What are you doing there then, Al?" Jack asked.

"Couldn't sleep," Sladky replied. "Just thought I'd try to keep an eye on things, talk some stuff over with some guys I know. Nothing productive, I guess."

"OK, Al," Brickman said. "I'll be home if you guys need me. I'll probably hit the rack early tonight, anyway. Thanks."

"Just lookin' out for ya, kid."

Brickman was relieved that he didn't have to head back to the office. He was glad Al was there to keep an eye on things, though. The veteran detective had been spending countless hours at the courthouse, which certainly helped the team and surely didn't hurt Al's pocketbook. Al was doing exactly what Jack had expected him to do – help the younger investigators stay on track.

Jack grabbed some leftover chicken out of the refrigerator, took it to his desk and started jotting down some notes about The Ninja. He didn't have all the information at home that he had at the office, but he worked predominantly from memory anyway. Mainly, he wrote down questions. He had those in abundance. What he was missing were the answers.

Karen came home just after seven. She had initially been happy to see him at home, but seeing him at work on the case was just too much. She had opened up the conversation with the phrase that all men loathe; "Honey, we need to talk."

For the next hour, she aired her concerns about his work. True, Jack had tried to back off a little. But that wasn't going to be enough, especially if they wanted kids. In the end, Brickman had finally convinced his wife to table her concerns about his career until after The Ninja was brought to justice. It had been a frustrating conversation for Jack, primarily because his wife had made several good points. Unfortunately, as Jack repeatedly told her, he was locked in, at least for the near future, and they were just going to have to ride it out. So, for all their talk, they didn't really resolve anything. Karen went up to bed to read, leaving Jack with his notes. The mood was noticeably tense when he finally turned in for the night.

Needless to say, by the time Monday morning rolled around, Jack was not in the best of moods. He had not slept well. He had discovered after getting married that it was almost impossible to sleep restfully when the person sharing your bed was mad at you. And he was worried about the case. Seeing The Ninja's latest hit as the lead story in both *The Plain Dealer* and *The North Coast Press* on his doorstep didn't help either.

As promised, he spoke to Stoddard as soon as he got to work. That had not gone well. Stoddard, apparently, had been getting heat from the mayor, the county commissioners and the governor's office concerning the lack of progress in the case. Jack was surprised to hear about the pressure. He had a few contacts in local and state government, and he hadn't heard a hint of complaint. More importantly, nobody had told him to cut back on expenses. He was still operating under the "blank check" mandate, and would continue to do so until told differently.

As he spoke to Jack, the detective noticed how frazzled the attorney looked. He had dark bags under his eyes and it looked like he had lost weight since they had first met. Jack hadn't noticed before, probably because he had other things to manage. The stress, real or imagined, was obviously taking a toll on Stoddard.

The true source of Stoddard's frustration, however, suddenly became clear as he lectured Jack about fiscal responsibility and leadership.

"And if you think I am going to jeopardize my future to prove your theories, then you are mistaken," he had said. "You may not care where you go from here, but I do."

By the time Jack had left his supervisor's office, all he had learned was that Stoddard had some kind of agenda. He hated making the call, but as soon as he was back in his own office, he dialed George Sellers. Sellers, of course, was curious about the progress of the case. Jack gave him a very brief version of the investigation before launching into a recap of his conversation with Stoddard. He felt a little like a snitch, but he had to cover his own ass. And he had to know exactly where he stood with the people writing the checks. If he were about to have the rug pulled out from under him, he wanted to know about it ahead of time.

Sellers listened intently before setting him straight.

"Jack, I know you wouldn't call if you weren't genuinely concerned," Sellers said. "First of all, don't worry about the team. Your stock may be a little lower today than it was last week, but the buck still stops here. I'm telling you officially – keep at it. I'll handle any flak from the bean counters."

Jack was relieved to hear his friend's support.

"As far as Stoddard goes, I've been hearing a few things lately, too," Sellers said. "Apparently, there's a federal judge's slot due to open up soon, and he's been lobbying pretty hard to get it."

"Damnit, George," Jack said. "I thought you said this guy was legit. I don't have time to worry about his career. That's exactly why NOSCU needs to be apolitical."

"Easy, Jack, easy," Sellers said. "Calvin came to me highly recommended. Plus, he's got a pretty good record. His political ambition, if you can call it that, is a recent development. Maybe he thought this was going to be a quick win onto which he could latch. If I had known, I would have found somebody else, believe me, unfortunately…"

"BOHICA," Jack said.

"I beg your pardon?"

"Sorry," Jack said. "Something Al taught me from the Marines. BOHICA – Bend Over, Here It Comes Again."

Sellers chuckled.

"Never heard that one," he said. "I don't mean to laugh, especially since it fits. Sorry, Jack, Stoddard is all yours until I can figure out what else to do. It might be hard for me to get rid of him anyway. The bureaucrats would all probably applaud his efforts to keep costs down. Sorry again, but that's the way it is."

"Great."

"Don't let him distract you, Jack," Sellers said. "You're my ace. Hell, it's your investigation. Run it the way you want. You need it, you call me, OK? No bullshit, Jack. As soon as you hear the word 'no' from Stoddard, you pick up the phone. I want The Ninja nailed, and my money is on you and your team."

Jack's mood improved considerably.

"Thanks, George," he said. "That's what I needed to hear."

"Tell you what," Sellers said. "I'm going to be in town later this week. Maybe I'll take Calvin to lunch, see if I can get him to back off a little. Wouldn't mind seeing NOSCU's setup, either."

"It's your money," Jack said.

"And don't you forget it," Sellers said. It was Jack's turn to chuckle.

Brickman had then sought out Ken Bright to bring him up to speed on both the situation with Stoddard and the latest murder. When he heard about their boss, he seemed indifferent.

"Don't act so surprised," Bright said. "One of the reasons I got into the Bureau was so I didn't have to put up with that kind of crap. Oh, we've got ambitious guys, but most of us just dream about bagging the elephants. But bureaucrats are bureaucrats. And I'll echo what Sellers said. You're the right guy for this job, Jack."

"Do the Feds feel the same way?"

"As far as you're concerned, I *am* the Feds," Bright said. "The team knows who's really calling the shots."

The FBI agent had gotten to the office very early that morning, and had peppered all the investigators he could find with questions. He had apparently received a decent overview of the Dupree murder, since he only had a few questions for Jack. His biggest concern was The Ninja's change in victim selection.

"White guy, huh?" he said. "What's that all about?"

"I guess we were right about this not being a hate crime after all," Jack said.

"Yeah," Bright said. "But how does that help us?"

They spent the better part of the morning trying to figure out what it meant. They were about to break for lunch when Therese Vidalia walked into the office carrying a banker's box from the coroner's office. Jack, Ken, and everybody else in the office immediately forgot about lunch and started diving into the box. Unfortunately, there weren't enough copies of the report to go around. Brickman finally had to put his foot down.

"Everybody stop before we lose something," he said. "Give me the main file. And stay out of the box."

Jack took the thick file to the copier and started feeding sheets into the machine. In short order, he had collated and stapled copies for the whole team.

"Those don't leave this office," he reminded them.

The file made for interesting reading. Contrary to what they had assumed at the crime scene, Robert Dupree had not been strangled, or at least he had not died from strangulation. He had died from a broken neck. That did not explain the chain-shaped ligature marks on the

211

victim's neck. Jack looked over to where Sam Rausch was sitting, reading the report. He had been about to ask the SWAT commander his opinion when the saw the lieutenant make a strange face and say "hmm?" He glanced up and saw Jack looking at him.

"Cause of death?" Rausch asked.

"Yeah," Jack said. "What do you think?"

Everybody in the room looked over at Sam except the slow readers who were scrambling to catch up with the rest of them.

"I'll tell you what it could be," he said. "Read a little further where it talks about the contusions on the top of his head. And the dirt ground into the wound. Dupree also had a crushed testicle."

Jack scanned the pages.

"OK," he said. "So?"

Rausch dug into his desk drawer and pulled out a heavy chain with a weight at either end."

"I'm starting to worry about you," Al Sladky said.

Sam just smiled.

"I need a volunteer," he said.

Bryce Cramer raised his hand.

"Is this going to hurt?" he asked.

"Probably."

"OK," Cramer said. "I just wanted to know."

Rausch positioned Cramer in an open part of the bullpen and started his demonstration. Calvin wandered in from his office to observe.

"OK," Rausch said. "I'm The Ninja. Bryce is Dupree."

They faced each other.

"We're pretty close to each other, face to face so Dupree can see my money," Rausch said. "When he looks down, I bring the folded twenty up to my mouth and blow the pepper in his face."

"Habanero, for the record," Terri Rome said, reading from the file.

"Right," Sam continued. "Two things happen when you're blinded. One, your head goes down to protect your eyes from another attack." Bryce dipped his head. "Two, your hands come up to rub the stuff, whatever it is, out of your eyes. That's what we wait for when we use OC." Bryce brought his hands up to his face.

"Dupree is blind, right, so he can't see The Ninja clearly now, but The Ninja can't do what he wants to do, which is get the *manriki* around Dupree's neck because his hands are up. So, The Ninja has got to bring Dupree's hands down. I think we all learned on the playground that the best way to do that is to go for the balls. Pardon me, Terri."

"Carry on, Sam," she said. "I've heard much worse."

"So, The Ninja is smart," Sam continued. "He's not going to throw away a kick to make a feint, especially since Dupree can't see anything at this point. So, he really lets him have it. My choice would be a front kick since it's about the fastest and most powerful kick you can deliver from head on. Now, watch."

Sam lashed out with his right foot. Even though Bryce knew it was coming, he flinched and immediately dropped his hands to protect himself. Sam had left the kick a good six inches short of contact, which was probably four or five inches farther away than he could have comfortably missed by, but it proved his point. As if by magic, the *manriki* appeared, stretched out in both hands.

"Freeze," Rausch commanded. Bryce did as he was told.

"Now that Dupree's hands are down, The Ninja can move in for the kill. Literally."

Rausch stepped in closer to Cramer, in effect clotheslining the younger man with the length of chain. He stopped and gave some safety tips to the detective before continuing.

"Bryce, before I keep going, bring your hands up and grab the chain, like you would if you were being choked."

Cramer brought his hands up, with the palms turned away from his throat.

"This might pinch your fingers a little, but I'll try to be careful," Rausch said. "Try not to resist, OK?"

With that, Rausch stepped past Cramer, stopping when he stood back-to-back with the other man. As he moved, he did something with his hands that Jack couldn't see and the loose ends of the chain crossed behind Cramer's back, held firmly by Rausch. Sam lowered his body until his hips were under Bryce's, crouching and tensing his legs as he got closer to the ground. With a push upward that seemed to accelerate as he rose, Rausch brought the younger man over his back and held him a few feet from the floor. The top of Cramer's head now pointed straight down. Sam held the position for a moment and then slowly straightened up and gently lowered his partner to his feet. They could all see where the move would have ended if Sam had not been a considerate partner.

"You OK, Bryce?" Sam asked.

"Yes," Cramer replied. "But that's the last time I volunteer."

"It's a variation of something we call a reverse hip throw," Sam said. "You could probably do it easier with your bare hands. We teach it that way and also let the kids take off their belts and try it. We don't use chains, of course, but it's the same principle. You'd have to do it pretty fast to break somebody's neck. The spine is hard to break, but compressing it is one way to do it. Probably be even more effective if you dropped the guy at a slight angle. I never thought about it until now. Anyway, if you were a little off, you'd probably at least stun the guy."

"If you teach kids, how hard is it to master?" Bright asked.

"Like everything else, it's a question of practice," Rausch said. "Most of the stuff we've seen this guy do is nothing fancy. What makes it stand out is that he does everything almost perfectly. That says plenty about his dedication."

"Sounds like you admire him, lieutenant," Calvin Stoddard said.

If the comment bothered him, Sam didn't let it show.

"Admire? No," Sam said. "Respect? Yes, I do. Respecting the capabilities of your enemy will keep you alive, Mr. Stoddard. On a personal level, I'm disgusted by the image he's giving to the martial arts, which have done a lot of good for a lot of people for thousands of years. I'd be tempted to say he's perverting the martial arts, but he's not, really. In a way, he's a purist. He's using *ninjitsu* exactly for what it was created to do. But I'll slap the cuffs on him or drop the hammer on him in a heartbeat if I get the chance."

There was no mistaking the quiet menace in his words.

It might have been wishful thinking, but Jack could have sworn he noticed Stoddard turn a little paler.

"Anyway," Sam said. "It makes sense. He keeps moving closer to his victims. I wouldn't be surprised to see him use his bare hands next. He likes the challenge."

"OK, everybody, you've got the file," Jack said. "Read it thoroughly, see if you agree with Sam and Doc Herlong. Then get back on the phones and on the street."

They did as they were told. Not that they needed much prodding. It may have just been the freshness of the crime, but they seemed re-energized by the latest activity. Jack had "Big Mo" – momentum – working for him, and he wanted to make the most of that driving force. He did not notice Stoddard slip back into his office.

Jack was back at his desk for about thirty minutes before his phone rang.

"NOSCU, Sgt. Brickman speaking," he said as he picked up the handset, his eyes still glued to the file in front of him.

"Jack, this is Elizabeth Carpenter," the voice said.

Brickman literally sat up in his chair.

"Yes, Mayor," he said. "How can I help you?"

"Actually, I was wondering if there was any way I could help *you*," she said. "It seems like you have your hands full over there."

"We're busy, Mayor," Brickman said. "But I think we've got everything we need. The FBI and the AG have been extremely helpful."

"How about manpower?" Carpenter asked. "Chief DiSanto tells me he can get you more people if you need them. A few more of our own detectives might smooth things out a little for you."

"I appreciate it, I really do," Jack said. "The team we've got is about the best we can put together, and CPD is short as it is."

"Understood, sergeant," Carpenter said. "Just make sure this is a Cleveland show and it gets wrapped up ASAP. A killer prowling our streets isn't exactly helping the tourist industry."

"I can't make any promises, Mayor," Jack said. "But the latest murder does give us a new beginning."

"Make the most of it then," Carpenter said. "And, Jack, there's no shame in asking for help if you think you bit off more than you can chew. The Chief and I both think you've been making an outstanding effort."

"Thank you, Mayor," Brickman replied. "I'll let the Chief know if I need anything."

"Do that," she said, and hung up.

Jack stared at the handset for a moment before he hung it back up in the cradle. He was left with two suspicions. The first was that Calvin Stoddard had already started casting doubt in Jack's direction, probably to minimize his own role in what he felt was, inexplicably, a doomed investigation. The second suspicion was that he and NOSCU had belatedly become a political football. The call had really served no useful purpose, other than to put Jack on notice that he and NOSCU were in the spotlight now. That was not really news to Brickman, though the Mayor or her advisers had thought it necessary to remind him for whom he was working. The call had deflated Jack's enthusiasm and basically ruined the rest of Monday.

By the time the team meeting rolled around on Tuesday morning, Jack's mood had improved, although it was doubtful that anyone except Al Sladky and Ken Bright, who had known Jack the longest, noticed. Part of his role as team leader, Brickman knew, was to deflect pressure and unnecessary distractions away from the team. And he knew how infectious a bad attitude could be, especially in a police organization. Seeds of discontent, once planted, could erode the resolve of even the most dedicated cops. So, when Jack addressed the team, he did it with a smile on his face.

Jack's presentation was brief, but detailed. He did not labor over obvious points since by now everybody should have been familiar with the Dupree murder. The facts of the crime were relatively straightforward. The Ninja had approached Dupree, peppered him, and broken his neck. Sam Rausch had discussed his theory extensively with Dr. Herlong, who agreed with lieutenant's assessment of how the crime had occurred. The angle of the neck at the time of impact supported Rausch's theory perfectly. Heath Moore and Therese Vidalia also ardently supported the fact pattern. It just made sense.

What most concerned the team, of course, was what they didn't know.

"What about the change in victim profile, Jack?" asked Terri Rome. "I know about serial crimes, mostly sex stuff, but don't you think that's a huge departure for The Ninja? So, what does it mean?"

"I could BS you, Terri, but I won't," Jack said. "We don't know what it means. We still don't know what he's getting out of this, so we're making educated guesses about his motivation. For the most part, Dupree fits the victim profile perfectly, except that he was white. Which, by the way, supports our belief that these aren't hate crimes, at least not hate crimes motivated by race."

"What about forensics?" Stan Lombardo asked. "Anything new there?"

"It's in there, Stan," Heath Moore said. "But yeah, we found some hair that looks like its going to match up. And we have a couple good shoe prints. Size nine Reeboks with worn soles. Probably part of the disguise since new shoes stand out a little, especially on a crack addict. We have some other fibers that need matching, but that's about it."

"How about the canvass?" Ken Bright asked. "Anything new?"

"Hell, Ken, the folks with the bird's eye view on the murder were watchin' free HBO," Al Sladky said. "You probably coulda set the building on fire without them noticing."

Around the table, the team members chuckled at Sladky's comment. All of them, that is, except for Bryce Cramer, who had a serious look on his face.

"What did you say, Al?" he asked.

"Free HBO," Sladky replied. "A promotion or something, I guess. Why?"

Cramer turned to Lombardo, who was sitting next to him at the table.

"Stan, do you remember when we went out to the Empire crime scene?"

Lombardo looked confused for a moment. Then his face broke into a grin.

"Son of a bitch, yeh, I remember," he said.

"You guys going to share or not?" Sladky asked.

"Look, it may be nothing...hang on a second, let me check my notes," Cramer said., rising and leaving the room. The rest of the team was left with little to do except exchange puzzled looks until Cramer returned with a file folder. He was already flipping through it by the time he sat down.

"I know it's here, I know it's here," Cramer kept saying to himself. He stopped suddenly and lay the file down on the tabletop, his finger pointed to an entry.

"Here it is," he said. "June 1. Stan and I were re-canvassing Empire. We had come up empty and were about to leave when Stan saw a truck from Cabletron and a repair guy up on a ladder. We were there anyway, and those guys are around a lot, so we got him down and asked him if he had seen anything. He hadn't, but we got to shooting the bull with him a little. Stan asked him what he was doing and he said he was fixing the main feed terminal or something. Apparently, somebody had rigged up free premium channels for the whole block."

"Yeah, yeah, I remember. Greek guy, right?" Lombardo asked.

"Lou Kastnokas," Cramer said.

"Yeah. Anyway, I remember him saying it was a little unusual, since people usually just try to rig up free cable for their own house, not for the whole block."

Suddenly the digitized voice of Andy Fulmer came through the intercom.

"Cabletron, right?" he said. "I'll have to check my notes, but I swear one of Rice's neighbors mentioned seeing a repair truck in the neighborhood a week or so before the murder. Shit, guys, I didn't think it was important."

"It wasn't, Andy, at least it wasn't important then. Don't worry about it," Jack said, finally starting to get the picture as something his father had said came back to him. "We all had the notes and files and we missed it. Ed?"

"Go ahead, Jack, we're listening," the Lake County detective said.

"Who provides the cable TV service where Dawkins was killed?"

"Cabletron, Jack," Payne replied. "They do the whole area."

"Same in Shaker," Lombardo confirmed.

The air in the room was electric. One by one, it started to sink in with the NOSCU cops. They finally had a clue. Most of the investigators had a weird half-smile on their faces, and expression not unlike a poker player whose pair had just become three of a kind. Only Stoddard looked a little lost.

"What exactly are we talking about?" he asked.

"We're going to have to confirm it, but Bryce may have just figured out how he's moving around without getting spotted," Jack said. "Ken, can you get on the phone to Cabletron and get their repair orders for the times around the murders? You know what we're looking for, right?"

Ken smiled.

"Yes, I do, Jack," the agent replied. "How hard do you want me to push?"

"Full weight of the Bureau, Ken," Brickman said without hesitation. "We need it fast. And quiet."

"Done," Ken said as he left the conference room.

"OK, Calvin, everybody, how does this sound?" Jack started. "We know he's casing these guys, right? That means plenty of surveillance. He's not going to rent a room or use a car like we might do because that leaves a trail and would make him stand out. Cops tend to notice a guy sitting alone in a car. So why not hide in plain sight?"

"Please get to the point, sergeant," Stoddard said.

"OK, OK," Brickman said, his slight annoyance with his boss swept away by his enthusiasm. "Telephone trucks, water crews, power company – you don't even notice them when you're on patrol. They're like part of the landscape, like other patrol cars. You never think they're suspicious because they're *supposed* to be there. We usually let them park where they want to because we assume that they know what they're doing, right? Chances are, nobody's going to think it's suspicious because we don't know what the guy is doing, either right? Everybody just assumes the guy is kosher. Plus, nobody's going to screw with the guy because they figure he's there to help, right? My dad used to work for CEI, and he says they almost never got hassled because people need their electricity. I guess they need their cable, too.

"The Ninja needs a way to scope out his victims, right? So, he steals a Cabletron van, or buys an old one, and starts posing as a cable repairman. Hell, he could sit on a pole day or night and nobody would give him a second thought. It's perfect. Sam?"

"Yes, Jack?" Rausch replied.

"What do you think, does it fit?"

"Yeah, yeah it does," Rausch said. "We might have been thinking about this all wrong. I know I kept picturing The Ninja sneaking around in a black suit, climbing roofs, and hiding in the shadows. I should have remembered they used disguises extensively. And it's a classic technique – show the enemy something familiar, something they expect to see, before you strike."

"And don't forget the free cable, either," Cramer said. "That's a nice touch."

"It's brilliant," Jack agreed. "Let's assume The Ninja's climbing poles or working on a cable box while he's plotting his moves. While he's up there, he rigs the feed or whatever so everybody on the street starts getting free premium channels. All of sudden, people have HBO and Cinemax and The Movie Channel for free and you know how it is when something's new – you make the most of it. It's no guarantee, but chances are it kept a few people inside who might have been witnesses.

Ken Bright re-entered the room with a smile on his face.

"We're in luck," he said. "Cabletron's got their own investigation going on. It seems somebody had been hacking their feed terminals to give entire neighborhoods free premium service. I spoke to the guy running the investigation and he was happy to give us everything he had. Coincidentally, all five cases occurred around the times of the murders and in those immediate locales. They haven't had anything stolen, so maybe The Ninja bought a used truck or faked one. He's faxing over all their records, but offhand, I'd say we've got a lead on the son of a bitch."

From around the table came a chorus of "yes."

218

"I would say celebration is premature at this point," Calvin Stoddard said.

"Easy, everybody, easy. Calvin's right," Jack said. But he was smiling as he said it. This was the break they had been looking for since the beginning. "Let's firm it up. Use your notes, get back on the street. But keep it quiet. This may be our best chance to snag this guy. Sam, get with me and Ken right after the meeting. We need to put out a teletype and a BOLO for cable trucks and I'd like your input on the wording and the distribution."

"Right," Rausch said.

"OK," Jack said. "This is what we've been looking for, so let's get on it. Excellent work, Bryce."

"When this is all over, I'm gonna buy you the biggest, coldest beer you ever saw, kid," Sladky said to Cramer.

"Nail The Ninja and the party is on me," Ken Bright said.

There were plenty of smiles to go around as the team poured out of the conference room. If they had been energized before, now they were positively electrified with enthusiasm.

Jack, Ken, and Sam Rausch were soon the only ones in the office. Everybody, including Sladky, had hit the streets again. It took the trio about a half an hour to draft a teletype they could send throughout CPD and other affected departments. Plainly, the message detailed what they were looking for and what would happen to the poor soul who leaked information. Above all, it stressed extreme caution when approaching suspicious people. Sam had Natalie Price type it into the LEADS terminal immediately.

"Well?" Brickman asked Ken when the SWAT commander had left the room.

"We still don't know how he's picking the victims, but it's a start, Jack, a damn good start," Bright replied. "But it's still a needle in a haystack. Cleveland's a big city and there's not enough cops to go around as it is. And he could have changed tactics by now, too."

"Why do you have to burst my bubble, Ken?" Jack said, smiling. "He's got no reason to think his cover has been compromised, so why change now? I say he sticks with what works."

"It's a safe bet, Jack, but somebody's occasionally got to be devil's advocate," Bright replied.

As if on cue, Jack's phone rang. The red blinking light showed it was coming from Stoddard's office.

"Speaking of which," he said as he picked up the phone. "Yes, Calvin?"

"Come to my office, please," the voice on the other end said before hanging up.

"I wonder why he can't just tell me anything over the phone?" Jack said, standing up.

"It enhances his perception of control," Bright replied, also standing.

"Sure, now you start using psychology."

"Good luck," Ken said as he disappeared into his office.

Jack was surprised to find his boss in a good mood. Stoddard was actually smiling, something Brickman hadn't seen in a while. The break in the case was obviously important to his career.

"So, sergeant, I am assuming the end is in sight?" he asked.

"Possibly, but not necessarily," Jack said.

"But you know how he is conducting surveillance now, you know his mode of travel," Stoddard said. "The rest should be simple."

"Agent Bright and I were just talking about that, Calvin," Jack said. "Yes, it's a big clue, if it pans out, and it probably will. But it doesn't guarantee anything."

The attorney seemed a little subdued by Brickman's response.

"I would like to call the Mayor and advise her," Stoddard said.

"Personally, I think that's a bad idea. Politicians will leak information for some good press," Jack replied. "But I can't stop you. Anyway, I'm sure you have her number."

Brickman's parting shot left Stoddard speechless. Jack thought the week was shaping up nicely after all.

CHAPTER 32

Patrolmen Shane Peterson and Lee Jackson had been partners for over a year.

Peterson had just under thirteen years on the job, notable because it meant he was more than halfway to retirement. Not that he was counting down the days on a calendar or anything, but it was nice to have more time behind you than ahead of you. There were days when that was a big deal, but for the most part, Shane liked his job. It beat sitting behind a desk all day.

Lee Jackson was a different story. He hadn't been in the department long, and had been out of the field training program for less than two years. But he paid attention to his senior partner, had good instincts, and didn't screw around, which was good for Peterson. The last thing he needed was some rookie know-it-all who wouldn't listen. They shared a love of sports, which made the slow moments, of which there were few, pass quickly.

Peterson was a good cop, not a great one. And Jackson was young and inexperienced. It turned out to be a dangerous combination.

They were on what the newspapers would call "routine patrol," though there was nothing routine about it, in the area of Buckeye Road. It was a run-down neighborhood where the decent people were slowly but surely being forced out by criminals and drug dealers. It was about two in the afternoon when Peterson spotted the van.

"What was that teletype about cable trucks we had last week, Lee?" he asked his partner, who remembered stuff like that.

"The Ninja thing?" Jackson said. "It said to check out all Cabletron trucks, and verify ID of the workers. And to use extreme caution."

"They always say that," Peterson said. "But let's check this guy out."

"Cool," Jackson said.

Peterson was driving. He pulled in behind the van, but didn't activate the overhead lights. Traffic was light on the side street and this really wasn't a vehicle stop. Just a check. The van was off the roadway, and a worker was up on a ladder resting against a pole. He seemed very intent on fixing whatever was wrong with the cable system. That wasn't true. He was much more interested in the two cops who had suddenly pulled up behind him than he was in the cable box opened up in front of him. Between his hard hat and wraparound safety sunglasses, however, it would have been difficult for Peterson or Jackson to see where he was really looking. Jackson ran the van's license plate on the car's computer, but it came back "NIF," or "Not In File." Jackson didn't find that unusual for a fleet truck.

Lee Jackson called in the stop to dispatch. He had been trained to keep his radio conversations short and direct, so he just told the communications center they would be checking on a suspicious vehicle. He did not mention it was a Cabletron van.

The man atop the ladder watched as the cops approached, pretending not to notice them until they called to him.

"Hey, buddy," the older cop, a white guy, said. "We need to talk to you."

"I'll be right down," the worker said. He closed up the box and secured it before descending to the ground. His movements were casual, unexcited. He noticed that the cops looked relaxed, the older one more so than the younger one, a Black kid who looked like a rookie.

"Sorry to bug you, but we need to see some ID," Peterson said.

"I have my work ID, officer, but not my license," the man said. "I don't like to carry a wallet when I work down here."

"I don't blame you," Peterson said. "I don't carry mine either. Just something else to worry about."

Cops meet dozens of people every day, so it was odd when somebody stood out immediately. This guy wouldn't have caught your eye. He was about five-eight, maybe 175, with dark hair and a heavy beard. He had a short-sleeved shirt on and Peterson noticed that his forearms were rippling with muscle. Not that he looked like a body builder. He just looked strong. What really caught Peterson's attention, though, was the voice. It was so high-pitched it was almost falsetto.

"I bet this guy got his balls busted all the time," Peterson thought.

The cable repair man had to move his heavy leather tool belt out of the way to dig into his front pocket to retrieve his Cabletron ID card. He handed it to Peterson, who handed it to Jackson.

"Go call this in," Peterson told his younger partner. "Man, they sure load you guys down with a lot of crap. Must get heavy on that ladder."

"It's not too bad," the cable man said, shifting his belt around. The leather pouches were filled with tools, including a heavy-duty power outlet strip.

"What's that for?" Peterson wondered.

"Can I ask what this is all about?" the man said, shuffling his feet a little. He sounded more curious than nervous.

"Just checking something out," Peterson said.

Jackson was just about to open the door to the cruiser when he had an inspiration. Why not run the guy's Social Security number, too?

"Hey, Pete," he called.

Shane Peterson looked at his partner, which was exactly the distraction The Ninja had been waiting for. The killer moved quickly, his hands a blur. In one swift, practiced movement, he grabbed the thick, foot-long cord of the power strip in his hand, pulled the heavy metal row of six outlets from his belt and swung it toward the cop's head. Peterson felt rather than saw the movement, far too late to avoid the blow. The metal strip struck him along this left jawline, directly under his ear in a location known as the mandibular angle. It is a highly sensitive bundle of nerves. The power strip also hit the side of Peterson's neck, at the origin of the brachial plexus, another sensitive nerve center. The patrolman was unconscious before he even knew he was in a fight.

Lee Jackson, of course, saw all this happen. There were any number of things he could have done. He could have drawn his sidearm and shot The Ninja, since this was clearly a life-threatening assault. He could have drawn his OC spray and used that, though he clearly would have been overmatched. He could even have retreated to the cruiser and called for help. In the end, he did none of those things.

Jackson's first reaction was sheer surprise. After seeing his partner hit the ground, he did what many cops might do – he rushed to his partner's side. Which was exactly what The Ninja wanted him to do.

The rookie took a step towards the attacker, finally trying to draw his pistol as he moved forward. The Ninja headed straight at Jackson. He covered the distance quickly. At the last moment, just as it seemed that Jackson might actually get the gun out of his holster, The Ninja spun and brought the improvised *manriki* around and down against the cop's wrist. The fragile bones shattered, rendering the gun hand useless. It is a credit to his training that Lee Jackson immediately tried to draw the gun with his left hand, a difficult maneuver under the best conditions. The second strike of The Ninja was a downward blow against the cop's left collarbone. An extremely painful injury, a shattered collarbone can paralyze the arm. Jackson nearly passed out from the pain.

The Ninja was not finished, however. As the young cop staggered forward, the killer spun the power strip under his arm and stepped around behind the man, executing a technique often erroneously labeled as a chokehold. It was, in reality, a sleeper hold, which cut off blood supply to the head, but not oxygen to the lungs. Jackson's struggles stopped almost immediately. The Ninja lowered him swiftly but gently to the ground. The entire violent encounter lasted less than five seconds.

He paused to retrieve his ID card from where it had fallen. The first cop he had hit groaned weakly. He was still alive. That was good. He had not wanted to kill the men. He did not want to go to jail, either. There was still much work to be done and it looked like the police were getting closer to finding him. That surprised him a little.

He was careful not to drive too fast as he left the scene. He didn't want to attract any more attention and the last thing he wanted was to get into a car accident.

CHAPTER 33

The attack on two CPD officers changed the tone of the investigation, if not its intensity.

When Peterson and Jackson failed to respond to the dispatcher's check-up calls, another zone car swung around to find them. It was not unusual for officers to forget to call back in from a traffic stop or fail to answer the dispatchers. Often, they are just too busy or too focused to make contact. Still, it has to be checked out. The zone car pulled up just as the first 9-1-1 calls started coming in, reporting two officers down. It had been slightly over ten minutes since The Ninja and CPD went head-to-head.

Nothing gets cops moving faster than hearing of another officer in trouble. Even cars that weren't assigned to respond headed to the scene. The watch supervisor immediately dispatched detectives to the scene, which was redundant since they were on the way regardless of orders. Everybody wanted to help. It was inspiring to see so many officers so concerned about their brethren. It also rendered the crime scene a complete disaster.

Lee Jackson didn't regain complete consciousness until they had him strapped down to a gurney. He probably would have been unconscious longer but one of the paramedics inadvertently pressed down on his shattered collarbone while adjusting the cervical collar, which had been applied as a precaution. While the pain was excruciating, it did wake him up. The paramedics wanted to give him something for the pain, but he insisted on talking to the detectives first. Jackson's display of courage was invaluable. The description he gave of The Ninja and his vehicle was very accurate. The investigating detective immediately made the connection and contacted NOSCU. The call was not one Jack Brickman welcomed.

"Son of a bitch," he said softly. He punched the number for Natalie Price's station and told her to send out a page to the entire team, less the far east and west siders. By the time they got in, it would probably be too late for them to help. Plus, since an alert patrolman had scribbled down the last plate Jackson had run on the MDT in the cruiser, they had a license plate to send out over the network. It was possible that they might get lucky and snare The Ninja outside the city. If that happened, he wanted a NOSCU member in on the pinch.

Jack called Sam Rausch's cell.

"Rausch," he said.

"Sam, this is Jack. Get your team up."

"What happened?"

"Looks like The Ninja beat the crap out of a couple of cops," Brickman said. "They're alive, thank God, but he really did a number on them. They were checking on a cable van, apparently."

"Christ, what part of 'extreme caution' did they not understand?" Rausch asked rhetorically.

"I know, I know," Jack said. "We got a vehicle description and a plate, so this may get hot really quick. I want you on deck, ready to jump, if it does."

"If we're ready in ten minutes, that'll be five minutes late," Rausch said. "I hope we get a crack at him."

"Me too, Sam."

Jack was aware of a flurry of activity in the bullpen as the cops who were in the office started heading out. He nearly bumped into Al Sladky and Ken Bright as he exited his door.

"Let's get a move on, junior," Al said. "Ken's driving."

As they headed through the reception area, Natalie Price stopped Jack.

"Sergeant Brickman? Mr. Stoddard's on the phone, he wants to speak to you," she said.

Jack never broke stride.

"I don't have time," he said. "Tell him what happened and tell him I'll call him back when I can."

Even with Ken Bright driving like he was trying to earn a pole position at Indy, they still got to the scene too late to do much good. The ambulances had already left the scene, or what was left of it. Dozens of well-intentioned police officers, EMS personnel and their assorted vehicles had contaminated the area around the downed officers and their car beyond repair. The ground, though dry, showed that many people had walked through the area. There were bandages and assorted medical waste blowing around the crime scene, along with a handful of cigarette butts deposited carelessly on the ground by nervous cops. When Jack saw the condition of the crime scene, he thought that all they really needed to complete the picture was a couple of half-full coffee cups.

Jack immediately found the supervisor, Lt. Clements, and told him to get his men out of the crime scene.

"I know they're worried, lieutenant, but all they're doing now is screwing it up for forensics," Jack told the older man a little more forcefully than he meant to. The officer finally got the picture and ordered his people to move away and establish a perimeter. They were in the middle of that process when Therese Vidalia and Heath Moore pulled up in the evidence van.

"Goddamnit, Jack," Vidalia said. "How are we supposed to process this scene?"

Heath Moore took it a little more quietly, though Jack could have sworn the technician was on the verge of tears.

Jack gathered the NOSCU members around him and briefed them on what he wanted.

"OK," he told them. "We know why he was here and we know what kind of victims he likes. If we get a witness, great. We probably won't, but try anyway. Maybe we can figure out who he was after. So, ID everybody and I mean everybody who lives in or stays in these houses." Jack waved his hand down the street. "He was here for a reason, and it sure wasn't to bring HBO to the masses. Don't take any crap from anybody. This may be our only chance to find a live victim. The trace evidence from the scene is probably fucked, so let's try to salvage something out of this mess."

Everyone on the team scattered except Terri Rome.

"Where are they taking the cops, Jack?" she asked.

"University."

"And these were contact assaults, right?"

"Yeah," Jack said. "Why?"

Terri didn't answer. Instead, she pulled out her cell phone and punched one key. It was obviously a speed dial button.

"Helen?" she said into the phone. "It's me, Terri...fine, busy though...how about you...oh, great to hear it...listen, I need a favor. EMS is bringing in two cops who got banged up by a suspect. It was a close contact assault. Could you pull a couple of rape kits and run them when they come in? Yeah, don't worry about the sexual swabs, but do the fingernails, hair, clothes, and everything else. Bag their uniforms, too. They'll bitch if they're awake but do it anyway. I'll be down to pick them up myself. Right. Thanks."

Terri pocketed the cell phone with a shrug.

"My specialty's sex crimes, Jack," she said. "My victims are usually still alive, even though sometimes they wish they weren't. Heath and Therese are used to having their victims still on the scene when they get there. I figure if The Ninja was close enough to these guys to hit them or choke them, he was close enough to leave trace evidence, the same kind of evidence we might look for in a sexual assault. I figure it's worth a try."

"Absolutely, Terri," Jack said. "I probably wouldn't have thought of it. Good call."

"I'm just glad I can do something," she said. "I've been feeling like a fifth wheel lately."

"Just because these aren't sex crimes? I read your dailies, Terri. You do great work. Don't let all these homicide guys make you feel like a second-class citizen."

"Actually, I'm so good, I think it was the other way around," she said, drawing a laugh from Jack in spite of the situation.

As expected, there was almost no usable evidence at the scene. Even the ladder he left didn't reveal any prints. There had been no witnesses to the attack itself, and the canvass had come up empty. Many people weren't home or weren't answering, which made finding The Ninja's target an even greater challenge. The detectives were going to have to make repeated visits to the neighborhood before they could even come close to figuring out who lived there. Stan Lombardo had called in a supervisor from Cabletron, who confirmed that the cable unit had indeed been tampered with. There was no doubt they were dealing with The Ninja, but outside of a good physical description, NOSCU was still batting .000.

"The press is going to have a field day with this," Jack thought as he watched his team work.

CHAPTER 34

From The North Coast Press

Page A-1

July 19

By Cliff O'Brien

CLEVELAND – The hunt for the serial killer known as "The Ninja" became costly for the Cleveland Police Department Wednesday as two police officers barely survived an encounter with the unknown assassin.

According to CPD spokesperson, Lt. Wilson Young, Patrolman Shane Peterson, 38, and Patrolman Lee Jackson, 26, sustained serious injuries while checking on a suspicious vehicle possibly connected to The Ninja investigation.

According to Young, the attack occurred Wednesday afternoon on Buckeye Road when the officers checked on a suspicious vehicle. Although Young would not elaborate on why the vehicle was suspicious, a source within the police department, who did not wish to be named, said officers were recently sent a teletype advising them to be on the lookout for utility vehicles, especially cable television repair trucks, in high crime areas.

Another source close to the investigation confirmed that NOSCUE and CPD had issued a "BOLO" for a white van, possibly disguised as a Cabletron repair truck. The source would not elaborate on what connection the vehicle has to the investigation.

Young stated that when Ptls. Peterson and Jackson approached the suspect, the man attacked both officers, Peterson, a thirteen-year veteran, received a broken jaw and concussion. His partner, Lee Jackson, who has been on the force for two years, was attacked when he tried to go to Peterson's aid.

According to Young, Jackson sustained fractures to his wrist and collarbone. Young said that Jackson was also choked into unconsciousness by the attacker.

"Both of these officers are lucky to be alive," Young said. "Only their training and courage brought them through this horrible situation."

Young said he had little doubt about the identity of the attacker.

"Who else could it be?" he said. "One unarmed man against two trained CPD officers? To me, there's no question about who attacked us. I'd say that's perfectly clear."

Both officers were listed in stable condition at University Hospital.

CPD Det. Sgt. Jack Brickman, who is leading the Northern Ohio Serial Crimes Unit tasked with tracking down The Ninja, would not confirm that they had targeted Cabletron repair trucks as part of the investigation, nor would he comment on the progress of the investigation.

"Obviously, we have reason to believe that this attack has some connection to The Ninja investigation," Brickman said. "Those reasons are best kept within the department at this time."

Brickman would not speculate on why The Ninja might have confronted the CPD officers.

"He's proven to be very flexible, very adept at changing his tactics," Brickman said. "Right now, of course, we're worried more about Peterson and Jackson. For the sake of CPD, I hope this isn't the start of new trend."

Despite the injuries to Peterson and Jackson, Brickman said the attack may actually help the investigation.

"We've got a good physical description now, thanks to our patrolmen," Brickman said. "And that description has confirmed much of what was just very educated guessing until now."

Brickman confirmed that the suspect is a white male in his mid to late 30s, approximately 5'8". The detective said he expected a detailed sketch of the suspect to be released to the media within the next 48 hours.

CHAPTER 35

From *The North Coast Press*

Page E-1

July 20

By Mike Pendleton

Just when you thought it was safe to go out...

Well, it seems like NOSCU was closer to getting The Ninja than we thought. I guess that's promising. Too bad two patrolmen had to get the daylights beat out of them as part of the investigation.

The latest development in The Ninja case is causing quite a stir in police circles, I can tell you. I was talking to a couple of cops I know. They said the attack on Shane Peterson and Lee Jackson has really changed their attitude about catching The Ninja. One of the cops, I'll just call him Joe if that's OK with you, says plenty of cops are angry now.

"Look," he was saying, "it's not like we didn't care before this, but you can't expect us to turn the other cheek. Yeah, some guys were secretly pulling for The Ninja. I wasn't one of them, but it's true. Anyway, I'm pissed off about it. Those guys were damn lucky. It could have been a lot worse."

I see what Joe means. My dad always said that there are two kinds of trouble - the kind that happens across the street and the kind that comes looking for your family. When it's family, it gets personal. Especially when your family wears blue polyester and carries guns.

But I have to disagree a little. With all due respect to Lee Jackson and Shane Peterson, the two cops who got in The Ninja's way, I don't think it's a matter of luck they survived. I think The Ninja just didn't want to kill them.

Now, before you start emailing me your cries of outrage, hear me out.

All six of The Ninja's victims were killed quickly and thoroughly. Despite the party line, it sounds like he got the drop on Peterson and Jackson and managed to work them over pretty good. It wouldn't have taken much to finish the job.

Heck, he could have used the cops' own guns against them if he really wanted to. How much easier than that does it get?

So, I'm still sticking with my original theory. I think The Ninja is still on the side of the angels. Why else would he leave two witnesses alive? It doesn't take a master's in psychology to figure out he spared two good guys for a reason.

CHAPTER 36

"Brickman, in my office," Calvin Stoddard said.

Jack, Al Sladky and Ken Bright all turned to look at their boss, who had poked his head into Brickman's office just after eight on Friday morning. Stoddard must have assumed Jack would be following him because he didn't wait for the detective to reply. Sladky and Bright, both veterans, were not impressed.

"Didn't he ever hear 'Death before dishonor, nothing before coffee'?" Al asked.

Indeed, they had all arrived at the office about the same time and had just gotten around to sipping the horrendously strong coffee Ken Bright liked to brew up if he got to the coffee maker first. He called it "Stakeout Blend." The "blend" part was apparently coffee blended with even more coffee.

"Ah, well, a little adrenaline jolt is just as good," Bright said. "Want a little company?"

Jack shook his head.

"I'm a big boy, Ken," Brickman replied. "Who knows? Maybe he just wants to talk about the Tribe game."

"Wanna bet?"

Jack took his time getting to Stoddard's office. He was pretty sure his boss wanted to ream him out about the lack of progress on the case, especially in light of the attack on Peterson and Jackson. Jack had paid a personal visit to the cops who were still recuperating at UH. It had been tough on Brickman, though it was by no means the first cops he'd had to visit in the hospital. Both cops had been in decent spirits, considering. Both cops were playing the role of the brave patient well, not easy considering their injuries.

As Jack interviewed Peterson, the older cop, it became clear that he blamed himself for putting his partner in danger. Through his wired-shut jaw, he kept repeating "my fault, never saw it coming." It was not grandstanding. He knew he had screwed up and was not afraid to take the blame despite the department's attempts to make him look like a hero. Peterson was showing a different kind of courage now, taking the blame when he really didn't have to. That went a long way in Jack's book.

"Look, Shane," he had said. "This guy had probably planned out the scenario and practiced his response hundreds of times. He knew exactly what he was going to do and you didn't. Human reaction time just isn't that good. Even Sam Rausch said you guys probably reacted better than most of us would have. And you got us one hell of a good sketch to send out, plus the freaky voice thing. This could be the big break."

Peterson said something that sounded like "mad fun." Jack finally translated and realized he had said "bad pun." But he sort of seemed to be smiling when Brickman finally left the hospital.

Jack had gone home feeling guilty that he hadn't caught The Ninja yet, and that two cops were hurt because of him. He knew logically that he wasn't responsible, but guilt doesn't always make sense.

Jack headed towards Calvin Stoddard's office prepared for the worst. As he walked across the bullpen, he noticed Bryce Cramer reading *The North Coast Press*. He nodded to the detective and took a deep breath, bracing for the onslaught.

Bryce Cramer was not the only one in the office interested in the morning paper. Once Jack had entered Stoddard's office and shut the door behind him as directed, the lawyer picked up a copy of *The North Coast Press* and tossed it onto the desktop in front of the detective.

"I assume you've found time to read the papers in between coffee breaks, sergeant," Stoddard said.

Jack let the thinly veiled insult pass without comment.

"Of course," he replied quietly.

"Then you can see we are being crucified by the media," Stoddard said. "And the papers are just the tip of the iceberg. The TV stations have been calling the Justice Center and the attorney general non-stop since the attack on those two officers. I have personally taken several calls from people who think you and your team are in way over your heads with this Ninja thing. And judging by your attitude since the attack, I find myself wondering exactly how much you care about solving this case."

Stoddard's statement was so flat-out wrong, Jack could no longer hold his temper.

"Enough," he said through clenched teeth. "I've told you before and I won't tell you again. Question my aptitude if you want. You can even question by integrity if it makes you feel better. But goddamnit don't you ever – EVER – question my dedication. I've been busting my ass since I got this job. I'm here before you every day and I'm here long after you leave. And how dare you imply that I don't care about Peterson and Jackson. I'm a cop, Stoddard, first, last, and always. That's something you don't understand because you were never a cop. But there isn't a cop in this city that doesn't care when another cop goes down. Did you sit with Shane Peterson at the hospital? Of course not. I did. And just so you know, I did it on my own time. And ask me if I give a damn about the heat you're feeling. I don't. You signed up for this assignment, and you knew damn well it could get a little hot. So, either do your job or quit now. Maybe you thought this was going to be a quick one, something you could tack on your resume and boost your stock a little. And, yeah, I hear you're looking for a federal judgeship. Big fucking deal. Campaign on your own time and get the hell out of my way."

"You are way out of line, sergeant," Stoddard said. "I have half a mind to replace you right now."

Jack smiled.

"Try it," he said. "Go ahead, call George Sellers. Better yet, I'll dial the number myself. I've got his guarantee, and Feds will back him up, that you'll go before I do. Bluffing won't work when I know you don't hold the cards."

That seemed to knock Stoddard off balance briefly. He quickly regained his composure, though.

"Maybe you've got friends, Brickman," he said, picking up *The North Coast Press* and pointing it at Jack like a weapon. "But eventually even they will start to run for cover if the media increases its scrutiny of this investigation and your conduct. We are not the only ones who read the paper, you know."

Jack was about to respond when he suddenly stopped.

"You're right," Brickman said. He turned abruptly and nearly ran out of Stoddard's office, leaving the attorney standing behind his desk with an idiotic look of surprise on his face. He didn't know it yet, but Stoddard had finally made a worthwhile contribution to the case.

Back in his own office, Bright and Sladky were both reading the morning papers and finishing their coffee. They looked up as Jack walked in with a huge grin on his face.

"That's a first," Sladky said. "You usually look like crap after you talk to the boss."

Jack ignored Al's comment.

"I know why he's doing it," Jack said simply.

"Who?" Sladky asked.

"The Ninja," Jack replied. "At least I've got a good theory."

"Yeah," Ken Bright asked, raising an eyebrow, and folding his paper. "Let's hear it."

"OK," Brickman said. "We know he's not taking souvenirs. Sure, he's taking weapons if they have them, but it seems like an afterthought. But he's not taking ears or fingers or eyeballs or anything. And from the lack of semen, we know he's not getting a sexual thrill out of the killings either. Simple revenge might have something to do with it, but look at his first two kills. He shoots Dawkins and Rice as easy as you please. They never really had a chance, right? So why make it more challenging if you just want to murder bad guys? Plus, these guys generally stick with what they know works. Serial criminals almost never vary their tactics once they've established a pattern unless they come close to getting caught.

"The Ninja gets away with a couple murders that seem so much like drug hits that nobody even connects the two," Jack continued. "Hell, I don't even remember hearing about either one. Do you guys?"

Ken and Al shook their heads.

"So, even though he's successful, he's still not getting what he wants," Jack said. "So, he changes his tactics and does Clayton with the *sai*. But even that doesn't do what he wants."

"What does he want, Jack?" Bright finally asked.

"Press coverage," Brickman replied. "He's getting off on being in the media spotlight."

Bright didn't say anything at first. Then he smiled.

"Yeah," he said. "Keep going."

"OK. So, he changes tactics and uses an exotic weapon on Clayton, probably thinking we'll figure it out right away. But we missed it, just like we missed the *shuko* he used for climbing into the first two apartments. And a guy killed in his apartment, possibly by an ex-roommate, just doesn't generate the kind of story he wants to read about himself. So, he kills Jameel Timmons in a relatively public place and he makes it very clear that he can handle a knife. That much we finally figure out and release to the media, so now he knows he's on the right track.

"But it's the Empire beheading where he really goes all out," Jack continued. "I think he needed to make a big splash so we would connect the dots. Cutting off a guy's head is pretty much guaranteed to get a lot of media attention."

"You think he wants to get caught?" Sladky asked.

"No," Jack said. "But if I'm right, he's got to give us enough clues to figure out his MO so we in turn will give it to the press. And there are some other things, too."

"Go, Jack, go," Ken Bright said.

"Look at his victim selection," Jack said. "First, they were all criminals of one sort or another. Not exactly sympathetic characters, right? And, except for Jameel Timmons, none of them had any family, at least nobody close. Think about the press coverage. If he was out whacking honor students from the suburbs, the papers would be full of stories about the grieving families and the outrage. Outside of Timmons' mother and his baby's mother, who mourned him? Even the sad mother angle didn't cause much of a ripple in the press. So somehow, he screwed up when he picked Timmons."

"So, The Ninja has a conscience," Sladky said.

"That's not what I'm saying, Al," Jack said. "But that kind of story takes away from the drama he's trying to create. It puts focus on the survivors and the victims, not on him. And then look what happened when the race issue starts to get more coverage. The Ninja lays low for a while and then kills a white guy, Dupree. Why? To shift the spotlight back on himself and his mission. I'm sure he was working on some kind of timetable but changed it in the interest of racial equality. It may have taken him a while to find a new victim or set up the kill, but I'd say the color of Dupree's skin had a lot to do with the timing of his murder."

"What about the vigilante or bully revenge theories?" Bright asked.

"That's probably part of it too, Ken," Jack said. "I just don't think it's the whole reason. I think he's more into his reputation as a master assassin than he wants to be regarded as a hero. But let's say he had targeted cops or random citizens. First of all, where's the challenge in killing ordinary citizens? Plus, there's the outrage. And cops? Sure, that's a challenge, but you know damn well we're going to go nuts looking for him as soon as he makes his first move. Look at the difference in attitude since Peterson and Jackson got smacked around."

"What about the mother thing?" Sladky said. "Didn't you think this guy had some issues at home?"

"Yeah, Al, and it still fits," Jack said. "He's looking for approval. I'd say that's a safe bet. He's not getting it from an intimate source so he's looking for it from the press and, I guess, from us, too. And that also fits with the victim selection. He doesn't seem to want to make anybody's mommy sad so he picks orphans. Plus, it fits in with the high-pitched voice, the vocal aberration Ken brought up, too. In his mind, he's just proving he can do something despite his difference."

"Christ, talk about overcompensating," Al said.

"So, what do you think?" Jack asked the cops.

"I think you're right," Bright said. "It makes sense. We should have seen it sooner. Hell, Ted Bundy and Ramirez were obsessed with press coverage, so this isn't really anything new."

"It makes sense to me, too," Sladky said. "He sure ain't the first guy to get off on seein' his picture in the paper…oh, shit…I just thoughta something."

"What's that?" Jack asked.

"Man, we started calling this guy The Ninja, right? That musta just got him going even more."

"Yeah, probably," Jack said.

"Don't sweat it, Al," Ken Bright said. "The papers might have come up with something even worse. Well, we better write this up, Jack. I want to make a few calls if that's OK with you."

"Sure, Ken, go ahead," Brickman replied as Ken stood up. The FBI agent was smiling.

"Nice work, Jack," he said. "How'd you figure it out?"

"You wouldn't believe me if I told you," Jack said. "Let's just call it divine inspiration for now."

CHAPTER 37

Following their leader's revelation about The Ninja's motive, the members of NOSCU shared the opinion that it was now only a matter of time before they snared the serial killer.

Armed with what everybody considered a solid intent for The Ninja murders, a physical description of the killer and his mode of transportation, the mood around the NOSCU office was one of restrained optimism. After weeks of unproductive interviews and telephone calls, some things had finally started to fall into place for the team. And Jack Brickman finally felt like he had lived up to the faith that had been placed in his abilities.

They had collected plenty of evidence against The Ninja. Hair fiber, DNA, footprints – they all matched up. Even without the murder weapons, the team generally felt that they had put together an airtight case against the killer. Ken Bright had carefully reviewed the files on each murder and pronounced them ready for the grand jury. All they needed now was the suspect.

A statewide search for the Cabletron van had come up empty. The plate had turned out to be bogus. That had not surprised Jack, though he had certainly wished differently. Police across the North Coast had stopped dozens of white vans after the attack on the CPD officers. Most cops were taking no chances with suspect vehicles. Their well-placed concern for their own safety had resulted in a few innocent civilians being ordered out of their cars at gunpoint during felony stops. Most took the unpleasant incidents in stride, especially after being told the reason for the stop. Inevitably, some citizens took it personally and filed complaints, all of which were duly investigated and dismissed. Police patience was not bottomless when it came to attacks on cops.

They had gotten some decent evidence from the attack, despite the condition of the crime scene. Therese Vidalia had lifted a couple of hairs that later matched up with the samples they already had gathered from the other murder scenes. Because of Terri Rome's inspired request to take the clothes and hair samples from the injured officers, they also matched a couple strands of hair from the victims. They also found several synthetic fibers that later turned out to be commonly used in theatre costumes. The Ninja, apparently, had been wearing a fake beard.

The fake beard created some problems for the sketch artists since they could only guess about the facial details. Based on the general shape of the beard, they could make educated guesses at the shape of the jaw underneath, but details were out of the question. The wraparound sunglasses didn't help, either. But they had good descriptions of the cheekbones, nose, and ears. Whether that would be enough to help identify The Ninja was anybody's guess. Still, they had a sketch and the media was more than happy to run it over and over.

There was a general feeling that all NOSCU needed was one lucky break.

It had been a week since Jack Brickman had put his theory on paper. Ken Bright had run the hypothesis past several sources in the Bureau. They had, for the most part, agreed with the detective.

The atmosphere in the office had greatly improved since Jack's confrontation with Calvin Stoddard. The lawyer had apparently made a phone call or two after Brickman had left him standing in his office. It had become obvious that somebody had made it very clear to Stoddard who was running the show at NOSCU. Calvin had spent all of his time in his office with the door closed. He arrived promptly at nine and left just before five, every day. He was still reviewing the daily reports and signing requisition checks, but that was it. For Jack, it was a welcome change.

It was early Thursday afternoon when Jack Brickman and NOSCU got the break they were looking for.

Jack was reading an article about media obsession that a friend from Case Western University had dug up at his request when there was a knock at his door. The knock was purely courtesy since the detective rarely closed his door. Brickman looked up and saw Bryce Cramer standing there.

"Hey, Bryce, what's up?" Jack asked.

"There's a guy in the lobby I think you should talk to," Cramer said.

"Who is he?" Jack asked.

"Guy's name is Carl Doyle," Cramer replied. "Lives over on Larchmont. He called on the tip line this morning, said he had something on The Ninja. The phone guys gave it to me and I called him back to get some more information. I asked him to come down in person."

"Is it good?" Jack asked. The last thing he wanted was a line of people who felt it necessary to explain their wild theories to the police in person. It was bad enough that they wasted so many man hours with bogus telephone tips. Still, Cramer had obviously thought enough about the man's information that he had invited him in for a sit down.

"It might be," Cramer said. "Guy checks out OK. Works in Willoughby as a machinist or something."

"Well, let's go hear what he has to say," Jack said, pushing his chair away from his desk.

Carl Doyle was in his early forties. He looked like many other Clevelanders. He was a little thicker around the middle than he should have been, and he had the rough face of a man who had weathered more than a few North Coast season changes. As Jack shook hands with Doyle, he could feel the strength and roughness that resulted from a lifetime of manual labor. Doyle seemed a little nervous as they ushered him through the lobby into a small, windowless interview room.

"Mr. Doyle," Jack began once they had sat down. "I understand you have some information that might help us with our investigation."

"Jeez, I hope so, but I don't know," Doyle said. "I almost didn't call. I don't want to waste your time. You probably got enough calls from the whackos without me putting my two cents worth in. And I sure didn't expect to be sitting down with you, detective. I mean, you're the head guy, right?"

"Don't worry about it, Mr. Doyle. Detective Cramer here obviously thinks you have something that could assist us, so just tell me what you told him. And I promise not to call you a whacko."

Doyle laughed a little.

"Sure, sergeant," he said. "And call me Carl, please. When I hear 'Mr. Doyle,' I start looking around for my father."

"Me, too," Jack said, smiling.

"OK," Doyle said. "Anyway, this happened about a month ago and it didn't seem like much then. Hell, it don't seem like much now. My wife's got this little pug dog, Curly. She thinks it's the cutest thing ever, you know. Let me tell you it's about the stupidest animal God ever put on this earth. Damn thing gets lost all the time, you know? Ever hear them stories about dogs crossing the country to get back home? Not Curly. He can't find his way home from across the street.

"Anyway," Doyle continued, "Curly got lost again, so I'm out walking through the neighborhood looking for him. He usually doesn't go that far – pugs have stubby legs – but I was two streets from my house, over on Falstaff, when I thought I heard him yapping. There's this house a good ways back from the street, you know, kind of secluded, big lot. That's kind of unusual for our neighborhood, you know. I guess I never noticed it before. It's getting dark out and I don't want to be walking around yelling 'Curly, Curly' all night so I figure, what the heck, I'll go check it out. Sure enough, the closer I got to the house, the louder that little bastard started barking. I could tell he was stuck inside the garage. I didn't want to break in, so I knocked on the door, rang the bell, but there was no answer.

"Like I said, it's getting late. I guess I was wrong, but I went around to the side door of the garage and tried it. It was open and there was Curly, all covered in grease and dust and stuff. Stupid thing must have gotten stuck in there or something. Well, while I was standing there, I noticed there was a cable van in the garage. First, I thought maybe somebody was getting laid or something, then I thought, hell, that's cool, letting guys take their work truck home. I was turning to leave when all of sudden, the door to the house opens up and here comes this guy. Scared the crap out of me. This guy was pissed off. Guess I can't blame him, but I tried to explain what had happened. I was holding Curly, not like I made up the story, you know. This guy wouldn't hear it, though, kept screaming at me, telling me he was going to call the cops and stuff. He was cursing like you wouldn't believe. I was backing out of there as quick as I could, but the guy started to piss me off, too, and I started to say, like, 'oh yeah, tough guy, let's talk about it outside' but then I looked at the guy – it wasn't too bright in the garage, just a little light bulb and the windows were painted over – and I said 'Carl, that ain't a good idea.'"

"Why was that?" Jack asked.

"You shoulda seen this guy," Doyle continued. "Look, I ain't no pussy, raised a little hell when I was in school, you know. Used to box, some, too. This guy was nothing but muscle, not too tall, but wiry, you know. Like I said, I boxed a bit back in the day, and I've seen what a lightweight can do. And this guy moved like he could fight, you know? So, I kept apologizing

242

and backing up. He slammed the door after me and that was that. I kept waiting for the cops to show up at my door, but they never did."

It was something, but it wasn't exactly a home run. Jack was about to thank Doyle for his time when the machinist started talking again.

"I gotta admit, it freaked me out a little," Doyle said. "I coulda swore the guy was going to kill me. And that voice, holy cow, that just made it worse."

Jack's ears perked up instantly.

"Voice?"

"Yeah," Doyle said. "Real high, like a broad, you know?"

Jack looked at Bryce, who nodded. The description of The Ninja's falsetto voice had not been given to the media. They had purposely withheld the information to help validate good leads.

"Have you told anybody about this?" Jack asked.

"Just my wife," Doyle said. "Like I said, I thought maybe I might be the one in trouble. Fact is, I was just hoping it would all go away until I heard about them cops getting beat up. Even after that, I wasn't sure, but Linda, that's my wife, kept telling me to call. I suppose I coulda left it anonymous, but I figured you might have questions."

"OK, Carl," Jack said. "You did the right thing by coming in. We're going to check this guy out. It might be nothing, but you never know. You kept it quiet this long. How about keeping it quiet a little longer?"

"Hey, half the guys I know would think I was a flake for calling in a tip in the first place," Doyle said. "I can keep my mouth shut. I know you want to catch this guy, 'specially after what he did to them cops, not that I blame you. Them drug guys, like who cares, right? But trying to kill cops? That just ain't right."

"No, it isn't," Brickman agreed. He stood and shook Doyle's hand.

"Thanks again for coming in. You gave the address to Detective Cramer, right?"

"Yeah."

"Bryce, would you walk Carl out?"

"Sure, sergeant. Happy to," Cramer replied. He tore off a paper from his pocket notebook and handed it to Brickman.

"That's the address," he said as he walked the witness to the lobby.

Jack knew the area, but not well. It was a neighborhood on the East Side, just west of the City of Euclid. It was a racially mixed area of what the media would call the "working class." It did not exactly fit Brickman and Bright's profile concerning The Ninja's financial status. It seemed unlikely that an independently wealthy man would be living in such an area. But you never know. And this sure as hell seemed like a solid lead.

Jack headed into the bullpen, stopping by a large bookcase in the center of the room. He grabbed two huge blue blooks off the top of the shelf and started flipping through them. Commonly referred to as the "criss-cross" books, the Haines Directories were priceless to law enforcement. One volume would tell you, if you had the phone number, which address the number belonged to. The other volume, the one Jack needed now, worked the opposite way. It would show him the phone number and name of the resident to a specific address. It did not take him long. Brickman ran his finger down the page until he came to the address Doyle had provided. The name next to it was "Plater, Nicholas."

Nicholas Plater. Now he had a name. Maybe.

Jack quickly scribbled down the information. Bryce Cramer came back into the office, a large grin on his face. Jack returned it. Yeah, maybe this was the guy.

"Listen up, everybody," Jack said. "Whatever you're working on, whoever you're talking to, wrap it up. We've got a hot one. Bryce, go grab Ken Bright out of his office, will you? Thanks."

It took less than a minute for the team to gather around the detective. He quickly briefed them on Carl Doyle's story.

"It may not sound like much, but I think it's the best lead we've had yet," Jack told the team. "A lot of this adds up. The physicals match, and so does the van. Plus, the voice fits. That's something we purposely left out of the press. Anyway, the suspect's name is Nicholas Plater. He lives at 8842 Falstaff. That's all we have right now but that's enough to keep us busy. Bryce, get with Natalie Price and run this guy through LEADS. I want his full driving history and a list of vehicles he owns or ever has owned. Run him through imaging, too. I want a photo of him ASAP. When you get that, run it over to Peterson and Jackson – they're both at home now – and see if they can confirm that it's him. And check and see if he's got a CCH, too.

"Ken, pull whatever strings you have to, but I want everything the government has on him. Income tax, selective service, service record if he's got one. I want it all and I want it yesterday.

"Al, do the same thing at the city and county levels. Tax statements, deeds, everything.

"Stan, you get to deal with the banks. They're not going to want to play ball, but run a credit history on this guy, see where his money is. If you run into trouble, go see Judge Ramallo, he's a friend of the team, or so I'm told. You're probably going to have to subpoena Plater's bank records, so expect a long day.

"Sam, I want some kind of surveillance on the house if you can set it up without tipping this guy off. Start working on a plan to hit the house, hard. And remember who we're dealing with. If you want tech support, check with Ken. I'm sure the Bureau has some toys they're not using."

Jack rattled off a few more directions to the remaining team members and then dismissed them with a warning.

"I want this fast, but I want it quiet, too," he said. "If this is The Ninja, I expect him to be extremely cautious, especially near his home. Let's get it done, people."

The team practically raced out of the office, leaving Jack to call Ed Payne and Andy Fulmer, and let them know what was going on. Before he could get to his office though, Ken Bright, who had lingered behind, stopped him.

"Kind of ironic, isn't it?" Bright said. "We bust our asses for a couple months then a lucky tip breaks the case wide open."

"You complaining?"

"Hell, no," Bright replied. "I'll take a win any way I can get it."

"If it pans out," Jack cautioned. "If it's the guy."

"What's your gut telling you?"

Brickman hesitated a moment. They were alone in the office.

"Plater's The Ninja."

CHAPTER 38

In the days that followed, NOSCU started to get a clearer picture of Nicholas Plater. And the added details all helped solidify the belief that he was, in fact, The Ninja.

Since Jack had given them a name, the team had worked feverishly to fill in the rest of the holes. They had nudged, cajoled, and threatened every source they could find in their quest for information. No detail was considered too small.

Nicholas Plater, 32, was single, never married. He lived alone in a house that had been left to him by his mother. His father had died in a car accident shortly after Nicholas had been born. His mother, Estelle Plater, had died five years ago due to complications from gall bladder surgery.

A lackluster student who, according to the yearbook had participated in no extracurricular activities, Plater had entered the military immediately after his high school graduation. He had done two years in the Army and received an honorable discharge. His service record showed he could follow orders, but not much more than that. He had rated high in marksmanship, hand-to-hand combat, and physical conditioning. There were several glowing reviews from his drill sergeants in basic training about his physical endurance. He had applied for advanced infantry combat training, the paratroopers, the Rangers – all had rejected him. The people who made those decisions repeatedly noted that Nicholas Plater, despite his physical skills, was not a team player and did not work well as part of a unit. His apparent inability to work in a small group of highly skilled individuals made his induction into the Army's elite forces impossible. Sam Rausch had confirmed that the Rangers, at least, prized trust in their teammates more than anything else. Plater instead had ended up in the clerical service, specializing in data entry. The few glitches on his service record had come from run-ins with soldiers from other units who apparently enjoyed taunting Plater about his high-pitched voice, at least according to one report written by his supervisor.

After leaving the military, Plater tried to get into law enforcement, even earning an associate's degree from Cleveland State University. The degree normally takes two years. It took Plater almost four. Just like his high school grades, Plater's college marks were not good. He had to take several classes more than once. He had never worked as a police officer and now worked part-time as a private security guard.

According to income tax returns, Plater worked for Cordall Security, a small local company.

Surprisingly, Plater was financially well off. The home, though not in the greatest of neighborhoods, had been paid off for years. When his mother had died, Plater had collected a meager life insurance payoff. A little digging by the team had revealed that Plater had also received a little over $200,000 in a medical malpractice settlement stemming from his mother's death. The hospital in question had slammed the door shut on them when NOSCU had sought more information about the settlement. Apparently, a gag order had been part of the out-of-court deal. Their lack of cooperation was fine with Jack. He had already found out what he wanted to know. Plater had plenty of cash.

Despite his windfall, Nicholas Plater didn't have much to show for his money. A check of his bank records revealed that he had about half of the money put away in savings accounts and CDs. Outside of his family home, he didn't own any real estate, at least none that they could find.

Plater had no arrest record. Even his driving record was clear, with only two speeding tickets in sixteen years of driving. He had only one vehicle registered in his name, a Honda coupe. If he had purchased a van, they couldn't find any record of it.

The initial information NOSCU had dug up on Plater had come in fairly large chunks. As the days progressed, the information slowed to a tantalizing trickle of intriguing facts that fleshed out their sketch of the man the team now universally believed was The Ninja.

A broad search of the newspaper archives had given them only one tidbit of information. As a child, Plater had once won a karate tournament in Cleveland. According to the brief *The Plain Dealer* had used as a one-paragraph filler in the sports section, Plater had taken two gold medals, one in sparring and one in *kata*. The article said he had been taking classes at the local YMCA. Either he had quit taking lessons or he had never stayed at one school long enough to make an impression since they couldn't find any record of him having enrolled at any dojo in the Cleveland area within the last ten years. Most schools, Sam Rausch had discovered, didn't keep class lists very long. And, according to Plater's bank statements, he hadn't written any checks for self-defense classes as far back as they could determine.

Despite Plater's poor performance in school, he was apparently a voracious reader, obsessed with current events. He had subscriptions to a dozen daily papers, as well as several periodicals.

NOSCU had also started a loose surveillance of Plater. Some of the detectives claimed it was so loose that was almost useless. Brickman didn't care. He believed, and Sam Rausch and Ken Bright supported him, that The Ninja was likely to notice any close surveillance. They didn't want to spook him. They had considered wiretaps on Plater's phone, although it was ultimately determined that would be a waste of time since it was clear that Plater did not have any close friends. Even if he did, it was ridiculous to think that a mysterious loner like Plater would discuss his crimes with anyone.

It fell to Jack and Ken Bright to sift through the information NOSCU brought to them and put it into some sort of meaningful order. It was a challenging process because, as the authors of The Ninja's criminal profile, they had to be careful not to force the facts to fit the profile. But even the most conservative compilation of the information at hand matched up to the letter.

Profiles, however, do not equal evidence.

They had plenty of information that made Plater a highly likely suspect, but they didn't have a shred of evidence that definitively identified Plater as The Ninja. Even Peterson and

Jackson had been unable to pick Plater out of a photo line-up. The disguise, apparently, had been good enough to throw off even the expert eyes of trained observers.

So, after almost a week of digging, they were still one piece of information short of getting a warrant for Plater.

Jack found the situation almost unbearably frustrating. To him, it was like having a name right on the tip of your tongue and just not quite being able to remember it. He felt they were that close to making the connection between the murders and Plater. Unfortunately, there were just too many pieces of the puzzle missing, not the least of which was the victimology. Plater, from what they could find out, clearly had not associated with any of the murdered men. They had even gone back as far as grade school enrollment records with nothing to show for it but some annoyed clerks. The link remained elusive.

Until Stan Lombardo figured it out.

Jack was sitting on Bryce Cramer's desk in the bullpen, discussing an interview with him and Ken Bright when they heard Lombardo mumble something under his breath. There was a flurry of activity as he shuffled papers around his desk, obviously looking for something. When he found it, he repeated his earlier comment louder.

"Holy shit," he said, standing up at his desk.

"What's up, Stan," Cramer asked.

"Hey, you guys are gonna love this," the detective said. "We've got a fairly good idea why he's doing it, right? The press coverage angle makes sense. But we still don't know how he's picking the victims, right?"

"Right," Jack said.

"I think it's all right here," Lombardo said, holding up a file folder.

"What is that?" Brickman asked.

"It's the Timmons file from the probation department," he said.

"And?"

"We sign these in and out like evidence, right?" Lombardo asked. "It's how they keep track of the files when they're brought over from storage."

"Yeah, but that's normal," Jack said. "Just about everybody has interoffice envelopes they transfer the same way."

"Right," Lombardo said. "I send it to you, you sign, you send it back, I sign, etc. But take a look at the jacket cover."

Jack looked at the manila envelope. There were places for signatures, but Jack didn't notice anything unusual.

"If you look at the top of the envelope, you'll notice the name SafeStor," Stan said.

"OK," Jack said. "Who's that?"

"Well, you know how it is for the court system, right? You generate tons of paperwork for anybody you arrest, especially a felon…reports, evidence sheets, court records, all kinds of stuff. I don't know how it is for Cleveland, but at Shaker, we outgrew our records storage a long time ago. Now we pay somebody to store our files. Judging from the paperwork here, Cuyahoga County does the same thing."

"Yeah, they do," Bryce Cramer chimed in. "I've seen the couriers from SafeStor bringing in boxes of the stuff."

"I never thought about it," Jack admitted. "I just assumed they kept all of that info locked away in a county building somewhere."

"I was taking a look at a list of companies Cordall Security has contracts with, places Plater might have worked. They have to keep an updated client list with the city to maintain their license," Lombardo explained, leafing through a stack of papers on his desk. He stopped and handed a sheet to Jack. "Check it out."

Jack took the proffered sheet and read down the list of names. There, near the bottom, was the name, SafeStor. Finally, it clicked into place.

"He's seen the probation records," Jack almost whispered.

Lombardo smiled.

"Yeah, I think he has," he said. "Look, it makes sense. We've all worked side jobs as security guards here and there. Usually, they're bullshit and you've got plenty of down time. Let's say Plater's working for Cordall, who contracts with SafeStor. Assume he works the occasional midnight shift. He'd have access to the files and plenty of time to flip through them. Plus, he wouldn't leave a trail like he might with a computer."

"We spent all that time looking for links and it was right there," Lombardo continued. "Every one of the victims was on probation, or had been recently. Probation hearings are formal – there's a transcript and everything, like court."

"But we checked all that," Cramer said. "We looked at the court clerks, stenographers, everything."

"Keep going, Stan," Jack said, noticing the small crowd that had gathered around them.

"You guys think he's purposely picking victims with no family, right? Well, that kind of stuff doesn't come out in regular court proceedings, but it does come up at probation hearings. Apparently, it has some bearing on whether or not they get probation."

"But Jameel Timmons had a family," Jack pointed out.

"Yes, he did," Lombardo said. "But listen to this. It's a transcript from his probation hearing. Somebody on the panel says 'What about family Mr. Timmons? Do you have someone you can stay with?' Timmons says: 'I got nobody.' I don't know why he said that, maybe he was on the outs with mom that day, who knows? But he said it. The probation department's own records list his mom as next of kin, but apparently the panel took him at his word because they never came back to the question. If The Ninja had access to the rest of the court documents, he'd have known that Timmons had family. So, I think it's safe to say he's just going off the probation hearings."

A smile crept onto Jack's face.

"Yeah," he said. "I think you're right."

"How about it, Ken?" Jack asked the FBI agent. "Is it enough?"

"Let's firm it up a little," Bright said. "I'd like to talk to somebody at Cordall Security, see if we can find out if Plater worked SafeStor. We can grab a supervisor at home, keep him quiet and go from there."

"OK," Jack said. He looked at this watch. It was late afternoon now. He picked up a phone and dialed Sam Rausch's number.

"Get ready, Sam," he said. "We're getting ready to cut a warrant for Plater."

"How soon?"

"Probably a couple of hours, then it's your show."

"Outstanding," Rausch said, then hung up.

Jack turned to the team members standing near him.

"OK," he said. "Let's go get him."

CHAPTER 39

It was almost the perfect raid.

True to his word, Sam Rausch had his SWAT team ready almost instantly. Since they already knew what their likely target would be, the unit had already worked out multiple strategies for assaulting Plater's home. They had very cautiously taken photos of the home from several different angles, including reconnaissance pictures taken from about courtesy of one of CPD's new helicopters. Somebody even had the foresight to pull the original house plans from the county engineer's archives so they could formulate plots for after entering the home.

They started compiling the information as soon as they had gotten the target information. The CPD SWAT team had experience conducting well-planned, specifically prepared raids. If they knew they were going to hit a house for drugs or a high-risk warrant, they generally had a day or two to work out the details. In the rare spontaneous high-risk situations, they usually did not have that luxury. When faced with situations that needed immediate action, such as active shooters or hostage events, the team and its leaders were forced to be more creative in their planning. In either case, the week Jack Brickman had given them to get ready had been put to effective use.

The reconnaissance had not gone as well as they would have liked.

Jack and Ken Bright had repeatedly warned them that The Ninja was bound to be paranoid and very aware of his surroundings. At least as far as the paranoia went, they could see that NOSCU was right. Every window of Plater's home was blacked out, either blocked with furniture or light-stopping blinds. Even the windows of the attached garage, as reported by Carl Doyle, had been blacked out with paint. Not only could they not see into the home, virtually no light escaped the home at night. Plater was apparently taking the Shadow Warrior's code to heart.

Even with the limitations placed on their recon, Sam Rausch and his team leaders felt they had several plans that would get the job done. It was just a matter of getting the "go" signal from Jack and picking their time.

It had taken little coaxing from the FBI agent to get Plater's supervisor to confirm that he had worked at SafeStor dozens of times during the last couple of years. By the time Ken Bright got the warrant ready and signed by a sympathetic judge NOSCU had enlisted from the beginning, the decision to arrest Nicholas Plater was already almost three hours old. Ken had been working on the warrant for a while, and it was just a matter of updating the information, but he had wanted a second opinion on it before having it signed. It was not a question of lack of confidence on his part; it was a sign of his professionalism. Ken Bright, despite his extensive legal experience, was not about to lose The Ninja because he had forgotten to cross a "t" or dot and "I." And after it had been checked, it had taken a little while to locate their judge. They had found him at the Lakeside Yacht Club, just returning from an evening sail. He had signed on the spot.

Even with the warrant in hand, they had decided to wait for nightfall, when the SWAT team would have their best chance at getting close to the home without being seen. They hoped that The Ninja's obsession with privacy would work in their favor, since it was unlikely that he could see out of the house any better than they could see in. Jack, Ken, and Sam had discussed waiting until three or four in the morning, when the usual suspect's reactions would be at their slowest. In the end, they had decided on hitting him two hours after sunset. The Ninja, they suspected, was probably a night owl anyway, so hitting him later probably would not make much difference.

Despite what they knew about The Ninja, however, there was still much they didn't know. Those unknowns were obviously foremost in the minds of the men who would be breaking down Plater's door. Jack had found that out when he had helped brief the SWAT team at Sam's request.

Jim McReedy, one of the team's shotgun operators, wanted to know if they could expect the house to be rigged with explosives or tripwires.

"What about booby traps, sarge?" he asked. "This guy's good with guns and knives, right? We can manage that, but to do this right, we're going to be moving pretty fast. I'd rather not plow through this house and find out he's a bomb maker, too."

The other team members nodded and murmured their agreement. McReedy's concern was well placed. Under the new formation they had developed specifically for The Ninja, he would be the first one through the door.

"It's doubtful, but it's a possibility," Jack admitted. "We know The Ninja reads a lot, and we know he can handle weapons. If he's patterned himself after the real ninjas, I think it's unlikely, but maybe Sam can explain why better."

"Jack's right, guys," Sam said, stepping up. "These guys moved in fast, hit fast, and got out fast. They might use stuff to slow down pursuit, like throw caltrops on the floor, but in general they relied on speed and stealth. Plus, this is the guy's home. They taught us plenty about booby traps in the Rangers, and one of the things they stressed was that you could never forget where you set the trap, for obvious reasons. Imagine Plater gets up to take a piss one night and steps on a *punji* stick. I don't see him risking it. And, as far as we know, this guy is not expecting us."

"So, it's a possibility, right?" McReedy persisted.

"Yeah, it is," Rausch replied. "Look, Jim, this is going to be a tough one, but nothing we all haven't done a hundred times. And it sure isn't going to be as tough as hitting a meth lab. At least we can shoot Plater without worrying about blowing up the house."

McReedy smiled.

"Yeah, L-T, good point," he said.

"What about night vision?" John Post, one of the team's MP-5 operators asked. "This guy going to have goggles or not?"

"Again, it's possible," Jack said.

"That's not going to matter," Rausch said. "We're going in loud and bright."

That raised a few eyebrows.

"Yeah, I know we usually pull the power first," Sam said. "But remember what we're dealing with here. Plater is used to working in the dark. I think we'd still have the edge with the night vision, but you guys know how those things can screw up your depth perception. So, we're going to move in fast with plenty of flashlights and we're going to use flash-bangs all the way through."

That told them much about how bad they wanted The Ninja. Flash-bang concussion grenades were less-lethal distraction devices intended to temporarily short circuit the nervous system. They were used sparingly, however, mainly because they presented a fire hazard. Like any "less-lethal" device, there was always the possibility of an inadvertent suspect death.

"The entry team won't be using NODs," Rausch continued, using the miliary term for night vision goggles, "Night Optical Devices." "But the perimeter team will be. We don't want Plater slipping past us in the dark. And we'll have both CPD choppers en route as soon as we make entry. If he gets out of the house, they can use their spotlights or their thermal imagers to track him. Not that that's going to be an issue, because I know you guys aren't going to let him slip through."

"Is this going to be a green light from the git-go?" sniper Lars Hendriksen asked. "I got a nice spot picked out and my ghillie suit's all pressed and cleaned."

That brought a few chuckles. The ghillie suit was a mesh hodgepodge of cloth strips and camouflage. Most snipers had them, though few urban police long gunmen ever needed them. There weren't many trees in major cities. Plater's yard, however, was a different story. It was heavily wooded and surrounded on three sides and in the rear by a slight rise. Regardless, if Hendriksen was looking forward to ending The Ninja's killing spree with "one shot, one kill," he was about to be disappointed.

"No," Rausch said. "We want to take him alive."

"What?"

"Our usual rules of engagement apply," Sam said. "If he gives a reason, drop him. We'll pick up the pieces later. But we want to get him in custody if we can."

"Why?" McReedy asked.

Jack Brickman took over on that point.

"We're operating under the assumption that Plater killed before he became The Ninja," Jack said. "With a little luck, we might be able to get him to talk to us, and that might close one or two murder cases. I know that solving some detective's case is not a big deal to you, but it can really help us and the families move on. Hell, they kept Bundy alive for years because he kept leaking information. But nobody is asking you guys to take any extra chances. Sam's given you your rules of engagement, and he's got my blessing. We're not trading a cop's life for a little information."

They may not have been happy about the situation, but Sam Rausch's response team was made up of pros who could follow orders. While they would have preferred "shoot on sight" orders, they also knew that was an unlikely directive for any police SWAT team. After all, they still had to follow the same use-of-force restrictions as any other police officer.

"We'll get it done, Sergeant Jack," Hendriksen drawled as Brickman left the SWAT staging area. Jack smiled and gave him a thumbs up as he walked out.

"I hope he's right," Jack thought.

They had decided to hit Plater's house at 2250, or ten minutes to eleven. That would give Hendriksen and the other perimeter units a chance to move in quietly under cover of darkness before the entry team hit the door. Jack left Sam Rausch to determine where he wanted to stage for the raid. They would be parking nearby and threading their way through the trees to hit the house from the front. Jack, Al, Ken, and Stan Lombardo would be following in an unmarked unit, followed by Bryce Cramer, Ed Payne, Andy Fulmer, and Terri Rome in another unmarked car. They, in turn, would be followed by three 3-man CPD units. The rest of NOSCU, including the evidence technicians and the docile Calvin Stoddard, would be staging at the Euclid Police Department, which would also have their SWAT unit on standby.

By the time they moved out, Jack was nervous. Not frightened, really, just nervous. Even though he intended to be well out of harm's way, he was wearing a Level III raid vest that was capable of stopping most handgun and some rifle rounds. In addition to his 9mm, Jack had retrieved his .38 from the safe at home and had it strapped to his ankle. Guns help calm cops' nerves.

At 2230, they checked in with Lars Hendriksen, who was somewhere in the trees behind The Ninja's house.

"Anything moving?" they heard Rausch ask over the radio. He did not use code. CPD had long since gone to an 800MhZ system that required an expensive and very sophisticated scanner for eavesdropping. On the chance that Plater had a scanner, though, they were careful not to give away too much information.

"Negative visual," the sniper replied. "Getting a warm spot on the thermal. Second-floor bathroom, looks like he may be in the tub."

"Perimeter?"

"Negative," came the replies from the other SWAT team operatives.

Jack's cell phone rang. It was Sam Rausch.

"What do you think, Jack? It's either wait until we see him move or go inside now."

"What's the downside?"

"The longer we wait, the better the odds that we'll be spotted," Rausch said. "We'll probably still get the evidence; we just might not get him."

"The windows must be keeping us from seeing if he's home," Jack said. "Any other way of finding out if he's in there?"

"If we had good enough microphones, we could listen for movement," Rausch said. "But we don't. We could always call him on the phone. That could tip him off, though."

Jack weighed the options. He wanted The Ninja caught more than anybody else, and he was trying to balance his desire for an arrest against the need to be sure. If they missed now, they might not get another shot at Plater for a long time. He almost asked his passengers what they thought but decided against it. This was going to be his decision.

"Make the phone call," he said.

Sam Rausch, who was riding with the rest of the team in CPD's SWAT van nodded to Jim McReedy.

"Dial him up," the lieutenant said.

McReedy punched in the number and waited. After several rings, the high-pitched voice of Nicholas Plater answered.

"Hello?" he said. "Hello? Who is this? Hello?"

McReedy hung up.

"He's there," the shotgunner said. Rausch relayed the message to Jack.

"What's your call, Jack?"

"Do it."

Watching an elite SWAT team work is an impressive sight. Until you see them in action, it's hard to imagine that a group of heavily armed, heavily armored men can move as quickly and quietly, or with such purpose. Occasionally, they acquire a reputation as prima donnas, with their special weapons and macho attitudes. Maybe they earned that reputation. But they could sure back it up.

Jack pulled in quietly behind the SWAT van and watched them move out into the tree line toward Plater's house. The six-man entry team moved silently through the wooded area while the other six members of the team fanned out across the front and sides of the home, careful to keep their fields of fire open. Jack and Ken Bright crept forward as far as they dared, aided by night vision goggles the special agent had borrowed from the Bureau. It was a hot night, and sweat immediately began to run down Jack's face under the goggles and down his back under the vest. He barely noticed.

Jack watched through the green tinged lenses as the entry team moved up to the house. Plater had no exterior lights on, which was a blessing. The unit crept silently up the stairs. Jack watched as two men with short-barreled shotguns moved up to the door. He held his breath as they fired their special breaching rounds through the deadbolt and hinges. Seconds later, he heard the definitive crack of the flash-bang grenades. And then the team disappeared into the house. Jack could follow their movement by the shattering of windows as the concussion grenades led their way into each new section of the home. By the time the second six-man team had moved up, Brickman started hearing the repeated calls of "clear" coming through the earpiece of the radio.

"Brickman, up," Sam Rausch's voice called.

Jack moved up to the house quickly but cautiously. Rausch did not look happy.

"He's not here," Rausch said. "We missed."

Yes, it was almost a perfect raid.

CHAPTER 40

Nicholas Plater, AKA The Ninja, had made the right assumption for the wrong reasons. Thus, he had not been at home for Sam Rausch's housewarming party.

Plater had been about to settle in for the evening but he had been restless sitting at home. A rigorous workout was followed by a scalding hot bath, Japanese style. Plater could not have known that his cast-iron tub would hold a heat signature long enough to fool Lars Hendriksen's thermal imager. The workout and bath had done nothing to calm Plater's nerves. What he really needed was a night of hunting. His fight with the police, however, had interrupted the stalking of his next prey, and there were no likely candidates ready for his attention. He needed to work more to dig up a new target, and lately Cordall Security hadn't been calling him to work. He was so eager to work, in fact, that he had calls forwarded from his home phone to his cell.

Plater had finally decided to go to the movies. He liked action films and the anonymity of sitting in a dark theater. It was one of the few places where you weren't expected to talk to anybody. Even better, you were encouraged not to talk. That suited him fine. Plater had just been entering the theater when his phone had vibrated. He had heard something on the other end, but nobody had answered. That had been weird. It was probably just a wrong number, but it made him nervous. Lots of things made him nervous these days.

He had been heading towards home in his Honda – his van had long since been repainted and tucked away in a self-storage garage – when he noticed a CPD unit and a Euclid PD car pulled off the road in a vacant lot about a mile from his house. It looked like they had just pulled up to shoot the breeze. Cops, he noticed, did that. They would pull driver's side to driver's side and BS for a while. If he could have heard their conversation, he would have known they played in a softball league together and they were just catching up on the latest standings. They had nothing at all to do with the raid. Anyway, it was not an unusual sight. But tonight, for some reason, it made the hairs on the back of his neck stand up. He made a left turn and headed for the freeway, towards his safe house.

Based on nothing more than a hang-up phone call and two cops sitting by the side of the road, Nicholas Plater, the worst serial killer to plague the North Coast since the Torso Killer, was going to ground.

CHAPTER 41

Jack did everything he could to hide his disappointment. He knew that NOSCU would take their cues from him, and the last thing he wanted to do was cast an air of defeat over the team. As veteran cops, they were used to disappointment, but it was still tough to keep going. Luckily, the treasure trove of evidence in Plater's home meant that NOSCU had plenty of work to keep them busy and keep their minds off the near miss.

After the SWAT team had declared Plater's house secure, they had gone through again and made sure. At Sam Rausch's direction, they had checked for tunnels, trapdoors, and secret rooms. His concern was that Plater, anticipating a police raid, might have created a hiding place somewhere in the house, a place where he could conceal himself and either escape or attack the cops scouring his home for evidence. That concern ultimately proved overly cautious, though it had taken a CPD K-9 unit to convince the lieutenant that the house was unoccupied before he would let Brickman and the rest of NOSCU enter the residence and start their painstaking hunt for evidence.

Jack would have liked some time to himself in the home. It was probably more from his sense of the dramatic than from any investigative technique, but he couldn't help feeling that he could somehow get a better sense of what made The Ninja tick. As he entered the house, though, Ken Bright and Al Sladky were right behind him. He was glad they were there, but he felt crowded. That crowded feeling would increase as the rest of the team arrived. At least he had the chance to walk through before they got there.

Brickman's first impression of Plater's house was that it was still very much his mother's home. The furniture in the living room, kitchen, and dining room was dated and shabby, not at all the type likely to be favored by a bachelor in his thirties. Either Plater had purposely maintained the house as his mother had left it as some type of shrine to her memory or he had just not bothered to change anything since her death. Jack suspected it was likely a combination of the two. On the second floor, Plater had even kept his mother's bedroom neat, though dusty. Her clothes were still hung in the closet.

Plater's room was plain, though it still had the air of an adolescent. His drawers were filled with neatly folded clothes and the bed was crisply made. Plater was apparently using a third bedroom on the second floor as a home office and computer room. There was little in it except for a chair, a file cabinet, and a rather expensive desktop on a wheeled computer station. Plater didn't seem to believe in decorations, since the walls in this room were blank.

The bland, everyhome feel of the house changed once they came to the third story.

To begin with, the door leading to the third floor had been replaced with a steel fire door. The breaching rounds of the SWAT team's shotguns had made short work of the reinforced door, but it was obvious that Plater did not want anybody entering his sanctum sanctorum.

The third floor of the house was a large, finished room. Unlike many houses with a finished attic, this room had high ceilings and hardwood floors. And it was big, big enough to house The Ninja's *dojo.*

Jack had been amazed at the amount of martial arts equipment in the attic room. Virtually every type of bizarre weapon he had seen while paging through catalogs of ninja supplies hung from the walls or in racks. In one corner stood a large wooden target bristling with throwing knives and *shuriken.* The room also had a rather lifelike sparring dummy and a huge mannequin hanging from a series of pulleys. Jack had never seen anything like it, and couldn't quite figure it out until Sam Rausch explained.

"It's an articulated training dummy," he said. "All the joints bend like a person's. You can even practice throws and takedowns on it. Put some free weights on the other end of the pulley and you can even increase the resistance. I've been trying to get one for the police academy for years, but they're too expensive. Guess we know how he brushed up on his techniques."

"Lifelike, isn't it?" Jack conceded.

"Tell me about it," Rausch said. "McReedy almost ventilated it when they hit this room."

As intimidating as the weapons were, they were not the most disturbing part of the third floor. Secreted behind one wall of the main room, they found a small door leading to what had probably been a storage room. Plater had converted it to a shrine to The Ninja.

The room, which was only about eight feet square, was plastered with floor to ceiling press clippings about The Ninja murders. Each murder had its own section of the wall. Each section was set up like a museum display, complete with the weapons used in the killings. And beyond that were the souvenirs…assorted items presumably taken from the victims. A few vials of crack, two handguns, several knives…all trophies taken by The Ninja. Jack hadn't expected that. He had thought that the media attention would have been enough to satisfy Plater's need for notoriety. Also in the room was a TV and VCR, positioned directly in front of a low futon chair. Dozens of videotapes sat in a rack next to the TV. Jack assumed they were tapes of local news broadcasts about The Ninja. He decided to let the evidence technicians find out for sure.

Brickman took his time in the room, just standing in its center, looking, careful not to touch anything. Finally, he left.

"Vidalia and Moore are going to have a field day in here," he thought as he headed back down the stairs.

The rest of the team was already swarming through the house, picking their way through the broken glass and debris left by the SWAT team's dynamic entry. It was a slow process. Literally everything in the home was considered possible evidence. Even contaminated by the entry team, mundane items such as carpet fibers could further solidify the case against Plater. Granted, they had physical evidence in abundance, including suspected murder weapons, but NOSCU wanted an absolutely airtight case.

For all the evidence, though, Jack was understandably depressed by the fact that they had missed their quarry. Over the next few hours, even the smiling faces of Therese Vidalia and Heath Moore, who were happily going through the painstaking process of bagging and tagging the mother lode of evidence, did little to brighten his spirits. Vidalia had checked in with Jack a couple of times, on each occasion expressing disbelief at the amount of forensic evidence Plater had left behind.

"It's like he wanted us to have this stuff, Jack," she had said. "Jesus, you can still see blood and bone on half the weapons. Why didn't he throw this stuff out?"

"Probably couldn't part with them," Brickman said. "He needed trophies, right? Plus, Sam thinks he probably attached some type of mystical qualities to the weapons. You don't just throw away an icon. And he probably likes to relive each murder."

"No kidding," Vidalia said. "We ran the light over his little sanctuary. The UV picked up hundreds of semen stains in the hardwood and the chair he had up there. He might not have left anything at the scene, but he sure as hell was getting off on the aftermath."

On top of overseeing the crime scene, Jack still had to figure out the next move. He sought out Sam Rausch, Ken Bright, and Al Sladky. They were the people he trusted the most. Jack had an idea and right now he needed advice.

He found them sitting in the rear of the SWAT van. Sam had released half his team. Those that remained were helping haul boxes of evidence out of the house.

"Hey, junior, how about a cup?" Sladky said, pouring him some coffee from an insulated carafe.

Jack sniffed it.

"Just coffee?" he asked. "I could use something a little stronger."

"Hey, we're still on the job, right?" Al said. "It ain't like you to get down, Jack. We've missed guys before."

"Al's right," Sam said. "Do you know how many houses I've hit and come up empty? Ask the team. It's feast or famine."

"They're right," Ken Bright said. "We've got this guy nailed. We know who he is, we know his MO. He's got to be on the run now, so it's just a matter of turning up the heat. Plus, he's now a fugitive from prosecution. That gets him on the FBI's most wanted list. I talked to the SAC and he said they'd approve it. That means there's going to be a hell of a lot of cops looking for him. Where's he going to go?"

Jack shook his head.

"I'd like to say I'm optimistic about our chances of nailing him soon, Ken, but you know Plater's different from most fugitives."

"How so?" Sladky said.

"For one thing, he's got money. Anywhere from fifty to a hundred thousand in cash. That buys plenty of running room. Plus, he's had a chance to plan his escape for a while, way before we started looking for him. And he's got good computer skills, so who knows what he's cooked up for cover. Working in our favor, he doesn't speak any foreign languages and he doesn't have any friends he can go to. Still, he could set up shop easily in another state and quietly start all over again. It took us what, four kills, before we figured out what he was up to. Could he get that many or more say, in Detroit or Chicago? Plus, he knows where he screwed up this time, mainly by leaving those cops alive. What if he decides the next blue suits are expendable?"

"But we'll get him, Jack," Ken said. "It's just a matter of when."

"No offense, Ken, but that's not good enough," Jack said. "We need to get this guy before he gets comfortable someplace else."

"OK, Jack," Bright said. "How?"

"I'm glad you asked," Jack replied, and started detailing his plan. When he was finished, the other three were nodding in agreement. It was a long shot, but it was worth a try. They were interrupted by a gentle tapping on the metal door of the van. It was Calvin Stoddard.

"I assume we're putting out arrest bulletins and such for Plater?" he asked. Jack assured him they were. "What about the media then? Should we call them?"

"Definitely," Jack replied.

CHAPTER 42

From *The North Coast Press*

Page A-1

August 4

By Cliff O'Brien

CLEVELAND – After more than two months of intensive investigation, the Northern Ohio Serial Crimes Unit has issued a warrant for the man they believe is the killer known as "The Ninja."

According to NOSCU's lead investigator, CPD Det. Sgt. Jack Brickman, they have positively identified Nicholas Plater, 32, of Cleveland, as their only suspect in a crime spree that has left at least six people dead and two police officers seriously injured.

NOSCU, along with members of the CPD SWAT team, raided Plater's East Side home late Thursday, armed with arrest and search warrants. While they did not apprehend Plater, Brickman said the team retrieved evidence that definitively linked Plater to the killings.

"For obvious reasons, I can't be specific about what we found in the suspect's home," Brickman said. "I can confirm that we recovered several weapons we believe were used in The Ninja murders, along with other physical evidence positively tying Nicholas Plater to this series of crimes."

Brickman said he believes Plater has left the Cleveland area, and could literally be anywhere. NOSCU's investigation has now sparked a nationwide manhunt for the serial killer, and the FBI has moved Plater onto its "Ten Most Wanted List."

While he could not elaborate on exactly how NOSCU tracked down The Ninja, Brickman did give most of the credit to his team, saying that it was the unique mix of investigators that brought The Ninja case to a close in a relatively brief period of time. Brickman praised the efforts of FBI Special Agent Ken Bright and CPD SWAT commander Lt. Sam Rausch.

"Ken Bright was instrumental in formulating the criminal profile of The Ninja and in making sure the team had all the resources it needed," Brickman said.

"Lt. Rausch gave us something different," Brickman said. "Sam's expertise in the martial arts really got us pointed in the right direction. It was his input that really got us looking at The Ninja as a serial killer."

Rausch came to national attention several years ago for thwarting a bank robbery while unarmed and facing three armed suspects. Off-duty and in civilian clothes, Rausch successfully disarmed one robber and used that suspect's gun against his accomplice. CPD SWAT team snipers stopped the third robber as he was about to execute the bank's manager.

Rausch shrugged off questions about that incident, saying he would prefer to focus on The Ninja.

"I just happened to be in the right place at the right time," he said. "I really should have been carrying a gun that day, anyway, but I was coming from my dojo and I have a strict rule against having guns at my school."

Rausch operates the West Side Martial Arts Center in Parma.

A long-time martial artist, the veteran SWAT commander admitted that his knowledge of ninjitsu was limited, but he was glad he had been able to help NOSCU.

"Ninjitsu is one of those fringe martial arts that creeps into the mainstream from time to time," Rausch said. "It really goes against the philosophy of most martial arts, which are defensive in nature. I mean, if you have to sneak up on somebody so you can win the fight, maybe you shouldn't be fighting at all. Maybe you should be walking away."

Rausch was reluctant to criticize other martial arts, but he did eventually admit he had little respect for ninjitsu.

"There's a mystique surrounding assassins that I could never figure out," Rausch said. "Historically, the ninja were second-rate when it came to face-to-face confrontations. Against a samurai in open combat? No contest."

Cliff looked up to see Leo Nelson standing in his cubicle, clearing his throat.

"Not exactly your best work, Cliff," he said.

"The sidebar?" Cliff asked. "Yeah, I know, but the main story's good, right?"

"Sure, sure," Nelson said. "I just don't know if we can fit in this story about Rausch."

"Try, Leo, it will mean a lot to me. And to other people."

Nelson's eyebrows raised a little.

"What are you up to, kid?" he asked.

"Me? Nothing," Cliff said.

"So, what's it worth to us?"

"An exclusive."

"About The Ninja? No kidding? OK, I guess they have their reasons. We'll make room."

"Thanks, Leo," Cliff said.

He hadn't been entirely honest with Leo. He knew why Brickman wanted the story to run. And his price had been more than an exclusive. Brickman was going to owe him a favor, too.

CHAPTER 43

As usual, Sam Rausch was the last person to leave the *dojo*.

He could have let one of his senior instructors lock up for him, but his work with NOSCU had kept him away from his students longer than he would have liked. His wife had kept up with the bookkeeping for the school, and his staff, who were accustomed to him being called away, had done an excellent job filling in for him. Still, he was glad to be back at the school. It was past ten by the time he had reviewed progress reports and scheduled classes for the next month.

He was a little stiff from the night's training. A very energetic brown belt had really given it her all in the sparring ring against him. There wasn't anything more dangerous than a student with a brown belt. They had plenty of speed and power, but lacked the timing and finesse needed to get them to the black belt level. And, since they weren't expected to win against a black belt, let alone the head instructor, they usually fought with the abandon of someone who had nothing to lose.

After Sam finished in his office, he went out to the main training floor. The room had been thoroughly cleaned by his students. That was one of things they all helped with, regardless of rank. It was quiet, and Sam loved it like this. So peaceful, so full of promise, the hardwood floor creaking ever so slightly under his bare feet. Inspired, he took a *katana* to the center of the floor and started running through *iaido* combinations. He only worked with the razor-sharp sword when the dojo was empty. It was too dangerous otherwise. By the time he had finished, he had worked up a new sweat. He replaced the sword in a leather case, knelt, meditated, and bowed before heading to the locker room to towel off and change into street clothes. He was feeling very relaxed and at peace with the world.

Sam shouldered his gym bag and long, leather weapons case and locked the front door of the school. The school, which was actually two storefronts in an older section of shops near Ridge Road, was blessed with fairly generous parking in the front and rear of the building. Sam usually parked in back. He had found it was easier, since the front lot was inevitably filled with parents picking up and dropping off their kids. Plus, they could sit and wait in their cars until classes were over. The rear lot was dark when Sam walked around the corner of the building toward his car.

The Ninja was about fifty feet away when he stepped from the shadows. He was dressed in traditional ninja garb, complete with cowl and *tabi* boots. In his hands he held a straight black sword, its edge gleaming in the faint lamplight. Sam's first reaction was to drop his right hand to his side where his .45 would normally be. He came up empty. Then The Ninja spoke. Sam recognized it as a line from a movie he had caught late one night.

"Baka, samurai," Plater said in Japanese. Foolish samurai.

Sam tried to buy a little time.

"It doesn't have to be this way, Plater," he said. As he spoke, he lowered his gym bag to the ground.

"That's what you think," Plater said in his strange, high voice.

Rausch could tell that communication was not Plater's strong suit. He talked like a kid on the playground. Except kids didn't carry swords and kill people. Sam watched Plater carefully. He was out of striking distance, but that could change in an instant. Sam cast a casual glance back toward the street. Plater, obviously not taking any chances, brought the tip of his sword up slightly.

"Uh uh uh," he said. "You know you'll never make it, lieutenant."

"What do you want?"

"Oh, I think you know," Plater said. "Time to walk the walk."

Sam hesitated before responding. When he did, his voice was calm and even. If The Ninja was expecting to scare him, he was going to be disappointed.

"Sure," he said. "Why not? Just let me get ready."

Plater giggled, a high-pitched noise punctuated by a little hopping movement.

Sam slid the leather weapons bag off of his other shoulder and knelt down facing Plater. He laid the case down in front of him. He placed his left hand then his right on the ground and lowered his head to the ground and sat back up. Plater was obviously impatient, hopping from foot to foot, but he didn't approach. Apparently, he respected ritual. Sam calmly unzipped the long leather case and removed his weapon.

It took a second for Plater to realize he had been duped.

Rausch brought the Remington 870 to bear on The Ninja as he raised himself onto one knee. The weapon was a short-barreled pump shotgun equipped with a Speedfeed pistol grip that looked like a teardrop, a design that had allowed Sam to conceal it in the narrow sword bag. In a smooth effortless motion, Rausch racked the slide, slamming a round into the weapon's chamber.

"Drop it," he ordered.

Plater, outraged, did not even hear him.

"Cheater!" he screamed as he charged Rausch, the sword coming up over his head.

Rausch fired, cycled the action of the shotgun, fired, and pumped again, his hands a blur. The muted roar of the weapon echoed dully in the muggy summer air as Plater went down. As one would expect from the commander of an elite SWAT unit, Sam Rausch's aim was clinically precise. The first round had struck Plater in the chest, just below the solar plexus. The second had hit him lower, just about the belt line.

Sam came to his feet slowly, the shotgun still pointed at the now prone suspect. Plater's sword had dropped from his hand after being shot and it was still a good ten feet from The Ninja.

Rausch did not close the distance with Plater. That would be a rookie mistake. The Ninja was about 25 feet way, and that was as close as he needed to get. He could tell from the sound of sirens and straining engines that help would be here soon enough. He forced himself to slow his breathing as a van and several cars screeched to a halt and SWAT and NOSCU members started hitting the pavement.

The SWAT team was taking no chances with Plater. Two arrest teams moved in from forty-five-degree angles in single file behind an officer laboring behind huge "body bunker" portable bulletproof shields. Once sure Plater was out of commission, they moved in quickly, cuffing, and shackling him. Two members of the team with cut resistant gloves thoroughly searched The Ninja. They turned up a half-dozen assorted weapons, from knives to throwing stars. Plater groaned as they rolled him to a sitting position.

"Good shooting, Sam," Jack said.

"Yeah," Rausch replied, finally relaxing. "The SIMs work pretty good. Most of the time."

Specialty Impact Munitions, or SIMs, once shunned by law enforcement in favor of chemical sprays or stun guns, have been steadily carving out a niche in the use-of-force options available to most police departments. Although they come in a variety of shapes and sizes, the most practical type of projectile can be launched from a standard 12-guage pump shotgun. Semiautomatic shotguns, which require substantial recoil to eject the empty shell and load a new round, won't function with the greatly reduced output of the SIMs. Some of the "bean bag" rounds were little more than lead shot in a square package, folded into a shotgun shell. Those types had the unfortunate characteristic of unfolding in mid-flight and veering off course, occasionally with fatal results.

For this particular mission, Sam had opted for the Federal Laboratories 23 DS round, which was significantly more accurate. The 23DS, which looks like a little yellow octopus once deployed, is a drag-stabilized pouch of #4 lead shot in a ballistic cloth cover. Weighing 1.43 ounces and travelling at 280 feet per second, the 23DS hits with about the same force as a surprise punch from a professional heavyweight boxer. The incapacitating effects of the "less-lethal" round are significantly increased by the fact that the suspect believes he has been shot with a "real" weapon. If television has done nothing else, it has taught generations of Americans how they're supposed to act when they're shot. Plater, no doubt influenced by his own experiences, responded as programmed. He assumed he was dead and went down.

As planned, an ambulance pulled up to the scene. One of the arrest team gave them an "all clear" sign. Jack felt a wave of relief wash over him, and the tension of the past several months lifted instantly. His mind felt clearer now than it had in a long time. As they strapped Plater down to a gurney and prepared to load him into the ambulance. Brickman noticed the rest of the team exchanging handshakes and high-fives. Al Sladky gave Jack a one-armed embrace that threatened to crush the younger man.

"See, junior?" he said. "You got the bastard."

"We got him, Al," Jack corrected. "It was a team effort."

"Yeah, but it was your idea, right?"

Jack shrugged.

"I thought the story would work," Brickman replied. "I just wasn't sure if he'd take the bait. I started thinking he was just going to write a letter to the editor or something."

Ken Bright, who had caught the tail end of the conversation, also chimed in.

"I don't know if I would have thought of it, Jack," he said. "Something this proactive, lots of things can go wrong. But it looks like your assessment was right on. A duel would appeal to Plater. He obviously wanted a chance to prove himself."

They had staked out Sam's *dojo* since the story had run in *The Press* in the hope that Plater would want to leave Cleveland in a blaze of glory. Jack had briefly considered using himself or Ken Bright as bait, since they had headed the investigation. In the end, though, Sam Rausch was the only logical choice. Plater probably wouldn't have seen any challenge in dispatching Jack or Ken, but Sam presented a real opponent. And they had purposely goaded Plater in the article. Sam had accepted the decoy role without hesitation.

Jack turned to Rausch.

"Sorry you had to stick your neck out like this, L-T," he said.

"Don't sweat it, Jack," he said. "It was worth the gamble to get him alive."

"Yeah, but the bean bag rounds might not have stopped him," Sladky interjected.

Sam smiled. He turned the shotgun over and extracted a shell from the tubular magazine under the barrel. That done, he cupped his palm over the ejection port of the weapon and racked the slide back, popping another live round from the chamber into his hand. He held the plastic rounds out so Jack and Al could read the words "#4 Buckshot, 3-inch Magnum" on their sides.

"Let's just say I stacked the deck a little," he said.

"I thought you weren't supposed to mix and match with bean bags and live rounds?" Al said.

Sam shrugged again.

"Special circumstances," he said. "I'm not much of a gambler. If I've got a choice, I'm not playing until the odds are in my favor. Which reminds me – can I use your radio, Jack?"

"Sure."

"C-1 to S-1, C-1 to S-2," he said into the microphone, calling the two sniper teams who had been positioned to cover their commander.

"Pack it in, guys," Rausch said. "Suspect's in custody, all secure."

"S-2 copies."

"S-1 copies," Lars Hendriksen said. "Dang, boss, thought we'd get a chance to dance tonight. You're too good with that shotgun."

"Maybe next time," Sam said. "Out."

Rausch handed the radio back to Jack.

"Snipers are a breed apart," he said. "They always want to take the shot. Might make a good thesis for your doctorate, Jack."

Brickman laughed.

"Like The Ninja isn't enough?" he said.

"Ain't you a little curious about who woulda won the swordfight, Sam?" Sladky asked.

Rausch thought a moment before responding.

"No. He had something to prove. I didn't."

By this time, the paramedics had loaded Plater into the back of the ambulance. Jack, Al, and Sam walked over to talk to the arrest team.

"OK," he said. "I want two of you in the back with Plater and four in an unmarked unit following. We'll have a marked unit from Parma PD get you to the Cleveland border, and CPD will take you the rest of the way to University Hospital. Once he's there, I want two of you in the room with him at all times, the rest outside. Remember what we're dealing with here. Don't take a chance with hm and don't let the hospital staff take any chances, either. We're going to move him to a secure facility as soon as he gets checked out."

Per CPD policy, anybody shot with Specialty Impact Munitions must be evaluated by a doctor to make sure there were no life-threatening internal injuries to the suspect. The label "less lethal" does not mean "non-lethal." When used properly, SIMs are unlikely to cause death, but the potential was always there.

"Anybody Mirandize him yet?" Brickman asked. The SWAT team shook their heads.

"Sorta thought you'd want to do that yourself," one of them said.

Jack smiled again. It was becoming a habit.

"Yes, I would," he said. "Al? Sam? Care to witness?"

"Hell, yes," Al replied.

"Count me in," Sam said.

Jack climbed up the rear step of the rescue squad and stood where Plater could see him.

"Nicholas Plater, I'm Sgt. Brickman of the Cleveland Police Department," he said. "You are under arrest for six counts of aggravated murder, two counts of felonious assaults against police officers and one count of attempted aggravated murder of a police officer. Do you understand what I am saying?"

Plater groaned. That was enough for Jack. He started the Miranda warning. Brickman didn't expect the SWAT officers guarding Plater to ask him anything, but he wanted to make sure that anything Plater said could be used in court later. Jack had probably read the legal rights advice warning hundreds of times in his career. It had never felt this good before.

When he finished, he hopped down and turned Plater over to Greg Giles and Jim McReedy, who would be riding with Plater to the hospital. Sam said something quietly to Giles before the ambulance left.

"What was that about?" Jack asked.

"Just a precaution," Sam said. "I told him to make sure they X-ray his whole body. This guy is just smart enough to have hidden a weapon somewhere we might have missed."

"Good idea," Jack said. "Let your team know they did a great job, and make sure Parma PD gets an attaboy, too. And thanks again. We couldn't have done it without you, Sam."

"You're a smart guy, Jack," Sam said. "You would have thought of something. I'm just glad I could help out. Now, if you'll excuse me, I need to debrief the team and write up an after-action report. After I make a phone call."

"Wife?" Ken Bright asked.

"Yeah, she knew something was up this week," he said. "I just want to let her know I'm OK. Probably wouldn't hurt you guys to call home, either."

They watched as Rausch headed toward his team members, who were standing around talking and gulping water. Even though they had not done much in the way of physical activity, it didn't take much heat, humidity, and tension to dehydrate a person wearing Level III body armor.

"Good man in a storm," Bright said.

"Good man any time," Jack replied.

The FBI agent looked at Brickman.

"Well, what now? We going to take a crack at Plater?"

Jack nodded.

"Yeah," he said. "I figure we've got four, maybe six hours until he's out of the hospital, then it's showtime."

"Do you think he'll talk?"

"Honestly? No," Jack said. "And with the evidence we have, we don't need him to, either. But I still need to try."

Ken checked his watch.

"All right," he said. "Let's get ready."

273

"Hell, yes," Jack said. "But I need to make a couple calls, first."

CHAPTER 44

The wait to interrogate The Ninja turned out to be closer to eight hours.

The SIMs had performed perfectly. Plater was bruised, but that was about it. They had been fired from optimum distances and the target selection had been perfect. If used under thirty feet, there was a chance for penetrating trauma to occur, likewise if they hit soft tissue such as the testicles. The doctor had prescribed ice and Tylenol.

Although Sam Rausch's concerns about a secreted weapon turned out to be unwarranted, the extra X-rays did turn out to be fortuitous. They had recovered not one but two handcuff keys hidden on The Ninja. One had been carefully inserted under the skin just below the left calf. Plater had obviously cut himself, put the key into place and allowed the wound to heal over it. He would have had to find a way to make a new incision to retrieve the key, but they figured he could have done so with minimal effort. The other key had been wrapped in plastic, sealed with a rubber band, and swallowed. The obvious plan was to wait until the package passed through his system and retrieve it from his own stool. An industrial strength laxative took care of that problem. They were giving him IV fluids to keep him hydrated, but he was obviously a little shaky.

Jack had headed home to grab a quick shower and shave before heading back to the office. He put on a shirt and tie. He wanted to look crisp and professional when he interviewed Plater. Ken Bright and he had discussed their interrogation strategy a dozen times. They had agreed that they were unlikely to bully him. Plater wanted to be seen as a pro, an expert in his field. They decided that the best course of action was to feign respect and appeal to his ego.

Jack knew that the interrogation was superfluous. They had enough physical evidence to convict Plater twenty times over and they had the eyewitness statement from Sam Rausch that all but convicted him of trying to murder a cop in the *dojo* parking lot. That alone would get him twenty to life. Brickman, however, had not abandoned his theory that Plater had killed before. Jack wanted to know for sure.

When he arrived, Plater was already waiting in an interrogation room nestled among the holding cells in the basement of the courthouse. Ken was pacing in the hallway outside the room. Despite the walking, he did not look especially nervous. Along with a trio of U.S. Marshals, two CPD SWAT team members stood outside the door of the room, still loaded for bear. Another pair, along with Sam Rausch and a couple of visitors, stood in the observation room separated from Plater by the one-way mirror that wasn't fooling anybody anymore. Jack was glad to see they weren't taking any chances. He slid his Glock from its holster and placed it in the lockbox outside the room. As an afterthought, he threw in his car keys, complete with handcuff key. Ken Bright eyed him and followed suit.

"You getting paranoid, Jack?" Ken asked.

"Just don't want Plater getting any ideas about hostages," he replied.

Sam had talked to Jack and Ken about what the SWAT procedure would be when they got The Ninja into custody. Plater would be cuffed and shackled, of course, but if he broke free of his restraints, the detective and the FBI agent were to hit the ground immediately. The two marshals would attempt to stop Plater with Tasers from the doorway. If they failed to drop him, the SWAT operators in the observation room were assigned to finish the job with their submachine guns. Jack hated to think what the press would do with a story about an unarmed prisoner being ventilated while in police custody. While the police knew that Plater, even unarmed, was highly dangerous, it was unlikely that the media would see it that way. In any case, Jack felt reasonably safe about confronting The Ninja.

"Ready?" Ken asked.

"Yeah," Jack replied. "Let's do it."

Plater was wearing an orange jumpsuit. The fluorescent light bounced off it and gave his face a sickly pallor, no doubt enhanced by the night long bout with an industrial strength laxative. Lack of sleep had apparently played its part, too, judging from the heavy bags under his eyes. Plater looked tired. Still, his face brightened considerably when he saw Jack and Ken walk into the room.

"Detective Brickman, Special Agent Bright," Plater said. "I'd shake hands, but…"

Plater gestured futilely. His feet were shackled together and a pair of handcuffs had been looped over that chain and connected to an eyebolt in the floor. Another chain ran from the leg shackles up to a belly chain that circled his waist. His hands were cuffed to the belly chain on either side of his body. Jack could see he needn't have bothered locking up his handcuff key. The Marshals had apparently broken out their high-security gear, including special restraints which would not accept a standard cuff key. Jack decided to keep his distance anyway. He sat down in a chair across the table from Plater. The tables and chairs, too, were bolted to the floor and walls. Ken lounged against a wall in the corner.

"I see you know us, Mr. Plater," Jack said.

"Of course, of course…the great *ninja* hunters," Plater said. "The press thinks highly of you. Well, most of the time." He trailed off into a giggle.

"OK, Mr. Plater, I read you your rights in the ambulance, but I'm going to do so again, just to make sure."

Plater waved his hand.

"Not necessary, but if it makes you feel better…" he said. "I'm sure it looks good for the cameras." Plater looked pointedly over Jack's shoulder toward the mirror, nodded and smiled. He was clearly enjoying this. He listened intently while Brickman Mirandized him again.

"So, will you answer some questions?" Jack said when he had finished.

"That depends on what you ask."

Brickman took a deep breath.

"Look, Mr. Plater, this is really a formality," he said. "Usually, I would dress up the interview room a little, throw some files on the desk, maybe a couple of videotapes too, so you would think we had all kinds of evidence against you. We call them props, just like Hollywood. But I don't need them, do I?"

"You tell me."

"I am. We don't need them. We had to make two trips with a van to haul all the evidence out of your house, including your little sanctuary on the third floor. We don't need theatrics. We've got the real thing."

"Maybe I had a roommate."

From the corner, Ken Bright snorted back a laugh. It was only half faked. The agent was purposely playing snob.

Jack held up his hand.

"No, bullshit, OK, Mr. Plater. I'm not going to bullshit you, so don't try it on me. We know you never had a roommate."

Plater shrugged.

"So why do you want to talk?"

"Maybe I want to save you from the needle."

Plater stared at Jack without emotion, as if the detective hadn't said a word. He was unfazed by the prospect of a trip to Ohio's lethal injection table.

"Do you want to hear my story?"

"Sure."

"I'm not going to tell you; I'm not going to tell you." The high-pitched reply came out in singsong fashion. It was unsettling.

"Why not?"

"Because you'll get it wrong!"

"Come on, sergeant," Ken said. "This is a waste of time."

"Wait," Plater said. "I'll talk a little."

"OK," Jack said. "Why?"

"Why what?"

"The big why. Why kill?"

Plater thought a moment before answering.

"Maybe somebody just wanted to be good at something."

"And get noticed for it?"

"Yeah. How else would you know if they were any good?"

"How good do you have to be to sneak up on somebody and kill them?" Ken Bright asked.

"Pretty good, I think."

"I'm not buying it," Jack said. "Killing somebody shouldn't be a publicity stunt."

"Every artist needs a canvas. The government pays people to kill. You get paid because you might have to kill somebody. Look at Lt. Rausch. He's killed a lot of people. Is he here? Bet he wishes he would have fought me. He's going to wonder about that."

"Wanna bet?" Jack thought. He was surprised at how talkative Plater was. He had expected a slower interview. Among other things, the killer was obviously enjoying a captive audience, especially one that was unlikely to make fun of his shrill voice.

Plater continued.

"Besides, who's going to miss them? They were all scum, criminals. They didn't matter. All they did was feed off the rest of us."

"Why stop there, though?" Jack asked. "Why not move up the food chain and knock off a politician or a CEO who stole millions from shareholders?"

"Where's the challenge? Prey that can't bite back isn't any fun. I know. I…"

Plater stopped short, suddenly realizing he had used the first person. His little verbal cat-and-mouse game had stumbled as he pumped up his ego. Jack pounced.

"What do you know?"

"Nothing."

"Oh, it's something, sergeant," Ken Bright said. "He did something he's not proud of. What's the matter, Nicky? Did you start on little old ladies for practice? Tough guy, right?"

Plater pulled against the restraints, veins popping out all over his neck with the effort. Jack wondered if the eyebolts would hold as he watched The Ninja struggle to control himself. After several tense moments, he appeared to have calmed down.

"I don't think I like you, Agent Bright, and I think this interview is over," he said. "I wonder how tough you are?"

Ken shrugged.

"Oh, I don't know," he said. "At least I never pissed my pants because I was so scared."

In spite of himself, Jack leaned back. Plater did his best to tear the chains out of their holders.

279

"That never happened! That never happened! Stone cold! I'm stone cold! I'm The Ninja!"

Plater was nearly uncontrollable with rage, screaming at the top of his lungs. In the enclosed space, it was frightening. Jack could feel the anger. He stood up and backed away. The interview was clearly over. But he had gotten what he wanted. He was about to open the door and leave when Plater went quiet. His voice was calm and measured when he spoke again.

"Detective?"

"Yes?"

"Will I get my perp walk?"

"I don't know," Brickman lied. The "perp walk" would lead Plater past scores of photographers and television cameras on his way to whatever permanent holding cell was waiting for him. The last thing he wanted was to give Plater his time in the spotlight.

"Maybe."

"I hope so," Plater said, and smiled. The smile would haunt Jack for a long time.

Jack exhaled when he reached the hallway, a long slow breath. Ken Bright seemed glad to be out of the room, too. He retrieved his pistol form the lockbox and turned to Jack.

"What do you think?"

"I think we were right," Brickman said as he holstered his Glock. "Get on the phone and wake everybody up. I want NOSCU going over everything we took out of Plater's house with a magnifying glass. We've still got somebody at the house, right? Good, the warrant should still be valid. Send part of the team back over there and start looking again."

"Newspaper articles, jewelry, body parts?" Ken asked.

Jack nodded.

"Anything," he said. "And they're probably going to find it hidden someplace. He's too proud to talk about it, but we know he keeps souvenirs. Let's find them."

Ken grabbed his cell phone and started dialing. Jack walked into the observation room.

"Jesus," Sam said. "I thought we were going to have to open fire."

"Scary, huh?" Jack replied. "There's a lot of anger in that guy."

Brickman turned to their visitors.

"So, what do you think Mr. Pendleton," he asked.

Mike Pendleton, despite the dim lights of the observation room, looked a little pale. It's not often you come face-to-face with madness.

"I...I don't know what to think," he said. "I guess he's not what I expected."

Jack nodded.

"Good enough, Cliff?" he asked the other visitor.

"Once I get my exclusive, yeah," O'Brien said.

"Sam, could you escort the journalists out of the building? I'm sure they have some writing to do."

CHAPTER 45

From *The North Coast Press*

Page A-1

August 12

By Mike Pendleton

If you're a fan of my column, even if you're not, I guess, you're probably used to seeing it on the opinion page, because that's where it belongs.

I asked my boss and he asked his boss and all the bosses agreed and said it would be OK to move today's column to the front page. I wish it were for a better reason, but I felt I owed it to the city to say something.

I was wrong.

Yes, you read right. A journalist admitting he was wrong. But I was.

I was wrong to make The Ninja look like a folk hero. He's not. Nicholas Plater, who has been charged with six murders, not to mention attacks on several police officers, is not a hero. He's not even a vigilante.

According to the police, he's nothing more than a glory hound, a publicity seeker who thought killing people would be a pretty neat way to get everybody's attention. Unfortunately, he was right.

Some of you are probably wondering about my change of heart. I can't say exactly what brought me to the light. Just let me say a couple of friends got me out of my ivory tower and back into reality. I'd be lying if I said I didn't like the ivory tower better.

Jack Brickman, he's the guy in charge of NOSCU, told me they have boxes upon boxes of evidence against Plater, evidence that all but guarantees multiple convictions for aggravated murder. In Ohio, that's enough to get you the death penalty. Plater will probably be convicted. I know I'm not supposed to say that, but it's true. When that time comes, I hope the death penalty is still Constitutional because I shudder when I think about a man like The Ninja getting back on the street.

And that, by the way, is the last time I call him that. And this is the last time I'm writing about Plater. At least until the trial's over. I think I've done enough to confuse prospective jurors.

George Orwell said something about decent people being able to sleep soundly at night because good men stand ready to do violence on their behalf. I don't know about the violence, but I do know there are good people ready to do a dirty job on our behalf. Jack Brickman, FBI Agent Ken Bright, CPD Lt. Sam Rausch, and the rest of NOSCU kept at a thankless job when half the city, me included, was pulling against them.

Sorry about that. Like I said, I was wrong.

CHAPTER 46

The Ninja trial was open and shut.

Plater's public defender mounted a valiant effort, but it was futile. Plater spent most of the trial smiling at the cameras and interrupting testimony, so often that the presiding judge had threatened to remove him from the courtroom. Plater obviously liked being the center of so much media attention. And, contrary to his lawyer's direction, Plater would talk to anybody who wanted an interview. He preferred not to be interviewed over the phone or on TV, however, since that would highlight his falsetto voice, he spoke to newspaper reporters.

Cliff O'Brien covered the trial but opted against a personal interview. His coverage of The Ninja, anchored by the exclusive Jack fed him for helping to bait Plater, earned him a national award from the Associated Press.

It took the jury four hours to return guilty convictions on all counts. Later, the jury foreman said they could have done it in about ten minutes, but he wanted it to look good, so they carefully reviewed each case. The mountain of evidence collected by NOSCU was overwhelming in both its quantity and quality. What had finally nailed Plater, though, was his shrine to himself. As the prosecutor walked the jury through the evidence, Jack knew they had a slam dunk.

The icing on the cake was the penalty phase. The judge decided that the death penalty was certainly in order. It still didn't seem to bother Plater. Jack wondered if that would change as the day of reckoning approached.

With the help of a ghostwriter, Plater would later sell his life story in a highly fictionalized biography that actually sold fairly well. The profits, according to Ohio law, went to Lumika Murphy and Jameel Timmons' son.

Jack's theory about previous murders turned out to be correct. NOSCU found two press clippings stuck in a thesaurus in Plater's house. Both dealt with the deaths of two elderly homeless men that had occurred several winters ago. One had been strangled, the other beaten with a blunt instrument. Neither, according to CPD's case files, had put up a fight. Most likely they had been asleep when the attacks occurred. Unfortunately, they didn't have enough trace evidence to charge Plater with the crimes, though the chief of homicide felt it was enough evidence to clear the cases with Plater as the probable suspect. Cleared homicides were always a good thing, though Jack found himself wondering if the result had been worth the risk.

The members of NOSCU started clearing out the office as soon as they had turned all the evidence and case files over to the Cuyahoga County Prosecutor's Office. Jack, Ken Bright, Sam Rausch, and Therese Vidalia did most of the testifying.

Sam Rausch got another Medal of Valor for acting as a decoy for The Ninja. He was getting quite a collection of them. He also got multiple letters from Plater, challenging him to duels. Those went right into the trash.

When the death sentence was handed down, Al Sladky marked the occasion by buying two countdown clocks that would mark the days, hours and minutes to Plater's scheduled execution and his own retirement.

Ken Bright received an official commendation from the Bureau. As promised, he personally funded a blowout farewell party for NOSCU at the Great Lakes Brewing Company. Jack attended the party with mixed feelings. He had spent the day with George Sellers, Calvin Stoddard, and the Ohio Attorney General, giving them a postmortem on NOSCU and The Ninja. Stoddard had been surprisingly supportive. Still, the meeting had given Jack much to think about.

After a couple of hours of steady beer drinking, Jack headed out to the patio of the restaurant for a breath of fresh air. It was cool and clear. Fall was just around the corner. Change was in the air. Al Sladky wandered outside and plopped down next to him. Jack didn't mind. The older man dug into his pocket and dug out two Cohibas.

"Here, junior, I been saving these for a special occasion," Al said. He cut the cigar for Jack and even lit it for him, swaying a little as he did so. "You done a good job, kid."

Jack took a long, thoughtful puff.

"Did I really, Al?" he asked. "Or did I just get lucky. Did *we* just get lucky?"

Sladky gave him a long look.

"I ain't saying we didn't get the breaks on this one, Jack," he said. "We sure did. But we did a lot of good police work, too. And let's be honest, if it wasn't for you, who knows how many guys woulda got killed before anybody figured out what we were up against? That goes a long way."

"That was mostly Sam, though," Jack said.

"Bullshit," Al said. "That was you thinking like a good cop. And you are one helluva good cop."

Jack's spirits improved immensely.

Jack Brickman had plenty to think about. Luckily, he would have the time to do it. He had earned much in overtime pay working for NOSCU and had also compiled compensatory time in lieu of pay. That, coupled with the fact that he hadn't used a single holiday or vacation day for months meant that head had plenty of time off coming. Karen Brickman booked them into the Wyndham Hotel in Aruba followed by a long leisurely cruise back to the United States. Somewhere between the blue water, rum drinks, and warm breezes, Jack and Karen remembered they were in love. They held hands and flirted and talked. And they had much to talk about.

One morning, about halfway through their vacation, Jack actually forgot about The Ninja for a while. He hoped it would become a habit.

About the author...

Jay Bender is a former newspaper editor and reporter, and a retired police detective. He attained the rank of *shodan* with the Japan Karate Association, and was a consecutive multiple medalist in the Ohio Law Enforcement Olympics. He was a six-time qualifier for the world law enforcement games. He lives in Northern Ohio with his wife, Katherine, and three children.

Made in United States
Cleveland, OH
26 April 2025

16443171R00160